A Tu

By Paul Walker

Table of Contents

.

Prologue

Wimereux, France
Monday, 6 January 1919

I huffed and hawed hot breath on to the frozen window in my room, then licked a fingertip to clear a small, circular spyhole through swirled patterns of frosted ice. Peering through, I caught a glimpse of Iris and Vanessa crossing the road on their way to Jock Carmichael's hotel. I should have been with them. It was our afternoon off, and Jock had invited us to join him and two of his doctor friends on a trip to central Boulogne in his motor car. We had been looking forward to our rare excursion and had talked of little else for two days. Our morning shift was into the last hour when I got the call that altered my plans. I had been dressing Lieutenant Harker's stump when I was given orders to stop, pack up my belongings, vacate my room and report to Colonel Faulkner. It shouldn't have been a surprise; I wasn't the first to go and knew my leave to return home was imminent. But why the hurry? I couldn't just drop everything and follow orders to the letter. Some procedures in a hospital can't be rushed; they knew that. The raw wound on Harker's right thigh was exposed and he was gasping in agony, not because of the wound or what remained of his limb; it was the missing, lower half, of his leg that drove the poor man to tear at his bedsheets. I had never heard of phantom pain when I first arrived there, but it was a common enough occurrence and I soon became familiar with the condition, along with other unimagined, mental and physical, consequences of war. Another half hour was needed with ointments, dressing and soothing of Harker before I could seek Matron's permission to leave the ward and return to my room for the last time.

I was conflicted. Often, I had returned to my lodgings, exhausted, numbed, questioning why I had ever volunteered. Now my turn had come, and I was about to leave the nightmare of a military hospital in northern France behind, I wasn't so sure. I couldn't rationalise my feelings. Of course, I wanted to see Mother again, and I had fond memories of our family home. There, in France, I had known discomfort, horror and sadness. It was contrary logic, but it was also where I felt secure and a sense of belonging. An imagining of our house in Whitstable – a distant peaceful place, untouched by the war – tied a knot of anxiety in my stomach. Would it be as I remembered? Had my experiences of the last few years left me too brittle and scarred to settle in the gentle contentment of small-town England?

I hefted the leather suitcase and closed the door to my room without a backward glance. The promenade at Wimereux was a grey and cheerless place. We temporary residents referred to it as *Pancake City*, and I had been unable to find a more interesting explanation on the origin of the nickname than our partiality for the offerings of traders on the sea front. Predictably, there were no carts or kiosks in sight at that time of year. I used to scoff at the old adage, *too cold to snow*; nonsense of course, but on that day I could believe it. The icy chill in the air seemed too stiff and unyielding for anything as soft and delicate as a snowflake. I shivered as the razor-sharp bite of the offshore breeze twisted and poked its way through my winter coat. I stopped in the shelter of a hut, tightened my scarf, raised my coat collar and stamped my feet. The beach was deserted and a crashing, resentful sea was empty save for the distant, blurred outline of a ship disappearing into the gloom. Destination Dover, perhaps. Kent. Home. A day or two more and I would be there. It was almost three years since I had said a tearful goodbye to Mother, and I would return a different person. For her sake, I would have to try and recover some of the innocence and joy I left behind when I crossed the Channel.

It was only a few hundred yards from my lodgings to Hotel Splendide, or Stationary Hospital 14, as it had been known since late 1914. Before the war, I was told the town was an elegant and lively place – *the Nice of the North*. Now, the smart hotels and villas along the front, empty if not requisitioned for hospital or military use, gave an air of anti-climax and melancholy. I passed the main hotel entrance and headed for the casino at the side. Offering a sympathetic smile to the sentry outside, I entered what had become the administrative and supply centre for the region. The entrance hall was stacked with blankets, mattresses, bed frames, pots, pans; everything an army hospital might need, except surgical instruments and medication. The sergeant outside Faulkner's office tapped the door, opened it, announced my name, then closed it behind me. The

Colonel barely lifted his head to notice my entry and continued to write in a ledger. A trim man in his late thirties, his appearance matched the laboured and precise progress of his writing. He finished, moved the ledger to one side, placed his pen inside a hinged wooden box, then gazed at me as though startled to see someone standing on the other side of his desk.

'Ah, yes, Miss Kiten, do take a seat.' He made an extravagant show of raising an arm to check his wristwatch. 'I was beginning to wonder what had delayed you.'

'Thank you, Colonel and my apologies if I kept you waiting.' I watched as he reached for a paper on top of a tray to his left. 'Am I going home at last?'

He looked at me over his spectacles, then removed them and cleared his throat. 'I'm afraid not. We had a telegram this morning.' He smoothed out the paper creases on his desk. 'You are due on the next train to Paris.'

'Paris? I thought...? Why? What does it say?' I couldn't understand. Perhaps there had been a mistake.

He raised an eyebrow. It seemed my initial reaction was unexpected. 'Of course, you don't have to go, Miss Kiten. After all, you're a volunteer.' He replaced his spectacles and scanned the paper again. 'Which is why it was such a surprise to get a telegram like this.' He paused and shook his head as though finding the words difficult to comprehend. 'Why on earth is the War Office sending a telegram to a volunteer nurse?' His question was a rhetorical one, spoken as though I wasn't present.

'The War Office?'

'Yes, it seems they have a position in mind for you.'

'A… position?'

He ran a finger along his moustache and stared into the distance as though trying to solve a mental puzzle, then clicked his tongue and said, 'One can only assume it's concerned with the Peace Conference, although it doesn't say as much. There is an urgent need for someone with language skills and apparently, you fit the bill.' He looked up from the telegram. 'You do have a facility with foreign languages?'

'Yes, yes, but who would know that? Surely there are others more suited?'

'There's very little detail about the position, but I shouldn't worry yourself unduly. These orders are often brief and to the point.' He sat back in his chair and clasped his hands together. 'I know any of my men would jump at the chance for a posting in Paris, and I would be delighted to be transferred there. Now hostilities are over, the theatres, galleries and restaurants will be ready and eager to entertain you.'

'I… this is… unexpected. I thought I would…'

'Yes, I understand this is a surprise, and I'm sure you want to get back home, but you may come to regard it as a reward; a thank you for your sterling efforts during the war.'

'Where do I go? Is there a contact name? Sir.'

'You are to report to Mr Arthur Burgess at the Majestic Hotel on Avenue Kleber. I understand the Majestic is one of the main hotels requisitioned for British delegates at the Peace Congress.'

Arthur. It started to make some sort of sense. I should have made the connection between Paris and Arthur. But why send a telegram to Faulkner? 'I know Mr Burgess, He's a long-standing family friend. Does he say… Is there a personal message for me?'

5

'Personal – no, I'm afraid not. The telegram is signed AB, Head of International Security in the War Office. So, he's a pretty important fellow, your Mr Burgess.'

'Yes, I know he works in the War Office, but I had no warning that he might...'

'Take a look for yourself, Miss Kiten.' He handed over the telegram.

I scanned it quickly. Abbreviated staccato phrases, much as Faulkner had reported; nothing remotely conversational or familiar. Disappointed. Intrigued. Whatever was behind the telegram, there was no way I could deny 'Uncle' Arthur.

'Thank you, sir. I'm ready to go. To Paris.'

'Good, that's the spirit.' He checked his watch. 'There's a train in forty minutes. See Sergeant Chambers out there would you. He'll organise your discharge, travel documents and with a bit of luck, there'll be a motor car available to get you to the station on time.'

'Thank you, sir.'

He stood, offered me a sloppy salute and we had an awkward handshake. 'My thanks, together with our patients and those of a grateful nation go to you, my dear Miss Kiten. Without you and your fellow volunteers, we would have been hard-pressed. So, very well done.'

It had the chime of a prepared speech, which I'm sure he had delivered many times before. Nevertheless, I was grateful for his words and pleased that there was no time for a round of goodbyes to nurses, doctors, patients and the soldiers who managed our busy little outpost. I had always hated the act of parting, knowing you may never meet again, and my close circle of friends there had made a pact to keep in touch after the war. I, for one, intended to hold true to that promise.

I was lucky to catch a ride with a motor car outside the Colonel's office. It was the daily collection of mail destined for the Dover ferry via a stop at Wimereux railway station. I took the opportunity, between bumps and bounces on the road, to write a hurried note to Mother. I handed it to the driver, a corporal who winked and said he would put it in the sack. Censorship was still in force officially, but general practice by then was to ignore it or pay lip service by a random check on a couple of letters each day. As a result, the speed of the outgoing postal service had improved with my letters usually taking only three or four days to arrive in Whitstable.

Monday, 6th January, 1919

Wimereux, France

Dearest Mother

I trust you are well and survived Aunt Winnifred's visit without too much fraying of nerves. Did you attend the New Year concert at King's Hall? I remember what a busy time of year this used to be for all in Whitstable, and how the concert was the much-loved climax.

Please excuse this hurried scrawl. I'm writing this on my knee while waiting for a motor car to take me to the railway station.

PAUL WALKER

In my last letter to you, I speculated about the date when my turn would come to return home. So, I was full of anticipation when summoned to see the Colonel today. But, surprise, surprise, my expectations were confounded by a telegram from Uncle Arthur on the Colonel's desk.

I have been ordered, or more correctly, "invited", to Paris in order to assist the British delegation at the Peace Conference. Apparently, my language skills are in demand. The telegram request was from Uncle Arthur, so I must suppose he has a treat in store for me. Or am I being too fanciful?

Did you know about this, Mother? I remember that you met with Uncle Arthur in December. Were you told then of his plans for me, and sworn to secrecy? Well, I will find out soon enough.

My address in Paris will be, The Majestic Hotel, Avenue Kléber.

With deep affection
Your loving daughter
Mary

P.S. Jock Carmichael and Vanessa Langley are engaged to be married. We had a little party to celebrate on Sunday. They are both frightfully excited and are planning on a wedding this Autumn in Oxford.

Once I had recovered from the shock of Arthur's telegram I could see the advantages of the unexpected change of plan. A short interlude in Paris before I returned home should be welcome; a half-way house between the heightened senses of fear and excitement in Wimereux and the mundane, pleasant existence waiting for me in Whitstable. It would allow me to adjust gradually. And it was an invitation from a well-loved uncle, not an order from a faceless bureaucrat. I knew, from Mother's letters, that Arthur was due to spend Christmas in Paris for the Conference, so I should have suspected he was behind the telegram. Of course, he would have been too busy to write himself and consult me in advance. Perhaps Faulkner was right, and it had been arranged as a sort of reward for service over the last few years. In that case, I was lucky as I knew many who were more deserving. Everything told me I should be positive and look forward to my time at the Peace Conference. Whatever Arthur's motivation, I was sure he wouldn't have sent the telegram unless he envisaged the position in Paris as an interesting and pleasant diversion for me. But, despite all my reasoning, I couldn't dispel a sense of unease that my time there was not going to be all sweetness and light.

One

Tuesday, 7 January 1919

Paris was the only place that mattered. Everywhere else was secondary and relegated to the margins. Those left behind in London, New York and Tokyo marked time, while fortunate thousands savoured the self-important and bored excitement that pervaded the French capital. The Great War was over; now, the scrabble for advantage in the terms of peace could begin.

*

I arrived at the Hotel Majestic on Avenue Kleber. The revolving door was stiff, and I was tired. It was three o'clock in the afternoon, and I had endured a journey of almost twenty-seven hours on a train from Wimereux, barely one hundred and seventy miles from Paris. Repairs to the track had forced an overnight stop and a sleepless night outside Amiens.

I had walked from the Gare du Nord, reasoning the air would clear sore eyes and relieve a headache, but my real purpose was to absorb an impression of the city from activity on the streets. It was almost eight years since my only other visit as an eager and innocent fifteen-year-old in the company of Father and Mother. Now, with the world changed and child-like wonder long gone, what would I make of Paris? The war had left its mark with piles of rubble, boarded windows and demobilized soldiers in frayed uniforms begging on street corners. There were also tantalising echoes of my earlier time: shop windows displayed the latest fashions; the tills in jewellers and bookshops chimed with confidence; forgotten smells of flavoursome food wafted through restaurant doors. That much I welcomed and had anticipated. It was a lightness and vitality in the cold air that surprised. Back at the hospital in Wimereux, celebration of a glorious, allied victory was muted and short-lived. There, we had settled into a mood of what could be described as contained disappointment. After all, it was an armistice, not a victory – not yet. Here, there was an unmistakable fizz of triumph in the streets. Why did I find this troubling? Was it so wrong? Despite attempts to rationalise and swim with the tide, I couldn't shift the thought that taking pleasure in a hard-won success was self-indulgent.

I stopped a couple of paces inside the foyer and lifted a gloved hand to my face to stifle a prickly scent of polish and bleach. The size was impressive and everywhere cut with the clean lines of marble: floors, walls; pillars; desks. Bright electric lighting lent a surreal aspect to the scene. No broken men in crumpled and muddied uniforms in view there; it was filled with the confident striding of stiff suits and scuttling attendants. Picking a way through choreography of urgent business, I arrived at the reception desk and bent to place my small, battered leather case on the pristine floor.

'Bonjour.' I offered an encouraging smile to the young man behind the counter who had watched my approach with nervous anticipation.

'Good afternoon, Mademoiselle, I'm afraid the hotel has been requisitioned by the British delegation. We have no rooms available for um... foreigners or casual occupancy.' He gave an apologetic, lopsided grin, hands fidgeting with a pen.

The English regional accent was unexpected. 'Oh, I see.' I hesitated, wondering where I would go if the hotel was full. The instructions were hurried and brief, but I assumed a place had been reserved for me at The Majestic. 'I am here to meet one of your guests – a Mr Arthur Burgess. Also, I am British, and Mr Burgess may have reserved a room in my name. I'm Mary Kiten; K - I - T - E – N.'

He gaped, then raised a finger and turned his back to examine rows of pigeonholes. Bruised, sunken eyes and edgy manner suggested he had seen action in the trenches. Was he a lucky one who had exchanged khaki for the burgundy livery of this hotel after a few days of retraining? Search completed; he returned to the desk.

'Here it is, Miss. I spoke to Mr Burgess this morning; he wrote this note, and you do have a room here. It's number 612.' He handed over an envelope and key with an expression that told of his pleasure in accomplishing the task.

'Thank you. Do you know how I can contact Mr Burgess?'

'Ah, yes, sorry Miss, I forgot. Mr Burgess said he had to go out and expects to be back here late in the afternoon.'

'And his room number?'

'Twenty-seven, Miss… Kiten.' His hand hovered over a bell, then his body twitched, and the hand was snatched away as though its ring would have been a dreadful mistake. 'Oh, and another thing, if you'll excuse me saying, you can't get to your room by the electric lift or the main staircase. You'll find your stairs at the end of that corridor over there.' He pointed to an unmarked door at the opposite side of the foyer.

'Thank you, and you've been most helpful, Mr…'

'Barnes, Miss, George Barnes. Happy to have been of assistance and, er, sorry about the foreigner thing.'

The door opened on to a corridor where it was apparent that cleaners and decorators had yet to begin their work. A conversation between two maids stilled as I approached. An enquiry of, 'Escaliers?' was met with blank looks. 'Stairs?' brought success with outstretched arms pointing in my direction of travel. Were all the staff here imported from across the channel? I climbed the stairs until reaching the sixth floor, then continued down a dimly lit corridor with a sloping roof and shafts of grey light from small overhead skylights.

Room 612 was narrow and cold. I placed the case on a thin bed and shivered. A bedside table, wardrobe and oil heater were the only other furnishings, but even they overwhelmed the cramped space. The window was cracked and the view outside blurred through layers of grime. I could see enough to know my room overlooked the main entrance to the hotel. Servants' quarters. Although disappointed that Arthur hadn't been able to secure a more comfortable room, I had occupied worse, and at least there was a heater. A box of matches sat on the top, and an inspection inside a hinged door confirmed it was ready for use. I struck a match, lit the wick and stood, waiting for signs of warmth to spread outwards and upwards.

I had forgotten the note in the strangeness of new surroundings. I retrieved the envelope from my bag and tore it open.

Maria
Meet in foyer.
Mum is well but needs care.
A

No hint on my role here, but what was meant by the cryptic comment about 'Mum'? I never referred to Mother in that way. No matter, I would find out soon enough.

The case was unpacked and stored on the wardrobe before the temperature allowed the removal of my coat, hat and gloves. I kicked off shoes, plumped the pillow, reclined on top of a grey, woollen blanket and stared at the ceiling. Why was I there? In Wimereux, it seemed an ideal next stop before home, and, of course, I was due to meet Arthur again after almost three years. But, having arrived, I felt drained and a longing for home. Legs and arms ached, and with eyes closed, I could have fallen into a deep sleep - a luxury I couldn't allow myself. A short nap, perhaps? A few moments rest - just five minutes.

I was alert, jolted into sudden action, needing a moment for mind to catch up with body. Had I been asleep? For how long? The same grey light filtered through the window, so perhaps only a few minutes or seconds. I swivelled my legs and stood by the bed. Now I remembered. The waspish crack of a handgun had disturbed my rest. Could I be sure? Yes, I was familiar enough with the sound. Only last week Iris and I were firing at tin cans on the beach with Jock

Carmichael's revolver. Was it a single shot or more? The window resisted initial attempts but eventually budged enough to poke my head out. A crowd had gathered in the street by the entrance; cars and carriages had stopped; a gendarme blew a whistle. I tried to lift the window higher, but it was stuck, and a full view obscured by a weathered stone ledge.

Curious but unhurried, I retraced the route to the ground floor. In the grand foyer, desks were emptied, and the expanse of marbled floor was bare. More than fifty people congregated by the entrance. Voices muttered, and necks were craned. I joined at the back. A man entered against the throng, pushed past and picked up a telephone on the concierge desk: nothing to see but heads.

'Excuse me.' I began to pick a way through. 'Forgive me, please…' Into the cold air. 'I beg your pardon, may I?' A burly figure in khaki halted progress; a British sergeant; one of a dozen or so outward-facing men, who had formed a protective circle. Beyond the bulk and splayed arms of the sergeant, I could see three or four men crouched over a horizontal, motionless figure.

'I'm a nurse. Can I help?'

'Too late for that, Miss.'

I peered under his arm and could see the legs of the prone figure, a man with dark grey, neatly pressed trousers and polished, black shoes, his top half obscured by the huddle.

'Are you sure I can't be of some assistance?'

'No, Miss, best turn back and get away from here. It's not a pretty sight.'

We were all ushered away, gently but firmly by the security ring; carried back on a wave of shuffling bodies into the foyer where the sense of hushed wonderment had grown to a gabble of chatter, shouted orders and ringing telephones. I scanned faces trying to gather sense from snatches of conversation. A middle-aged woman was headed my way, open-mouthed and hands tightly clasped around her middle.

'What is it? What's going on?'

The woman paused for a moment and made to reply, but words caught in her throat. She tilted her head and narrowed her eyes, then stopped, turned and marched away. The man at the concierge desk was waving his arms and shouting in broken French down the telephone. A large man in a heavy overcoat pushed through the confusion causing me to step back and cannon into someone behind.

'Pardon me; I couldn't help…'

'No matter.' The voice belonged to a young British army officer. He smiled and dipped his head, brushing a stray lock of fair hair back into place.

'Do you know the cause of this commotion? I've just arrived, and there appears to be an incident in the street outside.'

He delayed, seeming to assess how I might react, before replying. 'Unfortunately, a gentleman has been shot, Miss…'

'Kiten, Mary Kiten. How dreadful. Is he…?'

'I regret the gentleman died instantly.'

'And has the gunman been arrested?'

'I understand the attacker fled from the scene, and the police have taken control of the matter.' A suited man tugged at his sleeve and whispered in his ear. He half-turned, then stopped and asked, 'Are you a resident here, Miss Kiten?'

16

'Yes, I am and thank you for taking the time to inform me. I see you are wanted elsewhere - Major.'

'John Parkes, and it's a pleasure to meet you, even in these distressing circumstances.'

His brief hesitation was long enough for one more question. 'Did you know the gentleman in question, Major Parkes?'

'Indeed, I did, Miss Kiten. He was a fine man, attached to the delegation here. His name was Arthur Burgess. Now, if you will excuse me.' He marched quickly towards the entrance, followed by others in his wake.

Arthur. It took seconds for the information to register. Arthur. Arthur Burgess. Surely not. Fate didn't work like that – did it? Movement around blurred, and sounds merged into a dull thrum. Unsteady legs took me to the unmarked door. The corridor inside was empty. Closing the door, I leant against it with closed eyes to calm my breathing. All was quiet. I had become accustomed to the aftermath of sudden, violent death. But here? Now? Arthur?

Although I knew Arthur's work was *hush-hush* and probably involved spies, he was an administrator, not a field operative. Why would he be targeted after the armistice? Or was it simply bad luck: the random act of a madman; a robbery? Arthur Burgess wasn't just a name; he was my *Uncle* Arthur, a long-standing family friend; had visited our house; eaten Mother's cakes; thrown a ball in the garden for me to catch. After Father was killed at the Somme, it was Arthur who suggested I volunteer for nursing when I approached him with a naïve plea to do something meaningful for the war effort. Now he was dead, another pillar of my childhood had crumbled. And what was I to do there? He was my only contact.. What position was earmarked for me? Did Arthur have any other plans for me in Paris? I would have to improvise.

Two

Back in the bedroom, I examined Arthur's note again, trying to unscramble some significance. A knock at the door interrupted my train of thought.

'Hello, can I help…'

Two soldiers ignored me and entered, leaving my only option as a retreat to the other side of the bed.

'You must come with us, Miss.'

'With You? Where?'

'Just pack up all your belongings to take with you. Everything, please. Now.' A command, not a request.

What had I done? I stuffed the note up the sleeve of my blouse, retrieved the case from under the bed and began to unload the wardrobe under watchful eyes. Three in the room required a pantomime of shuffling and rearranging bodies before the task was completed. A soldier took the case in one hand, my arm in the other and led me to the doorway. Soldier number two performed a superficial search, then nodded to confirm that all had been removed.

Escorted to the foyer, then up the grand stairway to the first floor and a door marked 'Security', I was ushered inside. My guards followed, clicked heels, deposited the case and closed the door as they left. A generous space had been converted into a makeshift office with three rectangular work areas formed of cupboards, boxes, cabinets and desks. Surrounding it all were a dozen blackboards, some with chalked lists of names; others pinned with street maps, photographs and diagrams. A man and woman working in the area to my left paid no attention to my entrance. Seated at the central table was a middle-aged, thickset man with a heavy, drooping moustache, who surveyed me in the way a schoolteacher might consider an errant child. Major Parkes was standing at his side, hands behind his back, half-turned and in an attitude that suggested he was less than comfortable. Was he the reason for my detainment? Neither man spoke. I offered a meek smile and waited.

'Miss Kiten is it?' The voice was thick with phlegm. His flushed cheeks, ruby nose and deposits on the moustache told of a head cold.

'Yes, sir.'

'I am Sir Basil Thomson from Scotland Yard. I understand you have already met Major Parkes.'

'Yes, briefly, a few minutes ago. He had distressing news.' I would have told him then about my relationship with Uncle Arthur, but he held up a hand, screwed his eyes and gulped as though stifling a sneeze. So, I waited for his composure to return..

'Indeed.' He searched inside a dark jacket pocket for a handkerchief, fluffed it across his face, then smoothed his moustache with the palm of a hand. 'May I have your passport?'

I opened the bag slung across my shoulder, fished inside and handed it to Thomson. He unfolded and spread it on the desk, glancing up quickly to confirm the photograph.

'Our problem, Miss Kiten, is that your name does not appear on any list of approved residents in this, or any hotel requisitioned for the British delegation.'

20

'I was given the key to a room at reception, so someone was expecting my arrival.'

'We know, and the receptionist who handed you the key also has questions to answer.' He ran his finger over the description in the passport, then sat back in his chair. 'Kiten is an unusual family name – at least in England,' was framed as a question rather than a statement. 'Also, and please excuse my directness, you have certain Germanic features, such as blonde hair, fair skin, a statuesque build.'

I stifled a laugh. 'I don't know whether I should take that as a compliment.' I paused, but there was no hint of amusement on the face in front of me. 'My great grandfather was German. I was born in England and have never considered myself anything other than English - sir.'

'Tell me about your family.'

'Our home is in Whitstable, and we have an apartment in Ebury Street, London, which my father used when he was in town.'

'What business does your father have in town?'

'My father died at the Somme in 'sixteen. He was the senior medical officer with the East Kent Regiment. Before that, he had a general practice in Whitstable and also worked at St Thomas', which is why he bought the place in town. My mother… shall I continue, sir?'

Thomson raised a hand to indicate he had heard enough of family background. He turned to the man working at the far end of the room. 'Chivers, take this young lady's case and handbag to examine their contents. Quick as you please.'

Chivers jumped at the command, hurried to my side, picked up the case and took the bag from my shoulder between thumb and forefingers as though it may have been contaminated.

'Is all this really necessary?' I regretted my petulant tone as soon as the words were out.

He narrowed his eyes and leant forward. 'I am charged with the security of over one thousand persons in this city, Miss Kiten, and although the war is over, the incident outside this hotel should be enough to illustrate that mortal danger still exists.' The handkerchief was put to use again before he was ready to continue. 'You arrived here at the time of a brutal killing, and Major Parkes here was certain you recognised the name of the victim.'

I turned to Parkes, who remained silent. It seemed that distrust, even of those who appeared friends and allies, had become second nature. An understanding of Arthur's cryptic message dawned. Hide and seek games from my childhood were often accompanied by, 'Mum's the word,' from Arthur and a conspiratorial tap on the side of his nose. The reference was not to Mother; it was an allusion to something he had hidden; a secret between the two of us. But why? What could it be?

I said, 'I've known Arthur Burgess since I was a child. He was our dearest family friend. His was also the name I was given to contact at the Hotel Majestic.'

'A family friend, you say. I worked closely here with Mr Burgess, yet he never mentioned your name. I would have expected him to take special care to notify me of the imminent arrival of a – family friend.'

'It was all very rushed and last-minute. I was given only a few minutes to pack and be on my way.'

'On your way from where Miss Kiten?' Parkes had joined the interrogation.

'I was at Stationary Hospital 14 in Wimereux.'

'A nurse,' exclaimed Thomson. 'We are short of cooks and cleaners here but have ample medics and nurses. So why would anyone consider sending a nurse here?'

'I was a nurse there and before that at a hospital in Hastings, Sir Basil. As I said, my father was a doctor, and I picked up enough about nursing to be considered useful. I interrupted study at Girton, Cambridge, to volunteer. I'm numerate, have been told I write well, I'm fluent in French and German, and can get by with a few other languages. I can only guess that Mr Burgess, or one of his colleagues, thought I might serve a purpose here. Perhaps the need is urgent, and they were casting around for candidates within easy reach of Paris.'

'What were you told of your position here?' asked Parkes.

'I'm as much in the dark as you are, Major. I was told to report here for further instructions. The only clue I have is that my facility with languages could be useful.'

'You were passed a note at the reception desk. Might we see it?' Thomson spoke in a tone suggesting impatience to progress to the critical aspect of the interrogation.

'Certainly, I was reading it when your men invaded my room.' I retrieved the paper from the sleeve of my blouse and handed it to Thomson.

Both men stared intently at the note giving it more time than the few words warranted.

'Maria. It is addressed to Maria, not Mary.'

'As you can see from my passport, I was christened Maria, and although I am most often called Mary,

Arthur – Mr Burgess – preferred to use my given name.' I paused before adding, 'Do you find the name Maria significant, Sir Basil?'

Thomson waved his handkerchief in front of his face to stifle a cough. 'And what's this reference to "Mum is well, but needs care"?'

'My mother, Emily, has painful joints, especially in her hips, and her condition tends to worsen with cold weather. When his work schedule allowed, Mr Burgess was often kind enough to call on her and send me brief bulletins on her well-being. We have both tried to persuade her to employ a companion to assist with mobility, travel and light tasks around the house. Unfortunately, she has an independent mind and doesn't accept help easily.'

Both men appeared convinced by this explanation, nodding heads with understanding my last statement as though they had experienced similar frustrations. They exchanged a glance, then Thomson called Chivers over.

'Have you finished your rummaging in the case and handbag?'

'Yes, Sir Basil. All clear.'

'Then please accompany Miss Kiten and wait in the corridor while we confer.'

Thankfully, my interval with Chivers was short. An earnest young man, he was clearly embarrassed, constantly experimenting with the placement of arms and legs in order to appear unobtrusive. Finally, the door opened, and Parkes ushered us back inside. Chivers disappeared to his work area while I returned to face my interrogators, standing at the other side of Thomson's desk, with hands clasped behind my back.

'Miss Kiten, thank you for bearing the indignity of detention and examination with such calm assurance. But I hope you will understand the need for extreme caution in these uncertain times. We are satisfied with your credentials and offer sincere sympathy for the unfortunate coincidence of your arrival here with the loss of an intimate friend.' Thomson's effort in speaking without coughing or sneezing was too much, and he took some moments to compose himself before continuing. 'Please go with Major Parkes. He will see to your accommodation, coupons and any vacant position you may be able to fill.'

'Thank you, Sir Basil. Before I go, may I ask if you have discovered who killed Mr Burgess, and why?'

'It's a matter for the local police. We are... liaising...' Thomson looked to the Major for assistance in finishing his explanation.

'Yes, we're in touch with the local police. I understand they have witnesses and a good idea who the perpetrator may be. As soon as we know more, I'll...' Parkes left his sentence unfinished and looked at Thomson for confirmation.

When he didn't respond, I said, 'Thank you, I'd be very grateful for any news as soon as you have it.'

Thomson bowed his head, which I took as a sign of agreement. Parkes took my case, and I followed down a flight of stairs to room number 28 on the ground floor. He unlocked the door, stood aside and gestured for me to take a seat in an armchair. We were in the lounge area of a small suite with an unmade bed visible through an open door. His lounge also served as an office with two cabinets and a desk loaded with boxes and papers. He deposited the case, took a seat behind the desk and cleared a space.

'This room is next to - Arthur's,' I said, unsure how to refer to him, and pricked with a sense of guilt that the recent turmoil hadn't left space to grieve at his sudden passing.

'Mr Burgess was head of security at the Majestic. I was his deputy.'

'I thought...'

'It's complicated, Miss Kiten. There are two levels of security here. Sir Basil has oversight of confidentiality and security for the entire delegation, while there are separate protection units linked to each hotel, building and various apartments. With Mr Burgess gone, there are now eleven of us in the unit responsible for the more than four hundred souls in this hotel.'

'I see.' So that was Arthur's placement here. Wasn't it a little odd to insert a senior manager of the War Office in a hotel full of British delegates and their support staff? Unless. Enough. I resolved to put conjecture to one side until I was in a position to learn more. 'Sir Basil mentioned coupons.'

'Ah yes, food coupons.' He opened a drawer, removed a bundle of printed cards and counted out twenty-five. 'You need to present one for each meal in the main dining hall. We're not supposed to hand out more than a week's supply, but I've included a few spares in case you feel peckish. You can request more from room 26 when they run out. Also,' he opened another drawer and presented me with a closely-typed sheet of paper with the coupons, 'I'm afraid I'll have to ask you to sign this.'

The paper was headed, *Declaration of Security, Behaviour and Etiquette*. I read through it with a mix of bewilderment and growing disbelief. It contained a set of rules for residents who did not have official delegate status. I could understand the directions on security, but no loitering in city streets, respectful attitude to all delegates, curfew times for different classes of personnel, no raised voices during meals. My raised eyebrows were answered with a shrug.

'Who devised these regulations?'

'Sir Basil is responsible for the text on security; the rest comes from the office of the Organising Ambassador, Lord Hardinge.' He handed me a pen and ink bottle. 'I know it appears extreme, but a number of our contingent left their common sense in Dover before boarding ships, and it's not only we British. Delegates from over twenty nations are here, and a plague of reckless conduct seems to have infected many, especially during their leisure time. Regrettably, even a few of our most senior representatives have been rather - imprudent.' He paused to gauge my reaction, then quickly began to sort a pile of boxes as though embarrassed by the critical tone of his short lecture. 'Now, we must see if there is a position to suit your... education and talents, Miss Kiten.'

'Please, you must call me Mary now you have come to regard me as harmless.'

'Thank you, and I would be happy with John, in return.' A faint blush appeared around his collar, and my note of sarcasm was either missed or ignored. He opened a box, took out a set of bound papers and began to search through the pages with studied concentration.

Was there an attraction there? He was handsome in a traditional English way: square jaw, clean-shaven; blue eyes; fair hair; athletic build. I dismissed such thoughts from my mind. It was so long since I had considered men in *that* way.

'Might it be helpful if we searched the room next door to see if we can find a reference to my intended position?'

'That's a splendid idea.' He stood and stretched a hand towards the door.

He unlocked the door to room 27 and surveyed the space for a few moments before ushering me inside. Was Parkes checking for Arthur's ghost before signalling the all-clear? It was a room much the same as the one we had left, although the desk was less cluttered. I started to leaf through a neat pile of papers in the centre of the desk when Parkes cleared his throat and asked me to take a seat. The material on the desk was likely to be routine, but he couldn't discount the possibility that confidential matters were included. So, I sat and feigned patience, returning his occasional glances with encouraging smiles, as he examined individual sheets of paper, opened each drawer and checked every box. He was thorough and methodical. More than half an hour had passed when he leaned back in his chair, clapped both hands on the desk and announced, 'Nothing here to help us, I fear - Mary.'

'Should we take a look in the bedroom?'

He hesitated, seemingly unsure whether their situation warranted intrusion into a gentleman's private space. 'Very well, allow me a moment to check all is as it should be in there.'

He entered the bedroom and half-closed the door before returning after a few minutes to announce it was clear with a grand sweep of his arm. I joined him, peered into Arthur's bedroom and only then the full impact of his death struck home. He slept there only a few hours ago, unaware of the violent end that beckoned. A space in my middle emptied and memories of a man I had known and loved all my life created a sharp physical pain in my breast.

'I've checked the wardrobe and drawers.'

His statement startled and wrenched my thoughts back to the present. What had Arthur hidden that I was meant to find? I gazed at the orderly arrangement: a large bed; a wardrobe opened to show a tidy row of dark suits and two overcoats; a dressing table; cupboards. Nothing was out of place. A small bedside table held a pad of writing paper, roughly one inch thick, and two pencils. I lifted the cover to reveal a wad of blank paper and showed it to Parkes.

'Would you mind,' I paused for a deep breath, 'if I took this paper and pencils to write a letter? Arthur lost his wife when I was a child, and I'm sure Mark, his only son, would appreciate a note from me to soften the bland severity of a telegram.'

'Of course, there can be no harm in a letter.'

I scanned the bedroom one more time; then we returned to the office next door to continue the hunt for a vacant position. With Arthur gone, was there any reason for me to remain in Paris? Returning to Wimereux or home was out of the question until I learned the identity of the killer and the reason for Arthur's murder. Would I have to settle for the offer of work as a chamber maid or kitchen help? Or… Parkes was talking, but I wasn't listening. How stupid had I been? Arthur's reference, 'Mum', was not to anything he had hidden; it was our relationship that he wanted kept confidential. There must have been a reason why he wanted me kept at arm's length. Was it simply a matter of not wanting to be accused of partiality or nepotism in putting forward a candidate for the position there? Was that why the telegram was so impersonal; why my bedroom was so basic? No, it was unlike Arthur to be bothered by superficial considerations. Or, was he trying to shield me from some sort of danger?

'I'm sorry, what was that again?'

'I said, I knew there was something that may suit.' He waved a single sheet of paper with a look of triumph. 'The group from the Treasury are looking for a clerk with a working knowledge of French and German. Unfortunately, they had a fellow who was deemed unsuitable and re-assigned to shipping. How does that sound? Could this be the position Mr Burgess had in mind for you, Mary?'

A clerk. I supposed that meant typing, filing and acting as a general dogsbody, but it could have been worse. 'Yes... probably, and it sounds wonderful,' I said with as much enthusiasm as could be mustered. 'My typing and shorthand are no more than adequate, but I will certainly do my best.'

'Good, you will be reporting to the head of the Treasury Unit – a man named Keynes. I don't know him personally, but I understand he's well-regarded.'

'There was a Cambridge don of that name, I believe.' I had heard his name mentioned as a high-flyer during my studies there.

'It will be the same man, I'm sure, as I've heard he's from an academic background.' He eased back into his chair and folded his arms to indicate a satisfactory conclusion to his search. 'Most of the other units have offices and conference rooms set aside at the Astoria, but Mr Keynes has commandeered an old school not far from here. If we could meet at breakfast, say eight sharp, I'll introduce you to his number two, Gerry Pinchin. He's a friendly chap who I'm sure will be glad to show you the ropes.'

'Thank you again, John, you've been kind.' I made as if to rise, then as an afterthought added, 'There is a small favour I have to ask. Would you please see if you could arrange for me to pay my respects to... Mr Burgess... his body. I feel it is my duty to say a brief farewell to a man I've known for most of my life.'

'Are you sure that's necessary? The injuries would be extremely unpleasant viewing, and it may be best if you relied on memories of...'

'John, I have worked in hospitals, nursing men with hideous wounds. Naturally, I will be upset to witness the earthly remains of a friend, but I will not swoon at the sight of his injuries.'

'Very well, I'll see what can be done.'

When I asked for the key to 612 at reception, an attentive Parkes requested a room more suited to my status as a clerk rather than one for chamber maids and kitchen staff. Vacant rooms were in short supply, and the alternatives offered were no improvement. I was disappointed, but didn't want to show it, so made a show of insisting 612 was more than adequate. After all, with Arthur gone, my stay in Paris was likely to be short-lived.

Three

After an uncomfortable night, I was ten minutes early for the rendezvous at breakfast. Following the smell of fried food to the main dining hall, I met an incongruous sight. Amid chandeliers, marble and onyx stood regimented rows of flimsy, folding wooden tables of the type used in tented hospital camps. A group of tables at the far end stood out as the only ones laid with white cloth and ringed by chairs. The rest were bare, unvarnished wood with bench seats. Servers in white overalls were dispensing cooked food from a row of steaming metal cabinets to a queue of suits in various shades of grey, mingled with tweed jackets, woollen skirts, khaki uniforms and the occasional floral dress. The steady, low hum of conversation was broken by regular calls from supervisors to a conveyor belt of scurrying helpers from the kitchen to refill the hot platters. I fell into line at the back of the queue.

Two women in front, about my age or a little older, were chatting about their visit to a club last night. Their discussion was interspersed with wide-eyed disbelief, clicking of tongues, giggles and whispered confidences. Taking advantage of a short pause, I introduced myself as new to the Majestic, asked about the club and was informed it was the *Club Eloise* featuring a group of black men playing American music.

'Do you mean jazz?'

'Yes, have you heard it? It's quite new and - different,' said one.

I was beckoned into an excited huddle to discuss the thrilling experience of a night in a foreign city listening to strange music played by negroes. It was like listening to a confession of a schoolgirl's first kiss in a forbidden location. Eventually, I managed to steer the conversation away to mundane topics, learning about breakfast and work schedules and practices. Annie and Jane described their work in a typing pool based at the Astoria as though it was part of a glamorous, exciting adventure.

'Miss Kiten - Mary.' A tap on my shoulder and I turned to see John Parkes in the company of a large man with a round face, untidy moustache and a straggle of copper-coloured hair swept across a bald scalp. 'This is Mr Gerald Pinchin from the Treasury.' He bowed. I smiled. 'I've filled in Mr Pinchin about our meeting yesterday and your willingness to step in and help out with his clerical work.' He hesitated, unsure whether to add anything more. 'Well, I'll leave you to it, Gerry. As I said, Miss Kiten is new here and will need directions to your schoolroom.'

'Delighted to have you on board, Miss Kiten,' said Pinchin. 'Major Parkes informed me of the confusion around your position and it's almost certain you were recruited to work for us. Some of us just about get by in French, but the assistance of a linguist would be welcomed by all of us.' He paused and swept back a loose strand of hair. 'I should warn you that our boss is a stickler for detail and your predecessor failed to come up to scratch. I hear that you were up at Cambridge. That should help get you into his good books. Anyway, I see you are with companions, so I'll leave you to breakfast and see you in the foyer in, say, forty minutes.'

I nodded agreement, unsure whether to be pleased with a friendly welcome or uneasy at the high bar set for work standards at the Treasury Unit.

The closer I edged towards the food, the more my appetite waned. My plate of two boiled eggs with a small piece of dry bread was eyed with suspicion and queries on my health. In contrast, Annie and Jane met the challenge of fried food with vigour and enthusiasm. I left our table with a promise to meet again, armed with gossip about my colleagues - the 'money men'. They had a reputation for eccentricity, having chosen to ignore the comfort of the Astoria in favour of an old, disused school as their place of work.

Pinchin greeted me warmly and informed me it was a short walk to our destination on Rue Leo Delibes. He had an easy manner and responded willingly to questions. The Treasury Unit was a team of eight, and they had arrived in Paris two weeks ago. They moved their operations from the Astoria as Mr Keynes considered there were too many distractions, with constant interruptions from other units requesting assistance and information on finance.

It was only a few minutes before we arrived in front of an unmarked entrance to a four-storey terraced building.

'This is it. We only use a couple of rooms on the ground floor. I'm afraid you'll find it a bit spartan, but it's clean and secure.'

'Secure? Do you have men from the Majestic guarding it?'

'No, we have arranged our security with a couple of local ex-servicemen living on the first floor. There was a fair bit of discussion with Sir Basil and Mr Burgess to wangle it, but Mr Keynes can be very persuasive. Have you encountered our security masters yet?'

'Yes.' I decided further explanation could wait if it were needed. The news about Arthur's killing had clearly not filtered through to the Treasury.

He unlocked the door and led me down a corridor; past unused rooms piled high with desks and chairs until we reached a double door at the end. This opened to a large room, at least forty paces by twenty, which I guessed was the school assembly hall. It had been converted into a sort of library, surrounded by shelves of varying sizes, loaded with books, stacks of papers and binders. There were ten desks in the middle; six of them occupied by men bent over their work, while another was standing at the back scanning the shelves and puffing on a pipe.

'Hey everyone,' hailed Pinchin, 'this is our new help, Miss Mary Kiten. Say hello, mind your manners and be especially nice.'

I responded to a muted and ragged chorus of greetings with a wave and what I hoped could pass for an expression of eager anticipation.

'Come and meet the boss.' He pointed through an open door to an adjoining office where I spied a pair of legs resting on a desk.

The shirt-sleeved boss was reclining in a chair smoking a cigarette. A lanky figure with a high forehead, slick black hair and neat moustache, he was staring into the distance with an expression of deep concentration. He had a face that was hard to age; mid-thirties perhaps; younger than his exalted station would suggest. Pinchin made an introduction, and we waited as he blew a smoke ring, sat upright in his chair and stubbed the cigarette out with exaggerated care. His gaze remained unfocussed as he stood, took his jacket from his chair and slipped it on with a few unhurried shrugs of his shoulders. Finally, we had his attention. He bent over the desk and surprised me by reaching out for a handshake.

'Good morning, Miss Kiten, welcome to our little den.'

'Thank you, Mr Keynes, sir; I hope I will be able to assist with your important work in some small way.'

He held my hand in a firm, cold grip for a few moments before releasing it, taking his seat and pointing to a chair. Pinchin departed and closed the door.

'How much do you know about your duties here?' He placed elbows on the table and clasped his hands together.

'The position was described only as clerical.'

'There will be some secretarial work, but your primary purpose will be research. We have transported a considerable tonnage of books, files, committee papers, company reports, government statistics and academic studies to this place. You will familiarise yourself with our collection and assist the treasury officers in gathering information. You may be tasked to research the value of German exports of unmanufactured iron and steel in ten years leading up to the war, for example. Is that something you think you can handle?'

'Yes, sir, and I'm pleased there's more interest in the work than I had been led to believe.'

'Good.' He settled back in his chair and regarded me with a look of mild amusement. 'You're a very attractive young woman, Miss Kiten. Please don't excite or flirt with the men out there; we have a lot of detailed work ahead.'

A pity. I had wanted to warm to him. I should have been accustomed to treatment as ornament rather than functionary, so why did I expect him to be different? I spun on my heel and exited his office without acknowledging his last remark.

Despite low expectations, the work proved interesting, and my new colleagues were considerate and helpful in showing me the ropes. A young, bespectacled man was the most attentive. He was Derek, and I was Mary in our exchanges, but it was a more formal Mr and Miss for the rest. Pinchin had a reasonable knowledge of German, and a couple of his colleagues could get by reading French, but I was soon in demand for consultations over foreign-language documents. I was studying a report by the Belgian government when Pinchin announced it was lunchtime. Keynes, Pinchin and two others moved towards the exit, shouldering overcoats and wrapping scarves. It was almost half-past twelve, and Derek explained they were returning to the Majestic, but he was busy and would make do with tea and biscuits. Perhaps that was why so many plates were piled high at breakfast, and although lunch was tempting, I opted to stay and continue browsing the shelves.

An hour later, they started to drift back from the Majestic. Pinchin beckoned me to follow him into Keynes' office.

'I have a message for you from Major Parkes. Something about a visit to the local morgue.'

'Yes.' He was fishing for more information.

'He mentioned yesterday's dreadful incident outside the hotel.'

'I knew Mr Burgess. He is – was – a longstanding friend to my family. I asked if Major Parkes could arrange for me to pay my respects.'

'Ah, I see now.' He shook his head and tutted. 'Bad business. A good man. You have my condolences, Miss Kiten. Well, Major Parkes is waiting for you at the Majestic. You had better…' He waved his hand at the exit. 'One more thing before you go; the boss would like an informal chat. Could you meet with us in the delegate's bar after dinner at around eight?'

*

Parkes was waiting in the foyer. The morgue was adjacent to the nearest police station, a couple of streets behind the Majestic. I lifted my coat collar and tightened the belt as we stepped into the cold air. A gentle scattering of snowflakes had settled on the payments, and progress was deliberate and slow as we turned a corner into the Rue de Longchamp towards our destination. We passed the police station, turned down a side street, through a dark tunnelled entrance to metal gateway. Parkes pushed it open and rang a bell by a small wooden doorway. He handed a note to a man in a white cap and grey overalls. The door closed, and we waited outside. I stamped feet and clapped gloved hands to ward off the chill.

'Are you sure you want to go through with this?'

'I'm positive, thank you.'

The door opened again. I followed the white cap and Parkes along a corridor and downstairs into a long room with white-tiled walls and a low ceiling. I shivered. It was colder in there than outside. There was a row of a dozen metal tables in the middle of the room, and four were draped with black sheets over, what I assumed were, bodies. A clatter at the far end signalled a trolley barging through swing doors, pushed by a fat man in grey overalls and a fur hat. He waved an arm for us to approach, and, drawing near, I realised several layers of clothes magnified his size. Parkes took an arm and guided me to the head of the trolley.

'Maintenant?'

The query was directed at Parkes, but I answered, and the sheet was pulled back to reveal the top half of a body. The face was bound around the chin and head with a grey bandage, and the tongue protruded in a comical gesture of defiance. No attempt had been made to cover an ugly, jagged hole above the right eyebrow. The area around it was lumpy, swollen and disfigured. But there was no doubting who it was. I clasped hands tight, bowed my head and said a silent prayer for the soul of a man I knew as 'Uncle' Arthur.

I raised my head and asked the attendant if we could view the victim's belongings and received a short, gruff response of 'Commissariat' with an overstated Gallic shrug. Then, offering a brief acknowledgement to the attendant, I headed towards the exit. I had seen enough and was eager to be away from the cold reek of death.

'Thank you for arranging that, John,' I said once they were back in the side street.

'What was all that about "Commissariat"?'

'I requested sight of Arthur's belongings and was told they are kept in the police station next door.'

'I suppose that means…'

'Yes, please, John.'

He folded his arms across his chest and sighed. 'I will try for you, but it took a deal of persuasion to get you into the morgue. Inspector Roussel is a prickly so-and-so who makes no secret of his dislike of the invasion of *his* city by hordes of foreigners.'

'I'm sure you're more than a match for a prickly Frenchman, so I'll leave the talking to you, and I'll play the grieving relative.'

'Were you actually related?'

'No, but I always referred to him as "Uncle".'

Another deep breath, but he wasn't going to deny me.

Roussel was a small, clean-shaven man with a pasty face and thinning dark hair combed forward to a sharp arrowhead in the centre of his forehead. He reminded me of a portrait of Napoleon hanging in the National Gallery. Parkes had a hard time keeping up in his broken French, with Roussel making no effort to slow down for an easier understanding of his sharp, clipped speech. The hint of a smile played at the corner of Roussel's mouth. He was toying with the British major, who was becoming more confused and exasperated in an attempt to win the argument. It had gone on long enough. I stepped forward and proceeded to recount the story of my excitement at the prospect of meeting my favourite uncle in a wonderful city and utter despair at his cruel ending, minutes before our planned reunion. All this spoken with a wringing of hands and dabbing of eyes with a handkerchief. I bowed my head in meek resignation and waited for a response.

A keen silence hung in the air for a few moments before the scraping of a chair signalled Roussel had risen from his desk. He left the office and returned to deposit a small bag in front of me. The name 'Burgess' was written on an attached label. I opened the bag and took out a wallet, matches, an unopened pack of cigarettes, two handkerchiefs, a handful of coins and a penknife. The unfolded leather wallet exposed a photograph of Arthur's late wife, Diana, seated and their son, Mark, standing at her side with a hand resting on her shoulder. The photograph lifted to reveal a wad of new banknotes, perhaps eighty francs; nothing else – no letter or written note. Disappointed, I looked at Roussel.

'Has the killer been caught?'

'Yes, Mademoiselle, he was wanted for other serious crimes in this arrondissement.'

'Was?'

'He was identified at the scene and later located at an apartment in Auteuil. The arraignment was bloody, and he died of his wounds.'

'What were his other crimes?'

'He was a well-known thief and suspected of a grievous wounding in a bar brawl.'

I held the handkerchief to my eyes to give me a few seconds to consider my next question. 'May we see his body – the killer?'

'No Mademoiselle, that is not possible.'

I suppose I should have expected a denial. 'You say he was well-known. Was he... a big man? How tall?'

Roussel puffed his cheeks and answered, 'He was neither big nor small.' He inclined his head and continued, 'No bigger than me, and perhaps a little shorter. Why do you ask?'

'It's just that... No, I'm confused.' I struggled to find words that wouldn't offend. 'Do you believe robbery was the intention? There is money in the wallet.'

Roussel shook his head and spread his hands. 'The victim – your uncle – resisted; he was seen and stopped before... enough! I have complied with your request.' He rose from his chair and took a deep breath through his nose. 'The matter is closed. You have seen the contents. They will be shipped back to England with the body.' He slapped a hand on the desk. 'Good day, Major and Mademoiselle.'

'Just one more question, Inspector - was a gun found at the apartment in Auteuil?'

Roussel glared and growled his displeasure. Parkes held up his hands in a gesture of peace, declared our satisfaction, offered congratulations on solving the case, then guided me to the exit. Outside, everywhere was draped in a hushed covering of white. Parkes wanted to talk, but I needed emotions to settle and think clearly. I turned my back to avoid his questioning gaze and marched off but slipped on the snow and almost fell. He caught up and crooked his arm for me to hold.

'Why?' he asked.

'Why what?' I retorted, more sharply than intended.

'Why the interrogation of Roussel? I could follow most of your conversation. They have their man, he got what he deserved, and we need cooperation from the local police. I only hope he...'

'I don't believe Arthur was murdered by a petty criminal in a bungled robbery. It doesn't feel right.' We stopped, and before he could say more, I added, 'Eighty francs was still in the wallet. And the gun. I'll wager they didn't find a gun to match the calibre of the bullet in Arthur's head.'

He stared in disbelief. 'You talk as if... as if...' His voice trailed away. 'What other motive do you have in mind? And the gun. Masses of guns from the war have found their way into unsafe hands in this city. What am I missing, Mary?'

'I'm sorry for upsetting your Inspector chum and I'm no expert, but to my mind it doesn't add up.' I tugged at his arm. 'Come on, let's get back to the hotel. I need to speak to Sir Basil.'

*

I wanted to offer a more detailed explanation of my misgivings to John back at the Majestic, but he was dragged away by one of his soldiers to deal with a complaint from a delegate. He promised to join me as soon as he could, and the way he rolled his eyes suggested it wasn't the first time he had been tasked to placate that particular delegate. I was obliged to wait outside Sir Basil's office with two others and it was more than twenty minutes before I was ushered into his office.

'Ah, Miss Kiten, I was pleased to learn that your intended position has been found. I trust everything with the Treasury Unit is satisfactory?'

'Yes, thank you, Sir Basil, and I'm sorry to trouble you when you're so busy.'

He waved a hand dismissively and said, 'It's what we are here for. Now how can I help?'

'I've just returned from the mortuary and the police station on Rue de Longchamp with Major Parkes.'

He narrowed his eyes and ran a knuckle over his moustache. 'The mortuary – and with Major Parkes. Was that wise?'

'I had to say goodbye to Uncle Arthur's earthly remains and pray for his soul.'

'I see. Well, I would have advised against it, but you are clearly a determined young woman.'

'I don't believe Arthur – Mr Burgess – was killed by an opportunistic thief. I...'

A knock at the door and John entered. 'Excuse me, and my apologies if I was interrupting.'

'Come in, Major. Both of you take a seat.' He waited until we took seats at the other side of his desk. 'You were saying, Mis Kiten.'

'Thank you, yes...' I tried to slow my breathing, so that my arguments would be presented in a calm and measured way. 'I am grateful to Major Parkes for arranging the opportunity to pay my respects at the mortuary. Afterwards we went directly to the police station where I requested sight of Mr Burgess's belongings.'

'Who did you see there? Was it Inspector Roussel?'

John replied, 'Yes, Sir Basil, it was Roussel, and he was in a prickly mood, but Miss Kiten persuaded him to display the items found on Mr Burgess's person.'

Thomson was about to speak when he quickly retrieved a handkerchief and held it over his nose to suppress a sneeze. When the moment had passed he held up a hand by way of an apology and said, 'You were saying that you had doubts, Miss Kiten.'

'Inspector Roussel informed us they had identified a suspect, who had been apprehended and killed at a location in Auteuil. It seems the police consider the matter closed. But... how should I put this? I wonder if they are more interested in recording a crime as solved and ridding the city of a petty criminal than determining the reason for the attack and finding the actual killer.'

'That's a pretty extreme statement, Miss Kiten. What makes you say that?'

'There are a number of... inconsistencies. First, although the motive was robbery, Uncle Arthur had at least eighty francs in his wallet.'

'Ah well, it's my understanding that there were a number of people outside the hotel when the attempted theft took place. One must assume the thief was prevented from completing his mission.'

'Yes, but don't you see - the street outside the hotel is often crowded during daylight hours. Why then, would a petty thief choose that location for his crime. It would be destined to fail, and, at the very least, it's likely he would be seen, perhaps identified, and pursued.'

'One can't always use logic to explain the actions of someone who is desperate,' said John. 'And, as you say, he was identified.'

'By whom? By the police?'

'Now now, just because Inspector Roussel can be difficult, doesn't mean he doesn't do a good job.' Thomson leant forward and pointed a finger in my direction. 'You have no understanding of what is involved in policing, Miss Kiten.'

'I know, and forgive me for pressing the point, but there is the matter of the head wound.'

'Please explain.'

'Uncle... Mr Burgess was shot in the head at close range. As you know he was an unusually tall man, at six feet, three inches, with an erect bearing. According to Roussel, the suspect who the police shot and killed, was no taller than him. I measure five feet six inches and Roussel is at least a couple of inches shorter than me. All that adds up to Mr Burgess having a height advantage of about one foot over his supposed killer. It would have been, not impossible, but extremely awkward for short man to inflict such a wound.'

My little speech was met with silence. Thomson glanced at John, then sat back in his chair and folded his arms. 'Do you have anything to add, Major?'

'I did wonder why you asked that question about height. Now I see.' He thought for a moment, then added, 'How do you know the shot was fired from close range?'

'There was a circle of burned flesh around the wound, which would suggest... that...' I was distracted by Thomson's tutting and shaking of his head. 'That the gun was fired... very near to... his head.'

'Oh dear, Miss Kiten.' He fixed me with an expression of sympathy. 'I do understand how shocked and upset you must be. Forgive me for my directness, but it seems as though you have been carried away by an over-active imagination. You must try and refrain from making such accusations against the local police.' He clapped his hands together as though marking an end to my hysteria. 'And how on earth would you know about gunshot wounds?'

'From the hospital at Wimereux. Some of the doctors there were helpful in explaining the different types of wounds and how to treat them.' Both of them stared at me. 'Also, my father was a member of a gun club and he taught me how to use a handgun.'

A few moments of quiet followed before Thomson responded, 'Well, well, well, you are a surprise packet, Miss Kiten. Nevertheless, I must ask you not to get involved in police and security business. Interference by an innocent young woman, no matter how well-intentioned, is the last thing required in these circumstances. If you're finding it difficult to come to terms with Mr Burgess's death, then Reverend Blenkinsop has an office at the end of this corridor. He's a very good listener, so I'm informed.'

*

The same burly figure in khaki that had blocked my view of Arthur's prone figure now barred entrance to the delegate's bar. Offering the names of Keynes and Pinchin triggered a raised eyebrow and reluctant step to one side. I entered a room splashed with burgundy leather seating and matching velvet curtains trimmed with gold tassels, all through a wispy haze of cigarette and pipe smoke. About half of the thirty or so men were in lounge suits, with the remainder in formal dress. A bright pink silk frock belonged to the only other woman in the bar, sitting between two men holding an animated conversation. I looked away as she nudged the man to her right on noting my entrance.

'Miss Kiten. Over here.'

I turned right and saw Pinchin with a raised hand and broad smile standing by a group of three leather armchairs. I walked fifteen paces or so, feeling exposed and self-conscious as heads turned to follow my progress. I had taken trouble with my appearance; applying rarely-used cosmetics; and wearing my silk, turquoise, pleated dress – the only concession to high fashion in my suitcase. Pinchin gestured at an empty chair with self-conscious muttering, which I interpreted as a compliment. Keynes was slouched in the seat opposite with hands clasped over his belly, and one leg slung over the other in an attitude of languid indifference. Then, abruptly, as though he had suddenly remembered good manners, Keynes unravelled his legs and stood while I took my seat.

'Good evening, Miss Kiten; thank you for joining us.' He waited until all were seated before adding, 'Would you like a drink?'

It was clear from its tone that I was expected to answer his question with a polite refusal. Two cut-glass tumblers were sat on a small circular table in the middle, holding measures of pale amber liquid.

'I will have a small scotch, thank you, sir. Do they serve ice here?'

'Indeed, they do,' said Keynes with the hint of a raised eyebrow, 'and they have imported a fine selection of scotch whisky. Do you have a preference?'

'Now that is a question too far as you must know, Mr Keynes. I'm happy to rely on your experience for a choice of brand, served – on the rocks.'

A casual wave of an arm was enough to bring a waiter to his side. He ordered another glass of *Cardhu* and a bowl of ice.

'How did you find it in our schoolroom today?' asked Pinchin.

'Fascinating. I had no idea of the meticulous research and complex calculations you undertake to arrive at your financial estimates. Of course, I've only just scratched the surface and have a lot to learn, but I'm enjoying my work so far.'

'Gerry tells me you were acquainted with the recently deceased Arthur Burgess,' said Keynes.

'More than acquainted; he was my father's closest friend, and I've known him all my life.'

Keynes appeared unsettled by my response, and he took a moment to consider. 'I'm sorry, I hadn't realised the intimacy of your connection. My commiserations to you and your family. Are you quite ready for work? Wouldn't you like a few days rest or to return home?'

'Thank you, but no, I wish to remain here and prefer to work.'

The waiter placed a small glass of whisky and a bowl of ice on our table. I picked up a cube of ice with silver tongs, dropped it in my glass and swirled it around. Keynes waited, then raised his glass and offered a toast to 'absent friends'. I had tasted scotch whisky only once before at Cambridge. I didn't like it then and prepared for a shock to my tastebuds. I sipped carefully. It was much smoother than the one I remembered but still unpleasant. Pinchin was the first to replace his glass on the table.

'Your German is pretty good, Miss Kiten. How are you with other European languages?'

'I'm fluent in German and French. My Russian is adequate; no more. I can read Italian and speak a little but would not pretend to be anywhere near proficient.' I paused and took another sip. 'That's it. Oh, I started to read Greek at Cambridge, but I've probably forgotten what little I learned.'

Pinchin leaned back in his chair and exchanged a glance with Keynes, who nodded as though a decision had been made.

'Your expertise in languages puts the rest of our unit to shame, and it seems we have been fortunate in engaging your services.' Keynes clasped his hands together and gazed at me as though preparing a statement of some significance. 'Tomorrow, I'm due to travel to Germany with other senior delegates to extend the period of armistice and open discussions on reparations. Gerry was due to accompany me, but we have both concluded that your attendance would be more beneficial because of your grasp of languages, especially German and French.' He paused before adding, 'How would you feel about that, Miss Kiten?'

I had prepared for several possible questions and topics at the meeting but never envisaged a proposition such as this. Confused. In two minds. How should I answer? Despite Thomson's warning, I still had questions about Arthur's death and leaving Paris would feel like a desertion of duty. But where was I to start? I had no authority there. Keynes had presented me with an opportunity to learn more about the Congress, be at the heart of negotiations and make useful contacts. I knew what Uncle Arthur would have advised.

'I'm flattered you've considered me... and after such a short... I don't... Sorry, you've taken me by surprise, and I'm gabbling. What duties would I have on this trip to Germany, sir?'

'We travel by train and, as far as I understand, our business will be conducted on there once we reach our destination. You will be my Personal Assistant, attend and make notes at any formal or informal meetings where I am a participant and translate where necessary. Your main task, however, will be to mingle and listen to informal conversations, especially with French and German delegates. At the end of our visit, I should like to know what Germany, France and, indeed the Americans, have been saying in private about the Congress and the subject of reparations in particular.'

'You want me to act as a spy?' said too late to smother a reaction more forceful than intended.

Pinchin clapped his hands and exclaimed, 'Ha! No, nothing of the sort. It's simply a case of...' He looked to Keynes to elaborate.

'Gerry and I are delegates. Our faces are known, and conversation in our presence will be restricted. On the other hand, you are just another of the anonymous faces from the support staff and better placed to overhear unguarded comments.' Keynes hesitated and rearranged his position in the chair. 'Please don't take this the wrong way, Miss Kiten. You are a very attractive young woman, and men, especially those in high station, tend to believe that beauty and brains don't mix. We know in your case this is not true and would take advantage of this fact.'

'I understand and thank you for the explanation.'

'Are you comfortable with your role?'

'Yes, perfectly. It's an exciting opportunity, and I will do my best to repay the faith you have placed in me.'

Four

Four motor cars were waiting at the front of the Majestic, each with a uniformed driver and soldier in the front seats. The engines were running, billowing fumes into the chill, grey early morning. Keynes was waiting outside stamping his feet, fisting gloved hands and talking to two men I didn't recognise. After a brief nod of acknowledgement, he guided me into the back of the first car and instructed our driver to start the journey. It shuddered on the icy road, throwing us both forward, before settling into steady progress past the Arc and along the Avenue de Friedland.

Keynes appeared preoccupied, staring out of the window and providing only short, clipped answers to questions. I learnt we were taking a train from Gare de L'Est and our destination was Trèves, only a few miles over the German border with Luxembourg. I had been there as a young child when visiting relatives on Father's side near Kaiserslautern. My memory of the old town, known in Germany as Trier, was hazy. I remember the cathedral and ancient Roman ruins, including an amphitheatre. There would be no sightseeing on this trip. I had been tasked with mingling and listening.

A crowd was gathered at the station, held back by lines of soldiers in blue uniforms. The car stopped, and we made our way through a passage formed by the soldiers into a largely deserted concourse. A French officer directed us to a waiting train breathing long, uncomplaining sighs of steam. The front and rear carriages were a dark, muddy brown with small windows and central doors open to show a dozen or more soldiers in each. The six central carriages were of a very different character. Panels of deep red and cream surrounded curtained windows with sculpted frames of polished wood. An attendant held a door and bowed as we climbed into a carriage furnished as a drawing room with wood panelling, easy chairs, an ornate mirror and a table laid with decanters. Three men were already seated at the far end, reading newspapers. One looked up and waved at Keynes, who went to the far end to join him. Stranded, I removed my coat, draped it over a chair and took the nearest seat by a window.

A commotion of voices in French disturbed the quiet; two suited men peered into the carriage and disappeared for more conversation. From the fragments heard, it seemed a decision was made that the French contingent should occupy an adjacent carriage. I watched as more men boarded until more than half the chairs in my carriage were occupied.

'Pardon me, may I sit here?' The voice, spoken with an American accent, belonged to a slim, dark-haired woman in her thirties, wearing a smart, blue coat trimmed with fur.

'Of course.' I stood and picked up my coat from the chair opposite. 'I'm not sure where…'

'I'll take that.' She removed her coat, placed a bag on the chair and handed both coats to an attendant. 'I'm Sandra – Sandra Fairlight.'

'How do you do, Sandra.' We had the briefest of handshakes; our fingers barely touching. 'Mary – Mary Kiten.'

'Looks like we are the only women on the train. We'll have to stick together.' Her smile was encouraging and friendly. 'Which delegate or group are you with?'

'I'm assisting Mr Keynes from the British Treasury.' I paused, wondering whether to say more. 'I've only recently arrived in Paris as a replacement and feeling rather lost. I don't know any of the other delegates here.'

'I've been here for a few weeks, but it feels like much longer, meeting after meeting, even on Christmas Day. I'm looking forward to a change of scenery and this little adventure into enemy territory.' She rearranged her position in the chair, removed gloves and brushed down her skirt before continuing. 'I came over on the ship with our President, Mr Wilson. I'm the personal assistant to Colonel House, one of the President's advisors, here to listen and report back. I can put names to quite a few of the faces in here.' She leant to one side and peered down the carriage. 'I've met your Mr Keynes, and the man on his left is Norman Davis from our Treasury. I think the man next to Davis is another of yours – Sir John Beale, but I don't know the fourth man at their table. It looks like they're playing cards. Davis is a keen bridge player.'

I opened my bag, taking out a notebook and pencil. 'Do you mind if I take a few notes?'

The identifying continued for a few minutes until I had names, titles and rough sketches of more than half the twenty or so passengers in view.

'Thank you, that's been very useful. I wonder...' I paused and turned towards the door behind me. 'All the delegates in here are British or American. Are there others from France, Italy, Japan?'

'Ah, the French, led by Marshal Foch, have their own carriage, next to ours, and I understand the Italians and Japanese will not be with us. There's another carriage for selected press representatives, and two others have been set aside as meeting rooms for the German contingent.'

'You're very well informed, Sandra. I'm lucky you've been so open and friendly.'

'We all need friends in these strange times.' She leant forward and touched my hand. 'Now, tell me about yourself. You're very young to be in this company. Mr Keynes must have a high opinion of your abilities.'

'I don't know about that. It was probably my availability and knowledge of languages that persuaded him.'

Doors slammed, the engine huffed, and the train lurched into its first hesitant shuffles forward. We were on our way. I offered a brief and partial history of my time at Cambridge, volunteering as a nurse for the war effort and last-minute call up from Wimereux. I didn't mention Arthur's murder. We soon settled into a comfortable companionship, drinking coffee, gazing out of the window and drifting into occasional exchanges about Paris, the Congress and our families. Eventually, the carriage quietened as repetitive clacking and puffing lulled some occupants into dozing while others read or stared out of the windows.

I checked my watch. It was almost five hours since our departure from Paris. We had reached the outskirts of Trier, but progress was slow. The last few miles inside the German border had been a crawl. All of my fellow travellers had their attention fixed to the scene outside, no doubt curious to verify the tales of deprivation and starvation brought on by the allied blockade. There was nothing unremarkable in the structure or state of repair of buildings and streets; it was the slow, shambling melancholy of the inhabitants that struck me. Some stopped and stared at our train as it chugged slowly into the heart of the city. Nearing the centre, crowds thickened; lines watching deepened; arms waved, pointed; accusing. Someone opened a window, and I could hear the shouting from the masses outside, angry, threatening. A stone was thrown; then another. One thudded into a panel near our window; glass shattered at a distance. A shouted warning of, 'Everyone get down,' was obeyed, for the most part, with passengers crouching in their seats or kneeling on the floor. I leant back in my seat, out of full view, but still able to see the mob. The sharp retort of gunfire sent a shockwave through the throng - confusion, cowering; some stilled with open-mouthed horror; screaming; others defiant - then, more sharp rifle cracks. The train continued, unhurried, seeming oblivious to insults and danger. After no more than a couple of minutes, we slowed to a halt in the station. All was quiet. The angry crowd had been left behind and replaced by German soldiers lining the platform.

A man in naval unform, identified by Sandra as Admiral Browning, addressed the carriage. 'Lords, gentlemen... and ladies, my apologies for the disturbance. We were assured of a safe and protected reception here. That was most - unexpected. Please remain here while I consult with Marshal Foch to decide how we should proceed.'

Keynes was brushing down his jacket while others around him were righting a fallen table and recovering playing cards from the floor. A man I had not seen before entered the door behind Keynes, holding his bloodied head. Maybe it was the sight of blood that induced an automatic reaction. Without thinking, I found myself walking towards him.

'Excuse me… Please, allow me…'

Two men stood aside, and I confronted a tall, clean-shaven man in his late 'twenties or early 'thirties. His bleeding had spread under his hand on to his grey suit and white shirt.

'Let me take a look at that, sir.'

He appeared unconcerned and surprised at my attention. He shrugged, then removed his hand to show a three-inch gash on his forehead.

'Please sit.' I offered a chair and held his arm while he lowered himself.

I grabbed a round, embroidered cloth from a table, folded and pressed it against the wound. He followed my instructions and replaced my hand with his own while I gazed around the carriage for more material.

'Do you need more cloth?' He had an accent I couldn't place immediately. It wasn't British or American.

'Yes.'

'Then let's adjourn to the next carriage. That's set for the meeting and has long tables spread with plenty of white cloth.'

I picked up a decanter and followed him through the door. He handed me a handkerchief and penknife, then sat and watched as I ripped a large white cloth into long strips. Then, soaking his handkerchief in the spirit from the decanter, I removed the bloody compress and inspected the gash.

'It's a little early for brandy but go ahead anyway.'

I started to dab his forehead with the damp cloth. 'Was it caused by broken glass, or...'

'It was a brick or stone. My fault. I was at an open window, watching our welcome from the people of this city.'

'It's a clean wound and probably a blessing that shards of glass didn't cause the damage.' I started to wind a bandage around his head. 'You will need a couple of stitches eventually, but this should stop the bleeding.'

'Thank you.' He looked up as I paused the winding, reaching for the next strip. 'You must be Mary Kiten.'

'How... how did you know?'

'I'm sorry, forgive my rudeness. I'm Adam Visser, and I work for General Smuts, who advises your Prime Minister. I'm attending this conference on his behalf.'

'Ah, South Africa – that explains your accent.' I stopped myself from adding it was also the reason for his healthy, tanned complexion that shamed the pale, wintry faces of the rest of us.

'We met your Mr Keynes last night, and he mentioned you would assist him today.' I reached for the last strip of cloth, wondering if they had discussed more than my name. 'He is a clever man, much admired by some... and deeply mistrusted by others.'

'Mistrusted – why?'

'You don't know?'

'I know very little about Mr Keynes or the Congress. I arrived in Paris only two days ago and had no time to prepare.' I tied the bandage and stood back. 'There, it's not very neat, I'm afraid, but should serve until a doctor can be found.'

'Thank you again, Miss Kiten.' He used both hands to check the wrapping around his head. 'You should be aware that there are those who would wish to punish Germany by demanding extreme financial reparations that would likely bankrupt the country. They suspect that Mr Keynes will argue to limit reparations.'

'In that case, I should also thank you for filling a gap in my ignorance. Who are they - those who oppose Mr Keynes?'

He shrugged. 'Well, you could include most of the French delegates in that group. Also, some from your own country.'

I waited for names to follow, but it seemed that a vague warning was all I was going to be offered. 'Should we re-join the others/?'

He remained seated, folded his arms and looked at me as though considering an answer. 'I had a high regard for Arthur Burgess.'

'Oh...' A statement out of nowhere. Meaning what? A prelude to sympathy, or...? I met his gaze, wondering how much he knew. 'I was due to meet Mr Burgess when he....'

'Yes, I know.'

The door opened; Foch and Browning entered, followed by a French officer, Davis, Keynes and others. I stood back and let them pass down the carriage filling the seats on one side of the long table. Sandra came to my side as the door at the other end opened, and men filed in to take seats opposite. It didn't stop. Too many were entering from both ends. We were crushed into a corner as voices were raised by those being pushed. Newspaper men were jostling with cameras and notebooks for a better position. It became chaotic, and it was clear the meeting couldn't continue under those conditions. Someone shouted an order that all those standing should leave the carriage, which was echoed by the same command in French and German.

An hour or more of confusion followed until an announcement was made that the conference would take place in the station hotel. I wanted to ask Visser more about Arthur but couldn't find him. Sandra and I were among the last to exit the carriage and followed others in a short walk from the station to a hotel. Most of the angry horde had been dispersed and quietened by a show of force. Our soldiers guarded our progress on either side, keeping a sparse and sullen crowd at bay. We entered a cheerless, middle-sized room where odd tables had been hastily arranged in a rough rectangle. It was almost full, with about thirty seated and twice that number standing around the perimeter, but it was manageable, and introductions to each delegate had started. We took our places behind Keynes and Davis.

The grim-faced man in the centre of the German delegation belonged to Matthias Erzberger, the finance minister who offered a grudging apology for the attack on the train, adding that a few sticks and stones were no justification for warning gunfire from the train guards. Foch was in no mood to accept this version of events and loosed a tirade of complaints in return. Browning tried to calm the situation, but it was not a promising start to proceedings. The main business was simply to extend the armistice for another month, but both sides were eager to add conditions. The Germans wanted an end to the blockade and relief to their starving millions. At the same time, the allies, especially Foch and his deputies, were adamant the blockade would continue and also required the surrender of the German merchant fleet. Arguments were tossed back and forth across the table, becoming more repetitive and ill-tempered and without any sign of resolution.

Keynes' first contribution was made during a period of relative quiet. He proposed the meeting adjourned for an hour while he and a German banker named Melchior explored possible solutions to the impasse in a separate room. Browning was keen on the idea and persuaded Foch after a little grumbling. Erzberger consulted briefly with Melchior, then shrugged his acceptance. Keynes rose and signalled that I should follow.

We were ushered into a small office behind the reception desk. Not much bigger than a cupboard, it was furnished with two cabinets, a safe, a small table and two upright chairs. I was offered another chair but declined through lack of space and stood by the door. Melchior was a small, neat man with a high, stiff collar that gleamed remarkably white against his short, dark beard. His had been one of the more reasoned and less aggressive voices on the German side. In sharp contrast to the exchanges in the main meeting, the two men immediately struck up an easy, informal rapport. Melchior spoke impeccable English, and the discussion was brisk and to the point but friendly and without rancour.

An understanding was reached that neither of them would persuade their side to compromise at the current session. Still, they would both operate behind the scenes to argue for a more practical and reasoned approach to future negotiations. For his part, Keynes promised to urge his political masters to get food supplies moving to Germany, while Melchior would attempt to reconcile his side to surrender, at least part, of their merchant fleet.

*

It was past eight in the evening when the train pulled out of Trier. Our departure was delayed while refreshment was brought from the hotel. I found a seat next to Sandra in the carriage set aside for the meeting, but neither of us had much appetite, and the atmosphere around the table was subdued. The conference had satisfied neither side. An extension to the armistice had been signed, but the issues of shipping and the blockade were deferred to consideration in Paris. The subject of reparations was not discussed, and I overheard Keynes, in conversation with Davis, denounce Foch and Browning for mishandling the conference.

'It's been a long day, and you must forgive me if I doze on our return journey,' said Sandra as we returned to our seats in the delegates' lounge.

'I suspect you will not be alone,' I answered. The air had begun to thicken with cigar smoke, and attendants were busy with the decanters of brandy. 'Do you mind if I take a few minutes to check through my notes?'

I had been diligent but hurried in my notetaking, and there were many pages to scan for corrections and amendments to ensure I didn't forget context and meaning. Keynes had spoken no more than a handful of words to me all day, and I was dreading the prospect of having to type a fair record for him tomorrow. Sandra nudged my arm, and I looked up to see Visser.

'Pardon me, Miss Kiten, I thought you might like to know that I found a doctor to put the finishing touches to your handiwork.' A small white square had replaced his heavily bandaged head. It was the first time I had seen him since our encounter many hours before.

'I'm pleased to see he tidied up my clumsy dressing.'

'Not at all; it served its purpose well. I enjoyed your attention and our short conversation.' He bowed his head, clicked heels and turned to take a seat at the other end of the carriage.

'A handsome man,' said Sandra, 'and I don't blame you for going to his aid. Thank goodness our heated reception in Germany caused no serious injuries.'

'Yes, he's... interesting. I'll admit, I was surprised to find a South African on the train.'

'Colonel House has met with General Smuts a few times since our arrival in Paris, and Mr Visser has accompanied him on each occasion. He doesn't say much but has the air of someone with his ear to the ground and knows much of the intrigue going on behind closed doors.'

I was tempted to ask more about Visser but decided it was not the time to probe further. His unprompted mention of Arthur preyed on my mind, and I would try to find out more about the South African when we returned to Paris.

In another half hour the steady rattle and hum of the train had a dulling effect, and I was ready to join the majority in the carriage who were asleep. But I couldn't put it off any longer. I couldn't bear the thought of Mother hearing of Arthur's death from official or another source without notification from my hand.

PAUL WALKER

Thursday, 9th January, 1919

My Dearest Mother

I have struggled to find the right words for this note.

Uncle Arthur has passed to a better life. I regret his was a violent end, but I find comfort in knowing he is now reunited with his great friend, Robert; my father; your husband.

It happened within minutes of my arrival at the Majestic Hotel, and unhappily, before he had a chance to welcome me. The police have stated that Uncle Arthur was the unfortunate victim of an armed robbery outside the entrance to this hotel. After all we have suffered with the savage madness of war these past years, it is doubly difficult to accept his loss under these circumstances.

I have paid my respects to his earthly remains and I will write to Mark, although I expect he will already have been informed through official channels.

Uncle Arthur found a position for me in the British Treasury Unit. It has the potential of interesting work and I have decided to remain here, at least for a while, as my way of remembering and paying tribute to a dear family friend.

Most beloved Mother, it weighs heavily on me to impart such sad news to you in this way. I wish I could be with you, to share this melancholy, and hope you will understand the reason for my temporary stay in Paris.

With undying love and affection
Your devoted daughter
Mary

Five

I arrived at the school a little after eight on a cold, grey morning. Pinchin and two others were already at their desks, but there was no sign of Keynes. I received no hint from him on his expectations for our debriefing from Trier. It was less than six hours since we had arrived at the Majestic, and he was either too tired or preoccupied with his thoughts to manage more than grunts or nods in reply to my questions in the foyer before we retired. The bitter chill in my room and an active mind allowed only about two hours of fitful sleep before a reviving hot breakfast. Yet, to my surprise, once I arrived at the schoolroom, I felt alert and ready for the day ahead.

It was past eleven o'clock when Keynes breezed in and signalled for Pinchin and I to follow him into his office. We both stood while he removed his overcoat, hat and scarf, warmed hands over a heater, then made minute adjustments to the position of blotter, pens and paper. Finally, he took his seat behind the desk and gestured that we should take ours. The sheen on his neatly clipped hair and the fresh bloom on his complexion told of a recent visit to a barber.

'Bloody waste of time,' he said without any preamble. 'Reparations were not discussed; the French were mulish, and Browning was too weak. The conference was shambolic, and the only saving grace was a pleasant interlude with a chap named Melchior.'

'Did you at least get the armistice extended?' asked Gerry.

'Yes, but that was a foregone conclusion and could have been done without wasting the time of forty or more delegates.' He picked up a pen and jotted a few notes on a scrap of paper before turning his focus on me. 'How did you find our jaunt into Germany, Miss Kiten? I hope you found it useful in providing a background to the difficulties we face here.'

'I've typed up my notes from yesterday.'

He took the clipped sheets of foolscap from my hand and placed them on his desk in a manner that suggested they would not be read.

'Can you summarise the highlights?'

'I suppose the main findings overall were the belligerence of the French, the anger of the populace in Trier and a strong feeling of injustice felt by the German delegates.'

'Neatly put, Miss Kiten. Based on our experience yesterday, negotiations between France and Germany will not reach a successful compromise without significant urging and cajoling from Britain and America.' He paused and twirled a pen in his fingers. 'Anything else to report?'

'We were not in the company of the German delegation for long, but I did overhear muttered conversations suggesting they should continue the fight rather than submit to humiliation. Some amongst their number seemed to believe the original signing of the armistice was a mistake.'

'Yes, I'm not surprised,' replied Keynes. 'It will be difficult because they have already surrendered armaments, but we should be wary of believing that Germany has no military bite left. They may have had the worst of it on the Western Front, but few could argue their claim to victory on the East.'

'Is the blockade to be lifted,' asked Pinchin.

'Not yet, but it must come soon. Lloyd George and Wilson both know that Clemenceau will have to be persuaded.' Keynes paused and looked at us in turn as if ready to end our debriefing.

'There was something else....'

'What was it, Miss Kiten?'

'I heard reference to reparations and comments that the subject should be avoided at yesterday's conference.' That much I assumed he knew. 'Also, your name was mentioned in a... less than favourable light.'

'Oh, tell me more.'

'The terms "arrogant" and "head in the clouds" were used. You were said to hold dangerous views and should be "put in your place".'

Pinchin huffed and lurched back in his seat. 'Why, that's preposterous and insulting. Dangerous. How?'

'Those phrases stuck in my mind. I only heard snatches of conversation, but I understand Mr Keynes believes financial reparations from Germany should be - limited and not excessively punitive.'

'Your understanding is correct,' said Keynes. 'Who made those statements?'

'Some came from the French delegation, but I don't have names.' I hesitated before continuing. 'Similar sentiments were expressed in a conversation held with Sir John Beale and Admiral Browning, although the statements in question were not from either of their mouths.'

A silence hung in the air. I could sense Pinchin's discomfort, but he remained quiet. Keynes' expression was a mix of puzzlement and amusement. 'It seems my opinions are more widely known than I imagined and have ruffled a few feathers. "Dangerous" is an odd term to use, but I am gratified to learn that some believe I will influence the outcome.'

'Indeed, perhaps it should be taken as a compliment,' joined Pinchin. 'Well, Miss Kiten, it appears the decision to send you to the conference in Treves paid off. I hope you also found it to be a useful experience.'

'It certainly served to reveal how ignorant I was about the nature of Congress here. So, thank you for the opportunity.' Keynes' attention had wandered, and he clearly thought our debriefing was at an end. 'I wonder if you could help fill a few more holes in my knowledge.' Keynes tilted his head with mild interest inviting me to continue. 'Two delegates, who were not present yesterday but mentioned as significant advisors at the Congress were Colonel House and General Smuts. I know nothing about them and for my benefit....'

'Edward House is a close friend and advisor to President Wilson,' answered Keynes. 'We have never met, but he has a reputation as a man of good intellect and moderate views.'

'And General Smuts? I was surprised to learn that a South African advises Lloyd George.'

'Smuts is a good man, although many find his manner somewhat brusque. I imagine our Prime Minister values his advice as it is free from the petty squabbling of British party politics.' Keynes paused before adding, 'I noticed you attending to the head wound of his aide, Mr Visser. That was well done.'

'Do you know where General Smuts and Mr Visser are staying in Paris? I have a handkerchief from Mr Visser that I should like to return when cleaned.'

'They are at the Astoria, but they will be absent from Paris for a few days. I understand that General Smuts leads a delegation travelling to Hungary today.'

'Do we know why?' asked Pinchin.

'It's hush-hush, but I imagine it will be concerned with the Romanian conflict, or perhaps to gauge the extent of Russian influence.'

I was about to excuse myself, but reference to Russia stirred my interest. 'I'm ashamed to admit I know little about the Eastern front. Are there no delegates from Russia here?'

'Ha, the city is crawling with them, but not in an official capacity,' said Pinchin.

'Russia fought against Germany. Shouldn't they be represented here?'

Keynes took a cigarette from a silver case, retrieved a lighter from a pocket and sat back in his chair. He glanced at Pinchin as though expecting him to answer. When nothing came, he said, 'Gerry and I differ on the Russian question. The majority view believes we should have no communication with the Bolsheviks and offer increased military aid to the White Russians. I favour a more pragmatic solution. It is true that the Bolsheviks control only central Russia and are threatened by many opposing factions. But they are the *de facto* government of the largest country in Europe and will probably prevail in time.'

'Are the Bolsheviks or White Russians in Paris?'

Keynes lit his cigarette. 'There's no need to concern yourself with the Russian question at this stage, Miss Kiten. Now, I really must get on. Oh, and why don't you take the afternoon off? You had a long day yesterday.'

'Thank you; I will.'

I left his office, tempted to ignore Keynes' advice, and find out more about the Russians in Paris. I wasn't sure why; perhaps it was a reaction because his statement was so patronising. A visit to Visser would have to be put on hold, and that was a disappointment. I had no plan and knew it would not be easy, but I possessed a sense of purpose to discover who murdered Arthur.

*

Who was I kidding? I was not an investigator. I could handle a gun and had watched Jock Carmichael picking his door lock when he lost his key. Also, I had read some of the detective stories featuring Holmes and Watson. They were good fun, but far-fetched. And that was the extent of my background as a detective. Laughable. Cold logic told me that, as a young clerical worker in an unfamiliar city where I knew virtually no one, any attempt to conduct an enquiry into murder was a non-starter. What did I have: a cryptic note warning me to be secretive, and a conviction that Arthur's murder wasn't the result of a random robbery? It may have a connection with his work for the War Office – whatever that was. Would Sir Basil Thomson or John Parkes know? Even if they did, they were both reluctant to question the official police line. The throwaway mention of Arthur by Visser was tantalising, but may mean nothing. My idea of solving Arthur's murder was pathetic fantasy. I should continue my work for Keynes for a few months, or until the idea of returning home seemed more attractive than remaining in Paris. But – I couldn't rid myself of a sense of duty. I owed it to Arthur, Father and Mother, to persuade the competent authorities to carry out a thorough investigation. Failing that… I had to admit, I was at a loss to know. But somehow, I would find a way to avenge his murder.

I remembered my promise to write to Arthur's son. Mark Burgess was a banker, and a different character to his father. Their relationship was respectful and cordial but lacked warmth. He was seven or eight years older than me and my contacts with him had never gone beyond polite formalities. I would have to be circumspect and stick to the official police version surrounding the circumstances of Arthur's murder.

I picked up the writing pad and riffled the sheets a couple of times, preoccupied with composing the letter. I thumbed it again, but slowly. Had I seen something? There - in a sheet in the middle of the pad, an address was written in block capitals across the centre of the page – *18E, RUE GUSTAVE COURBET*. Underneath this, a less precise, hurried scrawl on a diagonal, followed by a question mark. It looked like a name: a Russian name. Was it *Chekov*, *Chavinky*, or…? No, it was two words or abbreviations – *Ch* and *Nivsky* or *Nevsky*.

My thoughts tumbled too quickly to process. Why write in block capitals and hide in the middle of the writing pad? Neither would be a regular practice for Arthur's neat mind. And then there was the untidy scribble of a name. Was it an afterthought? Was there a connection to his murder? There must have been a purpose in recording an address that way. Was there any other writing? I checked the other pages; all blank, except... I tore the top sheet from the writing pad and held it up against the weak light from an electric bulb. Faint indentations were visible with the paper at an angle. I could make out the shape of a capital 'L' and an 'M' but couldn't make out the other letters. Taking a pencil, I shaded the area over the writing with light strokes. Still unclear. I persevered with more delicate shading and holding the result against the light. Partial success. The first word began with 'Lit' and ended in 'ov', presumably the name of a Russian. Most of the following words were too indistinct. One may have been, 'inform' and another, 'danger' or dancer'. There was no doubt the last entry on the page was 'Maria' – me.

I forced myself to stop and consider if I was being fanciful. The message from the indentations could have been anything. Was that word really, 'danger'? Maybe it was simply a reminder to invite me to a dinner, the ballet or a concert. The address written in capitals may have held some significance in the context of his murder, although I supposed it was a long shot. But there was only one way to find out.

Six

One major disadvantage of importing all the Majestic staff from Britain was lack of local knowledge. The likelihood of any of them being able to direct me to Rue Gustave Courbet was slim. I wasn't even sure if I wanted anyone to learn of my interest in the address. I noticed George Barnes among those manning reception and waited until he was free.

'Good afternoon, Mr Barnes.'

'Miss Kiten, how can I help?'

'First, I'm sorry your assistance to me the other day landed you in hot water. I hadn't understood the necessity for such tight security here.'

'Don't worry, Miss, it was only a slap on the wrist, and the rules here take a bit of getting used to.'

'You're telling me, and I'm relieved we have both been forgiven.' I placed an elbow on the counter, leant forward and lowered my voice. 'I have been given the afternoon off, and I thought I might browse the shops but don't know my way around.'

'Ah, you want a street map.'

'Do you have one? That would be perfect.'

'We have four, one for each of the local ron…. rondi….'

'Arrondissements?'

'Yes, exactly. Sir Basil commissioned them for our residents, and we only have maps for the areas around the hotels and where the delegates meet. Exploring beyond these is discouraged.' He turned and unlocked a cupboard, extracted sheets of paper, each roughly a foot square and handed them over. 'They're hand-drawn, and we've had a few complaints of inaccuracies, but I suppose they're better than nothing.'

'Thank you, George, this is more than I had expected. Sorry, do you mind if I call you George? It's nice to have a friendly face in a strange city.'

'Of course, Miss, I would be....'

'And you must call me Mary.' He ran a finger around his shirt collar and looked uncomfortable. 'When you're off duty, I mean.'

'Thank you, Miss; I would enjoy that.'

I folded the maps, placed them in my bag and made my way to the exit. A small café down a side street was a convenient stop to study the maps and seek assistance from locals if the address in question was not marked. I reached into a coat pocket and removed the sheet of paper with the address. Although I didn't need to check the street name and apartment number, I wanted to have something with me that was relevant and personal from Arthur. It didn't take long to scan the maps of arrondissements one and two. George was right; the hand-drawn maps were only a rough guide with many streets unmarked. Despite poring over the maps for the eighth and sixteenth arrondissements, I could find no reference to Rue Gustave Courbet. It was either too small to be referenced or in a more distant area of the city. I beckoned a waitress and asked if she could direct me. I was in luck; she lived nearby, knew it well and pointed to its location on the map of the sixteenth. I calculated it should take no more than half an hour to walk there.

I set off at a brisk pace down Avenue Kleber. The air was cold, and a grey sky promised more snow to join the discoloured heaps piled at the kerbside. I crossed the road and headed towards Place Victor Hugo when my steps faltered as nagging doubts began to take hold. The excitement of finding the address had faded, and I came to realise my plan was hurried and thin. I intended to pose as a French nurse returned from a hospital in the Meuse region with a partial address given by a French soldier on his deathbed. I hoped this would allow a conversation, discovery of a name and other brief details about the resident. Of course, any progression beyond this subterfuge would depend on how I assessed whoever answered the door. Could I convince? Was my cover believable? But what if a man at the address was Arthur's murderer? Of course, it was possible, but unlikely. Could Arthur's contact be a woman? And how was I to navigate my way past the concierge? I couldn't turn back, but my enthusiasm was tempered by imaginings of all that might go wrong.

Rue Gustave Courbet presented as a typical residential street in central Paris; a paved road edged by six-storey cream plastered terraces, double wooden doors and shuttered windows for apartments, alternating with shop fronts, cafes and offices. The mid-afternoon sky had darkened, and the few pedestrians paid me little attention as they busied themselves, wrapped tightly into their collars and scarves. I passed number 18 mid-way on my right, continued to the end of the street and crossed to the other side. I walked back until I was opposite number

18 and stared into the reflection of a shop window. I saw five lights in windows on the second, third and fourth floors, but light was no sure indication of current occupation. I had resolved to take a seat in a nearby café to consider my next move when the door opened, and an elderly man appeared, gazed uncertainly at the sky and prodded a walking stick on to the pavement. There was my chance. I moved quickly over the street, with a hailed warning that the pavement was icy, offering him my arm to step out safely. He was surprised but grateful and grabbed my coat before placing a hesitant foot over the doorstep. I swung the bag off my shoulder with my other arm and put it behind him to stop the door from closing. We took a dozen steps together before I assured him it was safe to continue without my assistance. I watched as he progressed slowly, then I returned to number 18, picked up my bag and entered the hallway.

A single electric bulb lit a dim lobby and stairwell. The door to my left showed a brass letter A, and I assumed the unmarked door to my right was the domain of the concierge. I stilled myself and listened for any sounds of activity, holding my breath in the chill, bare space. Satisfied, I raised my heels and trod carefully up the stairs, grabbing my bag and coat tightly to deaden any rustling from cotton and silk. Apartment E was on the second floor. I tapped the door and waited. Nothing. I removed a white glove and knocked again; the sound echoed, brazen and harsh in the shadowy void of the stairwell. An ear to the door yielded only silence. What should I do? I cursed my lack of preparation; should have written a note in advance to slip under the door. I twisted the door handle in frustration. Was it unlocked? I pushed gently and the door opened.

As soon as I entered, I knew what I would find. The smell of death had become too familiar. I hesitated. Why wasn't I terrified? I felt a curious mix of nervous anticipation and calm certainty that I should explore the apartment. With a handkerchief to my face, I made my way along a dark corridor to a large room with pale grey light filtered through two windows. I flinched as I caught movement before realising it was my reflection in a full-length mirror. A large table and six chairs occupied the central space. An embroidered white cloth was arranged in a diamond shape on the tabletop, and a blue vase in the middle held an arrangement of dried flowers. Four easy chairs were set around a hearth at the far end with spent coal in the grate, and a neat stack of newspapers topped a smaller table. I examined a few. They were all *Le Figaro*, in date order with the most recent dated six days ago.

Four doors led off the main room; the nearest was half-open. I pushed slowly. A bedroom. An overturned cupboard. A trousered leg on a crumpled bed. I took a breath and entered a scene of bloody murder. A man formed a grotesque shape on the bed: arms outstretched; a hand raised with a finger pointing to the ceiling; one leg folded at an awkward angle underneath the other; his head hidden under a pillow covered in dried gore. I stood in the doorway, closed my eyes and steeled myself for a closer inspection. At hospitals, I dealt with the dead and dying in an environment far removed from the actions that caused their wounding or death. This was different. I bore witness to the immediate aftermath of an intimate and deliberate killing. I approached the body and tried to lift the pillow. Stuck to the head. I tugged, then wrenched, and it tore, leaving shreds of cloth around a gaping head wound. I imagined the scene; a terrified man held by strong arms, the pillow suffocating; one shot through the pillow into the forehead. Maybe a muffler or silencer was attached to the gun. It was not the work of one man. I don't know why, but I had an impression the mission was completed quickly and efficiently by at least three killers.

The mottled features with staring eyes, screaming mouth, and bulging tongue told me nothing. A short, thickset man in his forties with flecks of grey in his hair and moustache, I guessed he had been dead for two or three days. The cut and cloth of a dark suit were workaday, and a fob watch in his waistcoat pocket showed the name of a Swiss maker. I hesitated, took a deep breath, then opened the suit jacket to reveal the name of a French tailor but found no wallet inside.

I knew I should examine the body but looked away to suppress a feeling of nausea. Could I get clues on identity in another, more agreeable, way? I righted the cupboard and examined the drawers, two shirts in one: underclothes in the other. The initials A.C. embroidered in the shirts offered a tantalising clue to a name, but I needed more. Two suits and an overcoat in a small wardrobe revealed nothing about their wearer, so I moved back to the main room.

The next door was closed. I braced myself for another prospect of horror before opening. An anticlimax. Another bedroom, unoccupied, with everything neat and orderly except for a rumpled blanket on top of the bed. The wardrobes and cupboards were much the same as the other bedroom, with more shirts and underclothes, two pairs of boots and two fur hats, but no initials to offer clues to a name. A hairbrush, comb and small framed photograph of a middle-aged woman lay on top of the cupboard. Nothing was gained from what was clearly a studio photograph, with no inscription and an anonymous background.

Where was the second man? Had he escaped the terrible fate of his fellow resident? He may be an occasional lodger, or surely, he would have reported his death. Perhaps he could have met a similar fate, but at another location. Unless - he was one of the killers. No, that was unlikely. The sparsely furnished apartment gave the impression of a temporary residence, inhabited by men who had a cordial relationship at the very least.

The bathroom was narrow, damp and claustrophobic. A bar of soap, a shaving brush, two razors, three bottles of cologne and a jar of hair oil were arranged along a single shelf. Did this array of belongings and the shared use of soap and a shaving brush hint at a friendship? Possessions were few, and some could have been stolen, but there was no evidence of ransacking. Still, it was perplexing that I could find no identification, letters or other personal effects in the rooms.

The final room I entered had an air of little use and served as both kitchen and storage for items of broken furniture, a hatstand, lamp and a pile of woollen blankets. An empty sink and a small, rusting stove were in a corner, reinforcing my belief that occupation was short-lived and transient. A glass-fronted cupboard contained cups, saucers, bowls, plates and glasses. There was a strong smell of anise, which came from an uncorked, near-empty bottle alongside two full bottles of brandy, another bottle of clear spirit and half a dozen bottles of dark beer. No food. I manoeuvred my way past a broken dresser and opened the door to the stove. Empty? No, something nestled inside – a cloth bag tied with twine, containing what felt like a collection of paper and trinkets or coins. I took it into the main room for better light, placed it on a table and struggled to unravel the knot. Coins and banknotes. Roubles. So, the occupants were probably Russian.

I should have become accustomed to the stench, but it seemed to be getting stronger, my stomach was churning, and I adjourned to the bathroom. I forced myself to vomit, then splashed my face with cold water before returning to the bedroom with the body. What would a police detective do? How would he search for clues? I put on my gloves, opened a penknife, slashed the suit jacket and trousers, took a deep breath and fumbled in the lining. I found nothing in the folds or lining but touched a rigid object under the mattress and, after lifting and groping, pulled out a book. Another Russian connection: the author was Maxim Gorky, a name I recognised but had not read. The title translated as *Mother*. I flicked through the pages; no hidden notes, but there was an inscription on the inside front cover – three lines: the initials A C; a word I couldn't translate; initials M L followed by a date of August 1918. Those damned initials again. And who was M L?

I stuffed the book in my bag and stared at the earthly remains of A C. Not enough. What else should I do? I stifled a lurch in my middle as I imagined cold, injured flesh on a mortuary slab. Stop. I gathered my senses. There must be something I had missed. Shoes – I hadn't examined his shoes. The feet had swelled, and I was obliged to endure a bout of wrestling and tugging to remove them. Nothing. Using the penknife, I levered open the internal lining of both shoes. Success! A scrap of paper was concealed under the leather insole of the left shoe, an identification document. Most of the Russian on it defeated me, but I had a name at last – Alexander Chersky. Was that the name scrawled underneath the address on Arthur's pad? I couldn't be sure. Would check it later.

It was time to get out of the apartment. I whispered an apology to Mr Chersky for his undignified examination, then made for the exit. All was quiet as I descended the stairs. I reached the ground floor when a door opened, and a large, middle-aged woman appeared and blocked my way with hands on her hips. Bared arms, soiled apron and the belligerent set of her mouth suggested it would be a challenging encounter.

'Qui êtes vous? Pourquoi êtes-vous ici?'

I held the handkerchief to my face and coughed. 'Pardon, Madame, c'est mon ami... une maladie grave.' I coughed again. 'La grippe du soldat, peut-être.' I hoped the suggestion of what had been referred to as 'soldier's disease' would persuade her to retreat. Her eyes widened, and an expression of suspicion gave way to one of alarm. I added, 'Ou tuberculose,' feigned another fit, and that was enough to send her scurrying back to the safety of her apartment. I opened the door, stepped outside, took in a deep breath of the cold, clear air and marched down Rue Gustave Courbet as quickly as I dared without attracting attention.

What had I just done? Was it really me who had sneaked into an apartment uninvited, and discovered a corpse? With suspicions aroused, I guessed it was inevitable the concierge would investigate. Would she enter the apartment herself, or call the police to investigate? I had to assume the body in 18E would be discovered, and that police would be looking for a woman matching my description. There was no chance the hue and cry would be out before I was back at the Majestic, but might it be prudent to call in a shop and buy a new coat? In the end, exhilaration at my discovery, combined with the charm of Madame Voyance, proved irresistible. I left her shop on Rue de Longchamp with a navy-blue coat, matching hat, shoes and a pale pink dress. I bagged my old clothes and wore the new outfit, except shoes, for the remainder of my journey, justifying an outlay of almost forty francs through safety in my changed appearance.

A feeling of elation had subsided as I turned into Avenue Kleber. I had established a Russian connection with Arthur's murder. In my mind the address in the notepad and the discovery of Chersky's body confirmed the police were wrong in attributing the reason for his killing as robbery. The two murders were linked. It was also reasonable to suppose that Arthur and Chersky had met their end by the same hands and for the same motive. However, taking the investigation any further was problematic. How to discover more about Chersky and his background? Who was his missing co-tenant? Only then did it dawn on me that I may have been foolhardy to explore Chersky's apartment alone. No one would accuse me of Chersky's murder but breaking into the apartment and my confrontation with the concierge wouldn't present me in a good light. I couldn't simply present his identification paper to the police or Sir Basil and ask for their help in uncovering the intrigue behind a double murder. Could I spin a yarn to John Parkes and persuade him to assist me? Unlikely. I still hoped that Adam Visser would shed some light on Arthur's mission and reason for his killing but didn't know if or when he would return to Paris.

My mind was occupied with those thoughts when I entered the Majestic. I took my key from the reception desk and turned to be confronted by a uniformed figure.

'My apologies, Mary, did I startle you?'

'Ah, John, my mind was far away.'

'I see you've been shopping.'

'Yes, I'm afraid I spent more money than intended, but the shops here are so tempting.'

'I wonder whether you would like to celebrate your purchases and accompany me to dinner and a show tonight.' His words and fixed smile had the chime of a well-rehearsed proposal. 'Unless, of course, you....'

'No, I would be delighted.'

'Excellent. It's at a club not far from here. Shall we say eight in the foyer?'

Back in my room, I removed my old coat from the bag to retrieve Arthur's note from a pocket. It wasn't there. I searched every inch of the coat three or four times. Had I lost it in Madame Voyance's shop or Chersky's apartment? Did I need it anymore? I clenched my fists, shut my eyes and let out a silent scream at the ceiling. Of course I did. How else was I to explain my visit to Rue Gustave Courbet? It was evidence.

Seven

Le Baron had a modest exterior that belied the glitzy expanse we encountered after passing the doormen and cloakroom. A semi-circular dance floor was bordered by a small stage and at least fifty tables. Half of them were occupied, and waiters were swivelling, bowing and balancing silver trays of drinks and food aloft in a manner that deserved applause for safe arrival at their destination. A pianist was playing a tune I recognised but couldn't name. We were ushered to a small table at one end of the front row. With thoughts preoccupied, I hadn't paid much attention to John's small talk. It was only as we took our seats, it struck me that this wasn't a casual invitation. It was planned to impress, and I questioned how I felt about John's attention. In the subdued lighting and dark evening suit, he was uncommonly handsome and, despite our unfortunate introduction, he had been considerate and friendly. But was I ready for a romantic involvement?

'I think it's *I'm Always Chasing Rainbows*,' said John.

'Yes, you're right, but how did you know what I was thinking?'

'It's the way you wrinkled your nose and tilted your head in time to the music.'

'How observant of you, John.'

'Pardon me; I didn't mean to stare. I was just....'

'John, I was only teasing.'

'Ah, sorry, yes.' He was flustered, so I smiled and put a reassuring hand on his arm. 'Would you er... like a drink,' he added.

'Mm, that would be nice. May I have a sidecar?' It was the only cocktail I could name and had sampled once during an impromptu Christmas gathering at Wimereux.

With only a faint hint of surprise, he confirmed my order with our waiter and added a whisky for himself. We settled into a conversation I managed to steer around to John's background. His father was in business manufacturing glassware and had served a term as Mayor of Coventry. John attended Rugby School and Oxford, where he obtained a degree in history before joining the family business. He joined up at the start of the war and was promoted to his current rank by, in his words, 'filling dead men's shoes'. His recent posting came about through his father's connection with Sir Basil. John was evasive about the nature of the association, but I gathered it was something he either disapproved of or felt unable to disclose – a freemason connection, perhaps. He was, however, quite definite that Paris was to be his last posting before resigning his commission to take over the reins of the glassware business.

'Don't you find security at this Congress a sufficient challenge?' I asked.

'It's not why I signed up. I don't dismiss the need for security. This place has its perils, as evidenced by the death of Mr Burgess. But it's a policing role, not soldiering.' He hesitated, unsure if there was an element of mischief in my question. 'Of course, there are compensations: a soft bed; hot baths; no shelling; decent food; off-duty entertainment.'

'How long do you expect to be here?'

'Sir Basil has said he can see business here dragging on, and expects some form of British security presence will be required for two or three years. I hope he's wrong. I had assumed my posting would be for six months or nine at most.'

A waiter arrived with menus, and conversation ceased as we studied carefully before ordering. Both of us were hungry, and after what seemed an overlong delay and the inflated ceremony with which dishes were presented to our table we set about our food with relish. I enjoyed the evening; the cuisine was delicious, and, for the most part, we were at ease in each other's company. But Arthur's murder and the grisly discovery earlier that day were never far from my thoughts. I couldn't decide whether to confide in John and seek his aid in moving forward with an investigation. I wavered; sometimes in favour; then against a few moments later.

The place was filling up, the air had thickened with tobacco smoke, and the hum of conversation, fuelled by strong drink, was growing. The pianist was replaced by a five-piece band, who grabbed the audience's attention straight away with their stage presence and lively playing of modern favourites. Couples drifted on to the dance floor, and I couldn't ignore John's outstretched hand, so we joined them. He knew his steps, held me with confidence, and we moved well together. His earlier diffidence had disappeared, we had started on our third dance, and I was beginning to wonder what it would be like to kiss John when I felt a tap on my shoulder.

'Goodness… Sandra!'

'Yes, Mary, this is a surprise.'

'Sandra, this is John – Major John Parkes.' I had to raise my voice to be heard. 'John, this is Sandra Fairlight. Sandra is with the American delegation.'

John clicked his heels and offered an extravagant bow. Sandra tilted her head and smiled, seemingly amused at the military nature of his greeting.

'I'm sorry to interrupt, but when you're ready, please come and join our table over there.' She pointed to a large table in the middle with ten or more seated. 'A group of us from the Crillon decided we would have a night on the town.'

I sensed that John was not pleased to have his plans for the evening disrupted. We danced for another two numbers then, when the music stopped, I led the return to our table, where I insisted it would be rude to ignore Sandra's offer.

'How do you know her?'

'We met on a train to Trier in Germany a few days ago.'

'You were there - at the conference to extend the armistice?' He couldn't disguise an expression of bafflement and surprise.

'Yes, I was there as translator and note-taker for Mr Keynes.'

'That must have been an eye-opener with so many well-known and senior figures.'

'For the most part, it was a bore, and I was glad of Sandra's company. She is a Personal Assistant to Colonel House. Do you know him or any of the American delegation?'

'I've had very little to do with our American friends as my duties are centred on the Majestic.'

'Well, here's a chance to broaden your horizons, John.'

I made my way to Sandra's table, closely followed by a less than enthusiastic Major Parkes. Introductions were made. It turned out that a freckle-faced and sandy-haired American man was responsible for the safety and security of his colleagues and took the opportunity to compare notes with John, allowing me to converse freely with Sandra.

'He's very good looking, your Major Parkes.'

'Yes, he will be quite a catch for the right woman.'

'Does that mean you've excluded yourself as a candidate?'

'I don't know if I'm ready for competition like that.' I smiled and scanned the occupants of her table, with men outnumbering women, seven to three. 'What about you, Sandra; do you have an escort tonight?'

'We are just an informal group from the Crillon. I don't believe there are any romantic ties around the table. At least, not yet, but the night is young.'

'Is there anyone special for you back home in America?' Sandra opened her mouth to reply, then stopped, clamped her lips and bowed her head. 'I'm sorry, I shouldn't have asked such a personal question.'

'No, it's alright; I don't usually get upset when I think about him. I'm engaged to Max, a professor of history at Princeton. Ours has been a long engagement; too long. We had plans to marry six years ago, but my work for Colonel House, the war, Max getting promoted; something always got in the way.' She leant over, clasped a hand on mine and smiled. 'Whatever happens here, I am leaving in September at the latest and will be married before the year is out.'

A man appeared behind Sandra and tapped her shoulder.

'Excuse me, Miss Fairlight... Sandra... won't you... introduce...' He manoeuvred a chair between us and sat heavily. '...me to this lovely lady.' He was drunk.

Sandra rolled her eyes. 'Cody, this is Mary Kiten. Mary...' she shrugged her shoulders in an apology, 'this is Cody Becker.'

'Delighted, ma'am.' He took my hand and brushed it against his lips. He was a large man, tall and broad-shouldered, clean-shaven, with a round, fleshy face and thinning hair.

'Mary and Major Parkes are from the British delegation,' added Sandra.

He waved a dismissive hand as though that was already known. 'Dance,' he said as a statement rather than a request. He still had hold of my hand as he rose from his seat.

It was easier to comply than to make a fuss, so I trailed him to the dance floor. His breath reeked of alcohol, and he was strong, but I managed to keep a little distance between us.

'Cody is an unusual Christian name.' I ventured.

'Buffalo Bill. My father's fault. His hero.'

If that was an answer to my question, I didn't understand it. 'What is your role here in Paris?' If I could keep him talking, he was less likely to overstep the mark and get fresh.

'I'm with the Service.'

'What is the Service?'

He tapped the end of his nose and winked a bleary eye. 'Secret.'

'You work for the Secret Service.' I feigned an expression of admiring innocence, playing along with his drunken charade. 'How exciting. You mean you're a spy, or you catch foreign spies.'

He laughed and shook his head. 'No, it's just – the Service. We protect our elected leaders and....' He took a deep breath and put a hand to his mouth as though trying to stifle a hiccup. 'And the integrity of... the United States Dollar.'

'I see, you are here to protect your President, Mr Wilson?'

'Yes, ma'am.'

'So, nothing to do with spying or spies.'

'No ma'am, you'll have to ask Miss Fairlight about that. It's Colonel House who looks after all the cloak and dagger nonsense.'

'Is it nonsense? I understand there are concerns about security.'

'You're right; Paris is a dangerous place. Too many guns from the war here.'

'Is there a threat to your President?'

'Yes, ma'am, but we'll keep him safe.'

'That's very reassuring... Cody. But who would want to harm Mr Wilson? The Germans, or the Russians, perhaps?'

'All – all are potential threats.'

He was losing interest in our conversation and tried to pull me closer. I resisted. He was a big man but clumsy and uncoordinated with drink. I was able to steer him around the dance floor, then back to the table after a couple more numbers from the band. John beckoned me to a chair next to his, and I joined him with conflicting senses of relief and reluctance. I wanted to know more about Colonel House and spying, but I was separated from Sandra and unable to follow up Cody Becker's comments.

I was careful but probably had one drink too many as the night dissolved into a confusion of more introductions, music, dancing, talking, laughing. It came as a surprise when John suggested we leave and make our way back to the Majestic. I checked my watch – almost three o'clock. I circled the table until I reached Sandra, who seemed pleased to extricate herself from the middle of an earnest conversation between three men.

'I'm sorry we couldn't find more time to spend together tonight,' she said.

'Yes, but it was lovely to meet you again and thank you for asking us to join your table. You've come with a lively crowd.' It was noisy, and we had to shout to be heard.

'We will be following you out of here. Our taxis will be here soon.' She opened her arms and enveloped me in a hug, which I returned after a short hesitation. 'Have you enjoyed it?'

'Yes, it's been fun.'

'And John?'

'I think he has had a good time, even though the night has not turned out quite as he planned.' I wanted to quiz her about Colonel House and spying, but she was ushered on to the dance floor before I could continue. But then, what did I hope to gain? I couldn't expect her to divulge secrets, even if she had any. And there was nothing to suggest that Arthur was mixed up in spying – at least none that Sandra would know about. All I had was a connection to a murdered Russian and the disappearance of the man who shared his apartment. I stood, staring at the bar, but seeing nothing, when I felt a hand on my shoulder, and turned to find John, who guided me to the cloakroom. It was a five-minute walk back to the hotel, and there was no conversation as we had collars up and heads down to guard against the bitter cold and threatening wisps of snow. In the foyer, we headed for the reception desk to retrieve keys. I had anticipated the offer of a nightcap.

'Thank you, John, but it's late, and I'm expected at Mr Keynes' schoolroom at eight o'clock.'

'Yes, yes, I understand, and I meant in the bar, not....'

'There was something I was going to ask you earlier in the evening, but it slipped my mind.'

'Oh, what was that?'

'I wonder if I could persuade you to ask Sir Basil if he would investigate the circumstances surrounding the murder of Mr Burgess.' I saw doubt on his face and added quickly, 'I know he dismissed my suspicions before, and I'm not proposing he does anything that would offend the local police or interfere with the "official" outcome; just a few discreet enquiries, perhaps. The more I think about it, the more convinced I am that it wasn't a chance robbery. It was planned and part of a wider plot.'

'A plot; what makes you say that?'

'Oh, nothing I can put my finger on, just a... feeling.' I cursed inwardly at my clumsiness. I should have kept my mouth shut. It was not a good time to bring up the subject of Arthur. I couldn't mention Chersky, so what did I have to offer John, except an amorphous and unconvincing *feeling*. It was a foolish attempt, probably fuelled by too much strong drink. 'Sorry, forget I asked; it's the wrong time and...'

'No, I understand why it's been preying on your mind. I will have a word with Sir Basil. I will have to choose my moment with care, and I regret I can't offer you much encouragement that he will do as you wish. Right from the start we have been under orders that our security teams should work in harmony with the authorities in Paris. We've already had a couple of unofficial warnings from Hardinge's office due to complaints from Rousssel, so Sir Basil will not wish to ruffle French feathers.'

'That's good of you, and thank you for a lovely night, John. I hope that meeting Sandra and her American colleagues didn't spoil the occasion for you.'

'Not at all, it was… interesting. No, that's the wrong word; peculiar is nearer the mark. None of those I met tonight had actually fought in the war. To them, the Congress is a cross between political husting and a sales convention. It's as though all the filth, discomfort, horror and death of the last four years never happened.'

Eight

It looked as though I was the last one to arrive at the schoolroom. A quick scan told me everyone from the Treasury Unit was present except Keynes. It was eight o'clock. I wasn't late as start and finish times hadn't been discussed. I felt guilty and exposed, all the same; guilty for enjoying last night's entertainment; exposed as all eyes were on me as I hung up my coat and sat at the table in the centre of the room. I closed my bag, shoved it under the chair and returned a murmured greeting from Derek sitting opposite. His face was creased into more of a smirk than a smile. Had I interrupted something? Men talk? A smutty joke, perhaps?

'Good morning Miss Kiten.' Pinchin emerged from Keynes' office and slammed a pile of papers on the table.

'And good morning to you, Mr Pinchin.'

'I missed you at breakfast.'

'Oh, I didn't make breakfast today. But I'm not hungry.'

He muttered a few words I couldn't hear.

'I beg your pardon. I didn't catch…'

'I was just wondering if you had an enjoyable night out?'

I didn't know how to respond. Should I laugh it off, make a neutral reply or be offended that he was poking his nose into my private business? 'Has someone been spying on me?' I tried to keep my tone light-hearted.

'You can't have fun here without everyone finding out, you know.' He could see my confusion. 'Forgive me, I'm ribbing you, Miss Kiten. We're all jealous. *Le Baron* has a good reputation, but it's quite pricey.'

'How... how did you know?'

He tapped the side of his nose. 'Nothing much gets past the gossips on reception desk at the Majestic. You should use the rear staff entrance if you want to be discreet.' He winked at me, and I acknowledged his teasing with a smile. He hoisted his trousers and continued in a more serious vein. 'Give me five minutes while I search the shelves, and then join me in the office, would you. Our lord and master is attending a high-level meeting on reparations at the Quai D'Orsay this morning.'

I barely had time to look through notes left for me on information to research when Pinchin returned to the office. I followed and was asked to close the door before I took a seat.

'Now, Mary... do you mind if I call you Mary?'

'No, not at all.'

'I wanted a brief word about something you mentioned the other day when debriefing on the Trier conference.'

'Oh, did I miss something in my report?'

'No, it was nothing to do with your written report, which was excellent, by the way. You had questions about Russians in Paris, and I wondered what prompted that interest.' He paused, leant forward and rested his elbows on the desk. 'Did someone mention a particular name, or has a Russian man approached you, perhaps?'

'Oh no, nothing like that. Russia wasn't discussed at the formal session in Trier. I overheard a group of American delegates on the train discussing the different factions fighting in Russia, which led me to ask about participation here. It's such a big country, and they were on our side until....'

'Until they capitulated and signed that treaty last year. Yes – dreadful - bad show.' He adjusted his position in the chair and fixed me with a stare. 'I hear you met with one of General Smuts' men, Visser, on the train. Did he talk about Russia at all?'

'Mr Visser - no, not that I recall.' Why would he question me on Russian names so soon after my grisly discovery of Alexander Chersky? I couldn't believe that Gerry Pinchin had any involvement in murder, but it was a strange interrogation, and for reasons I couldn't fully understand, it put me on guard. Did he know more than he was letting on?

A subdued Keynes entered the schoolroom shortly after three o'clock. He loped through to his office without saying a word, proceeded to remove gloves, coat and hat with great care, examined his desk and adjusted the position of his blotter, then raised his head slowly and gazed at his staff through the glazed partition. I looked away quickly and sensed that I was not the only one following Keynes' progress. He came out into the middle of our room and clapped his hands to gain attention.

'Gentlemen... and lady. You may like to know the outcome of our deliberations this morning.' He waited for all heads to turn in his direction while resting a thumb in a waistcoat pocket. 'As you know, I have argued strongly against punitive reparations from the central powers. The collapse of the German economy would undermine the financial recovery of all countries in Europe, most particularly ours, due to the high level of our exports.' He paused and raised his head as though seeking how to formulate his following words. 'Unfortunately, I did not receive support for my views from Lords Sumner and Cunliffe. No firm consensus emerged from our meeting, and the Commission has set up three sub-committees to look at the extent of damage and reparations. We have been assigned to produce calculations and analyses of the financial damage caused by the war. We all know that this will produce a monstrous figure, which will be impossible for Germany to repay. However, I regret we must go through the motions. Clemenceau will not listen to reason, and France will have most to claim from damages, but I believe Wilson can be persuaded. For Lloyd George, it's a question of presentation to our electorate rather than numbers, and I must find a way to make him see reason.' He folded his arms, looked at Pinchin and a couple more of the senior men before continuing. 'So, as well as producing the damage calculations, we will continue to work on the analysis of economic recovery to support my argument. Gerry, will you see to the reorganisation and division of work, please.'

I was grateful for Keynes' little speech. I had been immersed in researching detailed information without a clear understanding of the overall purpose of our work. I knew that the French were opposed to Keynes' view on reparations, and it seemed that he would also have to deal with significant disagreement in the British delegation.

*

I wasn't hungry, picked at my plate and was poor company for Annie and Jane over dinner. I learned from John that Sir Basil had been called away to an incident at Calais and was likely to be absent for a couple of days. I was frustrated, unable to find a way to progress enquiries into Arthur's murder. I needed to find out more about Arthur's actions and contacts here, especially with Russians, before British security or local police would take me seriously. The only person I knew who may be able to provide information was Sandra. But was Cody Becker serious when he said her boss, Colonel House, managed the spying and intelligence gathering for the American delegation? Was he pulling my leg? Even if it were true, would Sandra be privy to any secrets, and would she be willing to discuss any of this business with me? There was only one way to find out.

I ordered a carriage to take me to the Hotel de Crillon. I could have walked to Place de la Concorde from the Majestic, but it was bitterly cold and more snow threatened, so I dipped into my depleted reserves of francs. The Crillon could easily be mistaken for a palace if one ignored the line of motor taxis, horse carriages and crowds milling at the entrance. Lights in the foyer dazzled after my journey in a cold, dark carriage. A large clock showed two minutes after seven. I walked to a marble pillar in a corner with a good vantage point, surveyed the scene and gathered my thoughts before venturing to the reception desk.

The hotel foyer was busy, and I joined the back of a queue to the desk. Progress was slow. Guests were becoming impatient; quarrels broke out when places were disputed, or others claimed seniority and priority in the lines. While waiting, I learned that the hotel staff in the foyer were French. Unlike the British at the Majestic, the Americans had not imported their own staff to work at the hotel in the name of security.

I was next in line. I gazed around the foyer again and watched as figures entered through the wide main doors, brushing down coats and stamping feet to rid themselves of the outside chill. One of them was familiar – a woman in a heavy dark grey coat and fur hat. It was Sandra. I went to meet her.

'Mary, this is a surprise. What brings you to the Crillon?' Her cheeks were glowing from the sudden uplift in temperature.

'It's something I didn't get a chance to ask at *Le Baron*. I'm sorry to arrive without warning. I hope this… isn't a bad time…' My voice trailed away as my confidence evaporated into the surrounding, jaunty chatter of American accents. In the gleaming grandeur of the Crillon, I felt small and foolish.

'Of course, no need to apologise, Mary. Let's go to my room. It's too busy here.'

I followed Sandra to the grand, carpeted staircase. She explained the hotel housed one hundred and fifty of the most important American delegates, but it was busier than you would expect based on that number. Delegates and staff from lesser hotels nearby often came to the Crillon to drink and eat. It had a reputation for fine dining, serving the city's best and most comprehensive selection of champagne and strong liquor. We stopped outside a door marked 'Suite 104'. Sandra unlocked the door, clicked the electric light switch, and I followed her inside. I halted after a couple of paces, marvelling at the luxurious prospect before me, then quickly shook my head and clamped my mouth to make sure I wasn't gawping like an idiot.

We were in an area with luxurious burgundy carpeting, glittering chandeliers, ornate, gold-framed mirrors, highly polished dining table and chairs, recliners, easy chairs and glowing coals in a stone fireplace.

'Help yourself to a drink and take a seat.' She pointed to a generous display of bottles and glasses on a gilded, circular table. 'Excuse me, Mary, I'll be a few minutes.' She disappeared through a door into, what I assumed was her bedroom.

I would have felt foolish standing in the same spot, looking helpless when she returned, so I removed my coat, hat and gloves and placed them on a chair. The drinks table presented a problem. I didn't want whisky or brandy, and, at the other end of the scale, a glass of fruit cordial seemed too timid and un-American. I poured a glass of sherry as the safest option and sat on a high-backed chair cushioned with burgundy and ochre velvet.

She reappeared after five minutes, looking refreshed and having changed into a loose, silk cream blouse and dark wool skirt. She offered to refill my glass and poured herself a small brandy.

'You don't mind, do you?' She motioned her head at bare feet.

'Of course not. This is your... suite.'

'I have a weakness for smart shoes, often at the expense of comfort.' She poured herself a brandy, sat on a recliner and tucked her legs up on the seat. 'Now, I'm intrigued to know why you're here.'

'It was something Mr Becker said last night.'

'He was drunk. I hope he wasn't offensive or indiscreet?'

'He told me that he worked for "The Service", which I now understand is the security unit protecting your president. Initially, I thought he referred to a "secret" service and Mr Becker was involved in intelligence gathering or… spying.' I glanced at Sandra, but her expression gave nothing away. 'Of course, I was wrong, and he informed me that Colonel House managed your intelligence activities in Paris.' Still no reaction from Sandra.

Had I misunderstood? I was about to give up and make an excuse to leave when she said, 'Why are you interested in the possibility of "spying" at the Congress?'

'Have you met, or did you know of a man named Arthur Burgess?'

The name produced an immediate reaction. She shifted back a fraction, tilted her head and narrowed her eyes. She was puzzled. After taking a couple of sips from her glass, she placed it on a table and looked at me directly. 'Yes, we knew Mr Burgess. I heard he was the unfortunate victim of a robbery outside the Majestic.' She paused before adding, 'Did you have a connection to him?'

'He was my late father's closest friend, and he met his end, not because of an unfortunate and random robbery; he was murdered in cold blood.'

'Oh, Mary,' She shook her head. 'I'm so sorry. You never mentioned this on the train. 'She swirled brandy around the glass and narrowed her eyes. 'What leads you to believe it was murder?'

'I went to the mortuary to pay my respects. An examination of the head wound and his wallet, still full of francs, led me to believe it was the work of a trained killer, not a petty thief.'

She shook her head in disbelief. 'That's a hell of a deduction for a young member of staff with the British Treasury to make. Why would anyone want to assassinate Mr Burgess, a temporary security manager at a large hotel?'

'I was sent to Paris at short notice. My contact here was Arthur – Mr Burgess. I arrived only a few minutes before his murder. He worked in the War Office and while I'm not sure of his exact role, I'm sure it was more than just security manager in a hotel.'

She stared, shook her head again and reached for her glass. No swirling or dainty sips this time; she drained the glass in two large gulps.

'Any answer I give is probably not going to be as helpful as you would expect or wish.' She stood and made her way to the drinks table and poured another brandy. I refused her offer of more sherry. 'We have a few agents or intelligence gatherers here who report to Colonel House. The arrangement is temporary, with no formal structure or control. It's definitely not a government department like your Secret Intelligence Service, and it would be stretching the definition to call our agents here "spies". It's simply that they have the right connections and are good listeners.'

'Do you have any information on the Russians in this city? I know they have not been invited to participate in the Congress, but I understand there are many here on the fringes.'

'Why do you have an interest in Russia?'

'I've discovered a link between Arthur Burgess and a Russian who was also murdered around the same date.' Sandra's eyebrows were raised. She tilted her head, inviting me to say more. 'I found an address on Arthur's notepad. I went there, an apartment in the sixteenth arrondissement. The door was unlocked. I found the body of a man with the same wound, a gunshot to the head. The murdered man was Russian.'

'I see.' She examined the brandy in her glass before bringing it to her lips, then placed on the table without drinking. 'I'm… amazed. Why? Were you alone?'

'Yes.'

She shook her head and said, 'What I don't understand, Mary is why you haven't already got this information from your own security services.'

'I haven't told anyone, except you, about my discovery of the murdered Russian. Also, I've lost the paper with the address written by Arthur. The Paris police have closed the case and Sir Basil Thomson is unwilling to offend them by asking questions or making his own enquiries.' I finished my sherry and placed the glass on a table. 'I suppose he doesn't take me or my suspicions seriously. He thinks I'm a silly young woman. I need to gather evidence and information on Arthur's movements. When I have enough I'll present it, hoping it will convince Sir Basil to order a proper examination of the circumstances around the murder.'.'

'At least you're not foolish enough to think you can see this through yourself.'

'If no one else will do it, I may have to.'

'I hope you're not serious. And if you find the murderer or murderers, what then?'

'I'm not crazy enough to consider myself as an executioner. I can use a gun, but hope I never have to fire one in anger. I'll pass on my findings to British security, and they will find a way to exact justice.' I was thirsty but didn't want a sherry, brandy or other liquor. 'Can I have a glass of water, please, Sandra?'

'Sure.' She rose, went through another door and returned a few seconds later with a glass of water. 'Sorry, I don't have any ice.'

I was tempted to make a smart remark about refrigerators, but kept my thoughts to myself and simply muttered, 'Thank you.' I drank greedily and emptied the glass. I could tell, from Sandra's thoughtful frown, she wasn't convinced I should be helped. Maybe she considered I had fallen into a situation beyond my capabilities and experience. 'I need to do this, Sandra. He was more to me than my father's friend. I called him "Uncle", but he was more like a second father. I know his death will haunt me if I don't try my best to find out who and why.'

'Could your escort from last night help? Major...'

'Parkes.' I hesitated; my thoughts still in two minds about seeking aid from John. 'Yes, he may be persuaded under the right circumstances.'

Sandra hadn't sat down again after fetching my glass of water. The way she stood, leant against a wall with arms folded and eyes watching a bare foot tracing a shape on the floor, reflected her indecision. 'Do you have a cigarette,' she said, shaking her hair loose.

'No, I don't smoke.'

'Neither do I. It's a shame; I thought smoking might help.'

I waited. The silence between us stretched; how long? A minute? More? 'Look, Sandra, I can see I've put you in an awkward position. I will leave now, and if, on reflection, you have any useful information you would be willing to share - well, you know where to find me.'

I started to rise from my chair, but Sandra held out her hand to stop me. She lowered herself slowly on to the recliner and, this time, sat straight-backed, cradling her brandy in both hands.

'My reluctance is nothing to do with secrecy, Mary. I have heard enough about the Russians in this city to know that even an innocent intervention or enquiry could be dangerous. They can be, and have been, ruthless to anyone who gets in their way or pokes a nose into their business.'

'You said, "ruthless". Does that mean you know they have committed illegal acts, assaults and even murder here?'

'Murder. Strictly speaking, I should refer to them as unexplained deaths among the Russian groups gathered in this city.' She sipped her brandy and took a deep breath before continuing. 'You have to understand that there are many factions here, and there is deadly rivalry even among those supposedly on the same side. Russian exiles have established a Russian Political Conference in Paris to speak for all non-Bolsheviks. This conference is a focal point for a broad spectrum of views, from conservatives to radicals, tsarist to terrorist. All of them united in their opposition to Bolshevism and their wish to be recognised by the Allies. We have heard of conflicts between participants at the Russian conference and several deaths, even in the few short weeks we have been here. The police are not interested in squabbles between the Russian factions, so the killings remain unsolved. Everyone knows it is either Bolshevik killing White Russian, White Russian killing Bolshevik or a dispute between the different factions of White Russian. We believed the killings were confined to Russians with no other nationals caught up in the crossfire. Now, you are suggesting that is not the case.'

'I am certain attempted robbery by a petty thief was a convenient solution to Arthur's death when the evidence points to a planned assassination. Does this result from police incompetence, laziness, lack of resources for an overworked force, or some other motive? I can't say.'

'We had no reason to query the police verdict, although Colonel House expressed surprise at the news of the death of Mr Burgess.' She clicked her tongue and shook her head. 'I'm sorry, Mary, that sounds callous.'

'Do you know if Arthur had a connection to any of the Russians here?'

'I don't. I'm sorry.' She lifted the glass to her lips and took more than a sip. 'It's unlikely that Colonel House will know, but I will ask.'

'Are there any names of significant Russians that may help my enquiries?'

'I only know a few; their names are confusing and difficult to remember. The most vocal representative of their Political Conference is Sergei Sazonov, a former member of the tsarist government. He is handsome, fashionable, has impeccable manners and has a reputation as both a lover and killer. I was on the fringes of a meeting when Lloyd George professed to admire the way his assassinations were undertaken with ruthless efficiency. Although this was said in a light-hearted manner, we all knew his statement was shocking and true. I haven't encountered many Russians here, but I have attended meetings where Sazonov was present. I found him unpleasant and untrustworthy, but he and his group of White Russians are desperate to find favour with our leaders. On the face of it then, he is unlikely to be involved in the murder of a senior allied administrator, unless you can find a hidden and compelling reason.'

'Any other names you can recall?'

She sighed, then levered herself up from the recliner. 'I will have to refer to my notebooks to get the names right.' She wandered off to her bedroom and returned a couple of minutes later with half a dozen notebooks, each roughly the size of a slim novel. She flicked through one of the books until she came to a page where she ran a hand down the middle to flatten the pages. 'The leaders of the other White Russian groups are Denikin and Kolchak. They were here only briefly last month, and they didn't meet with Colonel House. They have delegated others to speak on their behalf here, but I don't have names.'

'What about the Bolsheviks? Do they have representation in Paris?'

'We know they are here, lurking in the shadows and nameless, presumably to report back to their masters on White Russian activity. There has been communication with their leaders mostly at a distance, by telegram.' She picked up another notebook and turned the pages. 'A man named Litvinov, I forget his first name, met Mr Wilson, Colonel House and Lloyd George for a short meeting last month. It was a secure and hush-hush meeting with no one else invited. He was a charming man, and I know all were impressed with his talk of justice and humanity for all.'

'This man's first name; did it begin with an "M"?'

She scanned a few pages. 'I didn't record it. Let's see. No... but now you mention it, you're right; it was Maxim, Maxim Litvinov. How did you...'

'It fits with some other scraps of information I've picked up.'

'I wouldn't put Litvinov down as a candidate for the murderer of Mr Burgess or someone who would order such a killing. He seemed - well, normal and nice. I understand he is married to an English woman and has lived in London. He strongly supported Mr Wilson's fourteen points for peace.' She paused and breathed deeply, seeming to consider all she had said. 'Of course, having said all that in favour of Litvinov, the Bolsheviks are not to be trusted and have committed some foul crimes if the general opinion is to be believed.'

'Does this man, Litvinov, hold a position in the Bolshevik government?'

'Not an official one as far as I know. He came representing their commissar for foreign affairs, someone named Chicherin who had just replaced Trotsky.'

'What was the outcome of the meeting with Litvinov?'

'There have been several telegrams.' She turned a couple of pages, then stopped, and her eyes followed a finger as it zig-zagged down. 'A meeting was arranged between Litvinov and William Buckler, who is one of our diplomats. It's taking place as we speak.'

'Where is this meeting?'

'I can't tell you that, Mary. It's sensitive information right now, although it may be generally known in a week or two.'

'Is it at Budapest?'

She picked up her brandy and drank from the glass while keeping her eyes on me. She replaced her glass, sat back and folded her arms. She didn't intend to say any more on the subject.

'I ask because, in a conversation between Mr Keynes and Mr Pinchin, it was said that General Smuts and Adam Visser are currently leading a delegation to Budapest. Their purpose wasn't known for certain, and there was conjecture that it may have been connected to the Romanian conflict or the Russian question.'

Sandra's remained silent, and I couldn't read anything in her expression. Eventually, she brushed a hand over her skirt and said, 'That's about everything I can tell you on Russians in Paris, Mary. I doubt if anything I've said will help you identify the killer of Mr Burgess or even confirm your suspicion that his death was planned.' She hesitated before adding, 'My wish is that you stop your enquiries now. Pass on what you have discovered so far to Sir Basil Thomson, but for God's sake, don't go prying into Russian affairs yourself.'

'Rest assured; I'm not planning to charge into the middle of a Russian battleground. I confess I had hoped to learn more, and I don't believe I have enough to persuade British security to get involved.' I paused to consider Adam Visser's words about Arthur on the train to Trier again. 'I may have to wait until General Smuts and Mr Visser return from Hungary before I can progress enquiries any further.'

'Meanwhile, you have the task of looking after your Mr Keynes. His name crops up quite often in discussions. The President and Colonel House speak in his favour, but many distrust him and damn his opinions and arrogance.' She drained the last of the brandy in her glass. 'You should keep your eyes open for any threat against Keynes, Mary. He has made enemies, and you never know if they plan to harm him or his name in some way.'

It was time for me to leave. We hugged. I thanked her for the information on Russia and the warning about Keynes. I didn't rate the probability of any serious action against him as high. He knew many were violently opposed to his views on reparations, but he had an aura of confidence and certainty in his abilities. He could look after himself.

Tired and disappointed, I had come with high hopes that Sandra would offer vital clues on Arthur's killing and connection to Russia. Aside from a couple of names, I was no further forward.

Nine

Work at the schoolroom intensified over the next couple of days. Everyone seemed more active, more alert. The air hummed and crackled with a sense of urgency. It all started with Keynes, poring over half a dozen open books on the central table when I arrived. With shirt sleeves rolled up and tie askew, his muttering, scanning and exclaiming set an example that infected the rest of us. There was no leisurely break for lunch. Instead, Derek and Jack were despatched to the Majestic at noon with orders to return with a supply of bread, cheese and ham. Fewer cigarettes were smoked, and half the cups of tea were forgotten and left untouched.

I had little time to brood. My services were in constant demand. The few times I allowed my mind to wander on to the subject of how I should proceed in the Arthur investigation, I was quickly prodded back to the reality of tabulated data, francs, deutschmarks, exports and gross domestic products. I enjoyed the industry, the teamwork, and the satisfaction of a problem solved; a number justified; a task completed. Only once or twice was I pricked with shame, the shame of taking pleasure in work and letting the death of Arthur slip from my conscious thoughts.

I was working with Derek when he stopped and looked behind him. Jack Livsey was holding his coat and gloves, suggesting it was time for them to go. Derek checked his watch, then scrambled into his jacket, and they both left in a hurry, muttering apologies about meeting friends for drinks and dinner. I sat back in my chair and surveyed our schoolroom. It was a quarter past seven, and I hadn't realised most had already finished and departed. Three of us were left; me Keynes and Pinchin. I yawned. Keynes saw me and followed suit. He stretched, flexed his shoulders and said, 'Come on, Miss Kiten, we've done enough for today. We will walk you back to the Majestic. Ready, Gerry?'

'No boss, not yet. I'll be another hour or so.'

I tidied my desk, gathered coat and bag, then waited for Keynes, who made a few adjustments to a pile of books, brushed his suit jacket with exaggerated care, then hoisted a heavy overcoat, grabbed his trilby and closed the door to his office. I shivered as I stepped out into the cold of Rue Leo Delibes. Keynes pulled on leather gloves, raised the collar of his overcoat and joined me. I was soon hurrying to catch up with his long, loping stride. Neither of us had spoken a word, and we were only a few hundred yards from the Majestic when Keynes stopped, pointed to a bar along a side street and asked if I would like to join him in a drink. I would have much preferred to head straight back to my hotel room but felt obliged to accept his invitation.

Inside, *Bar Felix* was warm, more extensive than expected and busy. The light had a curious subdued quality as though a delicate veil had been draped before my eyes. I followed him to a table and was about to settle there when Keynes waved a hand of recognition. He guided me round tables, to a corner where two men and a woman were seated and introduced me to them as his research assistant. Laughter from the next table prevented me from hearing names of the two men. I did hear enough to learn both men were British, and I assumed they were also in Paris for the Congress. The woman was Lucille. I removed my coat and followed Keynes' example by hanging it over the back of a chair. A waiter arrived; I ordered a sidecar and sat down between Keynes and Lucille.

After a cursory enquiry into my health and enjoyment of Paris, the two men began an animated conversation with Keynes. At least one of the men was a recent arrival in Paris from Athens, and the main topic of their discussion concerned a mutual admiration of ancient Greek monuments. They were odd companions for Keynes. One was middle-aged with thick wavy hair and a neatly trimmed moustache. He was sitting with chin raised, straight-backed, his eyes darting this way and that as though he was expecting another, imminent arrival at our table. The other, a slender, clean-shaven man in his late twenties with slicked, black hair, seemed determined to find anything Keynes said amusing or insightful. My attention wavered; I turned to Lucille and asked if she had a room at the Majestic. Her reply took me by surprise. She was French, worked as a seamstress and had an apartment nearby; all this stated in a thick accent, with blushing cheeks and rather shamefaced but defiant manner. It took a few seconds, and then I understood. She was pretty and beneath overused cosmetics around my age or even younger. She was paid to be with one of the men, perhaps both.

I continued my chat with Lucille in French, and she seemed grateful for the language switch. We discussed the local area and her experience of the war. Hers was a sad story; father killed in the first months, and mother recently succumbed to what she termed the 'soldier plague'; she was 'surviving'; said with a shrug and an absence of self-pity. It also emerged that Lucille was not her given name. She was Estelle. I liked her. I was sorry for her situation, but even a few minutes with her was enough to understand she would not take kindly to any expression of sympathy.

'Damn!'

An exclamation from Keynes silenced our table. He patted his jacket and searched inside the pockets of his overcoat.

'Have you lost something?' No one else had asked the obvious question, so I was obliged to fill the quiet space.

'My pocket book.' He shook his head and tutted to himself.

'Did you leave it at the school?'

'I suppose I must have.'

'Would you like me to go back and retrieve it for you?'

'Oh, would you? That would be a great help, Miss Kiten.' He paused, sat back and scratched the back of his head. 'It's a small dark blue leather book with my initials embossed in gold. If it's not on my desk, then look at the central table in the main room, where I was working with Gerry.' I gulped a mouthful of my cocktail and started to put my coat on. 'Please take it back to the Majestic and leave it at reception, will you? Thank you again, Miss Kiten.'

115

I exited the bar with a nagging sensation that all was not quite right. I suppose I shouldn't be shocked that even a man of Keynes' status was content to be seen with a young girl paid for her company. And those men. Why did I feel uneasy? They were not the type of companions I expected Keynes to seek out. Most of all, it was the thought of how one, or all of them, might take advantage of Estelle's situation that produced a nauseous feeling in the pit of my stomach.

I arrived back at the school to find the front door locked. I was sure it was open when we left. I had a key but never had to use it before. I fumbled in my handbag, then stopped as I heard activity from the other side. The door opened, and a figure emerged wearing a dark coat and hat. It wasn't Pinchin; too tall, almost a head higher than my five and a half feet. My eyes caught the outline of a face with a livid scar running from forehead, through half-closed left eye, then disappearing into a turned-up collar. He stared at me for a moment, then pushed past without a word and strode with purpose down the street.

I stepped cautiously along the corridor towards our room, wondering what I would find. Was Pinchin still there? Had he met with the stranger? Why meet there and at that time of night? I could see the light from our room filtering through the closed door. Someone was inside. I opened it slowly and peered around before entering. The main room appeared empty. I closed the door behind me. Ah, there was Pinchin, in Keynes's office, sat at his desk. I knocked and entered.

'Sorry to disturb you, Mr Pinchin. I'm looking for Mr Keynes' small leather notebook.'

His body jerked back into the chair, his eyes wild and gaping with surprise. 'Miss... Miss Kiten... Mary... how?'

'I encountered a strange man at the front door. I thought he might be up to no good. I'm pleased to see you're alright.'

'A man?'

'Yes, a tall man in dark coat and hat.'

'Oh... I see... not here.' He seemed flustered; his neck coloured. 'There was no one here. It must have been... one of our resident security men.' He shuffled and straightened a collection of papers on the desk. 'Why did you say you are here?'

'Mr Keynes left his notebook; said it might be in his office or on the central table in the main area, where he was working with you.'

'Ah yes, yes, I have it here.' He patted the chest pocket on his jacket. 'I'll bring it back with me.'

'No, he may need it now. I said I would retrieve it for him.' As soon as my words were out, I knew they sounded too argumentative. But I had only given voice to my sense of growing unease: I had been introduced to the two security men at the school, and I knew neither was the man at the door. I felt uneasy about Estelle and the two men; and now, there was Pinchin to consider, sitting in Keynes' office with the notebook in his pocket.

'Well now, Miss Kiten, I can see you've had a wasted journey, but I'm disappointed that you question me in that way. Rest assured, I will be finished here soon, and I will return the book to Mr Keynes as soon as I arrive back at the Majestic.'

For reasons I couldn't rationalise, I was irritated by Pinchin's manner. Or was it simply that I didn't want

117

to return empty-handed? 'Very well, I will leave it to you.' I tried to appear contrite, but the words and tone weren't right and, to my ears, sounded petulant. I held up my hand by way of an apology, then turned and made my way to the exit. I could feel his eyes fixed on my back as I walked away.

Out in the cold streets again, I walked briskly on the route back to the hotel. Nearing the side street with *Bar Felix*, I noticed Estelle turning the corner with the younger of the two men. I slowed my pace, then stopped, shackled by indecision. Should I follow Estelle, check in the bar to see if Keynes was still there, or return to the Majestic? An immediate continuation of my journey to the Majestic was the only sensible choice, but not the one I took. I turned right and walked thirty yards to the Bar Felix entrance. Trailing Estelle and checking on Keynes would only satisfy idle curiosity, but the latter option was less sordid and could be excused through concern for the welfare of my employer.

I raised the collar on my coat, lowered the brim of my hat and entered the bar. I turned right without pausing, having a vague recollection of an empty table in that area. I was in luck; two small tables beckoned with vacant chairs. I intended to stay only a few minutes and hoped to escape the attention of waiters, so I could slip back through the doorway when I had seen Keynes. I lifted my head to find my view was blocked by a huddle of men playing cards at the next table. I shuffled to my left and caught a glimpse of the rear view of Keynes about twenty paces away. I removed my hat and brushed the felt lining while peering around its edge. He was talking to the man with wavy hair and another who I couldn't see as my vision was partly obscured. I replaced my hat and, as I was adjusting it, moved to the chair to my left. Now I could see; the side view of a man with blond hair, a much younger man. They were laughing. The young man patted Keynes' back. More laughter. The blond man stood and buttoned his suit jacket; now, all three were standing, shaking hands. I had to leave - quickly.

I walked to the end of the street and retraced my steps on Avenue Kleber, intending to wait there until they emerged. I could either join them, saying I was on my way back from the school, or track them to their destination. A man walked past, twisting his head to inspect me. Two women, arm-in-arm, followed. I stepped into a doorway, removed a shoe and tapped it against the wall, and the same routine for the other shoe. There he was – the blond, young man – alone. At the end of the street, he stopped, looked left and right, then, seeming to recognise someone, he walked away from me toward the Majestic. Two men emerged from a shop doorway. They greeted the blond man and formed a huddle. I set off towards them, hoping to catch a fragment of their conversation. Too late. I was too far away. I reached them as the blond man turned and almost knocked into me.

'Excusez moi, mademoiselle.' He touched his hat and walked back in the direction of the bar. He was even younger than I had first thought; probably no more than eighteen or nineteen; medium height; clean-shaven.

I glanced at the other two men in the shadows. A fleeting impression told me they were older, burlier; one had a heavy moustache, both wore berets and were hard-faced.

I continued for another few hundred yards without looking back until I arrived at the Majestic. A quick check confirmed I hadn't been followed, so I pushed the swing door and headed to the reception desk. I was in luck; George Barnes was there.

'Good evening, George.'

'Ah, good evening, Miss Kiten. Would you like your key?'

'Yes, please, George, and may I have a sheet of paper and envelope to write a note for a guest.'

I scribbled a note to Keynes, advising that Pinchin had his notebook and planned to return it that evening. I folded the note, inserted in the envelope and handed it to George. 'It's for Mr Keynes. I don't know his room number, but no doubt you do.' He nodded his head. 'And George, if you are still on duty, would you do me a favour and note the time when Mr Keynes receives my note.'

I checked the clock in the foyer. I had only thirty minutes before last orders for dinner. I realised I was hungry and thirsty. There was no time to freshen up in my room; I would have to make my way directly to the dining hall. Once I had eaten, I would retire and consider all that had happened today. Was there any significance in Keynes' diversion to *Bar Felix* and Pinchin's discomfort at my appearance back at the schoolroom? Or had Arthur's murder led me to imagine intrigue and deception when there was none?

Ten

I slept until an hour after midnight, then woke with a start, eyes open before my mind was ready; upright in bed, panting for breath, my skin hot and sticky, despite the cold. Arthur. Chersky. Images of their wounded and disfigured heads flickered and pestered. A strange noise buzzed like a siren. Stop. I shook my head and ran fingers through my hair. The noise that roused from sleep was me, moaning.

I got out of bed, wrapped myself in a blanket and lit the fire. Shivered. Teeth chattered. My skin had turned cold and clammy. Goosebumps. My thoughts were a jumble of disorganised events, characters, motives and conjecture. It wasn't only Arthur and Chersky; the Keynes puzzle added to the confusion. I would have to write it all down and let a structure emerge from words, lines and diagrams. It was a routine I had used before to solve problems or clarify the logic of an academic argument. Of course, it didn't always work, but what else was I going to do for the next couple of hours? I couldn't sleep until the room warmed up.

I grabbed the notepad and a pencil and started to write names, places, dates, injuries, scraps of evidence, all written without any indication of significance, connection or priority. The next stage involved questioning and logic, resulting in lines of connection, circles of importance and arrows of direction. Finally, I rewrote the tangled chaos of letters, lines and shapes into a format that could be understood. That wasn't strictly necessary as I had formulated it all in my mind by then, but habit and superstition were persuasive companions.

The mode and date of killing, together with the address in Arthur's notepad, left no doubt in my mind that Arthur and Chersky were murdered by the same hand. The partial name indented on Arthur's notepad began with an 'L', ended in 'ov' and together with the ML inscribed in Chersky's book linked them both to Maxim Litvinov. Everything pointed to a Russian connection, but which faction was responsible for murder? If Chersky was an associate of Litvinov, that suggested one of the White Russian groups. I couldn't imagine Chersky as a Tsarist or White Russian. There was nothing in his possessions to suggest wealth or privilege. His lodging gave the impression of someone of modest means wishing to be inconspicuous. Sandra spoke of disputes and killings between the different factions. But Sazanov and the Russian Conference were desperate for recognition and aid from the allies, so would they risk the scandal and disgrace from discovery of their murder of a British security chief? I hadn't thought too deeply about the Russian situation and communism, but all the talk I had heard could be summarised as Bolsheviks dangerous and bad; White Russians deserving of help and good. Did I harbour an unconscious bias against the Bolsheviks and unwillingness to accept a conclusion that the Whites had killed Arthur? Sandra's description of Sazanov as unpleasant and creepy swayed opinion the other way. I tried to remain objective, and it wasn't easy, but I arrived at a sort of conclusion in the end.

Remembering Sandra's mention of a conference arranged between Litvinov and an American diplomat, Buckler; could Arthur have been involved in the arrangements and contacts with Bolsheviks? In that case, his murder was probably arranged by one of the anti-Bolshevik factions. Sazanov? I tore off the pages from the notepad, opened the heater and held them until the flame took them. It was the best answer I had to the puzzle of Arthur's murder. And I had to admit it was flimsy.

Keynes was a mystery. I wanted to like and admire him. There was no doubting his formidable intellect, and I could forgive his occasional arrogance, but there was also something darker in his character. I wasn't naïve, and I knew some men of high standing liked to seek pleasures in the more dubious margins of society. On reflection, I reasoned that my mind had become fevered with imaginings of conspiracy and devilry after the discovery of Chersky. In that case, I could dismiss Estelle and the men in the Bar Felix as odd companions for Keynes, but essentially harmless. By the same token, I discounted any significance of finding Pinchin in Keynes' office and the mystery man exiting the school. It was the rendezvous of the blond young man with the two hard men in Avenue Kleber that troubled. Although Keynes wasn't my main concern, I would have to keep an eye on him.

Back to bed, and I slept fitfully until shortly after five o'clock when I dressed and wrote a note to Adam Visser. I planned to catch Annie and Jane at breakfast and ask them to hand it in at the Astoria on their way to the typing pool there.

I was early in the dining hall and had started on my third cup of tea before I spied Annie in the queue. Jane wasn't far behind, and they sat at a table with three other women. I waited a couple of minutes before I went over and joined them. I owed them gossip, so told them about my night at *Le Baron* with exaggerated and lurid details of drinking champagne, jazz music and dancing with an American. They were enthralled and readily agreed to deliver my note to the Astoria. I was about to offer my excuses and leave them when I saw George Barnes heading my way. He raised a hand in recognition and weaved his way through the tables.

'Hello, George, do you have something for me?'

'Good Morning, Miss Kiten; I've been sent to find you. Sir Basil would like to see you in his office. He says it's urgent.'

I thanked George for his message. But, instead of leaving, he hovered by the table. It seemed he had been given instructions to hurry me along and accompany me to Sir Basil's office. I rose from my chair, leaving a collection of raised eyebrows and followed George, wondering why I warranted the attention of Sir Basil himself.

George stopped outside Thomson's door and said, 'You asked about Mr Keynes.' When I didn't respond, he added, 'Yesterday evening.'

'Oh yes, forgive me, George, I had forgotten about my note.'

'He came to reception about half an hour after you. He read your note, muttered something about keys and Mr Pinchin, then went off to the bar.'

'Thank you, George. That was helpful.' I searched in my bag. He realised I was about to tip him and became flustered but accepted when I insisted and pressed a couple of coins into his hand. He tapped the door, waited for a rasped command from inside, turned the handle and gestured with an outstretched hand for me to enter.

'Ah, good morning Miss Kiten, do come in and take a seat. My apologies if I have interrupted your breakfast.' I returned a muttered greeting and took my seat at his cluttered desk. 'How are you finding your work for Mr Keynes and his Treasury men?'

'I'm enjoying it, thank you, Sir Basil. It's more of a challenge than I expected as it's mainly research in unfamiliar subjects using my language skills.'

'Good, good,' he said as he sorted through a pile of papers. He wasn't really listening, and my answer could have contained a reference to rabid dogs and received the same response. I was relieved to note his head cold had eased its grip since our previous encounter.

'Now.' He adjusted his jacket, ran a finger around his short collar and leant back in his chair. 'I've been speaking to Major Parkes.' He waited and I suppose he wanted a reaction from me, but I remained impassive. 'He suggested we should examine the circumstances surrounding the killing of Mr Burgess. Although the Major denied his approach was made at your behest, I assume that you and he have discussed the matter.'

'Yes, Sir Basil, I am grateful to Major Parkes for his discretion. I cannot deny that it was probably my pleading that led him to broach the subject with you. But, I'm sure he only made the suggestion because he believes there is good cause to doubt the police case.'

'Maybe you're right. However, whatever opinion Major Parkes or I hold is irrelevant now. Matters have been taken out of my hands. I have a letter here from a fellow named Smith-Cumming in a section of the

War Office. Apparently he has arranged for an agent to look into the killing of Mr Burgess.'

'An agent?'

'Yes, I don't think I will be disclosing any state secrets if I tell you Smith-Cumming heads the section dealing with intelligence gathering.'

'You mean... spying?'

'I'm not sure they would ever use that word. His section is now referred to only by initials – SIS. Decide for yourself what words they might signify.' He took a deep breath and smoothed his moustache with his fingers. 'I'm advised it will be a few days before the agent arrives to begin an enquiry. When he does I'm sure that, as a close friend of the deceased, you will be interviewed with others. Meanwhile...' He leant forward and fixed me with a stare that I guess was meant as a warning. 'Meanwhile, I want your word that you will not get embroiled in any investigation into the death of Mr Burgess.'

'Why would you ask...?'

'I have no inside information on your intentions, Miss Kiten. Put it down to intuition if you like. There's a scent of reckless spirit about you and I've a feeling it would be prudent to keep you well clear of any hint of danger.'

'I can assure you, Sir Basil, I have no wish to get involved in any situation that could be regarded as dangerous.'

'Nevertheless, I will have your word on it. Aside from any peril, your close relationship with Mr Burgess will not allow you to view evidence and circumstances objectively. You must leave it to the agent sent here by Smith-Cumming.'

I had no wish stand back from Arthur's murderer and stop gathering information, but neither could I lie easily. Still, I had no idea on how I was going to follow up my discovery of Chersky's corpse and the Russian link. All I had in mind was to question Visser, and it seemed unlikely I would make any progress until he returned. Perhaps I could find a form of words that would ease my conscience.

'Very well, Sir Basil, I give my word that I will do nothing about the killing of Mr Burgess without first making contact and discussing the issue with the agent due here in the next few days.'

'Don't try to confuse with clever phrasing and conditions, Miss Kiten. I could make your position here extremely uncomfortable if you cross me.'

'I apologise again, Sir Basil. It is not my intention to wriggle out of a promise. I take an oath seriously and would be placed in an awkward position if the agent sent here to investigate requested my assistance in the matter of Mr Burgess.' I hesitated as he raised his eyebrows. 'I do realise that is unlikely given your message, but my conscience would be troubled even if I was asked to provide minor administrative or clerical assistance. You see my dilemma?'

He stared at me. I met his gaze, not with any challenge, but a directness that I hoped spoke of openness and sincerity.

'Very well, Miss Kiten, I accept your word and the force of your argument. Please do not give me cause to regret my trust.'

He gestured with his hand that I was free to leave. I acknowledged with a nod of my head and murmured thanks as I rose from my seat. I left Thomson's room to find John in the corridor outside chatting to one of his soldiers. I didn't want to talk and kept my head down, not intending to linger, but I could see him break away and follow me at the margin of my vision. He called my name. I turned and smiled a greeting.

'Good morning, John.'

'Mary, were you with Sir Basil?'

'Yes, only a short meeting.'

'Was it… is there a problem?'

'Sir Basil informed me about a communication from London.'

'So, everything is alright?'

'Yes, John. I will be glad to explain. But not now, I'm going to be late.'

He checked his watch. 'Oh yes, I see. Then perhaps we could meet for a drink in the bar this evening?'

'That would be perfect, John. Sorry, must dash.'

He held out his hand. 'I almost forgot. Here.' He handed a letter to me. 'The mail has just arrived, and I was hoping to catch you before your departure to the schoolroom.'

I thanked him and slipped the letter into my bag. A quick glance at the envelope confirmed the handwriting was Mother's. She wouldn't have received my letter about Arthur yet, but had she heard from another source? Mark? The newspapers? I stopped in a shop doorway on my way to Rue Leo Delibes and read the letter.

Friday, 10th January 1919

My Precious Mary

Thank you for your letter of 6th January. Let me inform you straightway that your suspicions are unfounded. I knew nought of your unexpected call to Paris. I met with Arthur last in early December when we had a very pleasant lunch at the Star Hotel. I'm sure I would have told you in my letters, that we shared a delicious lobster. He had a couple of days here to sort out business in town before heading to Paris. He mentioned the Conference, but didn't elaborate on his position there, and he certainly didn't confide in any plans he had for you. Perhaps he didn't want to disappoint me, knowing how I long to have you back home. Oh well, I suppose I will have to put up with a few more weeks of rattling about in this draughty old house on my own.

New Year was a muted affair. Winnifred and I did attend the concert at King's, but it brought back such painful memories of your father that I rather think I spoiled the enjoyment for both of us. Overall though, I enjoyed Winnifred's visit and I rather think we will do the same again next Christmas. You will be surprised to learn that I have given in to insistence that I spend Easter with her in Bristol. I am determined not to give in to my fear of train journeys. I know it is irrational, but the memory of that accident lingers.

There was a disgraceful incident at the bridge club last Thursday...

I stopped and stuffed the letter back into the envelope, then into a coat pocket. Couldn't read any more. A knot had been tied in the pit of my stomach. It didn't feel right to have such familiar and innocent correspondence with Mother without any mention of Arthur's murder. She should have received my letter of 10th by now, so her next reply would be full of shock and horror at the news. I dreaded receiving it. But oddly enough, I felt it would be easier to read than the one just received.

    *

Another busy day in the schoolrooms, and I had little time to dwell on the interview with Sir Basil and the communication from London. I wasn't surprised that the letter was from the intelligence section of the War Office. I didn't know the exact nature of Uncle Arthur's position there, but I guessed it was *hush-hush* as he rarely mentioned his work. I suppose I should have been pleased that someone in England thought his killing was worth an investigation. But the trail of evidence may well have turned cold when the agent arrived. It was too little, too late – an afterthought by a Whitehall bureaucrat..

Most of the day, I worked with Derek and Jack, the two youngest in the unit, on population and mortality statistics for all countries except the Central Powers. The exercise was time-consuming as we had to collect the latest estimates by long-distance telephone and telegram. Additional complexity was found due to a high number of deaths from the viral disease currently causing havoc in Europe and the different ways it was referenced or classified in each country. Pinchin left early, and I kept my eyes open for other leavers as evening approached.

We three were still struggling with our tabulated statistics when I saw Keynes grab his overcoat and prepare to leave his office. I waited until he was out of the door before I complained of a headache and said I would have to finish and get some fresh air.

I had to hurry down Rue Leo Delibes to catch sight of Keynes about seventy paces ahead. I had closed to about forty paces when Keynes turned down the side street to *Bar Felix*. I stopped at the junction and watched as he entered the bar. I waited another couple of minutes and was about to make my way to the bar, with the prepared excuse of a mislaid glove, when I saw movement in a doorway. Two, three, then four figures emerged. The first two were the hard-faced men from yesterday, and the third looked like the blond young man I had seen patting Keynes' back. I had difficulty viewing the fourth as they formed a huddle. It broke; the blond man headed for the bar while the others went in the opposite direction. I followed the three men as we left Bar Felix behind and turned into Avenue Kleber. The man I hadn't seen before came into view as they passed a shop window. He was carrying something, a bulky shape, under his arm. Was it... a camera? I quickened my steps to get closer. They crossed the road and headed down Rue Copernic. They slowed; I held back, looked in a shop window, then followed a couple walking arm-in-arm. At a crossing, the three men turned left and stopped in a doorway on Rue Lauriston. The man with a camera seemed to be receiving instructions from the other two. The door opened, and he disappeared inside with, what I supposed, was his camera. The two hard-faced men spoke some words then split, each stopping in the shadows about twenty yards either side of the doorway.

What had I just witnessed? The actions were innocent enough, but I couldn't shake the notion of an elaborate trap being laid. No, that was fanciful, surely? I was gripped with indecision for a few moments, then knew what I must do. I turned and walked, then ran as fast as I could, back to the Majestic.

I slowed in the foyer, gasping to catch my breath. Two men stopped their conversation and stared. Other eyes were on me as I crossed the foyer, up a few marble steps, and down a corridor to room number 28. I knocked and waited a couple of seconds before trying the door handle. It was open. I edged into the room, calling his name. His bedroom door opened, and John came out hoisting up braces over his shirt.

'Mary, what is it?'

'Please John… please come with me. It's urgent. I'll explain on the way.' I picked up the khaki jacket hanging over the back of a chair and handed it to him. 'You'll need your overcoat as well.'

'Where… just a minute. Wait.'

Too slow. I grabbed his arm and pulled him. Desperation must have shown on my face because he submitted to my urging, slammed his door shut and wrestled with his coat as he followed. He caught up and matched my steps as we arrived at the exit.

'Where are we going?'

'It's only a few minutes away,'

'Where?'

'Down here, then across the road.' We were walking too quickly for a proper conversation. 'It's Keynes.'

'What about him?'

'In trouble – I think. Come on.' I tugged at his arm, and we broke into a run.

We stopped by a haberdashery before the junction with Rue Lauriston.

'Now, tell me what's going on,' he said.

'I think a plan has been laid to harm Mr Keynes in some way.'

'Harm him – how?'

'I'm not sure.' I grabbed his coat and guided him towards the shop window. 'I've seen a group of men... they seemed to be conspiring... to lure him....'

'You're not making a lot of sense, Mary.'

The shop was still open, and we were too conspicuous in the light. 'We need to move into the shadows. Shall we - can we pretend we are a couple?'

'My pleasure.' He smiled and crooked his elbow, allowing me to slip in a gloved hand. 'Sir Basil told me about your meeting this morning.' I started to respond but stopped myself, and all that escaped my mouth was a puff of air. Now was not the time. I inclined my head as an encouragement to move on, and we strolled down the street until the doorway in Rue Lauriston came into view. I stood with my back to the wall, grabbed the lapels of John's overcoat and pulled him closer.

'Not too close; I need to be able to see the other side of the street.'

'We need to make this convincing,' he whispered in my ear. I gave him a playful punch on the chest. 'Seriously, Mary, are we talking mortal danger here or some form of practical joke?'

'It's not a practical joke. Wait...' I noticed two figures walking this way on the other side of the street. One had a long, loping gait that I was sure belonged to Keynes. 'He's coming.'

I peered around the other side of John. I couldn't see either of the hard men.

'Don't look behind you. Another ten seconds, and we'll cross the road and follow him.'

It was the blond young man with Keynes. They were sharing a joke. Animated. Close. Then, I think I understood.

'Come on, let's go.' I took John's hand and crossed the road. We were only fifteen paces behind Keynes as they headed for the door in Rue Lauriston. Blond man slowed, searched in his pocket and produced a key; smiled, put the key in the door.

'Stop!' My voice; harsh, discordant, unexpected, in the night air.

Keynes turned and stared, open-mouthed. Blond man froze, looked at me, glanced left, then right. I let go of John's hand, walked to Keynes, started to speak - and felt rather than heard the noise – a crack like a whiplash; thin; fierce; brutal. A gunshot. Was I hit? I sensed something on the back of my neck, my shoulders. I turned slowly, all motion sluggish and deliberate. John had fallen, crumpled on the cold paving, mouth wide, shouting; surprised. The noise was faint, distant. I knelt and stretched out my hand, not quite reaching him.

Then, a sudden rush of movement, feeling and hearing. Too quick. Too loud. Blood. I had blood on my hand from John's wound. Voices shouted. John said something. 'Gun.' His gun was in its leather holster. I unfastened it, took the gun, flicked the catch. Then, still kneeling, I swivelled to my right. He was there, one of the hard men, a dark shape, aimed - at me. I pulled the trigger and fired; once, twice, three times. He fell.

I stood. Keynes was motionless. His blond companion ran. Another man stepped out of the shadows and followed him. A dozen yards back in the other direction, a man was on the ground, arms outstretched, and one leg bent under the other. Had I shot and killed him? Me?

I heard footsteps behind. People edged closer, peered at the body. I closed my eyes and clenched my fists to clear my mind so that I could tend John's wound. He was holding his right shoulder. I knelt and moved his hand. He drew a hard breath and grimaced. The injury was high in his shoulder, and it looked as though the bullet may have broken a bone. Thankfully, there was an exit wound and a fair chance the injury would be clean and free from infection. I lifted my head and shouted, 'Docteur. Hopital. Rapidement,' to anyone who would listen. I would have to staunch the bleeding, but what was I to use?

'John, help is coming. First, I will have to put something on your wound.' He nodded his head and gritted his teeth. 'If I can stop the bleeding, you will mend.'

I stood, unbuttoned my coat, then lifted my skirt and tugged at my petticoat. No, that wouldn't do. I scrabbled in my bag and retrieved a knife. I cut and tore until the bottom half of my petticoat was free. More cutting until I had lengths of cloth I could use to wrap his shoulder. I pulled at the sleeve of his overcoat. No good, I couldn't do it alone.

'Help me, Mr Keynes... please.'

Keynes' body seemed to shudder with surprise at my words. He took off his coat, threw it on the ground and lowered himself on to one knee, so he was able to tug at John's overcoat and jacket sleeves while I supported his shoulder. After much painful pulling and yelling, I was able to get at the injured shoulder and could see the exit wound.

'Good news, John. It's a clean injury.' He attempted a smile that didn't quite make it. I looked at Keynes. 'Brandy or whisky?' He nodded, produced a small silver hip flask. I dribbled contents on the entry and exit wounds, then handed it to John. He gulped three or four mouthfuls before I prised it from his fingers and returned to Keynes. Then, it was a question of wrapping as tightly as I could around John's shoulder while trying to minimise his pain.

I finished by tying a rough sling to hold his injured arm. I checked my handiwork, kissed him on the forehead and announced, 'Bravely done, John. That should do the trick.'

I looked up and, for the first time, saw the crowd that had gathered around us. Keynes was talking to a man with a notebook, and two uniformed gendarmes were inspecting the body of the man I had shot. Gun: where was the gun I had used? I mouthed the word silently at John. He narrowed his eyes, seeming not to understand, then nodded in recognition and tapped his holster. He had replaced it while my attention was taken up with tending his wound.

He held out his good arm. 'Here, give me a hand to get up.' I helped him to his feet. Although he appeared to have recovered from the shock, his teeth chattered with cold, and I could feel an unsteadiness and frailty in his limbs. We had to get him to a hospital quickly. He pulled me close and whispered, 'I shot him. If the police ask, it was me. My gun. I shot him.'

'Why?'

'Easier. You would have too many questions to answer.'

He staggered over to Keynes and asked him to help him with his overcoat to guard against the cold. I went to help, but John held out a hand, saying they could manage. He muttered something to Keynes as he settled the heavy coat tentatively on his shoulder. I couldn't hear but suspect he was repeating his claim to be the one who shot our attacker.

A motor car edged its way through onlookers and came to a stop. The driver was another gendarme. The passenger was a large man in a grey coat, bowler hat, heavy jowls and a snub nose. A pencil-thin dark moustache seemed out of place, as though borrowed from another, leaner face. The gendarme immediately went to the man with a notebook, who was trying to get Keynes' attention again; angry words were exchanged until the gendarme pointed a hand and the notebook man stepped back into the crowd. I gathered from the few words overheard that he was a newspaperman. Three gendarmes then gathered around the heavy man; a short discussion ensued before they were interrupted by the arrival of another motor car containing four more of their number. Over fifty people had gathered in the street with windows and doors opened, others joining, leading to elbowing and jostling to gain a vantage point. They shuffled back reluctantly when coaxed by the uniformed policemen, but the urging to disperse fell on deaf ears.

The policeman in the grey coat was in no hurry. He ambled over to the body, ordered one of the gendarmes to lift the cloak placed over his head. He shrugged, looked over to our group briefly before returning to discuss something with his colleague. I glanced at Keynes, then John. We were all keenly focussed on the activities of the burly policeman. Finally, he made his way slowly and deliberately towards us.

'You are all British?' He spoke English with confidence and one who had been well educated. 'Forgive my presumption, but I notice the uniform of a British major. My name is Bonnet, Inspecteur Principal in this arrondissement.'

John started to respond, but Keynes interrupted, saying, 'Yes, Inspector, we are with the British delegation at the Majestic. My friend, the major has been wounded by a gunshot and should be taken to a hospital without delay.'

'Who has tended your injury, Major?'

'It was me,' I answered, impatient for him to move quicker. 'I have experience as a nurse. The bullet passed through his shoulder, but he has lost a lot of blood, and the shoulder bone is broken.'

'What has happened here?' He took a pipe from his coat pocket and proceeded to tap and prod, readying it for smoking.

'We were attacked,' I answered.

'By that man and for no apparent reason,' added Keynes, pointing to the prone figure.

'You were fortunate, then.' He lit his pipe with a lighter, remaining calm and unhurried despite our mounting agitation.

'Do you know the attacker, Inspecteur?' I asked.

'Yes, Mademoiselle, he is known to us.' He took a couple of thoughtful puffs. 'Who fired the shots to kill that man?'

'It was me,' said John tapping the holster with his good hand.

'Hmm, you did well to fire three shots after being wounded yourself, Major. Or – forgive me - did you, perhaps, shoot first?'

'No, of course not. Maybe his gun jammed, or… I don't know… it happened quickly,' said John.

'The hospital, Inspecteur, please.' I took hold of his good arm to support John and highlight his need for attention.

He nodded acceptance of my plea, then beckoned to two gendarmes and gave instructions between puffs of smoke. Bonnet took our names. One of the gendarmes was instructed to take John to the Clinique du Parc Monceau in a motor car, and the other to escort Keynes and me in a short walk back to the Majestic. There, we were to wait for Bonnet, who would call at the Majestic and interview us within the hour. I wanted to accompany John, but there were only two seats in the car, so let him go with a promise to inform Sir Basil of the incident.

As we entered the foyer of the Majestic, no words had passed between us, but I could sense Keynes, like me, was struggling to come to terms with what had just happened. I felt as though I was emerging from a dream-like episode, where I was more spectator than participant. Perhaps Keynes shared this feeling as all traces of his authority and arrogance had vanished.

'I will go and inform Sir Basil about Major Parkes. Shall we take a seat over there and wait for the inspector?' I pointed to a table and four chairs in a corner. He nodded dumbly. 'Mr Keynes.' I raised my voice.

'Yes, yes.' He shook his head. 'Do you mind if we meet in my room for more privacy?'

'What is your room number?'

'Room number eighty – on the first floor.' He started to move, then stopped and said, 'And Mary, thank you. Your quick actions saved me; saved us all.'

I nodded my head and mumbled a noncommittal reply. I couldn't be sure he fully understood that he was the reason behind the attack. But it wasn't the right time. I would explain at a later meeting.

As soon as Keynes left, I went to report the incident to security. Sir Basil was not in his room and the sergeant manning his office advised he would probably not return until tomorrow. I wrote a short note advising John was injured, recovering well, and he could have more detail by contacting me.

I didn't bother to go to my bedroom. Instead, I sat on an upright chair, noted the time as almost eight o'clock and waited for Bonnet. He promised an hour, but his languid manner led me to suspect he would be much longer.

I was wrong. The inspector emerged from the swing door at ten minutes to nine o'clock. I met him on his way to the reception desk and explained that Keynes was waiting for us in his room.

'Thank you, mademoiselle; I should like to speak to you both, but separately. Let us talk now, and I will see Mr Keynes when we are finished. Shall we go to your room?'

'I regret my room is too small, Inspecteur. Would you like to sit at one of these tables in the foyer?'

'I would prefer somewhere... quieter if that is possible.'

I hesitated, wondering how I could arrange a meeting room. Sir Basil was away and approaching him or his stand-in for an interview with a policeman did not seem a good idea after his warning to keep out of trouble. Then I remembered; John and I left his room in a hurry, and I was sure he didn't stop to lock his door. I guided Bonnet across the foyer and down a corridor to room number 28. I tried the handle and was relieved to find it unlocked. I went inside and closed the door behind Bonnet.

'Shall we sit here,' I said, pointing to two armchairs on either side of a small table. I removed my coat, waited to receive Bonnet's, then hung both up on a stand by his bedroom door.

'This is not my room.' Better to confess than be found, out, and it relieved me of the obligation to offer a drink.

'Yes, it is a gentleman's room; that much is clear.'

'It is the Major's room; Major Parkes who has been taken to the hospital.'

'So, you are a friend of the Major... or perhaps more than a friend?'

'Just a friend.' He took his notebook from one pocket and his pipe from another. Thankfully, the pipe was put to one side as he flicked the pages in his book. 'Do you have any news of his condition from the hospital?'

He shook his head and readied his pencil. 'Now, please tell me why you were at the scene of the shooting.'

'I was walking with Major Parkes when we saw Mr Keynes in Rue Lauriston. We had hailed him and crossed the road to meet him when suddenly a shot was fired.'

'You were walking. Where was your destination?'

'I had endured a busy day in a stuffy office and simply wanted a brisk walk in the fresh air.'

He raised an eyebrow and paused his writing. 'So, it was pure chance that you encountered Mr Keynes.'

'Yes.'

'And you had no end point in mind so that it could be termed… an aimless walk.'

'I suppose so.'

He put down his notebook and started to prepare his pipe, all the while with a thoughtful demeanour as though he was assessing what had been said. I found myself watching his hands, fascinated and lulled into a numbed state by the careful, deliberate movements. The pipe was returned to a pocket unlit.

'Why do you think you were attacked? Were you wearing precious jewels or carrying a significant amount of money?'

'I had no jewellery, except this ring and very little money.' I held up my left hand to show a ring given by my mother as a token of good fortune. 'I believe the major is from a wealthy family, and Mr Keynes has a certain reputation in academic and political circles. I suppose both men appear affluent and therefore could be possible targets for an opportunist thief.'

'Tell me what happened when the first shot was fired.'

'I realised that the noise was a shot from a handgun, but I had no idea who had fired it. I remember wondering if I had been hit and saw John – Major Parkes - had fallen to the ground, so I bent to help him. There was blood. His shoulder…'

'How did he fire his gun? It hangs on the left side of his belt, so I presume he is right-handed, yet it was the right shoulder that was hit, rendering his right arm useless.'

'I have trouble remembering all the detail. It was a blur; happened so quickly; dreamlike.'

'Who fired the gun at your attacker, mademoiselle?'

'Major Parkes. He shouted, "Gun", and motioned his head at the handgun on his belt. I may have unclipped the gun and handed it to him. Yes, I'm sure that's what happened. The gunshots were quite disorienting, and it took a while to recover my senses.'

'Why do you think your attacker delayed firing another shot, allowing the major to return fire?'

'I really couldn't say. Perhaps his gun jammed. Or he hesitated to shoot at an unarmed woman. Maybe I was in the way, and he didn't want to shoot me.'

'From what we know, that man would not be squeamish about shooting a woman, even one as young and as beautiful as you.'

'Who was he?'

'An unpleasant man named Maxim Fabre from a well-known criminal family.'

'There may have been another.'

'What did you see?'

'There was a man, about 20 paces in the opposite direction. He ran away when shots were fired.'

'Can you describe him; the other man?'

'No, it was too dark, and I only saw his back.'

He clicked his tongue, wrote a few more words, then finished with a flourish of the pencil, snapped his notebook, bowed his head and smiled. 'Thank you, Mademoiselle Kiten, most interesting. I congratulate you on your escape from a deadly attack and your admirable treatment of the major's wound.' It required an effort to heave his considerable bulk from his chair.

'Will you be visiting the major in hospital this night?'

'Yes, after I have spoken to Mr Keynes.'

'Would it be too much to ask to take me with you? I am eager to learn a doctor's opinion on his wound and what treatment he may need for a full recovery.'

'By all means. Shall we say thirty minutes at reception?'

There was little point shivering on the sixth floor, so I returned to room 28 after showing Bonnet the way to Keynes. Only then, did I begin to appreciate the importance of synchronising our reports to the police about the attack. Up to that point, being vague and confused by the danger had seemed plausible and I assumed would be accepted by Bonnet without further questioning. I wasn't too concerned about crediting John with firing the shots that killed Fabre. After all, few would believe a young woman capable of such action. No, any doubt in Bonnet's mind would probably result from his understanding the reason for our encounter with Keynes and the purpose behind the attack. How would Keynes explain his presence in Rue Lauriston? I hoped he would be persuasive, and John would follow my lead in reporting a chance meeting during a stroll for fresh air.

I supposed all that was important, but not matters of life and death. More troubling thoughts concerned guns being used in the entrapment of Keynes. I had presumed the intention was to catch and photograph Keynes in a compromising position to blackmail or discredit him and his views on reparations. I hadn't considered the use of extreme force or even the possibility that assassination might be a fallback position if problems with the entrapment occurred. The dismissal of the newspaperman by the gendarme was another aspect I hadn't deemed significant at the time. On reflection, I had to wonder if his attendance at the scene was coincidental or did he have a part to play in the elaborate scheme as witness and reporter. If that was the case, then it was likely he had observed the entire drama.

I was at reception only a few minutes before Bonnet appeared and guided me to a police motor car waiting outside the entrance to the hotel. I sat in the back while Bonnet had a conversation with the driver. I wasn't paying full attention, but I gathered there was concern about a disturbance at a club. Bonnet clambered into the front seat and turned his head.

'I regret we must stop on the way to the hospital, Mademoiselle Kiten. There has been an incident nearby.'

'Of course.' Unwelcome news. I was eager to see John but not in a position to complain.

We continued up Avenue Kleber, past the Arc and along Avenue Hoche, a well-lit street lined with bars, cafes, clubs and restaurants. The car stopped outside a club where a crowd of fifty or more were gathered. Gendarmes were already in attendance. Bonnet ordered me to stay in the car while he and the driver both joined the throng outside. From my position, most of the people in the crowd appeared good-natured, with animated conversations, huddled groups, feet stamping, hand gestures and some laughter. I could also see at least one broken window and two men using brushes to clean the glass. After a few minutes, the crowd started to drift back into the club. Bonnet shook hands with a tall, well-dressed man carrying a cane, then returned to the car.

'I hope it was nothing too serious.'

He sighed, shook his head and answered, 'Les Russes.'

'Russians. I have been told there is often trouble with the different Russian factions in the city.'

'You are well informed. I regret it is a regular occurrence in this neighbourhood.'

'Is this where the Russians tend to gather?'

'The orthodox church is in the next street, so there are Russians here in normal times, but many more now we have the Congress.'

I took a mental note of the name *Club Margot* as the driver started the engine. 'Was there a fight or shooting at the club?'

'Poof!' he waved his hands in the air. 'We were informed there was a possibility of a bomb, but only bricks were thrown through the windows. No one was hurt.'

'Thank goodness. A bomb would have been terrible in an enclosed and crowded area.'

'There was a bomb – a small one – at a property nearby a few days ago. The Bolsheviks were blamed as a Tsarist minister, Sergei Sazanov, owned the damaged house. There was a genuine concern that this could have been another one as the club is a gathering place for all those Russian groups opposed to the Bolsheviks.'

'The man you shook hands with at the end - I'm sure I have seen him before at the Majestic.'

'Quite possibly, mademoiselle. That was Sazanov, the man I mentioned a few moments ago. I understand he has a reputation with many delegates as a charming and entertaining companion.'

'Your tone suggests you are not an admirer.'

He chose not to answer, and from my rear view, I couldn't see his expression.

A TURBULENT PEACE

The hospital was only a short distance from *Club Margot*, in a typical Parisian street of cream, plastered facades. The entrance was busy with a collection of horse-drawn and motor vehicles blocking our progress. Bonnet and I got out of the car, leaving the driver to negotiate the impasse and find a place to park. Inside the main entrance, it was chaotic with doctors and nurses trying to bring order to a scrimmage of would-be patients with their helpers vying for attention above the general babble. I stood back while Bonnet struggled to speak to a nurse and uniformed man behind a desk. He beckoned to me, and I followed down a short corridor to stairs, where the fray had quietened.

'Major Parkes is on the third floor. The British delegation has reserved a few beds. It is unusually busy here, and I was informed it is because of the influenza,' said Bonnet. 'It is quite alarming how many are seeking hospital care.'

I murmured an agreement with his last statement. The spread of a new and deadly strain of 'flu was widely known, despite a lack of coverage in the newspapers. I had come across a few cases of this new disease in Wimereux, but they were sent to isolation wards as soon as they were diagnosed. I had no experience of its treatment or prognosis.

At the top of the stairs, we were directed along a corridor to a room at the end containing about a dozen beds in each of two rows. Bonnet enquired at a circular desk in the centre, and we were pointed to the far end where I could see a nurse tending to John. He saw us coming and raised his good hand, looking pale and tired but smiling and clearly pleased to see us. We exchanged greetings and waited until the nurse had

147

finished tying the new sling. The neighbouring two beds were unoccupied, so Bonnet had a fair degree of privacy for his questioning.

'Has a doctor examined your shoulder yet, John?'

'I've had ten minutes with two doctors, and a nurse has cleaned and dressed the wound. But, so far, all I have been told is that I have a broken bone that may take a while to heal.' He glanced at Bonnet, then turned to me, cleared his throat and said, 'May I have a private word with you when the interview with the Inspector is finished?'

I murmured my agreement, thinking he probably wished to see if our accounts tallied. Bonnet asked a nurse to arrange screens around John's bed. I wasn't sure if I would be allowed to stay while he interviewed John, but he made no sign I was to leave. I took half a step back from Bonnet, hoping to be inconspicuous, as he took out his notebook.

I could have predicted his first question. 'Major Parkes, please tell me how you came to be at Rue Lauriston earlier this evening.'

John made the mistake of looking at me over Bonnet's shoulder before answering, and I was asked to step outside the screens. I could hear the conversation, and thankfully his answer more-or-less coincided with my explanation, with John saying I had requested his company on a short walk to get an appetite for dinner. *And no, we had no destination in mind. He was acquainted with Keynes but had only exchanged a few words. It was Miss Kiten who acknowledged Keynes. No, he couldn't understand why they had been attacked. He wasn't carrying much cash. He saw a flash at the same time he was hit, so he knew the general direction of his attacker. He couldn't remember exactly how he had managed to handle the gun and fire three shots. Yes, he was right-handed but had been trained to use a gun in either hand. Yes, he supposed it may have been possible that Miss Kiten helped move the gun from his holster to his hand. The circumstances of the attack were confusing, and the shock of being shot may have affected his accurate recall of events.*

From my hearing, John's answers should have satisfied the inspector. Nothing he said contradicted my statement, and Bonnet hadn't queried anything after his interview with Keynes. We waited until Bonnet had ambled his way through the exit before we spoke.

'I said, 'That seemed to go well enough.'

'Yes, although he has a disturbing aura about him that suggests he can see through inaccuracies and untruths. I couldn't help a feeling of guilt. Even so, I do think our little white lie about who fired the gun was for the best, and it shouldn't impair his investigation, should it?'

'No, you're probably right, who fired your gun shouldn't make any difference to their search for the other attackers.'

'Good, good, Anyway, that wasn't actually the reason I wanted to talk to you. The two doctors I saw here... well, they are both... women... British women would you believe?'

'Why should that be so outrageous, John?'

'It's not, as you say, outrageous. It's just very... uncommon. I knew there were a few female doctors back home, but I didn't think...'

'Didn't think they would be allowed to do any serious doctoring here, with war casualties.'

'No, no you misunderstand, Mary. I don't object to women doctors at all. I know there are old-fashioned attitudes and I thought… well, I thought you would be interested.'

I'm sorry, John. I didn't mean to be snappy, and I am interested.' I placed my hand on his as a gesture of appeasement. 'There's a small hospital in Wimereux run by the Women's Hospital Corps, and I understand there's a hospital in an abbey about 30 miles north of here run by a group of Scottish women. But I didn't know of any working in central Paris.'

'I believe the doctors I saw here are both Scottish; Doctors Morton and Inglis if I recall their names correctly.'

I stayed for another twenty minutes or so, hoping to see one or both of those doctors, but neither appeared. I wasn't surprised when John had trouble keeping his eyes open. He was still in shock, and despite weak protestations, he was fast asleep a matter of seconds after I helped a nurse tuck him into his bed. I had reacted badly and been too short with him when he mentioned the women doctors. My father talked of the pig-headed attitude of our War Office to women doctors before he left for France. It was our last conversation and perhaps that was why I was so touchy on the subject.

Eleven

Wednesday, 15th January, 1919

My Dearest Mother

I have always imagined the to and fro of our letters as a conversation and reading your letter of 10th January produced an extra heaviness in my heart. Of course, I know it would have been impossible for you to receive the dreadful news contained in my letter of 9th January before your writing. Nevertheless, your letter was a difficult read without any acknowledgement from you of Uncle Arthur's passing.

While I would not wish to prolong the hurt and upset, I feel duty bound to inform you that there is some doubt over the police verdict on the circumstances of Arthur's killing. I assume an inquiry is underway. I have struck up a cordial relationship with Uncle Arthur's deputy, a Major John Parkes, and I was rather hoping he would keep me informed on the progress of any investigation. Unfortunately, he suffered an injury yesterday and has been hospitalised. I hope he will be discharged soon, for his own sake as well as for any assistance or information he may provide. He is a very pleasant man, and I confess there may be an attraction between us, even after our short acquaintance.

Meanwhile, I have been undertaking interesting work for the Treasury Unit. The head of our section is John Maynard Keynes, a one-time Cambridge academic who has a reputation as a highflyer. My knowledge of languages is coming in handy, and you could best describe the nature of my work as a research assistant. Altogether, we make up a happy and effective team, I think. We operate out of a converted local schoolroom to avoid distractions and requests for help from other units, which are mostly sited in the Hotel Astoria.

Please excuse the abbreviated nature of this letter, but I am sure you understand it is hard to write a 'newsy' letter with the pall of Uncle Arthur's passing casting a shadow over thoughts and actions.

Your ever-loving daughter
Mary

I woke early and spent a good half hour deciding how I would inform Mother of an inquiry into Arthur's murder. Of course, there was no investigation; it was simply me poking my nose into matters that were not my concern. At least that was the general opinion, and certainly Mother would be horrified to learn of my presence at the scenes in Rue Gustave Courbet and Rue Lauriston. In the end, I was circumspect and hoped that a fascination with my mention of an attraction to John would mean she didn't dwell on the possibilities surrounding Arthur's killing.

I was outside Sir Basil's door a few minutes after six. My knock was tentative, not wanting to disturb his morning ablutions but knowing it had to be early enough to request security cover for Keynes before his departure to the school. I needn't have worried. My knock was answered with a prompt and authoritative invitation to enter.

'Ah, Miss Kiten, I have your note and had intended to catch you at breakfast for clarification.' He gestured to a chair. 'Please sit.' He picked up my note from his desk and waved it between thumb and forefinger. 'At our previous meeting, you promised to desist from any involvement in an investigation of the circumstances of the death of Mr Burgess and to keep a low profile. I hope that, whatever happened last night, does not signify you reneged on your word.'

'No, Sir Basil, the incident last night had nothing to do with Arthur Burgess.'

Under Thomson's scrutiny, my response to his command to explain was less composed than I had hoped. Instead, I was hesitant and stumbling over words I had rehearsed in my bedroom. I suspected that John would eventually disclose the truth to Thomson about who shot our attacker, but without the opportunity to confirm this with him, I stuck to the story I had told Bonnet.

'Tell me again. Why did you suspect Mr Keynes was in danger?' He screwed up my note and threw it in a basket by his feet.

'I was taken to *Bar Felix* by Mr Keynes before and suspected the motives of men he had befriended. I had previously been warned of a possible threat to Mr Keynes by Colonel House's assistant, Miss Fairlight.'

'But you were nowhere near *Bar Felix* when you were attacked. And why was Major Parkes shot if Mr Keynes was the target?'

'I don't know. Perhaps it was because we shouted a warning to Mr Keynes.'

He shook his head. 'I get the feeling there's something you're not telling me, Miss Kiten. However, we must deal with the situation as presented. I am mightily relieved to learn that Major Parkes will recover from his wound, although healing may be a long process. And, I should not forget to congratulate you on your foresight, which may have prevented a deadlier outcome for the innocents. Remarkable.' He paused, shook his head again and puffed air as though this was all beyond his comprehension.

'Will you provide extra security for Mr Keynes?'

'My resources are stretched, and you are suggesting permanent cover for one man.' He drew in a sharp breath through clenched teeth. 'Under the circumstances, I suppose it must be done.'

*

There was no sign of Keynes at breakfast, and he wasn't in his office when I arrived at our schoolroom. It was almost ten o'clock before the door opened, and he entered, shuffling off his overcoat, followed by a corporal from the Majestic. He placed coat and hat on a central desk, cleared his throat to get our attention and introduced Corporal Hincham as his security guard. He tried to make light of last night's incident and suggested the extra security was a temporary measure, apologising to Hincham for burdening with a tedious duty. Heads turned to me when my name was mentioned, and there were gasps at his description of the wounding and heroic return of gunfire by John. We heard him out in silence, followed by clicking tongues and murmurs of disbelief and shock as Keynes headed to his office. Hincham was handed a chair and newspaper to wait by the door.

Pinchin followed Keynes through to his office, and they were entrenched in there for over half an hour before he left, and I was beckoned to replace him. I closed the door behind me as requested.

'I understand I have you to thank for my escort, Miss Kiten.'

'I simply reported last night's incident to Sir Basil as requested by Major Parkes. It was Sir Basil's decision to allocate corporal Hincham to your future security, sir.'

He offered a cigarette. I refused. He lit his and drew deeply. 'Why were you following me last night?'

'I didn't like the look of the men you met in *Bar Felix*. I watched one of them behaving furtively with two dubious characters and a cameraman. I suspected they were planning to entrap you and take a photograph, which would be used either for blackmail or to bring down disgrace on your name.' I shrugged. 'Reparations. We know some strongly oppose your views, and it seems there was a malicious design to taint you and your position. I didn't anticipate a deadly attack with gunfire, or we would have been better prepared. I was naïve. I thought we could warn you, and the attempt at entrapment would be abandoned.'

'A cameraman you say?'

'Yes, I believe he was ensconced in an apartment reserved for you, and we must assume he slipped away in the melee that followed the shooting.'

'So, you knew my intention in accompanying that young man to an apartment?'

'Yes.'

'Yet you make no comment.'

'I have encountered too much of the dark side in human nature over the last two years to be concerned about particular preferences in private affairs.' He raised an eyebrow in surprise at my statement. I wondered if I had answered too quickly, and my words had offended. 'You will understand this is not an easy subject to discuss, and I hope you don't regard my answer as impertinent.'

He stubbed out his cigarette with more than half of it unused. 'Not at all. You're a remarkable young woman, and I owe you a deep debt of thanks for your concern and actions. Mere words cannot express the admiration I hold for your bravery and resourcefulness in shooting that man.'

I didn't know how to respond and bowed my head to hide my awkwardness. 'Do you have any idea who may be behind the attack?'

'There are many with opposing views, but before the attack, I would not have considered any might stoop so low to win the argument. Now it has happened, my imagination overflows with possibilities. I confess that it would ease my mind to know where the responsibility lies.'

'What about the men in *Bar Felix*? They could provide an answer.'

'Of course, I have considered them, but confess I took no care to learn their backgrounds. My only interest was in the transaction.' An unintentional huffing sound escaped my mouth at that phrase, which seemed to put Keynes on the defensive. 'I can assure you, Miss Kiten, that our encounter with them in *Bar Felix* that night was unexpected. It was not my intention for you to meet with them but suppose I should be thankful you did.'

'Where and how did you first come across the men.'

'It was at the same bar a couple of days before the evening you and I visited. I was on my own, and accidental spillage of whisky was the excuse to engage me in conversation.' He slapped a hand on the desk and clicked his tongue as a rebuke to his own gullibility. 'I knew I was being played but never suspected their target was anything other than a grubby banknote or two.'

'What about the girl, Lucille?'

'A pretty girl, but I was not attracted.' He paused and raised his eyes as if trying to recollect the scene. 'She appeared uncomfortable, as though not fully in tune with her role. At the time, I thought it was simply nerves, and she was new to the game, but it may be that she was recruited as a mere decorative accessory and knew nothing of their real objective.'

'I understand your desire to know who is behind the conspiracy against you. I would like to help, but there are limits to how far I can go. I don't shoot assailants every day, and I'm not equipped to investigate a gang of hardened criminals. Even if I was, I am under strict instructions by Sir Basil to keep a low profile.'

'Gracious no, I was only thinking out loud when musing who may be behind the attack. My stupidity has placed you in great danger once, and I would not dream of...' He stopped suddenly and narrowed his eyes. 'Ah, you must forgive me, Miss Kiten. You're joking, of course.'

'Yes, I'll admit it was a weak attempt at humour and probably inappropriate given the deadly nature of the attack.' He waved a hand to dismiss my concerns. I

wanted to uncover more, and not only for Keynes'
sake. John had been shot, and it could have ended up
much worse. Most of all, I was intrigued. Maybe there
was something I could do. 'Also, while I have no
intention of confronting any more men with guns, I
should like to make a few discreet enquiries – with the
girl, perhaps. Do you have any objection?'

My words were unexpected, and it seemed another
cigarette was required. He reached inside his jacket for
the case and went through the process of lighting up,
slowly and deliberately. 'I shouldn't be surprised at
your suggestion after witnessing you in action. But all
logic screams caution.' He paused for two thoughtful
puffs on his cigarette. 'I would be grateful for your
"discreet enquiries", but I beg you to withdraw at any
hint of mortal danger.'

'Of course.'

'I also wonder if you would agree to discuss any
findings you uncover with me before sharing more
widely with Sir Basil and others concerned with our
security.'

I paused before replying. 'I see no reason to deny
your request. However, I'm sure you understand that
the odds are against my enquiries bearing fruit.'

'You will not be damned by me, either way, Miss
Kiten. It will take a good deal to knock you off a
pedestal in my eyes.' Another drag on the cigarette and
deep exhalation before he adds. 'You must tell me if
there is anything I can do to support your efforts.'

'No, I don't think so.' I smiled inwardly at the image
of the sophisticated, drawing-room intellectual that is
Keynes, scrambling up a drainpipe with a dagger in his
teeth. 'Then again, it may be helpful if you could,

maybe… provide a little money to help jog memories and open doors.'

'How much will you need?'

Twelve

Derek accompanied me to *Bar Felix* after work had finished in the schoolroom. He took some persuading. Derek was my choice of companion as he had a sweetheart back home, wrote to her every day, and I was certain he would not use the occasion as an excuse to proposition me. I hadn't considered the contrary possibility that Derek would suspect my motives were less than pure. It was easy to forget that, before the war, only a young woman of loose morals would consider inviting a man to a bar. But so much had changed in the last few years. I felt a pang of guilt using Derek to make my appearance in a bar less conspicuous. I couldn't tell him that was my real purpose, and I had almost given up trying to convince him when he finally consented, for one drink only and no more than an hour.

We were there before six o'clock, and there were only a few customers; a couple lounging against the counter and half a dozen others scattered around the twenty-odd tables. I didn't recognise any of the faces. Derek guided me to a central table, then took our coats to the small cloakroom. A waitress sidled her way over. She looked bored. Derek ordered a scotch, and I asked for a sidecar. I was developing a taste for the mix of cognac with citrus fruit. Derek smiled nervously and asked me about last night's incident.

Had only twenty-four hours elapsed? So much had happened; the memory felt more distant.

'It was shocking,' I said. 'I think the fright jumbled my thoughts, and I have trouble remembering the exact sequence of events.'

'Major Parkes was shot.'

'Yes, and despite being hit, he managed to shoot and kill our attacker.'

'So, you were with Major Parkes?'

'Yes

'Are you and he... seeing each other?'

'No, we were just having a short walk and getting a breath of fresh air after being stuck inside all day.'

'Do you have a special gentleman friend at home?'

'No, I was too busy studying before the war and then... while I was nursing, it was difficult not to think of men as patients. Now...' I was going to suggest we had returned to normal times, but our current situation could hardly be described as commonplace or ordinary. 'Now and in the future, I hope friendships and relations between men and women can take a more natural course.'

The waitress placed the drinks on our table. I wanted to talk to her, and that quiet time would have been ideal, but I had to find an opportunity away from Derek. The conversation turned to our colleagues in the office. Derek had studied under Keynes at Cambridge and had taken up a lecturing post there himself until he was recruited to the Treasury by his former teacher only a few months ago. It was clear from the way he spoke that he was a fervent admirer of the great man.

'Is Gerry Pinchin from Cambridge as well?' I asked.

'I don't know about his background. I believe he has been at the Treasury for over twenty years.'

'How do you get on with him - Mr Pinchin.'

'Oh, he is -' a pause while he sips from his glass, 'a bit of a stickler for following the rule book.'

I waited for more, but nothing came. Had Derek and Pinchin had a falling out or disagreement that he was unwilling to discuss? I could see the waitress had taken a seat at an unoccupied table during an idle moment. I excused myself, telling Derek I had to visit the powder room. I walked past the waitress then turned as if remembering something.

'Excusez moi, mademoiselle.' My accent was good enough to pass for native French, although not perhaps a Parisienne. 'Do you know Estelle?'

She drew on her cigarette and studied me carefully before replying. 'No, I don't know anyone by that name.'

'That's a shame. I have something of hers.'

I had kindled a spark of interest. 'No one named Estelle works here.'

'She is here often; also, in other bars and clubs in this arrondissement.'

'What is it you have for her?'

I moved a chair close to hers and sat down, opened my bag and placed a folded banknote on the table. She feigned disinterest and drew on her cigarette again.

'I met Estelle a few nights past. I mean her no harm. I need to speak to her urgently.' I placed another note on the table. 'All I want is her address.'

'How did you say you know her.'

'I met her here. She was paid to be in the company of two men. I know she didn't want to be with them.'

I hesitated, then added, 'She calls herself Lucille, although her real name is Estelle.'

She gazed at me, examined the notes, took a deep breath and turned her head away.

'How much?'

'Twenty.'

'I'll give you fifteen.'

We had an agreement. I made sure her description of Estelle fitted mine before handing over the money. Rue de Chaillot, 37c, was a ten-minute walk in the direction of the river.

Back with Derek, I sipped at my sidecar and contributed mechanically to our conversation for another thirty minutes until he started to look at his watch. We soon departed and arrived back at the hotel a few minutes after seven o'clock. Derek must have been baffled when I offered thanks, informed him I had forgotten my gloves at the bar and politely declined his offer to act as escort for my retrieval mission.

The instructions I had been given by the waitress were a little too brief. I took a few false turns and needed directions from pedestrians before I found Rue De Chaillot. It was a typical and respectable street for this area of Paris, with seven storeys on both sides housing a mix of residential apartments, shops, offices and restaurants. Number 37 was sandwiched between an optician and a bakery. My fingers were crossed that she was still at home. The night was young, and I assumed she didn't set out to the clubs and bars until later. I had stopped at a florist on the way and purchased a winter bouquet of hellebores, narcissi, anemone and berries.

The front door was ajar, showing a thin strip of light. I could hear voices from inside. I knocked and entered. Two elderly women were gathered around an oil heater. They stopped their conversation and stared at my unwelcome intrusion.

'Mademoiselle?' said one, who I took to be the concierge.

I brandished my bouquet. 'Pour Estelle. D'un admirateur.'

She stepped to the side, blocking my progress to the stairway and held out both hands to receive the flowers.

'No, Madame, I must deliver them personally.'

'Not possible. You will give them to me, and I will deliver to the young lady.'

'That will not do. My client has insisted that I hand them to Mademoiselle Estelle and report back on her reaction and any message she may have.'

She folded her arms and stood her ground. Around sixty years old, five feet tall and weighing probably no more than six stone, she nevertheless presented a formidable obstacle.

'Will this help, Madame?' I pressed a one-franc banknote into her hand.

She looked at it, raised her eyes to me, then back to the money. She closed her fist, peered over my shoulder to check if her companion had spotted the transaction, then inclined her head and stood aside.

I climbed the stairs to the first floor and tapped boldly on the door. The ears of the two women below were undoubtedly closely attuned to my actions, and I would have to play out my part with conviction. I stood with the bouquet held in both hands in front of my face. The door opened; I exclaimed Estelle's name and a short message of devotion, then quickly barged my way in, pushing her backwards. I closed the door behind me and lowered the bouquet. The woman before me was not the Estelle I remembered. She was younger, her hair was shorter, but she had the same neat features in a pale oval face.

'My name is Mary. Do you remember we met at the Bar Felix?'

'The flowers?'

'Here, you have them. They were used to get past the concierge.'

'I remember you from the bar, but why are you here - Mary?'

'Forgive me; this must be a surprise.' I paused to catch my breath. 'I have a question. It's important.' I smiled in a way I hoped would offer reassurance. 'Those men, the English men, you were with in the bar - do you know them?'

She frowned and made as if to reply, then stopped and beckoned me to follow. I was ushered through to a room at the end of the corridor. As far as I could see in the poor light of a single electric bulb, we were in a spacious but somewhat frayed and rundown drawing-room. I took a seat on a worn leather armchair while Estelle sat opposite on a chaise longue with the bouquet resting across her knees.

'You must tell me why you ask this question,' said Estelle.

'We were attacked yesterday evening. The man I accompanied has opponents in the Congress, and I believe those men arranged a trap.'

'The English men assaulted you?' Her tone was sceptical.

'No, I saw the older one conspire with two other rough, intimidating men in the shadow of a doorway near the bar. It was they who led the attack. I think they planned to compromise and threaten their victim, but they were discovered, and shots were fired.'

Estelle stifled a gasp bringing both hands to cover her mouth. 'Was anyone hurt by those shots?'

'My friend, a soldier, was hit in the shoulder. He will mend. One of the attackers was shot and killed.'

She gaped with an expression of disbelief and horror. 'I am sorry, but I don't know the men or anything about a plan to trap your friend. I do not want any police here. If you give the police my name, I will deny everything.'

'I am not here for the police, and I promise your name will not be given to them. The target was my boss, and I only wish to know who plotted against him so he will be safe in the future.'

'This man, your boss; is he important? Is he deserving of your consideration and protection?'

'He is…' I hesitated, wondering how to describe Keynes. 'He is a brilliant man, a professor, a man of reason and logic. His words would help bring a safe peace for the many, not just the privileged few. His enemies are those who seek advantage for themselves or narrow interests, and they do not wish his arguments to be heard by our leaders.' I paused again. Had I been too flattering? 'He is also a man; with the frailties and vices we associate with many men. But on balance, he is a good man and, in time, may be recognised as an important one.'

My little speech had an effect. Estelle inclined her head and gazed at me in a manner I found difficult to interpret. Puzzlement? Concern?

'I accept what you say, but still, I cannot help you. I met those English men only once, knew them only as George and Edward, and I am sure those were not their real names.'

'How and where did you meet them?'

'In a bar on Avenue Hoche. I had no choice; I was ordered to go with them by Fournier.'

'Who is Fournier?'

Estelle's shoulders sagged, and she sighed. 'He offers me protection, and in exchange, I am bound to him. He controls many clubs and bars in the eighth arrondissement and the northern part of the sixteenth.'

'A pimp?'

'Yes, he is a pimp; a thief; a thug; a criminal; all those.'

'What instructions did Fournier give you?'

'I was to go with the English men and meet another man in *Bar Felix* who may want to spend time with me in one of Fournier's apartments. In that case, I was to be at my most obliging, and I would be well paid.' She stopped, lowered her head and examined the bouquet.

'Please, carry on.'

'It seemed that I was not wanted.' A deep breath before continuing. 'That night was not convenient, and anyway, your boss has a preference for young men. I was escorted back to the bar I had come from by the one named Edward. I was paid my regular fee by Fournier; no more.'

'If you had been... required, was there a particular apartment of Fournier's intended for your use?'

'There is one on Rue Lauriston that is the closest to Bar Felix. I have used it before and have a key.'

It crossed my mind for a moment to ask for the key, but what could I expect to find there to aid my search? No, there was nothing to be gained.

'Have you seen the English men since that night?'

'No, and I do not expect to.' She folded her arms with an air of finality. Her answer was definite.

It looked as though my enquiries had come to a dead-end already. The two English men were probably long gone, and I wasn't equipped to go to war with a local criminal. I had a name, for what that was worth, and could do no more. Besides, the War Office agent was expected soon, and I was determined to assist in any way I could in the hunt for Arthur's killer.

'Here.' I took most of Keynes' remaining banknotes and offered them to her. 'This is not my money. My boss gave it to me to help discover who was behind his attack.' I stood, ready to depart.

Estelle's eyes widened in surprise. She gaped, then grabbed the notes and counted out eighty-five francs, probably more than two month's earnings.

'Thank you, Mary.' Estelle rose and kissed my cheek.

I smiled, regretful that I couldn't do more. 'One final question before I go. You said you were in a bar on Avenue Hoche. What do you know of *Club Margot* there?'

'Too many Russians. I had a bad experience with one.' She closed her eyes and shook her head as if to dismiss the memory from her thoughts. 'You should not go there. It is a dangerous place. Sometimes I work in *Bar L'Espoir* nearby, but I don't go in the *Margot* unless I can't avoid it.'

'Thank you for the warning.' I paused, thinking I would have liked to stay a little longer and done more to help her. 'May I call here again if I have the opportunity?'

'Of course, Mary. I am here most evenings until about nine o'clock. To avoid Madame Concierge, you can use the rear entrance via the fire escape.'

Thirteen

I had nothing substantive for Keynes, he didn't press me for a progress report, and I didn't bother passing on the name of Estelle's pimp. It was only two days since my visit to her, but time dragged. I was impatient to make headway and at a loss to know what steps to take. Also, there was no sign of the SIS agent yet, and I began to wonder if it was a false promise, designed as a ploy to keep me from any involvement in an investigation of Arthur's murder.

I had some time before the canteen opened in the morning and resolved to write a letter to John. After several false starts I gave up. A letter would not ease the pricks of guilt I was feeling. I would have to make time to visit him in hospital.

I sat at a breakfast table with Jane and Annie. The chatter seemed more excitable than usual, and there was something odd in the air. I couldn't put my finger on it, but they looked different. As I gazed around, many, if not most, of the people at breakfast were energised, expectant. The air was heavy with scent; lipstick was brighter, creases in skirts were sharper, white, bristly necks denoted men's new haircuts, shirt collars dazzled in their stiffness. Then I remembered. I had seen a notice yesterday evening, but its importance hadn't registered as my thoughts were whirling with political and criminal intrigue. The press had been invited to the Majestic that morning; our notables were to be interviewed, and photographs of every person in the delegation were planned.

'When and where do they intend to take the photographs,' I asked Jane.

'In the ballroom, straight after breakfast.'

'It said eight-thirty sharp on the notice,' added Annie. 'If you want to go back to your room and change or touch up, there's still time.'

'Yes, they say our photographs may end up in the newspapers back home, and it would be a shame not to look our best.'

'You both look wonderful, and you're making me feel rather threadbare and plain.' I checked my watch. I had plenty of time, but did I want to bother getting changed and spend twenty minutes staring into a mirror and preparing my face in a freezing bedroom? Annie and Jane smiled encouragement. I decided it would appear churlish to ignore their advice, and I may have invited suspicion by refusing to go with the general flow. So, I finished my toast and headed back to my room. I was crossing the lobby as a group of men picked their way across the marble floor bearing tripods, heavy leather satchels and boxes. The cameramen and their entourage were being fussed over and guided by uniformed hotel staff with a couple of John's soldiers looking on. I was climbing the final flight of stairs before reaching my floor when I slowed, then stopped and realised what my subconscious had been struggling to tell me; one of the cameramen was familiar. Could it be?

My immediate impulse was to run down to the ballroom and check the cameramen before they started to take photographs. I steadied tumbling thoughts. The impression I carried in my mind of the cameraman from that night was fleeting and imprecise. Could I be confident, even with a close inspection of the men here today? It would be safer to examine them in a crowded room. I could not discount the possibility that if one of them was party to the entrapment, he might recognise me from the melee at Rue Lauriston. I spent the next half hour changing into my turquoise frock, applying makeup and pinning up my hair. Not exactly a disguise, but it was the best I could manage given the time and circumstances.

I returned to the foyer to find groups forming and a loose-straggled queue snaking a crooked passage to the ballroom entrance. Men and women with clipboards were bustling, pointing, calling names and cajoling those waiting into some semblance of order. I was about to join Annie and Jane when someone tugged at my sleeve. It was Derek. He ushered me over to our Treasury group. All were present from the schoolroom, except Keynes. Our group was supplemented by half a dozen women and three men from the General Register Office and Board of Trade. Small groups like ours were being combined to reduce the number of photographs – a blow to our sense of importance.

We waited in our chattering clusters until called to enter the ballroom. A small platform had been erected at one end. Three cameras were placed close to each other about ten paces from the platform. Keynes and two men I didn't know, arrived and were directed to chairs placed centrally on the platform. Our instructions were to stand behind and to the side of the seated subjects, tallest in the middle, smallest at each end. My allocated place was behind Keynes' right shoulder, and only then was I able to survey the men operating the cameras. I dismissed further consideration of two cameramen straight away, and the third - I wasn't sure. He was the right build; his face had a thin, prominent nose and dark moustache. Both features matched my recall, but here in the bright electric lights of the Majestic, it was hard to compare this man with a memory from shadowy streets on a dark night. All three cameras were moved a couple of yards nearer. He seemed to be changing the lens, lifting something heavy from a box and - yes, I remembered that movement. The way he bent his body and hefted the object in the box clicked a switch of recognition. I was sure – almost.

Our positions and poses had to be exactly right. An interpreter was employed to convey their frantic instructions, encouragement and last-minute minor adjustments before our ensemble was judged ready for exposure to their lenses. The long moments of capturing our image filled with hypnotic stillness and gawping silence. I waited for a cough, giggle or sneeze to fracture the quiet, but none came. At last, it was over, and we could disperse.

I needed a minute with the cameraman on his own, but he was deep in conversation with others. It wasn't going to be easy. The notice had stated the photography session would be completed by half-past-ten. Could I wait until the end? I lingered in the doorway for an opportunity to approach Keynes. I asked if I could delay my appearance at the schoolroom until eleven o'clock.

'Would you like to tell me why?'

'I'd rather not say at this point, sir.'

173

He worked his tongue around the inside of his mouth, then breathed deeply a couple of times as though he had concluded a tricky problem. 'Let's cut out the "sirs", shall we? The formality of address sits oddly between us in light of our recent experiences.' He placed his left hand in a jacket pocket about to retrieve something, perhaps cigarettes, then changed his mind, withdrew it and stroked his chin. 'How are you at proofreading?'

'I can check grammar but may need help with technical terms. Would I be reading something written by you, concerned with politics and economics?'

'I have written a paper and intend to submit it to the Congress next week. If you come to my room at noon, you can proofread it before we leave for a meeting at two o'clock.'

'You want me to accompany you to a meeting?'

'Yes, I have been invited to a briefing with Colonel House at the Murat's palace where the President has set up residence. I understand our conference with the Germans at Trier will be discussed. You were there and so may be useful at this meeting with House. I trust you are happy to tag along – Mary?'

'Yes, I will be with you at noon - and thank you.'

The timeline fitted nicely with my intended enquiry with the cameraman. I surveyed the numbers waiting in the queue outside and guessed the photographers would be finished in about one hour.

I returned in time to see the last group trailing out of the ballroom, pleased with their morning diversion and speculating on which newspapers and on which page their photographs would be displayed. The supervisors with clipboards had disappeared. When I poked my head around the doorway, I saw the cameras were in the process of being dismantled and readied for their return journey. I approached my target. He had his back to me.

'Excusez moi.'

He turned and swept a hand through his thick, dark hair. He looked younger close up, in his twenties, with sunken eyes and a skin pallor that hinted at too many late nights and overindulgence in hard drink. 'What is it, Miss. I am very busy.'

'May I talk with you for a few moments, in private?'

He puffed his cheeks in exasperation but followed as I beckoned him away from the others. 'So, what is it?' said with a shrug of his shoulders and open hands.

'I wondered if you have a studio where you could take photographs of me.' His eyes widened with interest, then he stepped back and scanned me from head to foot. He had the manners of a monkey, but I detected no recognition of me in his expression or actions, so it seemed I was safe to continue. 'The photographs would be a gift for my special gentleman friend back in England.'

He nodded slowly as if weighing up the possibilities. 'Of course, Miss. Here is my card.'

I took a small card from him with the name and epithet, *Vincent Crozier, Artistic Photographer*, embossed in blue and silver letters. 'When would be the best time to visit your studio?'

'For you, any time is good.' He smiled, and I shrank inwardly from a display of blackened teeth. 'I am inspired to do my best work in the evening. Try me around seven o'clock.'

*

The proofreading was surprisingly easy to read and understand. Keynes had a way of presenting complex matters in an engaging and straightforward but non-patronising style. His paper was not a detailed argument for restraint on the subject of reparations; it was a plea to the leaders at the Congress to keep an open mind and make decisions based upon an analysis of data, rather than emotion or capitulation to populist sentiment.

A motor car had been commandeered by Hincham, and his driving through the streets of Paris was an adventure I would have gladly foregone. Our driver appeared to take on a new persona behind the steering wheel, regaling us with his driving escapades at the front while at the same time swerving around carriages and alarmed pedestrians. Keynes feigned indifference, but hands hovering above his knees and twitching, ready to grab for safety, confirmed we were of one mind. I recognised Avenue Hoche and *Club Margot* as we headed in the general direction of John's hospital. We stopped in the Rue de Monceau outside a grand residence flying the American and French flags. Hincham was directed through an elaborate wrought iron gate to an entrance at the side. I noticed only two guards, one by the gate and the other at the front door, both in civilian clothes, and I assumed they were from Cody Becker's unit. I had expected there to be a larger and more overt security presence.

We were ushered by uniformed staff through a grand hallway, then down a marbled corridor lined with spectacular furnishings, gilded mirrors and oil paintings to carved double doors. Our guide knocked, and they opened by unseen hands to reveal a bright expanse lit by crystal chandeliers but lacking the extravagant detail we had encountered so far. It was a functional space, an office, a place of business. Sandra was standing by a table looking over the shoulder at a paper held by a seated man, who I assumed was Colonel House. He stood to greet our entrance. A small, neat man, he was dressed in a light grey suit with a colourful cravat. Regular features and an almost oriental set to his eyes gave him the appearance of a shop window model in miniature. Keynes shook hands with House, nodded to Sandra and introduced me as his personal assistant. House bowed his head and took my hand in his for a brief moment. Sandra gave me a welcoming hug and guided me a few paces away from the two men while they exchanged their opening pleasantries.

'You're looking very glamorous today, Mary. I love the hair and the frock,' was said in a hushed voice.

'I can claim no credit in preparing for this meeting. Our photographs were taken at the Majestic this morning, and I was shamed into making the best of myself.'

I declined her offer of tea or coffee and waited while she served Keynes and House. The subject of the attack in Rue Lauriston was broached by House, who was full of sympathy for Keynes' unpleasant experience.

'It was shocking, and the outcome could have been much worse had it not been for the brave actions of Miss Kiten here and her companion, Major Parkes,' said Keynes.

House turned his head towards me, slowly and deliberately, as though a mechanism controlled it. 'I had heard that your rescuer, a British major, was injured, but I was not informed you were present at the incident, Miss Kiten.'

Unsure how to reply, I nodded my head and muttered, 'Yes, the Major acted bravely.'

'And you, Miss Kiten, did you witness the whole affair?' asked House.

'I did and it was awful. Thankfully, the injury to Major Parkes is not life-threatening, but he will be out of action for many weeks.'

'Goodness.' House raised one eyebrow a notch and pursed his lips. 'But all to the good that you are both here now, unharmed.' He took a cup handed to him by Sandra. 'Shall we all sit at the table?'

Sandra signalled to the servants to exit our room. She closed the door behind them, then passed me a glass of water as she sat down. I mouthed, 'Thank you.'

'I was told of your recent conversation with Miss Fairlight,' House said, looking directly at me. 'In particular, you enquired about the various Russian groups here for the Congress and their possible involvement in the killing of Mr Burgess. I understand he was a close family friend, and I am sorry for your loss, but I have to admit we have no information on who was responsible. However, I am not giving away any confidences now by advising that one of Mr Burgess' responsibilities was to handle communications between our two countries and the Bolsheviks.' He clasped his hands together and inclined his head as if waiting for my reaction. I mumbled my thanks. 'Good, then let us proceed to the main business of this meeting.'

House explained they had some communications with Germany about reparations. They were from Matthias Erzberger, the finance minister, who described President Wilson as the most trustworthy and influential of the Allied leaders. As the sole recipient of Erzberger's messages, his plea to Wilson was to use his authority and counter strident calls for punitive German reparations. Erzberger argued that not only were these unjustified morally and logically, but excessive reparations would encourage those factions in Germany that wished to end the armistice and prolong the war. House confirmed that President Wilson had sympathy with the rationale for modest reparations and was alarmed at the issue's potential to undermine the fragile peace.

Keynes was mentioned as the German's choice to present the case for modest reparations. The message to Keynes was routed via Wilson rather than Lloyd George as Erzberger claimed the British lords Sumner and Cunliffe would inevitably be informed and sabotage Keynes' arguments. It was hoped that Keynes would agree to work with Carl Melchior, who he had met in Trier, to produce the most persuasive case. Further, it was hoped that this collaboration should be undertaken in secret so as not to arouse suspicion and possible disruption.

All this was heard in silence by Keynes, who sat back in his seat with legs crossed. We waited for his reaction. He took a few moments, then uncoiled his legs, straightened his back and placed both hands flat on the table.

'I have begun my work on the justification for sensible and moderate reparations, and I welcome the opportunity to cooperate with Melchior.'

'Would that be wise?' questioned House. 'Such cooperation could be presented as a reason to disregard your arguments.'

'Hence the request for secrecy,' said Keynes. 'On balance, I believe it will be worthwhile enlisting

Melchior's assistance. He is likely to have access to information that could strengthen my case. His involvement may also help Erzberger mollify some of the more extreme elements in Germany threatening to break the armistice.'

House clasped his hands together and bowed his head in agreement. 'That is a major concern of our president, and we believe the danger this poses to our plans for peace is not well understood by the other leaders here in Paris.'

The decision had been made. The discussion continued but was primarily concerned with the detail of lines of communication, timetable, reporting and security measures. I listened as Keynes explained that Hincham had been assigned as his guard and, while he found it tiresome, he understood he must bear the inconvenience. When no further comments were received on security, I had to intervene.

'Hincham is not enough.'

Heads turned to me; questioning; surprised. Nothing was said, but the incline of his head indicated that House wanted me to elaborate. Surely I wasn't the only one concerned? It was common sense, wasn't it?

'We cannot suppose that because the first attack failed, there will be no further attempts to silence Mr Keynes through assassination - or some other means. These new responsibilities magnify any danger he faces. There can be no guarantee that news of his cooperation with Melchior will remain a close-guarded secret.' I gazed at Keynes. His eyes were narrowed, sceptical, despite our shared experience. 'Hincham is a military man and will guard you in a military manner. But the threat against you is not a military one; there will be no bombardment of guns or charge across muddied fields. Any approach is likely to be sly, devious and may go unnoticed by an untrained mind. Local criminals were employed in the assault in Rue Lauriston and may be again because of their special knowledge and contacts in these arrondissements.'

'What are you suggesting, Mary?' asked Sandra.

'You have security men who protect your president here. Might it be possible to redeploy someone from that duty without compromising the safety of President Wilson and other senior American delegates? They, at least, will be more accustomed to guarding against unspecified risks to one man.'

House and Sandra exchanged glances. House would have spoken, but Keynes was quicker. 'Your concern is appreciated, Mary. But, we should leave such judgements to the professionals.'

He was probably right. I lowered my head and didn't protest. I had surprised even myself, by speaking on the matter, but surely I wasn't the only one with concerns about his extra exposure. It was common sense, wasn't it?

House finished conferring with Sandra, announced that he agreed with my suggestion and confirmed security personnel would be assigned to watch over Keynes, in a discreet rather than overt manner. House wrote a note for Keynes to hand to Sir Basil to keep him in the picture. After a few more minutes, our meeting was finished. House had another appointment and remained at the table while Sandra accompanied us back to the grand hallway. There she greeted a delegation from Egypt and escorted them to the room we had vacated.

'I am sorry if I spoke out of turn with my proposal for your security. I could not forgive myself if you were harmed because I failed to speak on your behalf.'

He opened his case, took out a cigarette, tapped it, then, unhurried and with care, lit it with his lighter. 'No, you must not apologise. I have no experience dealing with a bizarre situation like this, where I am in danger simply for my opinions. However, I'm sure you are right and thank you again for looking after my interests, Mary.'

'In that case, may I beg a favour?'

'What is it?'

'If you wouldn't mind a short diversion on your journey back to the Majestic, you could drop me off so I can visit Major Parkes. His hospital is no more than a half-mile from here.'

Fourteen

A line of carriages, vans and ambulances waited outside the Clinique du Parc Monceau. Gendarmes were directing traffic away from the hospital entrance to a side street. I left the car with some trepidation, wondering how to navigate the expected crush of patients and helpers clamouring for attention at the hospital reception.

I needn't have worried. The free-for-all during my last visit had been replaced by a queue, which had a semblance of orderliness and fairness in its make-up. I progressed to the stairs with mention of the 'injured British major on the third floor' to a couple of attendants. When I entered John's ward, I had to stop and check I was in the right place. The ward was busier. Additional beds had been brought in and placed between existing ones, so there was virtually no space between most of the beds. I spied John at the far end, lying on top of his bed, reading a book. As I got nearer, I could see he was one of the fortunate few with a strip of open floor on either side of his bed.

'What are you reading, John?'

'Ah, Mary, you are a welcome distraction from these pages. It's one of Conrad's – *Lord Jim*. I've read it before, but the choice of English language books here is very limited, as you can imagine.' His right shoulder was heavily bandaged with his arm in a sling.

Otherwise, he looked healthy with good colour to his skin and an air of humour in his eyes.

'It's more crowded in here than I remember.' The patients on either side of John appeared to be asleep. Even so, our conversation would have to be constrained.

'Yes, they're short of beds for those ill with the damned virus. About half a dozen in this ward are residents or staff from the Majestic, and the rest are locals from this region of Paris.'

'Shouldn't they be isolated from other patients if they have the virus?' As soon as my question was out, I realised it should not have been directed at John. Three or four patients were visibly very ill, and two other beds were screened from general view. I was sure my expression must have betrayed concern.

'I don't know, Mary. You should know better than I. Perhaps it's not infectious, or they have nowhere to isolate them.' He patted his bed, inviting me to sit beside him. 'How did you travel here? Are you on your own?'

'I was driven in a motor car with Mr Keynes. We finished a meeting at President Wilson's residence, only a short distance from here. I begged a diversion on our return journey in order to visit you.'

'The President, indeed. You keep exalted company, Mary.'

I turned and gazed at him directly, but there was no mocking in his voice or expression. 'Our meeting was with Colonel House. Have you met him?'

'Sir Basil introduced us at a Christmas function, but that was my only contact.' He adjusted his pillow to sit more upright on his bed. 'Can you tell me the purpose of your meeting, or is that hush-hush?'

'Walk with me, please, John.' I stepped away from his bed. He swung his legs over and adjusted himself as best he could with one hand. I helped tie a drawstring around his robe, and we walked together down the middle of the ward. 'I can relate the outcome of our meeting to you. In view of the incident on Rue Lauriston, it was decided to provide Mr Keynes with enhanced security. One of your men, Corporal Hincham, plus another from the service that guards the American president, have been assigned to protect him.'

He turned and fixed me with a questioning stare. 'Isn't that a little over the top?' He shook his head. 'Would he really be attacked again? I can understand Hincham. The other chap – well, I don't know. Is Keynes regarded as so vulnerable and important to warrant diverting presidential guards or secret service men?'

I waited as we stood back to allow two nurses and a patient with a hacking cough to pass by in a wheelchair. 'Yes, I do believe that a high level of security is necessary for Mr Keynes, and I'm sure Colonel House wouldn't have consented if it leaves their president exposed.'

He stopped and adjusted his sling, looked at me and bowed his head as though he was going to speak, then decided against it. He shivered and drew his robe around him with his free hand. Why did he do that? It wasn't cold inside the hospital.

'Is everything alright, John? You seem troubled by something.'

'No, I'm fine, thank you.' He looked up and offered a weak smile. 'I'm just… pleased that you came to

185

visit me. After all, you must be busy with, Keynes and the Treasury chaps.'

'Don't be silly, John. Of course, I was always going to come and visit you. I'm only sorry I couldn't have come before now.'

We reached the doorway. I was ready to turn back, but John opened the door and inclined his head, inviting me to step through. He closed it behind us and said in a low voice, 'I had another visitor here earlier today.'

'Oh yes, who was it, someone from the Majestic?'

'Inspector Bonnet came to see me, to clarify a couple of points from our interview on the night of the incident.'

'Oh. what did he -.' I didn't expect that name. 'What were his questions?' I had to hope that John had convinced with our original version of events. 'Was it a difficult interview? Did you change anything from your initial statement?'

'Steady on, Mary, one question at a time.' He made another minor adjustment to his sling, wincing with a gasp of air as his shoulder moved. I laid a hand on his other shoulder for reassurance, hoping the pain didn't signify an infection in his wound. 'Essentially, Bonnet doesn't believe I shot and killed our attacker. He explained in great detail why he thought I couldn't have fired the shots from my handgun.'

'How did you respond?'

'I insisted it was me; said it was confusing; my recall may be a little mixed up.' He smiled apologetically. 'I'm afraid I might not have been terribly convincing. He didn't appear to believe my story. Asked about you.'

'What did he want to know about me?'

'Your job here, your background and er... our relationship.'

'Any what did you say?'

'The truth. I've only known you for a short time; you were a nurse in the war and sent here at short notice mainly because of your proficiency in languages.'

'How did you leave it? Did he go away satisfied?'

'Honestly – no. He made it clear that he didn't believe my story. Although not explicit, he also suggested that it didn't really matter who shot our assailant. He is a strange chap. Said that if it wasn't me who shot him, he would not necessarily feel obliged to change his report on the incident. He wanted to know what actually happened for his personal understanding.'

'Do you believe him?'

'I do. Even if we admit it was you who fired the gun, it will not alter the fact that we were the innocent party, set upon by a criminal or gang of criminals.' He shook his head and sighed. 'I'm sorry, Mary. I probably shouldn't have arranged our little white lie. At the time, it seemed to be the easiest way to avoid a lot of unnecessary questioning.'

'Don't blame yourself, John. You were trying to protect me, and I am grateful for that.'

He looked at me. I could see it in his eyes. He wanted to hold me, to kiss me. Should I...? The door slammed open; a wheelchair barged through, pushed by a nurse with another woman supporting and instructing the patient. We watched as they disappeared through a door further down the corridor.

'Was that one of your doctors?'

'Yes,' he answered, 'that was Doctor Morton with Kitty McNab, one of our nurses.'

'I should go now.'

'Already?'

'It's getting dark outside.' I took his free hand and held it in mine. 'Also, I thought I might visit Chief Inspector Bonnet. You don't happen to know which station he works from, do you?'

'Actually, I do. He left me a card, and the address on there is the Préfecture de Police for the eighth arrondissement. It's in Rue du Faubourg Saint-Honoré, about halfway between here and the Majestic. You will be pleased to know it's not the same station where we met the delightful Inspector Roussel.'

We returned to the door of his ward, stopped and faced each other. We kissed lightly, on the lips. It felt good. There was no awkwardness in the quiet moments between us. I turned slowly and trailed my hand in his as I said goodbye.

I didn't leave the hospital straight away. It wouldn't have been right to ask John's doctor about his health while he was present, so I hung around in the corridor hoping to encounter Doctor Morton. It seemed I lingered too long and had begun to attract strange looks from nurses, orderlies and others. I was about to leave when a door opened, and she appeared muttering to herself and writing on a clipboard.

'Doctor Morton?'

'Yes, can I help? Are you here to see a patient?'

'I've just left one of your patients – Major Parkes.'

She put a pencil into a breast pocket and lowered her clipboard. 'You must be Mary.'

'Yes, how do you…?'

'A lucky guess. He talks about you. You're the one who was with him when he was shot aren't you?'

'Yes, I was there.'

'And tended his wound?'

'Yes.'

'He told me. You did well to staunch the flow of blood and dress the wound – with scraps of your petticoat, I would guess.'

'Yes, you're right. I should admit that I've have had a lot of practice tending to wounds like that one. I was a nurse at Stationary 14 in Wimereux.'

'Ah, Wimereux.' She nodded her head slowly as if sifting her memory. 'I know a friend and colleague who was there back in 'fifteen. She worked in a small, converted chateau on the edge of town. It was run by the Women's Hospital Corps'

'I didn't arrive there until 'sixteen, but I know the place you mean, and I believe it's still operational.' We both moved to the side to make way for a bed, wheeled down the corridor by two orderlies. 'I confess, I'm surprised to find you here. I had heard about the hospital set up by the Scottish Women's group at Royaumont Abbey but didn't know any British women doctors were working in Paris.'

'I was there, at the Abbey, until a week after Christmas, then two of us were asked to help out here as cover for the Conference. This place is - I was going to say mundane, but that would be unkind and tactless. It's just - easier. There are no wounded soldiers here, so it's a routine of broken limbs, heart disease, childbirth, pneumonia, old age problems and, of course, the new respiratory virus.'

'It may be easier, but it's still busy' I said. 'I assume you're getting a lot of patients with the virus. I don't know much about it as those infected at Wimereux were put in an isolation unit.'

'It's the same with me. We didn't treat any cases at the Abbey. Any infections were transferred to other hospitals.' She smiled and put the clipboard under her arm, ready to move on,

I touched her arm and said, 'How is Major Parkes? Does the wound show signs of infection?'

'The wound is clean and should heal in four or five weeks. His broken bone may take a little longer, but we expect a full recovery, at least from his physical injuries.'

'Physical injuries. What other…?'

'Like many who fought in the trenches, his mental state is fragile.'

'I came across many cases of disturbed minds and shell shock in Wimereux, but I haven't detected anything like that in John – Major Parkes.'

'It's not always obvious and some sufferers are very good at hiding it.' She shrugged her shoulders. 'His nights are far from peaceful; constant nightmares; screaming; cold sweats. He's had a couple of trembling fits during the day, where he's unable to speak and his mind is – well, I'm sure you know what I mean. On the positive side, these periods haven't lasted long, and I've seen far worse.'

'I didn't know.'

'Perhaps, that's because he's been very careful not to let you see him when he has been in that state. As I say, he has mentioned your name quite a few times…'

She carried on talking, but I wasn't listening. Poor John. I had no idea. I had seen it often enough at Wimereux; some patients, so mentally disturbed that it was difficult to imagine how they would ever recover. But John? He had never given me any sign. I must have appeared dazed as I remembered Doctor

Morton guiding me to the stairs when she was called away by a nurse.

*

It was almost five o'clock when I arrived at the police station after a short carriage ride. I had waited for another ten minutes or so at the hospital until my thoughts had cleared and I felt ready to call on Inspector Bonnet. Still, my intentions were uncertain. All I knew was I wanted a frank conversation with him, and I would improvise. If I owned up to the shooting and offered a little more detail about my part in the incident, would he be willing to share information that might help me discover who was behind the attack on Keynes? Would he even be available to see me?

My enquiry at the reception desk was met with bored indifference by the gendarme on duty. My name and request to see Bonnet on an urgent matter was scrawled in a ledger with painful, unhurried precision. I was directed to a wooden bench occupied by half a dozen others. I begged a space between two men, both wearing an air of slumped resignation for a prolonged wait, then perhaps, an unpleasant ordeal.

I had barely two minutes to settle on my seat when my name was called, and I was guided down a corridor to a door marked with the brass letters, 'X Bonnet'. Xavier. Bonnet's Christian name brought surprise and amusement; he was so far removed from my imagining of someone with that name. The gendarme rapped the door, opened it, offered a weak salute and disappeared back along the corridor. Bonnet was facing me, sitting at an extravagantly large desk, both ends piled high with papers, while the space in the

191

centre was deserted, save for a well-used blotting board with blue leather edging and corners.

'Miss Kiten, it is a pleasure to meet with you again. Please take a seat.' I sat on one of three upright chairs as he pushed his pipe, a penknife and an ashtray behind the pile of papers to his right as though to set them aside from temptation. 'Thank you for taking the trouble to come to my place of work. Do you have new or changed recollections from the night of your attack?'

'Good afternoon, Chief Inspector. I understand from Major Parkes that you dispute his version of events.'

'There are elements of his story that do not ring true. The same can be said for the statements from you and Mr Keynes. It leads me to wonder if there is a conspiracy to conceal the true circumstances of that episode.'

'You reported that the man who attacked us was named Fabre. Have you discovered any other names of those who may have been involved in the assault?'

'No, Miss Kiten, we have not. Do you have any other questions? I was hoping that you had come here to provide information, not to interrogate me.'

'Just one more question; who do you believe shot Fabre?'

'I know shots were fired from Major Parkes' gun, and in my view, he was incapable of pulling the trigger.'

'How would it be received if you reported that a woman fired the shots and killed Fabre?'

He sat back in his chair and gazed at me for a few moments before answering. 'Eyebrows would be raised; questions asked; it would add to the pile of papers on my desk.' He paused and reached across his desk to retrieve his penknife. 'Even if I found that occurrence was true, I may decide not to include it in my report. After all, it is the least probable of the alternatives, and what would be gained by drawing attention to a minor detail at this stage?'

'In that case, I can inform you that I have been trained in the use of firearms..'

I had thought I would be merely confirming his suspicion, but the revelation seemed to unsettle him as he reached for his pipe and began to press and tap vigorously until satisfied it was ready to be lit. He relaxed visibly after the first few puffs, and there was even a hint of a smile through teeth tightly fixed around the stem.

'You need to say no more on the shooting of Fabre, Miss Kiten. Do you have any information for me on the possible motive for the attack?'

'On reflection, the likeliest target was Mr Keynes. He holds influential views on the subject of war reparations, and there are those who would wish to weaken his arguments or remove them from consideration altogether.'

'Is your opinion shared by others?'

'Yes, and to guard against any future attempts, extra protection has been assigned to Mr Keynes.'

Bonnet drew on his pipe and considered for a few moments. 'Now you are telling me the views of one man, Mr Keynes, are considered so dangerous that action was taken to murder him on the streets of Paris? Can this be true?'

'I believe the initial intention was to discredit him by tempting him into a compromising situation, then threatening public exposure unless he remained silent or changed his position.' I considered what I had said.

'More likely, they would bypass the threat, make his weakness public, expect him to slink away in disgrace and go into hiding.'

'I am sorry, Miss Kiten, but you have me at a disadvantage. I know nothing of a "weakness" in Mr Keynes or his "tempting". You must explain.'

'It is a delicate matter, Inspector, and perhaps I chose my words unwisely. You are a man; this is Paris. Here, the natural inclinations of men are more easily discussed and forgiven. We British find it more difficult to talk about such matters.' I paused to emphasise my apparent embarrassment. 'I omitted to reveal at our previous interview that a cameraman consulted with the attackers at the scene of the crime. I believe it was intended to capture the result of the enticement on film.'

He nodded his head slowly, drawing on his pipe again and sitting back in his chair to consider all I had said. 'In that case, I must assume your encounter with Mr Keynes was not an accident, as you stated. Did the shooting occur because of your unexpected disruption to the planned entrapment?'

'I think that is the likeliest explanation, either as a contingency measure or an instinctive reaction by criminals whose scheme had been disturbed.'

Bonnet removed the pipe from his mouth and made a strange, indeterminate sound in his throat, like a groan, but with an undertone of approval. He stabbed the pipe stem in my direction and said, 'I cannot condone your initial withholding of this information, Miss Kiten, yet I must give credit for your voluntary correction. I suspected there was more to the incident than any of you would admit but would not have guessed you were trying to protect Mr Keynes'

194

reputation.' He ran a finger along both sides of his thin moustache as though wiping away non-existent sweat. 'You stated that extra protection has been provided for Mr Keynes. Are you part of that security?'

'No, Inspector, you give me far too much credit.' I put a hand to my mouth and supressed a laugh. 'My role here is to assist Mr Keynes and the rest of the Treasury unit in their research and production of support material for the British delegation – nothing more.'

He narrowed his eyes and placed his pipe in the ashtray. 'Then you are a very talented – and lucky – young woman..'

'You don't believe me?'

'Not entirely.'

'I didn't expect to be working with Mr Keynes when I arrived in Paris. My assignment with his unit was not arranged before my arrival, or at least not to my knowledge. It came about due to unfortunate circumstances.' I paused, remembering the shock of learning that the victim at the front of the Majestic was Arthur. 'It would be a great relief to Mr Keynes and the British delegation as a whole if you could make progress in your investigation and bring all those involved in the attack at Rue Lauriston to justice.'

'Of course, but you should not expect too much. The war has depleted our numbers, and we do not have the manpower to give all crimes the attention they deserve.' He was about to say more, but words died in a weary exhalation of air and shake of his head. Should I offer the name mentioned by Estelle – Fournier? Or Crozier the cameraman? I wasn't certain about Crozier, and could I avoid giving Estelle's as my source for Fournier? Before I could decide either way,

Bonnet sat back in his chair and picked up his pipe again. 'You mentioned "unfortunate circumstances". What were they?'

'I was sent to Paris to work for a man I knew as an uncle – a dear family friend. He was murdered outside the Hotel Majestic within a few minutes of my arrival.'

'I am sorry. That must have been distressing for you. What was the name of this man – your uncle?'

'Arthur Burgess.'

'Ah yes, the name is familiar. I remember it was recorded as a street robbery. The murderer was apprehended and killed in an exchange of gunfire.'

'I'm certain it was not a chance, spur-of-the-moment robbery. It was a planned killing.'

'What makes you think so?'

'The gunshot wound in the forehead from close range; an untouched wallet stuffed with francs; and the nature of his work'

'His work was….'

'I don't know his exact role, but he worked in security for the British War Office. It may have involved some… clandestine or confidential duties.' I hesitated before divulging more. 'I have a name and address for you. In his room, there was a notepad with writing that may be significant. Does the name "Chersky" or an address in "Rue Gustave Courbet" mean anything to you? Have they appeared on any of your reports?'

He was motionless for a few moments, but I could see recognition and surprise in his eyes. The pipe came into action again. He took care to make sure it was well lit before speaking.

'The body of a man with that name was found in an apartment at Rue Gustave Courbet a few days ago. The cause of his death was, without doubt, murder.' He took a long, slow draw on his pipe and watched as the smoke wafted into the air. 'I suppose that connection would reinforce your belief that Mr Burgess was also murdered. But why did you not bring this information to the police before now?'

'I was with Major Parkes when we met with Inspector Roussel at the police station on the corner of Rue de Longchamp. His attitude was - unhelpful. He made it clear the case was closed with the arrest and killing of a suspect – a known petty criminal.' Bonnet muttered something indistinct while keeping his teeth clenched around the pipe stem. I said, 'May I ask how the man Chersky was killed and who discovered or identified the body?'

I expected to be told it was none of my business, and the interview brought to an end. But he continued to smoke his pipe in silence. The quiet between us had continued for too long. I was about to repeat my question when he leaned forward and said, 'Chersky was shot in the head. Perhaps you know that already?'
I didn't respond and hoped my face gave nothing away. He removed a slim file from near the top of the pile to his left, opened it and started to leaf through the papers. 'His body was discovered by his wife, Monique, who claims she married Chersky in St Petersburg four years ago but could not produce any documentary evidence to that effect. Her maiden name is Deschamps.' He stopped reading and looked at me directly for a reaction.

'I haven't heard that name before. Does she live in the apartment in Rue Gustave Courbet?'

He returned to the file and examined the papers. 'She gave her address as Rue de Montevideo – so either they lived separately, or Chersky was killed in someone else's apartment.'

'Might that be significant?'

'Possibly.' He sighed. 'As I have said, our resources do not allow exhaustive investigation of all crimes.' He paused. 'I will be honest with you, Miss Kiten, we had marked this murder as a dispute between the different Russian factions here and have assigned low priority to these crimes. I have a note here that Chersky was a Bolshevik, and they have many enemies among the various groups from Russia gathered here for the Congress.'

'Do you have a statement from Madame Chersky in your file of papers?'

'The investigating officer recorded her extreme distress, erratic behaviour and....' He scanned two remaining pages in the file, 'an accusation against an unnamed Russian man or group.' He closed the file and shrugged. 'That is all we have.'

'If you are not actively investigating this murder, would you have any objection if I talked to Madame Chersky?' I saw the hint of a frown appearing and quickly added, 'This would only be to confirm a connection between Chersky and Mr Burgess. I would not wish to interfere in police business or the private vendetta of opposing Russian factions.'

He removed the pipe from his mouth, placed it in the ashtray and adjusted his seat. 'I could not object to a private conversation between two individuals, assuming it will be as harmless as you describe.'

'It would be helpful in that case if you have an apartment number in Rue de Montevideo.'

He re-opened the file. 'Apartment 61A. And Miss Kiten.'

'Yes.'

'If you do happen to uncover any relevant new facts about the murder of Chersky, you will make sure to inform me, won't you?'

'Of course, and thank you, Inspector Bonnet.'

Fifteen

I never imagined that my visit to Bonnet would produce a piece to fill a gap in the puzzle of Arthur's murder. Following up the clue may lead nowhere, but I had to try. I hesitated when giving the destination to my taxi outside the police station, but only for a second. I had promised Sir Basil not to get involved in searching for Arthur's killer, but the interview with Bonnet had jolted my sense of loss and the urge to discover more. I couldn't wait for the agent from the War Office; my blood was up, and I had to act. Besides, any conversation with Madame Chersky would be about her husband and the circumstances surrounding his murder. Arthur's name would only be mentioned in passing.

My journey took me via the Arc, down Avenue Kleber past the Majestic and west towards the Bois de Boulogne. The taxi had to navigate piles of rubble as it turned into a dark and silent street. It could have been uninhabited, save for a cluster of lights and a few pedestrians some fifty or sixty paces from where the taxi had pulled up. We were outside a narrow doorway in a tired building with flaking plaster and boarded windows. I paid my driver and offered a generous tip if he would return in one hour. He agreed; reluctantly.

There was no bell-pull at the doorway, and a closer inspection showed the handle was broken. The door opened with a gentle shove. A pale light filtered down the stairwell from the first floor, too dim to illuminate any detail in the hallway. I waited until my eyes became accustomed to the gloom and could distinguish the outline of the letter 'A' on the door to my left. I knocked. Again. I put my ear to the door, wondering if I had heard a faint shuffling from the other side. I couldn't be certain. I imagined someone with their ear matching mine, separated only by two inches of wood. Funny. An involuntary, 'Nuh,' sound escaped my mouth before I could suppress it. Now was not the time for laughter. I took a deep breath, tapped and said, 'Monique,' as loud as I dare through cupped hands. There – a definite sign of movement from the other side of the door. I waited silently, hoping. With a click, the handle turned, and the door opened a fraction.

'Who is it?' hissed a voice.

'My name is Mary Kiten. I am English. My uncle knew your husband.'

The door closed. Another metallic sound. The door opened again, and the shadowy figure of a woman appeared. She was small and, with her head and shoulders wrapped in a black scarf, I couldn't make out her features.

'What do you want?'

'To help...' I stopped; decided I should be more direct. 'I want to know who killed your husband and my uncle so their murderers can be punished.' All was quiet. No response. 'May I come in and talk to you?'

'Who was your uncle?'

'Arthur Burgess.'

The door opened, and I followed down a corridor towards a flickering light. I shivered. It felt colder inside than the night air on the streets. We entered a space lit by a single candle on a square table. She muttered an apology for the cold and darkness, then grabbed a box of matches from the table and bent to adjust and light a small oil heater. She removed the scarf from her head and sat at the table. Older than I expected, I guessed her age about fifty. Her greying hair was scraped back from a pale, unmade face with a sharp nose and sunken red eyes that betrayed the distress of her loss.

'I met him, your uncle; he came here.' She dabbed the corners of her mouth with a handkerchief. 'It was only last month but seems an age ago now.'

I looked around, spotted a small stool, pulled it closer to the table and sat on it, carefully. How should I begin? 'Your husband, was he… was he here representing the provisional government in Russia?' I chose not to use the word 'Bolshevik' as I had heard it used as a term of abuse.

She looked at me as though I had said something of special idiocy. 'I did not know your uncle had also been murdered and, for that, you have my sympathy.' She huffed a mocking laugh. 'But how do you expect to avenge his death when you know so little?'

'Please forgive my ignorance in these matters. I have learned much in these past few days, and I am determined to find the killer. It would be helpful to learn about how you met your husband, your links with Russia and how you think your husband was murdered.'

She gazed at me directly as though assessing whether the telling would be a waste of her breath. After a prolonged and awkward silence, she sighed and began to speak. 'My first encounter with

Alexander was ten years ago when he came to Paris with Lenin and others. He was speaking at a conference on the Paris Commune. I was a widow then, and we married on a short visit to St Petersburg in 'fifteen. We had intended to stay, but it was too dangerous for Alexander, and we fled back to France, barely escaping with our lives. We lived here until early 'seventeen when he returned for the glorious revolution. Plans were made for me to leave France and make our home together in a Bolshevik Russia. Alexander returned here three months ago to help set up lines of communication for negotiations with Allied leaders. One of his contacts was your uncle, Arthur Burgess.'

'He had other contacts?'

'Yes, I believe there was one other. Mr Burgess was the only one I met in person.'

'Do you have a name for the other contact?'

She considered for a while. 'I cannot remember. Is it important?'

'No matter, please continue.'

'We knew of danger from the Tsarist factions in this city, but we were careful; your uncle's security was good, and progress was made. Maxim returned to Russia with one of Wilson's men....'

'Who is Maxim?'

'Maxim Litvinov. Alexander was one of three men sent by Lenin to persuade Wilson and Lloyd George to negotiate terms. Maxim was another. Georgi Brinkov was the third man.'

'So, Litvinov is no longer in Paris?'

'Maxim left over three weeks ago with William Buckler, the Allied representative and a friend of Wilson.'

'Is Litvinov still there?'

'Yes.'

'I'm sorry for interrupting. Please…'

'All was quiet. We waited for news from Russia, hoping for a recall after successful negotiations. Then, almost two weeks after Maxim's departure, Alexander had an urgent message from Georgi. He left immediately and returned worried: frightened; spoke of danger; a conspiracy. A meeting was arranged with Mr Burgess. Alexander told me to lock the door and stay here. He would take Maxim's place and lodge with Georgi at Rue Gustave Courbet until the threat had passed. He warned me not to go out. It was too dangerous. He would send a note.' She shook her head and dabbed her eyes. 'No note came.'

'And so, I assume; eventually, you went to Rue Gustave Courbet and discovered….'

'Yes.' She blew her nose into the handkerchief. 'Alexander. My poor Alexander.' A pause and a dab of her eyes before she cleared her throat and continued. 'At least it was quick. Someone - someone had been there before me. His body was - disturbed.'

A stab of guilt hit, but now was not the time or place to admit that someone was me. 'What about the body of the other man, Georgi - Georgi Brinkov?'

'Gone.'

'Gone where?'

'I don't know. Maybe he fled. Is he hiding? Was killed, and his body moved? I have heard no word from Georgi. It is a mystery.'

Is it possible that Georgi murdered your husband?'

She lifted her head and stared at me with an air of disdain. 'No. They were fellow Bolsheviks, deeply committed to the cause. They had worked together for many years. He trusted Georgi. I trusted him.'

'You mentioned a conspiracy. Did Alexander tell you what that was?'

'No.'

'What was the nature of the danger he faced?'

'He wouldn't say. According to Alexander, it would be safer for me if I knew nothing about it. All I knew was it was something big, and it had to be stopped.'

'Do you remember the date when this happened – when Alexander left and instructed you to stay here?'

'It was a Friday.' She counted silently on her fingers. 'Friday the seventeenth.'

The same day I arrived in Paris, and Arthur was murdered. Ten days had passed since that date. It felt like weeks, not days. 'That was the day Arthur Burgess was murdered. He was shot in front of our hotel. I believe Alexander was killed on the same day.'

'How do you know that?'

'The er... police report estimated the date of death.' I cautioned myself to be careful how much I disclosed to Monique. 'Who do you think was responsible for the murders?'

She leaned forward and cupped her face in her hands. 'It can only be Sazanov and his cronies.' She paused and closed her eyes as though sifting through memories. 'But it was not the usual threat from Sazanov.'

'What do you mean by "not the usual threat"?'

'We had become accustomed to the ways of Sazanov and other Tsarist reactionaries. It was not easy to guard against their threat, but at least we knew the faces and how they would seek to intimidate, terrorise and kill. Alexander said a "devils' contract" had been made.

Their methods would be less predictable; more dangerous.'

'What did he mean?'

'I'm not sure. He often referred to Sazanov as a devil. But a contract...? I don't know. Perhaps Sazanov had joined with another evil force.'

'Did he mention any names?'

'No, he was... in a hurry... and scared – for the cause, me and himself.'

'The cause? You mean Bolshevism?'

'Yes, of course.'

So, the danger she talked of was not just personal; it could jeopardize the Bolshevik government in Russia. It would need a significant conspiracy or event here in Paris to realise that outcome. It seemed unlikely. Despite all she related to me, Monique didn't have anything more definite than pointing an accusing finger in the general direction of Sazanov. That only confirmed my suspicions, but there was no proof, nothing more definite than - *it must be him because he was a hated enemy*. I needed more than that to exact revenge. I did have a name for the other occupant of the apartment on Rue Gustave Courbet – Georgi Brinkov. But whether he could be found and alive was another matter altogether.

I broke a period of silence and said, 'Will Maxim Litvinov return to Paris?'

'I don't know.'

'If he does, might he be able to explain the "devils' contract" and who was responsible for the deaths of your Alexander and my Uncle Arthur?'

'I cannot help you with your questions anymore. I am tired. Please go and leave me to mourn in peace.'

I guessed I wasn't going to get any more helpful information that night. Reluctantly, I rose from my stool, offered my condolences once more and thanked her for allowing me into her home. She followed me down the corridor with her candle. I opened the door, exited into the hallway and turned to see Monique as an eerie and wraithlike figure at the door illuminated by candlelight. I would have said my farewell, but she spoke first.

'I have remembered something. Alexander thought it odd that the other Allied contact was not British or American. He was a South African.'

Sixteen

Tuesday, the day after my visit to Madame Chersky, I had been distracted and couldn't concentrate on my work at the school. Wednesday promised to be as unproductive. I managed to sleep for two or three hours. Once awake, Visser's image was there: in the frosted glass of my bedroom window; at the breakfast table; by the schoolroom bookshelves. How closely did he work with Arthur? Surely, if he had known who was behind his killing, he would have offered more than mere sympathy on the train from Trier. I regretted my promise to Sir Basil. It had been eleven days since Arthur's murder, and there was still no sign of an agent to investigate. I was frustrated and also angry. Angry with Smith-Cumming, with the War Office and the entire British government for the casual and uncaring way they had reacted to the killing of a senior and devoted servant. I resolved to wait until Saturday, as the first day of next month. If there were still no sign of an SIS presence here, I would... I wasn't sure exactly what, but I had to do something.

I had a letter from Mother, picked up at the hotel after breakfast. I knew what it would contain and had delayed its opening until arriving at the schoolroom. I wasn't sure why I hadn't read it at the hotel. Perhaps I thought a brisk walk in the cold morning air would stiffen my resolve, or being surrounded by friendly faces in my workplace would somehow soften the impact of Mother's words. I sat down at my desk and opened the envelope.

Wednesday, 14th January, 1919

My Dear Mary

Please, please, please abandon any idea you have of staying in Paris for a few weeks and return home. Surely, there is nought to be gained by prolonging your stay there.

The news in your letter was a dreadful shock. I had not been informed by Mark or Ellen and there was no mention in the national or local newspapers. Poor, poor Arthur. What awful bad luck, as you say, after all the war had thrown at him. It has taken me several hours to compose myself enough to pen this letter, and I'm sure you can deduce from my uneven scrawl that my hands are less than steady.

If the police case is closed and you have paid your respects, then I see little value in your remaining in Paris. Oh, I know too well that you have a restless spirit and will likely find reasons to travel far and wide beyond dear old Whitstable. A few weeks or months together is all I ask. Until I have you by my side, I will be unable to come to terms with the senseless conflict that has marred so many lives. Also, I am eager to hear about Wimereux first hand, even if you think my fragile senses will not withstand the horrors you have experienced.

Will you return to Cambridge and finish your studies? Or do you have other plans? I assume that you will have had enough of nursing. I know you have hankered after an academic way of life, and I have always thought you would make a good teacher of virtually any subject. Perhaps your few days acting as a research assistant will rekindle your appetite for academia.

You should know that that I have agreed to rent the apartment in Ebury Street to Mr Morrison, one of your father's ex golf partners. He is spending more time in town now as his legal practice has expanded. The extra money will come in useful, and your Uncle Peter keeps nagging me to be thrifty now we have lost your father's regular income.

....

No need to read on. It was much as I anticipated. I had no intention of being persuaded to return home at that stage, but I couldn't prevent a knot of guilt twisting uncomfortably in my middle. My sigh was unintentional and disturbed Jack, sitting next to me.

'Anything wrong, Mary?'

'No, sorry Jack, just daydreaming.'

'The boss is waving at you.' I looked up, and Keynes was in his office with Pinchin. His hand was raised, beckoning for Jack or me. 'Yes, I think it's you he wants,' said Jack. 'It must be you because he's smiling. My invitations normally come with black, disapproving looks followed by a humiliating dressing down.'

I punched his shoulder playfully. Jack and Derek had been ribbing me for a few days now about Keynes being unusually polite and friendly. I wanted to tell them I wasn't his type, but that would be indiscreet and might lead to more questions. I knocked and entered.

'Was it me you wanted, Mr Keynes?'

'Yes, Miss Kiten, come in and take a seat. Thank you, Gerry, and we'll discuss that over a drink tonight in the bar.'

I stood aside and let Pinchin through the door, then closed it and took a seat at his desk. Keynes had his cigarette case out, and I waited in silence while he continued with unhurried preparations to smoke. At last, Keynes sat back and drew on his cigarette.

'I have some news for you,' he said, looking rather pleased to have my attention. 'I remember our earlier discussion about Russia when you were dismayed to learn that General Smuts and his assistant, Visser, had left Paris on a mission for Lloyd George.' I nodded confirmation. 'Well, they're both back in Paris. I had an appointment at the Astoria yesterday evening and greeted them in the foyer on their return.'

'Thank you, can I make arrangements to....' My voice trailed away as I could not think of a fitting way to finish my statement. My heart was thumping on hearing Visser's name spoken. Simply saying I had a handkerchief to return would sound very lame. 'I think you said you have met General Smuts.'

'Yes.'

'What manner of man is he?'

He showed a hint of surprise at my question but answered after only a brief pause. 'As you may expect, he has a military bearing and can appear severe and forbidding on first approach. But I can vouch from personal experience that he owns a wicked sense of humour coupled with good intellect. He is fine company with a cigar and whisky.' He glanced at me and added quickly. 'Of course, I speak as I have found him in the company of other gentlemen. I would expect his behaviour towards women to be proper and restrained.'

'I wonder if you would write a letter of introduction for me?'

'What would be the purpose of the introduction?'

'I need to learn more of the Allied attitude to the various Russian factions. I heard that his recent absence from Paris may be connected with Russia and events in Eastern Europe.'

He nodded his head slowly as he reached an understanding. 'No doubt this follows from our conversation with Colonel House and his mention of Mr Burgess' role in communications with Russia.'

'Yes.'

'Then I'll ask no more.'

The letter was written quickly in the untidy scrawl I recognised well from proofreading his paper. His signature was completed without any extravagant flourish, and blotting paper was applied before folding and inserting into an envelope. He handed it to me, swivelled his chair and looped his right leg over his left.

'I hope that will do.'

'Thank you.'

He stroked his moustache, turned his gaze on me and said, 'Forgive my impatience, but have you made any progress in your enquiries about the assault on Rue Lauriston?'

'I'm sorry, but there is nothing significant to report at the moment.'

'Oh, I thought you may have something for me. I overheard a conversation out in the main office a couple of days ago about you and a cameraman.'

'A cameraman?'

'Yes, Gerry was questioning Derek and Jack about your conversation with one of those photographers at the Majestic.' He took a final draw on his cigarette and stubbed it out in the ashtray. 'Perhaps I shouldn't say this, but they assumed you had arranged a private photography session. I, on the other hand, wondered if it was connected to the cameraman you spotted at the Rue Lauriston incident.'

'I did have a conversation with one of the photographers. I can't say for certain that he is the one who was party to your entrapment. I plan to visit his studio and find out more, but - I didn't want to inform you until I could be more definite.'

He accepted my explanation with good grace, and I was thankful he didn't press me for more information on other developments into the Rue Lauriston case. My priority was Arthur's murder. All other issues would have to take a back seat for now.

*

I skipped dinner. The weather was fine when I began a short walk from the Majestic and then, without warning, it began to rain heavily as I turned right down the Champs-Elysées. I arrived at the Astoria just before seven o'clock with hat and coat soaked, and stockings spattered with mud. I did not present at my best. Nevertheless, I was determined to go ahead with my plan to meet Smuts and Visser - assuming they were here and available, of course. For all I knew, they could be dining privately, meeting with other notables, or enjoying a night at the opera.

The grandeur and elegant exterior of the Astoria impressed. It stood comparison with the Crillon and outshone the Majestic. It promised refinement and luxury, but the interior was a disappointment. It had been used as a hospital during the war, and ample evidence of its recent utilitarian function was on display. Any redecoration attempted was hurried and incomplete. Most of the walls were still covered in a flaking and indeterminate grey blue with white arrows and stencilled signs to, 'Unité d'Isolement' and 'Amputé'. It conveyed the air of a place for business, rather than rest and relaxation.

I asked for General Smuts at reception. Unlike the Majestic, the staff in the foyer of the Astoria were French. My receptionist called a colleague to join him. Both surveyed me with expressions of surprise. They turned their backs and, after a hurried and whispered exchange, I was requested to write a note, which would be delivered to the General. I handed over Keynes' introduction. At least Smuts was there. All I could do was wait to see if I would be granted an audience.

I barely had time to rehearse my opening statement before I was summoned to follow an imperious figure from the concierge desk. I was led to the first floor, where my guide flourished a hand at a door, then swiftly departed. I knocked. A voice inside responded, and although I couldn't hear what was said, I turned the handle and opened the door. Lights were bright, and I was immediately hit by the welcoming aroma of pipe tobacco and something else, which reminded me of home. Was it Christmas pudding? A man was stood facing me at three paces. A tall, angular man with intense blue eyes, he was in shirt and braces with no tie. His beard, in the style of a 'goatee', together with waxed and twirled moustache, recalled an illustration of a pirate from a childhood book. One hand held a glass of amber liquid while the other rested casually in a trouser pocket.

'General Smuts, thank you for receiving me.' I had to stop myself from performing a full curtsey.

'Ha,' he shook his head, 'Miss Kiten, you are welcome. Ha.' Far from being reserved and severe, he looked amused, as though he was about to break into a hearty laugh.

'I hope the letter from Mr Keynes explained. I was hoping to talk to you and Mr Visser to learn more of the status of Russia in the eyes of the Allied leaders at the Congress.'

'Adam Visser, yes, yes.' He shook his head again and chuckled to himself. 'I am sorry, Miss Kiten, you must think I am very rude. You appear to be... damp. Here, let me take your coat and hat.'

I unpinned and removed my hat, then he helped with my coat, hung them on the back of a chair and placed it by a large, ornate steam radiator.

'Now, would you care for a drink, Miss Kiten?'

'I don't... yes, a small cognac, please.' I wavered. I couldn't expect Smuts to prepare a cocktail, and the safest option would have been to decline. In the end, I decided a sociable glass of cognac may help the conversation flow more easily. He presented me with a generous measure in a cut-glass tumbler, glinting gold and copper under the electric light. I was guided to a seating area, and we sat in deep leather armchairs on either side of a low table carved in an oriental style.

He raised his glass and declared, 'Gesondheid, Miss Kiten,' with a bow of his head.

215

'Cin cin to you, General.' I returned the toast, sipping my cognac while attempting to keep a straight face. It was fire water. 'Do you have any ice?'

'Ah, you must have been spoiled by visits to the Crillon, where they have refrigerators. I regret we do not have such luxuries at this hotel.' He twirled the glass in his hands. 'Tell me about yourself, Miss Kiten. I know you work for Mr Keynes in the Treasury Unit. How did you end up there, and what were you doing in the war?'

'I was a nurse during the last two years of the war. I arrived here less than two weeks ago, having been sent at short notice from a hospital at Wimereux. I was due to meet Arthur Burgess for instructions on my posting here. He was murdered minutes after I checked in at the Majestic.' I took a deep breath and exhaled before continuing. 'Mr Burgess was a long-standing family friend and I... I want to find out why he was murdered. Although I wasn't certain what position was earmarked for me here, the position with Mr Keynes was offered, and I accepted.'

'How unfortunate for you, and what a tragic death.' He nodded his head slowly. 'Adam Visser informed me about your encounter on the train to Trier. How did you find the Germans at your conference there?'

'A general feeling of injustice was the main message from my viewpoint.'

'And how would you say the Allied side managed discussions?'

'Opinions on our side are divided. There are those who wish to punish Germany with the harshest possible terms, while others take a more pragmatic view.'

'Which position do you favour, Miss Kiten?'

'Me? Oh, I am firmly in Mr Keynes' camp, which calls for modest financial penalties to allow for a recovery in international trade.' I was indebted to my proofreading of Keynes' paper for adding undeserved gloss and assurance to my statement.

'As am I. Your report confirms the one from Adam. Negotiating from a divided position against a belligerent Germany, united against unjust terms, does not bode well for the outcome.'

He uttered those words in a low voice as though speaking as an aside to an invisible colleague. I was becoming impatient to begin my questioning on Russia. And why was he interested in my inexpert views? 'Will Mr Visser be joining us?'

'Ha.' He shook his head and slapped a hand on the arm of his chair, seeming to find my question amusing.

Someone tapped, the door opened, and Visser entered. This was too much for Smuts, who clapped his hands and roared with laughter. Nonplussed, I gazed at each man in turn for a clue. Smuts continued to rock back and forth in his chair, snorting, howling and helpless. What had he found hilarious? Visser appeared to share my bemusement for a moment, then a realisation dawned. He shook his head, smiled broadly, and said, 'Miss Kiten, what a pleasure to meet you again. I see you have been entertaining General Smuts.'

I didn't know how to respond. I stood and offered my hand to Visser. He took it both hands, winked, then sat in the chair next to mine. The scar on his forehead was still visible, although it had faded. He was taller and thinner than I remember, and his hair had more of a reddish tinge under those lights. There was no denying he cut a striking figure in mid-winter Paris, with his handsome, tanned and clean-shaven face.

Smuts was trying to control his mirth. 'Forgive me… Miss… Kiten… I couldn't help myself… laughing too much… Ha! Adam will explain.'

I turned to Visser. Had I breached some arcane and unwritten rule? Was there something comical about my appearance?

He said, 'No more than twenty minutes ago, I was in this room about to take my leave of General Smuts.'

'Where were you going?'

'To the Majestic, to call on you. I received your note.'

Then I understood. A coincidence. To my mind, it warranted a wry smile, not the side-splitting hilarity displayed by Smuts. Still, better an easy sense of humour than one carved with hammer and chisel. 'Perhaps we passed in the street,' I said.

'Unless you have local knowledge of side streets and alleys, then it's a certainty we did.' He eyed Smuts, then continued. 'We received a note from the War Office while on our travels in Eastern Europe. They asked me to make contact with you and take a closer look at the events surrounding the killing of Arthur Burgess.' He removed his coat and scarf and placed them on the chair near mine. 'I understand you have misgivings about the official version of his death.'

Had I heard correctly? 'So, are you…?'

'Are we what?' asked Smuts.

'I was instructed to cease asking questions or making enquiries into the murder of Arthur and wait for an SIS agent. Is it - you, who I've been expecting?' My question was directed at Smuts, but I should have known he was far too important a figure to be a mere agent. 'I apologise, General. I meant…' My voice trailed away as I struggled to organise tumbling thoughts and impressions.

They exchanged a glance before Smuts said, 'I confess, I am too much of a coward to be considered as an SIS agent, Miss Kiten. However, like most government departments, the War Office and SIS complain about lack of manpower, which could go some way to explaining the delay you have experienced. Adam Visser here may be described as a freelance operative who from time to time has undertaken work for SIS.'

'I'm not sure I understand. Are you the expected SIS agent or not, Mr Visser?'

'I'm sorry if you find me a disappointment, Miss Kiten. I worked closely with Arthur Burgess for a few weeks from mid-December. He was a fine man and a great loss to SIS. I was certainly asked to contact you on our return, although reference to an investigation into Arthur's murder confused me. When we met on the train I believed the police had found the culprit, and it was a case of wretched bad luck with Arthur happening to cross the path of an armed and desperate criminal.'

'No – that's wrong.' My tone was tetchy, and I spilt brandy moving forward in my seat. I took a deep breath and continued, 'There was no proper investigation by the local police. They conspired to make events fit a convenient outcome. Arthur's murder was planned by a Russian faction here in Paris. My purpose in coming here to see you was to understand more about the power struggle in Russia and the Allied attitude towards the various opposing groups. I assumed that your recent absence from Paris was connected to the Russian question.'

I had stunned them into silence. All traces of amusement had disappeared from Smuts, and Visser was gazing at me with arms folded and a quizzical expression. Smuts cleared his throat and said, 'I understand your intimate connection to Mr Burgess will give you a keen interest in understanding why and how he was killed. But you talk as though you yourself are conducting an investigation.'

'I apologise if my remarks were too forceful and gave the wrong impression. Of course, I realise that I'm not in a position to do the work of the police. That would be - absurd. But I don't see why I shouldn't have civilised conversations with certain relevant people if they are willing to talk.'

Smuts opened his mouth to speak, then stopped, muttered something under his breath and turned to Visser. 'Adam?'

Visser shrugged, looked at me, smiled and replied, 'That seems reasonable.'

Smuts took a deep breath. 'So, you say there's a Russian connection, Miss Kiten. I'm not sure we have any information that could help. Our recent enquiries have taken us to Budapest, Prague, Minsk and Kiev. And while it is true that part of our mission was to gather information on Russia, our remit was somewhat broader. Nevertheless, we are acquainted with the current state of play in Russia and the representation of the different parties here in Paris. So, why don't you take your time and relate all you have discovered about the death of Mr Burgess.'

Where to start? Memories of my first entrance into the Majestic seemed distant. How much did they know? I began with the sound of a gunshot in my garret, the general confusion and my disbelief that 'Uncle Arthur' could have met his end only moments after my arrival. My description of the examination of Arthur's body, his possessions and the attitude of Inspector Roussel was met with muttering of disapproval by Smuts. It was Visser who reacted when I told of the address on Arthur's notepad and my discovery of Chersky's body.

'I met with Chersky not long before we departed for Budapest. What date was he killed?'

'It was the seventeenth, the same day as Arthur – Mr Burgess. Have you also come across his colleagues, Litvinov and Brinkov?'

'Yes, are they…'

'I understand Litvinov is still in Russia. He went with President Wilson's representative, someone named Buckler. Brinkov disappeared and has not been seen since the day of Chersky's murder.'

Smuts rose from his chair and offered me more cognac from a decanter. I declined. He poured generous measures into his glass and Visser's from another decanter. Visser waited until Smuts was seated and asked, 'How do you know all this, Miss Kiten? You are remarkably well-informed. Some of the evidence you have gathered could only have been known by the police or close associates of Chersky.'

'I was given the name and address of Chersky's widow by a policeman. She was the one who reported his murder. When I visited her, she provided information on the date of his death, the whereabouts of Litvinov and the disappearance of Brinkov.'

'I thought you said the police were unhelpful and had closed the case for Arthur's murder.'

'It was another policeman, Chief Inspector Bonnet, who provided the information on Madame Chersky, or Monique Deschamps as she was referenced in the report.'

'Wait a minute, Miss Kiten,' said Smuts. 'Take it slowly and go back to when you discovered Chersky's body.'

I hadn't explained it well, was too rushed, too excited, and I had missed important events. I tried to compose myself, took a large sip of cognac, grimaced and restated the story in meticulous detail, day by day. I had intended to omit all reference to Keynes and the attack in Rue Lauriston as it added to the complexity. It wasn't possible. Arthur's death and the Keynes incident were linked by Bonnet through the Chersky murder. Besides, I had spent so much of my time working for Keynes, seeking to protect him or trying to determine who was behind the entrapment attempt, that to ignore it all would be a distortion. Despite striving for clarity, logic and brevity, I feared the result was an overlong and tortuous exposition.

'You have been busy during our absence, Miss Kiten,' said Smuts. 'I hardly know where to start. Adam, perhaps you…'

Visser had been taking notes as I was talking. We waited as he ran a pen down his paper making marks that I assumed highlighted questions or significant aspects. 'It's complicated. If I understand you correctly, you suspect Sazanov was behind the murder of Arthur Burgess, and the motive was to break the line of communication between Allied leaders and the Bolsheviks.'

'Yes, Sazanov is the leader of the Tsarist group suspected by Madame Chersky. Arthur and Chersky

222

were linked by their mandate to establish an arrangement to enable contact between their respective sides.'

'In that case, I should also have been one of Sazanov's targets as I helped Arthur set up those channels. Yet, as you can see, I'm still here.' He glanced at his notes. 'The date of both murders was the seventeenth. Arthur and I were working with Litvinov, Chersky and Brinkov from the end of December. Agreement for meetings with the Bolsheviks was reached on the ninth of this month, and Mr Buckler accompanied Litvinov to St Petersburg on the twelfth. While these arrangements were not trumpeted to all and sundry, it was no secret. Sazanov and other Tsarist opponents of the Bolsheviks would certainly have been aware of them. In light of this, I must disagree with the motive you ascribe to Sazanov. There would have been no sense in taking the risk of killing Arthur Burgess out of malice. From their point of view, the damage had already been done. Cruel and ruthless they may be, but stupid they are not.'

Dismayed and taken aback by such a comprehensive demolition of my argument, I couldn't speak for a few moments. Both men looked at me for my reaction. 'Does that mean you also dismiss Sazanov as a suspect? Surely, you don't go along with the police version of Arthur's murder?'

'No, Miss Kiten,' answered Smuts, 'you have convinced me at least that there was more to the killing of Mr Burgess than bad luck and an impulsive robbery.'

'And you, Mr Visser, are you convinced by anything I have presented to you?' I regretted my peevish tone as soon as it was out. I sipped at the cognac to hide my embarrassment, but that only served to produce a cough as it caught in my throat. I felt foolish.

Visser placed his pen and paper on the table and leaned back in his chair. 'Forgive me if I appeared negative. I believe you have put forward persuasive evidence to indicate that Arthur's murder was planned and there is a Russian connection. Sazanov would be the most obvious threat from the Tsarist factions here. However, he is desperate to win over Allied support, and we must question whether he would jeopardize that by murdering a prominent servant of the British government.'

'I agree,' joined Smuts, 'Sazanov and his kind must be regarded as the prime suspects, though nothing springs to mind regarding their objective.'

'The disappearance of Brinkov is an added complication. Did Madame Chersky have any explanation?' asked Visser.

'No, she did not. He has vanished. It's a complete mystery to her. I remember she used the term "devils' contract" to describe the reason behind her husband's sudden alarm. It was as though something new and more threatening had been discovered about their enemies.'

'But why should that peril also concern Arthur Burgess?' A rhetorical question from Visser. None of us had an answer.

A period of silence settled. I felt no sense of discomfort in the quiet. Each of us was tied up in our own thoughts. For no other reason than passing mention of him in my narrative, mine had wandered to images of John; in his uniform; in a coarse, woollen gown at the hospital; on the dance floor at Le Baron. Smuts broke the quiet by clearing his throat. 'Well, if you will both excuse me, I need a wash and brush up before I change. I am dining at Rue Nitot tonight with Lloyd George and Nobuaki from the Japanese delegation.' He rose from his chair. 'Adam, perhaps you can continue with Miss Kiten in your room or one of the bars.' He bowed his head stiffly. 'It has been a pleasure, Miss Kiten. Your efforts to this point have been quite remarkable.'

I followed Visser to the door, exited and waited for him to join me in the corridor.

He said, 'My room is next door. Would you like to continue in there, go to one of the hotel bars, or find a decent restaurant nearby for dinner?'

That presented me with an easy choice from the alternatives offered. Even if it was still raining, I needed little persuasion to explore the streets around the Astoria for a restaurant. I was hungry.

*

Le Pistolet Fumant was an odd name for a restaurant located only a few yards from the Champs Elysees. Some may have considered it strangely appropriate to the subject of our intended conversation. The interior was warm, welcoming and tempting. A subdued light gave an intimate air to an arrangement of ornate tables and chairs cosseted with a flush of maroon velvet trimmed with gold. The only concession to its intriguing name was a pair of ancient muskets hung on the wall facing our entrance. The rich smells wafting from waiters' trays and filtering through kitchen doors teased my senses and banished all other thoughts as we studied our menus in silence.

Visser had decided. He folded his menu and placed it on the table. He said, 'Would you consider me too forward if I suggested we use each other's Christian names instead of the "Mr" and "Miss" from now on?'

'Not at all.' I was surprised and pleased he had asked. 'I would be happy to be called Mary or Maria.'

'And I am plain Adam with no variant or nickname, I'm afraid.'

We smiled, then I quickly returned to the menu as a waiter approached. Our orders given, both of us seemed to be waiting for the other to initiate a resumption of unfinished conversation from the Astoria.

Eventually, he said, 'Tell me more about the attack on Keynes and how you came to be following him that night.'

'Oh, we haven't finished with the enquiries into Arthur's murder, have we?'

'No, but there is no more to be done until I have made a few enquiries. Sazanov heads the most influential of the anti-Bolshevik groups in Paris, but there are others. I need to gather information on the current activities of all of them.'

'Who would have that information?'

'I have the SIS dossiers we used for briefing before our assignments in Eastern Europe. The French intelligence service should be able to help, but the Americans will probably have the most detailed information.'

'I've already spoken to Colonel House's assistant, and the information she offered was helpful but brief and incomplete.'

'It's Lansing and his entourage who have the data I need.'

'Excuse my ignorance, but who is Lansing?'

'He is Wilson's Secretary of State, although Wilson doesn't appear to have much faith in him. Lansing is fiercely anti-Bolshevik and opposed all contact with them. I am assured he holds current and voluminous files on all the parties fighting against Lenin, Trotsky and the Red Army.'

I supposed it made sense, but I had an uneasy feeling I was being side-lined. I related the story of my first visit to *Bar Felix* with Keynes, the retrieval of his notebook, my suspicions aroused by the scheming in street doorways and a sudden realisation of a possible entrapment with a camera. He heard me patiently and without interrupting while we were served with our aperitifs. Finally, I paused my narrative to tackle the mussels we had both ordered.

'Tell me, Mary,' he said, wiping his fingers on a napkin, 'were you and Major Parkes surprised at the attackers use of weapons? You knew a trap had been laid.'

'I didn't anticipate weapons would be used in anger for the entrapment. I imagined threats would have been sufficient if needed.' I paused, remembering the shock of the gunshot. 'Put it down to my naivety. I should have explained more to Major Parkes, then he would have been prepared. But... we were rushed... there wasn't time.' I shook my head to dismiss images of John's wound. 'No, please ignore those excuses. It was my fault. I was too eager to scupper their plans. I didn't think it through properly.'

I was half expecting him to protest that I was blameless and say words to ease my conscience, but he didn't. He didn't react at all. I wasn't sure if he approved of my actions or thought I was foolish. His expression told me nothing. The mussels were finished. Delicious. I dabbed my lips with the napkin, then continued to recount the Keynes incident and its aftermath.

He listened carefully and waited until I had finished before his next question. 'How sure are you that you correctly identified the cameraman at the entrapment as one of those hired to take photographs at the Majestic?'

'I'm not absolutely certain.' Directly after my conversation with Crozier, I was sure it was him. Since then, doubts set in. 'If you are asking me for odds, then I would say I am about eighty per cent confident it was the same man.'

'And you have his contact details on a card?'

'Yes.'

'Have you passed his name and address to Inspector Bonnet?'

'No.'

'What do you intend to do with this information, Mary?'

'I had thought to visit Crozier under the pretence of sitting for a photographic portrait.'

'And if he refuses to reveal all when you question him – then what?'

'I… I hadn't finally decided how to threaten or persuade him. At one time, I had considered asking Major Parkes to help me, but in his absence, one of his men might be willing to intimidate Crozier in exchange for a few francs.' As soon as I said the words, I recognised how flimsy and foolish they sounded. 'Please, Adam, ignore my last remark. I realise that I don't know how to handle Crozier.'

'I think you should let Inspector Bonnet interrogate him.'

228

'Of course, I had considered Bonnet, but you know how hopeless the police were investigating Arthur's murder.'

'From all you have told me, Bonnet is not from the same mould as the other inspector you encountered.'

'Roussel.'

'Yes, contrary to your experience with Roussel, you have portrayed Bonnet as intelligent, thoughtful and with an objective for justice rather than a quiet life.'

'Yes... yes, it is true. He is quite... different.'

'There is something else he should know – the criminal boss and Estelle's pimp. Have you disclosed his name to Bonnet?'

'Fournier. No, I haven't, but I assume you believe that I should?'

'Yes. When confronted by political intrigue, the police may be found wanting, but they should be competent in dealing with local criminals. Bonnet will certainly know more about Fournier than you or I.'

'Then your view is that the investigation into the Keynes incident should be handed over in its entirety to the police.'

'Yes, we should concentrate on finding out the reason for the murders of Arthur Burgess and Chersky, together with the disappearance of Brinkov.'

Of course, he was right. Dealing with Fournier was a police matter, and if we were to solve Arthur's murder, we needed to focus without the distraction of another investigation. 'You said, "we". Does that mean you're not telling me to keep out of the way? You want me to help you uncover the truth?'

'Well, you haven't been doing too badly so far. Besides...' He swirled the wine in his glass, 'from everything I've heard, it would take an armed unit to stop your involvement.'

'Funny, ha, ha, but thank you for not shunting me off into a siding, Adam. Most men in your position wouldn't have been so understanding. And you're right about letting the police handle the Keynes matter.'

He smiled, reached forward and placed his hand on mine. I froze for a moment, wondering how to interpret his gesture. Then I dived into my handbag. 'I nearly forgot,' I said. 'Here, this is yours.' I produced his handkerchief from the train at Trier.

Seventeen

I had to tell Keynes. The next day, as soon as he had hung up his overcoat and dumped a box of papers on his desk, I tapped on the door of his office. I explained the reasons why any further investigation would be better handled by Bonnet. Keynes agreed and was fulsome in his thanks for my actions and resolve up to that point.

I wrote a letter to Bonnet to outline why I suspected the involvement of Fournier and Crozier. I detailed how I chanced upon Crozier but offered nothing on the source of Fournier's name. Surely, Bonnet would understand why. I sealed my note in an envelope, addressed it as, "Privé et Confidentiel", and "Seulement Pour le Destinataire" on the reverse, then hand-delivered it by taxi during my lunch break.

I expected to hear back from Bonnet, but perhaps not so quickly. It was shortly after five that same day. Most had just left the schoolroom. Keynes, Pinchin and two others had departed earlier that afternoon to meet French and American finance teams at the Quai d'Orsay, leaving me to finish and tidy up the main office with Jack.

'Mademoiselle Kiten.'

I heard Bonnet before I saw him. I turned and saw his bulky frame filling the open doorway, standing with sad, wide eyes gazing around our schoolroom, slowly rotating a bowler hat in front of his middle.

'Chief Inspector Bonnet, this is a surprise. Welcome to the British Treasury's temporary home, or as we like to call it, our "research library".'

He nodded his head slowly, then started towards me with his curious, lumbering and unhurried gait. 'I attended this school as a young boy.' He shook his head. 'More years have passed since than I care to count. Of course, it is a school no longer. I was thinking; the place had hardly changed until I opened this door.' He lifted his head and circled a hand in a wide arc to encompass the entire space. 'The assembly hall has quite transformed from my memories of morning worship, the headmaster's daily oration and his... special punishments.'

I made no comment, not wanting to disturb his recollections and musings. The way his body appeared to shudder as he spoke the last words led me to wonder if he was the subject of one or more of those "special punishments". When he finally directed his attention at me, I asked, 'Did you receive my letter?'

'Yes, of course. May we talk; somewhere more private?'

I signalled to Jack that it was alright for him to leave. I arranged a couple of chairs by my desk, and we waited in silence until Jack closed the door behind him, and we were alone. Keynes had got into the habit of locking his office when he wasn't there. I apologised to Bonnet, explaining that I couldn't get into Keynes office to offer him more comfort and a drink. He looked at his watch and shook his head vigorously as though a drink at that hour was an absurd suggestion. He was in no hurry and continued to

232

contemplate his surroundings before delving into the ample folds of his suit jacket to retrieve a sheet of paper. I guessed it was my letter.

'Thank you for the name and address of the photographer, Miss Kiten. Have you visited Mr Crozier in his studio?'

'No.'

'As I understand from your letter, you recognised this man when he came to the Majestic some two days past. Later that day, you came to my office, but you failed to mention him then. Was there a reason you delayed the disclosure of his name?'

'I wasn't absolutely sure it was the same man I had seen at the incident on Rue Lauriston. I had a half-formed plan to meet him again, to settle the matter one way or the other, but I thought it better to inform you now and delay no further.'

'It is a great pity you did not advise me of your suspicions the same day.'

'Why?'

He placed the paper on my desk and smoothed it deliberately and gently as though stroking a lover's hair. 'An unnecessary death may have been avoided; a life saved.' Finished with the paper, he directed his gaze at me. 'When my men arrived at Crozier's studio, they found him dead.'

'Dead. How? How did he die?'

'Crozier was known to be a morphine addict. An initial report stated that circumstances indicated a probable accidental overdose of the drug using a hypodermic syringe. I went to Crozier's studio myself with a doctor and came away with a different interpretation. There was bruising around Crozier's wrists and neck, with traces of blood and skin under

233

his fingernails. Taking account of broken glass and overturned furniture as signs of a struggle, we were left in no doubt that an overdose was the cause of death, but it was not self-administered.'

'A murder?' I knew from experience how quickly addiction came and how easy it was to end a life with an over-generous measure of morphine. I had dispensed a fatal dose myself once, out of kindness to relieve horrific suffering when there was no chance of recovery. But why would anyone murder Crozier, and was his killing connected to the attack on Keynes? 'You mean... he was murdered by... injecting with morphine?'

'Exactly, Miss Kiten. You will understand now why you should have given me his name as soon as you were able.'

'Yes, I see I was foolish, and I am sorry.' I hesitated before asking, 'Do you think his killing was linked in any way to the attack and entrapment planned in Rue Lauriston?'

He puffed air through his lips and looked at me as though I should be ashamed to ask. 'Why not? Of course, it may have been a coincidence, and he was involved in another dangerous intrigue that led to his killing.' He shrugged. 'But until and unless we learn of an alternative explanation, we must assume he was murdered to make sure he could not inform on his partners in the crime against you and Mr Keynes.'

Yes, it was an inane question, but the murder of Crozier so that he couldn't talk to the police was - extreme. I hadn't anticipated anyone would be so ruthless. 'I was the only one who saw the photographer in Rue Lauriston and suspected he was the same man at the Majestic. So, how...'

'Did you disclose his name to anyone before you wrote the letter to me?'

I knew that question was coming. 'When do you believe he was murdered?'

'The doctor estimated Crozier died between twenty-four and thirty-six hours before we examined his body.' He checked his watch. 'That calculation was made approximately three hours ago at two-thirty.'

I sifted tumbling memories of recent conversations. Was I the inadvertent cause of Crozier's murder? Had I spoken his name to someone? And had that person had gone on to inform others he was suspected of involvement in the Rue Lauriston attack? Somehow this had leaked back to the murderer. Or... No, I couldn't believe anyone I had talked to would inform the murderer directly. Keynes. I had told him, but only a few hours earlier. Also, it couldn't have been Visser or Smuts as they learned of his name less than twenty-four hours ago. No one else came to mind. Unless... I recalled there was a meeting in Keynes' office a couple of days before when.... Yes, I had mentioned a cameraman to Keynes at that meeting. But I hadn't spoken Crozier's name then, had I? Would the knowledge that one of three cameramen at the Majestic was under suspicion be enough to order a killing? Surely not.

'I don't think I spoke the name "Crozier" to anyone,' I said, 'at least not within the timeframe you have given.'

'Perhaps you were seen in his company. Can you remember?'

'Yes, that would include the other photographers at the Majestic and their assistants.' I hesitated, trying to recall the scene during my short conversation with

Crozier. 'There may have been others. We were in the hotel ballroom for a few minutes together, and anyone may have looked in there momentarily without my noticing.'

Bonnet folded my letter carefully and inserted it back into a pocket. 'If there any other facts I should know about this affair, then please inform me now, Miss Kiten.'

His reproach hurt more than I expected. 'You have shamed me, Inspector, and I apologise again for the delay in communication. I am not withholding any information about this case, not intentionally anyway. If my memory is at fault and I recall any new facts, then I will let you know in a timely fashion.' I instantly regretted my choice of words; the apology sounded insincere and a little pompous. 'You haven't mentioned the other name in my letter. I suppose Fournier is well-known to you.'

'You suppose correctly, Miss Kiten.'

'If he was behind the attack on Mr Keynes, presumably he is also the chief suspect in the murder of Mr Crozier?'

'If only it were that simple,' said Bonnet. 'Fournier takes care to keep his hands clean and distance himself from any criminal offence. Fear is his most potent weapon. People in these arrondissements will not give evidence against Fournier, and without their cooperation, mere accusations and suspicions will go nowhere.'

'The attack on Mr Keynes was not a run-of-the-mill local crime. It has political manoeuvring and intrigue on a national level at its heart. Does it surprise you that someone like Fournier would get involved?'

'Yes, it does. The inducement must have been significant.'

'The entrapment and attack failed. Do you know Fournier well enough to understand whether he will shy away from a repeat attempt or take up the challenge and redouble his efforts?'

'Ha, you do me too much credit to believe I can read criminal minds.' He puffed his cheeks and expelled air, slowly. 'I am not a betting man, but if you were to force my hand, I would place money on a second attempt.'

Bonnet had confirmed my suspicions. I should have been reassured by the two-pronged protection Keynes was receiving but couldn't suppress a feeling of unease that it was not enough. The news about Crozier had also given me a jolt of anxiety for the safety of Estelle. I dreaded the thought of Fournier discovering she was the one who had dared to utter his name in my presence.

Eighteen

I hauled myself out of bed early the following day with a pounding head and limbs of jelly. I doubt if I had managed more than a few minutes of genuine sleep. My thoughts were filled with troubling images of Estelle, her routine abuse at the hands of strangers and the possibility that my enquiries and seeking her out may have prompted steps to ensure her silence. Given her occupation, it would be easy to arrange a throat cut, a strangling or suffocation with blame placed on a wayward client. Police like Roussel would simply shrug and put the case of her murder on a pile of the undeserving and unsolved.

But worry about Estelle was not the primary cause of my lack of sleep. I simply couldn't position my body for any comfort. I was tired, but the ache deep in my bones was more than a match for exhaustion. I was also forever on the point of vomiting but unable to complete the action and therefore caught in a cycle of rest, cramp, prepare to retch, fail and rest again. I put it down to a bout of food poisoning. What had I eaten and when? It was unlikely to be the two poached eggs I had for yesterday's dinner, preceded by a ham sandwich for lunch and toast with blackcurrant preserve for breakfast. Initially, I dismissed the previous dinner at the restaurant as too far removed, then eventually concluded it must have been the cause.

Adam also had the mussels, so, I assumed, he was probably suffering too.

I went to the washroom, splashed cold water over my face, scrubbed my body with a brush covered in a wet flannel before finishing with a vigorous rubbing dry with a towel. I returned to my bedroom and, despite a splitting headache and wheezing chest, convinced myself I was feeling well enough to prepare for work and make an appearance at breakfast. I dressed and made my way down to the corridor leading to the dining room, where I hovered for a few seconds before a hurried escape to the powder room. The odours of cooked sausage meat, bacon and kippers brought the lurching in my belly to a long-awaited and, ultimately, satisfying conclusion. I took that as a good sign and the beginning of a recovery from a temporary upset.

It was early; the cloak of night had barely lifted, with lights from horse carriages and motor taxis reflecting brittle yellow shards in the wet surface of the streets as I walked to our workplace in Rue Leo Delibes. I stopped mid-way, short of breath and uncertain whether to proceed or to take the safe and sensible option, to go back and retire to my bed. I forced myself to continue, persuaded I would improve by lunchtime.

Pinchin was the only one who had beaten me to work. His response to my greeting was a grunt of acknowledgement without lifting his head from the papers on his desk. I retreated to the large walk-in cupboard, modified to act as a makeshift kitchen, put a match to the small gas stove and waited for the kettle to boil. My legs buckled, and I grabbed a shelf for support.

'Are you alright, Mary?'

It was Derek. He was with Jack. I hadn't heard either of them enter. 'Yes, thank you, Derek, just a little peaky. I think it's something I ate.'

'Fancy French grub with all those herbs and spices, no doubt,' said Jack. 'You should stick to the good, wholesome British fare from the Majestic dining rooms.'

He expected me to disagree and initiate a conversation about food in general – his favourite topic. I wasn't in the mood for small talk; a noncommittal murmur my only response. I turned away and kept my sight firmly on the kettle, hoping they would take this as a sign I wasn't feeling sociable. I could hear them behind me and imagined an exchange of disappointed and knowing looks as they hesitated briefly then shuffled off to their desks. I didn't want to, but I was there, tending the kettle and teapot, so felt obliged to offer a cuppa to all the early starters.

The tea was brewed, four steaming cups and saucers were on the tray. I picked it up and took a few steps into the office when it suddenly became so heavy; I could barely hold it. I stopped; a low moan escaped my mouth; the effort was too much. The tray rattled. My whole body sagged under an oppressive weight, and I crumpled to the floor. I heard the shattering of crockery as a distant but sharp sound and felt heat in my legs as I slid down into a spinning grey mist. I could have shouted for help, but a gentle, dark descent seemed so natural and inevitable that I welcomed the coming oblivion. Black came, then - nothing.

*

It was sleep – and it wasn't sleep. I hovered at the edge of wakefulness, knowing at any time I could open my eyes, and I would be there. Present. Sleeping was easier; restful; warm. I sank into the welcoming folds of soft lambswool, denying all urgent calls to wake. I lay in swaddled comfort, uncaring. The sounds of a conscious state could be heard, sometimes harsh and rasping, but mostly soothing and hushed. Voices sang lullabies as I lay in a boat, bobbing gently on the waves of a tranquil, black ocean. A door opened. Murmuring. Footsteps – coming or going?

'Mary.'

'Mary Kiten.'

I recognised that voice. Was that me – Mary Kiten? I wanted to answer. I wanted to be left alone.

'Mary. Mary, please open your eyes.'

'No… leave… me…' My mouth was too dry. My throat hurt.

'Mary, it's me, Adam – Adam Visser.'

A light dazzled. Too bright. 'Adam?'

'Yes, thank God, you're awake.'

'Why. What's wrong?' One eye was open. Everywhere was white. 'Where am I?'

'You've been ill. You're in bed.'

My other eye lifted, fluttered, opened. Colours crept into view; green, brown, black, and - red. 'This… this is not my room.'

'No, you have been moved to a more suitable room. We insisted. It's the same hotel – the Majestic.'

'Why aren't you… the mussels… poison?'

'The doctor thinks you have caught the new strain of influenza rife in the city. At least, that was his best guess. He did consider food poisoning, pneumonia and another illness I can't pronounce but dismissed them in favour of influenza.'

'Where… how did I catch it?'

241

No reply. I couldn't see him, so I turned my head. He was on my right side, sitting on a chair. The room was – big, clean and appeared to be newly decorated. The wall behind Adam was covered in wallpaper with a floral pattern. The door and ceiling were brilliant white, reflecting glare from the windows. I sniffed, clutching at a faint scent - of freshly applied paint? I repeated my question.

He shrugged. 'It could have been anywhere. I understand more than two dozen people at this hotel are laid up with the same illness.'

I struggled to lever myself up on an elbow. I was in my nightdress. How? Who undressed me and put me to bed? Why didn't I remember? 'Water. Could I have a glass of water, please?'

He leant over me to the other side of the bed, took a glass of water from a bedside cabinet and handed it to me. I closed my eyes as his smell filled my senses. A muscular, healthy smell, attractive and intense. I drank greedily, with my actions uncoordinated, so that much of the water spilt on my bedclothes. I handed back the empty glass and subsided, spent by the effort.

'How long have I been like this?'

'Three days. You were brought here by taxi. Apparently, you were just about able to walk with support, but not making a lot of sense. I heard that some even suspected you were drunk from the previous evening. I called on you that lunchtime, shortly before the doctor arrived. You were conscious but delirious with a fever. The doctor prescribed bed rest and plenty of liquids.'

'What day is it now?'

'It's Thursday,' he checked his watch, 'and two minutes to eleven o'clock in the morning.'

'I don't… remember anything, except… the tea tray falling.'

'Tea tray?'

'Never mind.'

'How are you feeling now?'

'I'm tired, but otherwise… I think I'm alright. The aching bones and the urge to retch have gone.' I paused to consider my physical being. Mind and body felt curiously detached, and it was as though considering the sensation of limbs, fingers, toes, breasts and other body parts for the first time. 'I am very tired, also hungry.'

'I'll go…' He started to rise from his seat.

'No, stay for a while, Adam. Food can wait. You said that you came to call on me almost two days ago. Was there anything you wanted to report or ask?'

'You shouldn't concern yourself with that now, Mary. There will be ample time for investigating once you are recovered.'

'No, Adam, time is not on our side. Arthur and Chersky have been dead for almost a fortnight now. If their murders were part of a devious plan then, whatever is intended as the climax, may be imminent.' I think I surprised both of us with the strength of my denial and the confident tone in my voice.

He sat back in his seat and took a few moments to reflect before responding. 'You want to know the reason I called on you?'

'Of course.'

'I simply wanted to see you again, and I was going to suggest dinner at another restaurant.'

'You wanted to…'

'Yes, is that so outrageous? I had no new information to discuss with you at that point.' He stroked his chin and appeared to be contemplating whether to say more. He leant forward and said, 'Now, I have examined all the intelligence reports on the Russians in Paris. It seems that you were right to mention Sazanov the other evening. The consensus is that his faction is the strongest, wealthiest and most active. All the other anti-Bolshevik groups in the city appear to have recognised Sazanov as their best chance of gaining Allied support and, while they don't exactly stand with him shoulder-to-shoulder, they are happy for him to make the running.' He tilted his head and smiled. 'So, when you are recovered, perhaps we can put him under surveillance.'

I heard all the words he spoke, but it took me a while to piece them into an intelligible format. I was still fixed on his reason for calling. Dinner? Was there an interest? Desire? I tried to shrink beneath the bedclothes, to hide my awkwardness and, possibly, blushing cheeks.

'Yes, yes, thank you, Adam. Sazanov. Surveillance. We should.' I cursed inwardly at my lame and clumsy response and decided that I should be more positive. 'I'm sure I will be ready tomorrow. Once I've had something to eat and drink, I will recover quickly.'

He nodded his head slowly, but there was doubt in his eyes. 'Very well, I will call again tomorrow, around six. Please don't even consider going to work in the schoolroom. You need at least another full day's rest.'

He rose from his seat and was about to take his leave. There was something else to discuss with Adam. What was it? I held up a hand as a signal for him to stop. I cast my thought back to – the tea tray, Derek and Jack, and Estelle. Yes, I remembered.

'Adam, I need to ask a favour.'

'Of course, what is it, Mary.'

I explained that I followed his advice and had written a letter to Chief Inspector Bonnet providing the names and context for Crozier and Fournier. Then, my shock and surprise to hear of Crozier's murder and Bonnet's suspicion that it was connected to the Rue Lauriston incident. Finally, I arrived at the point of my telling; to request that he seek out Estelle and warn her of the possible danger from Fournier and if she was asked, to deny she had ever met with me.

He breathed deeply, raised his head to the ceiling, then turned his gaze on me. 'I have obligations for General Smuts, but I will try and do as you ask, Mary.' He stood transfixed for an instant as though unsure what he should do next.

'Thank you, Adam.'

He bowed his head in a strangely formal manner. 'Get well. I will see you again tomorrow evening.'

Nineteen

I slept most of what was left of the day after Adam called. A girl named Edith had been assigned to check on me periodically, to bring meals and see if I needed anything. I was ravenous, and I had never tasted anything so good as the lamb chops served for lunch shortly after waking from my delirium. Edith was happy to watch me eat and gossip about her other charges. She, and her friend Margaret, had volunteered to look after the sick in the hotel as they both held an ambition to be nurses. They each had eleven guests in their care, and, Edith confessed, she was sure I was a 'goner' a couple of days ago. She had three guests who she described as in a worse state than me, with their skin turned a grey-blue colour and gasping for breath. It sounded terrible, made more so by how she described their condition in a matter of fact and unemotional manner.

I woke early on the following day – Friday, according to Adam's account. I felt refreshed and impatient. My incapacity had wasted four days, and I was eager to make up for the lost time. Refreshed I may have been, but vigorous I was not. As soon as I slid out of bed, I realised that my legs and arms were weak and unsteady. I had the luxury of a new room with space and warmth, so I decided to exercise. My father had taught me a routine of stretching, running on the spot, sit-ups and press-ups that I practised in full each morning before leaving for France in 'sixteen. But good intentions faded, and I had started days in that way only intermittently in the past year. After five minutes, my limbs were trembling, and I struggled with breathing. I rested for ten minutes, then began again.

Almost two hours later, there was a knock at my door, and Edith came in to find me in my underclothes, mid-press-up, red-faced and perspiring heavily. She stared open-mouthed at the antics of a woman who had clearly lost her mind. I reassured her that I was much improved, and that strenuous exercise was an aid to a quick recovery. She knew I had been a nurse, so she didn't dismiss my claim outright but was unconvinced and scurried away with a shake of her head to fetch my order of eggs and bacon for breakfast. I ran a hot bath to celebrate the unaccustomed indulgence of my private bathroom.

I finished my ablutions, primed to tackle a hearty breakfast, and was pleased to find a fully laden tray waiting for me on a table. A letter was tucked under the saucer. Intrigued, I tore it open with a knife and unfolded a single sheet of paper with a handwritten note in blue ink. It was from John. The writing was odd, beginning in a neat, flowing hand and gradually deteriorating to an uneven and unsteady scrawl. The corrections gave it the appearance of an edited draft. If that was the case, where was the final version and why send this one?

~~Thursday~~
~~Date~~

My Dear Mary

I trust that you are well. I often think of your last visit here. Although that was only a few days ago, it feels like another age in a different world. Time passes slowly when there is little to occupy hands and mind. Thoughts of the best and worst kind are free to run riot.

~~I hope My most earnest wish~~ Please forgive my presumption, but I write this letter in the expectation that you may plan to visit me again while I am confined in this place. Nothing would please me more than sit with you, but I fear that will not be possible, at least for a week or two. I have been diagnosed with influenza, and it seems that almost everyone in my ward is suffering from this damnable disease. ~~Writing this letter is a monumental effort. I fear that I may~~

~~Darling Mary~~ You, my dear Mary, must not come near this hospital until the all-clear is given as I am informed that others may become ill through proximity to those already infected. ~~God willing~~ My shoulder is healing nicely, and as soon as I am free of influenza, I will discharge myself from this hospital.

~~Dearest~~ You are ~~always~~ often in my thoughts, and I confess I have dared to dream of a future together, even though we have known each other for only a few days.

~~With love and affection~~
~~Deepest I~~
With sincere regard and warm affection
John

~~Major John Parkes~~

I wept. My breath came in deep, heaving gulps. The tears wouldn't stop. Tears for John. His wound and illness were my doing. If only I hadn't asked him to accompany me to Rue Lauriston, he would be whole, unblemished, healthy. Tears for my father, for my mother's loss of her partner and lover. Tears for all who died and suffered in the calamity that was termed The Great War. Tears for me – for what I had become. There was nothing soft and feminine in me now. My whole being was focused on blood, scheming and revenge. When did my heart last yearn for happier times, for normality, family life and love?

Yet, John's letter was an unmistakable declaration of his affection. To him, I must have appeared... womanly... desirable. We had known each other for only a few short days, and I knew we had stirred feelings in each other but never imagined it would have gone so far as to think of a 'future together'. Was I in denial? I did not doubt that an attachment to him could grow, given time.

My tears subsided and breathing calmed. I attempted to rationalise my emotions. Guilt. That was it. Guilt because of the feeling I experienced when Adam hinted at his interest the previous day. Was my imagination running wild, or were two men competing for my attention? I knew almost nothing about Adam. Maybe he was married? Had I misread his signals? No, I wasn't being fanciful. I could see it in his eyes. But why now? Perhaps this sudden and unexpected entanglement was due to our situation. The war, at least on the Western Front, was over. Imminent peril had faded, and here we were cast into the city of romance, free to wonder about pleasure, tenderness and passion.

I splashed cold water on my face, metaphorically, slapped my cheeks physically, and instructed myself to stop those fantasies. There would be time enough for a rediscovery of softness and femininity once Arthur's murder had been avenged and my time in Paris was finished. Meanwhile, I decided to see if Sir Basil knew anything about John's letter and his current wellbeing. Then, there would be little to do but wait for Adam, his news on Estelle and our promised joint endeavour to place Sazanov under surveillance.

*

'Miss Kiten, are you quite well?' I recognised Sir Basil's voice.

My new room number was 44, along the same corridor as his and the other security offices. I had taken barely three paces from my door when I was stopped by the question behind me.

'Yes, thank you, Sir Basil. I believe I am almost fully recovered. More to the point, experience tells me that I should no longer be infectious, so I have taken the opportunity to venture from my room.' I waited until he stood alongside me. I realised I hadn't seen him on his feet before; he had always been seated across the other side of a desk or table. He was quite short and tubby, perhaps three inches below my height. 'In fact, I was on my way to your office. Could you spare me a couple of minutes, please, Sir Basil?'

'Very well, but do try and keep it quick; I have a particularly busy morning. President Wilson is expected here this afternoon, you know.'

I didn't know, but I could understand why he was busy arranging security. We entered his office, and he gestured for me to take a seat at his desk. I waited a few minutes in silence while he sifted through papers on the middle of his desk and consigned them to a fresh pile on his left, a smaller one to his right, or discarded into a bin at his side.

'Now, how can I help, Miss Kiten?'

'I received a letter this morning from Major Parkes. I understand he is ill with influenza and wondered if you had any news on his condition.'

'Yes, it is most unfortunate. We were informed that there are no places left in the ward where we reserved beds, so I sent Jenkins to see how the land lies at the hospital. He was instructed to visit Major Parkes, but he was unable to gain access. The entire hospital has been placed under quarantine.'

'That's an extreme measure. At the hospital in Wimereux, we confined those with symptoms to a single ward, but the rest of the hospital functioned normally.'

'I gather it is precautionary and only temporary. Jenkins was told limited access would probably be allowed in a few days.'

'So, Jenkins didn't actually meet Major Parkes. Did he get a report on his condition?'

'Jenkins had a note from me for Major Parkes. He was obliged to hand it to a nurse who promised to deliver it into his hands and return with a reply. There was no verbal response from the Major. Jenkins was advised he was sleeping after a restless night. My understanding is that the nurse returned with the letter addressed to you and pressed it into Jenkins' hand.'

'Do you know if the nurse had any verbal message for me from the major?'

'That I don't know. You would have to ask Jenkins if anything was said.'

'Thank you, Sir Basil; I will if I can find him. As a matter of interest, what time is President Wilson due here this afternoon?'

'He is due at one o'clock, but I have been that warned he is notorious for his relaxed attitude to timekeeping. So, we will be prepared for his arrival from mid-day until four or even five. Now, if you will forgive me, Miss Kiten, I must get on.'

I knew Jenkins as the corporal who confronted me when I approached the security cordon around Arthur's body at the hotel's front. He and I were on informal greeting terms, a smile or a nod on my part and a wink or sloppy salute from Jenkins. He was one of John's men and, no doubt, had noticed John and I were often seen together. I hovered in the corridor outside the security officers for about fifteen minutes, but there was no sign of Jenkins.

I retired to my new room. The novelty of its opulence continued to delight in a childlike manner. So much space; three rooms, each one four or five times bigger than my old one; a large bed with a deep, yielding mattress, fresh linens and plush eiderdown; deep pile rugs; heating radiators; and a bathroom we could only dream about at our lodgings in Wimereux. I kicked off my shoes, flopped on the bed and stared at the stucco ceiling, my thoughts a tangled mess of events from the last few weeks in Paris. Were memories of Mother and home real? They seemed so distant. Even my time at Wimereux felt remote, detached, faint. A knock on my door startled me. I had begun to doze.

'Ah, good morning, Jenkins. I've been looking for you.'

'Hello, Miss Kiten, Sir Basil told me you had asked about the letter.'

'Thank you for delivering the letter from Major Parkes. I wondered if… I know you were not allowed to visit his ward. Did you gather any more information about the Major's condition – from the nurse, perhaps?'

'No, I'm sorry, Miss, she was too busy.'

'Was there any message from the Major when the nurse gave you his letter?'

'Not really, she just said something like, "he would have wanted to send this".'

A statement like that implied he was too sick to finish, address and send the letter himself. I couldn't remember if the address on the envelope was in the same handwriting as the letter. It could also mean that John hadn't intended that version to be sent, but the nurse took it on herself to decide, because of – what? I realised I was staring at Jenkins.

'Sorry, Jenkins. I was wondering… No, it doesn't matter.'

'Do you want to send a letter in reply, Miss? Sir Basil has said he will probably want me to go to the hospital again. He corresponds with two other patients there as well as Major Parkes.'

'Oh, yes, please, but I'm not sure when I will write it.'

'That's fine, Miss, just leave it at Sir Basil's office when it's ready.'

Twenty

President Wilson and a procession of motor cars arrived around noon. Crowds had gathered in the streets outside and within the Majestic. I viewed events from halfway up the central stairway among rows of onlookers, glimpsing Wilson with Lloyd George at his side and Colonel House following. A lot of handshaking forced smiles and introductions were made. It appeared that Wilson was meeting British notables, and the few I recognised included Hardinge, Sumner, Cunliffe, Balfour, Sir John Beale and Keynes. They hung around in the foyer, doing not very much as far as I could see. I learned, from conversations around me, that it was only a temporary halt at the hotel. Wilson and those he met in the foyer were planning to travel on for a short visit to Versailles. I couldn't see Sandra, and after half an hour, I extricated myself from the crowd and retired to my room.

Most of my hours that day were spent alone, toiling with pen and paper, interspersed with occasional bouts of physical exercise. Desperate to shake off the effects of my bout of influenza, I was relieved to sense a measure of vitality and strength returning to my body.

Friday, 24th January, 1919

A TURBULENT PEACE

Most Beloved Mother

I am sorry not to have replied sooner to your letter of 14th January. I have been laid low in bed for a few days with a bout of influenza. A doctor advised it was the latest strain of the disease, which has been so prevalent in France this last year or so. There have been several cases in our hotel, and some of the hospitals here are having difficulty coping with an influx of those suffering with its symptoms. Have there been any outbreaks in our part of Kent? Anyway, it was most unexpected, unpleasant, and inconvenient. But, I am recovered now, although still a little weak and not yet back at work with the Treasury Unit.

Oh Mother, I do understand your concerns and desire for me to return home. I too, am eager for the comforts of home and your closeness, but I must beg you to be patient a little longer. Here, I am near to the investigation into Uncle Arthur's attack and to leave now would feel like I'm deserting him at a critical time. I regret there has been no further news from the investigation, but I am sure something will be unearthed before too long.

You ask what I intend to do, once I am back in England. If you had put the question to me only a few days ago, then Cambridge and teaching would have been near the top of my list. Now, I am not so sure. Nursing is hard work, but I would not dismiss the possibility of continuing in some way out of hand. Perhaps it is only now, separated from hospital and patients after over two years, that I have come to

realise I hold a fascination for all things medical. I am
rambling Mother – please take no notice.

As an end to this brief note, I request your
indulgence once again. Please bear with my little
idiosyncrasy in wishing to tarry here while any
mystery surrounding Uncle Arthur is uncovered.

With much love
Your devoted daughter
Mary

My latest letter to Mother was straightforward.
However, I failed dismally in many attempts to find
the right words for a return letter to John. Phrases were
trite, paragraphs formulaic, pages I read aloud seemed
over emotional and gushing, or stilted and formal. In
short, the tone and content of the letter I wanted to
write were impossible to achieve. I aimed to respond
positively, while falling just short of declaring open-
hearted encouragement. I dithered; needed more time;
but couldn't disappoint. It was a minefield, especially
with the tortuous examination of each word to ensure
there was no possibility of misinterpretation.

I skipped dinner at the Majestic because I couldn't
face a chattering throng at the canteen. At the back of
my mind, I suppose there was also a hope that our
endeavours that night might leave time for dinner at a
restaurant. It was after nine when Adam called. I was
impatient, hungry, and preoccupied. Few words were
exchanged until we entered the motor taxi outside the
hotel. Adam's enquiries after my health were met with
short, absent-minded affirmations that I was recovered
and ready. My thoughts were still absorbed in

composing the letter. I must have puzzled him with my attitude of detachment and indifference.

He said, 'Are you interested to know whether I was able to meet with Estelle?'

'Who?' I paused, and to my shame, had to concentrate my thinking for a few seconds before recognising the name. 'Oh yes, I apologise, Adam. Did you manage to meet with her?'

'I went to her apartment and used the fire escape as you suggested to avoid the concierge.'

'I hope you didn't frighten her?'

'I'm sure I did at first sight. I took a square of card on which I wrote your name and pressed it to her window, hoping she would understand who sent me and that I was not just a brute of a man trying to crash into her apartment.'

'That was thoughtful of you.'

'Thankfully, she recognised your name and let me in. Despite your fleeting acquaintance, she seemed to hold you in high regard and spoke your name warmly. I explained your concerns around the incident at Rue Lauriston.' He sat back in his seat and spread his hands. 'You didn't tell me that the man Fournier was her pimp.'

'Didn't I? I'm sorry, Adam, it must have slipped my mind. I can only offer my bout of influenza as an excuse?'

He turned to face me, unsure how to react. I smiled, and although it was dark, I could sense that he reciprocated. He placed a hand on mine. I wondered if he would leave there for the duration of the taxi ride, but it was removed after a few seconds. 'Well, it seems Fournier questioned her about her brief encounter with Keynes in Bar Felix, but as she was elsewhere on the

257

night of the incident, she said he didn't appear concerned or suspect her in any way.'

'I hope her assessment can be relied upon.'

'She was shocked and saddened to hear about Crozier, who she had seen a few times, though they had never exchanged more than a few words. Despite the suspicious circumstances surrounding his death, she told me to reassure you that she felt in no danger – at least not from Fournier.'

I was comforted by Adam's report. Although not entirely free from worry about Estelle, I could concentrate on helping to discover the reason for Arthur's murder and hold those responsible to account. The taxi stopped in a line of traffic, waiting to navigate the twelve-road junction that circled the Arc.

'Where are we going?' I asked, my mind now focussed on our task ahead.

'I am indebted to Estelle's knowledge of the area around Avenue Hoche. She avoids bars and clubs where Sazanov's pack tend to gather as she regards some of his men as brutish and rude. So, those are the places we will explore. She mentioned *Club Margot, Bar L'Espoir* and *Bar Alfredo Quinze*. We will start with the last-named.'

We stopped outside a narrow-fronted entrance. I could distinguish faint lettering of 'Quinze' above the door, but Alfredo was either missing or overpainted with the dark blue that had been recently applied. I raised the coat collar as my breath clouded in the chill night air. Adam opened the door, and I entered first into a dimly lit and surprisingly large space scattered with small, round tables, most unoccupied.

'We're too early,' I muttered to Adam.

He didn't reply and guided me to a table against a wall, mid-way between the door and the bar - a good place to watch the comings, goings and interaction with the bar staff. He asked what I wanted to drink. We could have been in for a long night, and I dared not start with alcohol as I wanted to stay sharp. I noticed a sign for *Compagnie de Limonadiers*, so I requested a lemonade.

'Are you sure?'

'Yes, thank you, I may have wine or a sidecar later, but for now, a lemonade is all I want.' I hesitated, then added, 'I haven't eaten since breakfast, so a small plate of food would also be welcome.'

He folded his arms, our eyes met, and he was about to speak, but I looked away quickly and pretended to retrieve something from my bag. A handkerchief would do. I didn't want to answer any awkward questions about what I had been doing that day and why I had skipped meals. A waiter came, and Adam ordered my lemonade, a cognac and the only food on offer - bread, crudités and cheese.

We had been there for over an hour before deciding to move on. Although more customers had drifted in, the atmosphere remained sedate. *Bar L'Espoir* was no more than one hundred paces away on the same side of the avenue. The frontage was more expansive, and, with a bold electric sign, the outside suggested a more stimulating and extravagant interior than the bar we had just left. We were disappointed. It was roughly the same size, and the only feature that distinguished it from the 'Alfredo' was a small, raised platform, which I assumed served as a stage.

Instead of taking a seat, I followed Adam, who made his way to the bar, weaving around occupied tables.

There, he made a show of examining the different cognac brands on offer and said he was surprised to see so many bottles of vodka. Two of the French barmen were happy to inform about their Russian clientele and enter into a discussion with Adam on the pros and cons of cognac, whisky and vodka. I had lost interest, and my mind wandered until it was brought back sharply with the unexpected mention of 'Sazanov' by one of the barmen.

'What was all that about?' I asked Adam as we took seats at a table. This one was also against a wall and close enough to the bar to overhear snatches of conversation.

'Sazanov has his special supply of the most expensive cognac here. No one else can use it. Apparently, he doesn't touch vodka, which is most un-Russian. I thought they were weaned on the stuff.'

'Does he come in here every night?'

'They say he is in here three or four nights each week, and normally he puts in an appearance around midnight. So, there is a fair chance he will be in later.'

'You have seen him before and can identify him, can't you?' I asked, realising I had only assumed Smuts and Adam had been present at Allied meetings with Sazanov and other Tsarist groups.

He stared at me with an expression of mock horror before sitting back in his seat and suppressing laughter with a hand to his mouth. 'I have met Sazanov a few times and, rest assured; we will not miss him. He has a very distinctive appearance, like a dandy. Did you think I was relying on you to recognise him?'

'No, of course not.' His confirmation was a relief, for although I had observed Sazanov, that was only a momentary glimpse on one occasion from the inside of Bonnet's police car.

I tried to act naturally and relax, but I was on edge waiting for Sazanov. The minutes dragged, and I had to stop fidgeting with my glass, bag, gloves, anything. Adam, on the other hand, was composed, calm and watchful. The majority of the voices I heard either spoke Russian or French with a Russian accent. After about half an hour, three men took to the stage to a smattering of applause. After a brief tuning up, one brought a stool on the platform, and the other two placed themselves on either side. An odd trio, the one seated played what I assumed was a balalaika, while the other two had an accordion and some form of tambourine. The songs were Russian – old folk songs, I guessed, and although unfamiliar, the music was melodic and pleasing.

Adam nudged me and pointed covertly to a group of men at the bar. I had noticed them as they entered; a heavily bearded one, in particular, had a swagger that suggested a kind of rough authority. Sazanov was not among them. The bearded one was gesticulating and seemed to be giving orders to others.

'Why are those men of interest to you?' I had my mouth close to his ear as though whispering endearments.

'I am sure one of those men accompanied Sazanov to Hotel Crillon for a conference last month.' He placed his arm around me. I felt his hot breath on my neck. 'The one with a full beard. He is giving instructions on some matters. Maybe important.'

'Shall I...'

I interpreted his raised hand as an indication that we should wait to observe and listen. We couldn't overhear anything while the music was playing and my attempt at lip-reading Russian failed. I waited until the band finished a number, then whispered, 'Powder Room,' to Adam and set off, weaving my way around the tables. I passed within a couple of paces of the group at the bar when I dropped a lipstick from my bag and made a pretence of trying to recover it. I would have lingered longer, but a man from a nearby table insisted on helping me.

I regained my seat next to Adam a few minutes later.

'Well? Did you learn anything useful?' His tone suggested only grudging approval of my furtive bid to eavesdrop.

'The man with a beard was angry. I gathered it was about an arrangement with the other men that hadn't been honoured. Or there was some problem in delivering what had been promised.'

'Did you discover the nature of the dispute?'

'No, not exactly. The bearded man spoke in Russian and French. I believe the three men he was arguing with were French. His cursing, insults and side remarks were in Russian.'

'You heard no reference to Sazanov?'

'No.'

'Then, perhaps it's of no significance for us.'

'But you said you recognised the man with the heavy beard as an associate of Sazanov.'

'I cannot be certain.'

'You were sure a few minutes ago.'

He stifled a response, sat back in his chair and frowned. 'Why would Frenchmen be involved?'

I shrugged. 'Local knowledge. Or...' I hesitated, thinking through what I was about to say, 'maybe the Russians want to distance themselves from whatever conspiracy they have in mind.' The idea took hold, and I could see it sparked an interest in Adam. 'There was talk of "la récompense", and the delivery of whatever service the Frenchmen were to provide was "plus tard". The bearded one also mentioned "les barils" more than once.'

'Barrels.' He paused, and I could imagine the possibilities running through his mind. 'Barrels in connection with what?'

'I don't know. I could only pick up fragments of the conversation. I may have misheard, and it could have been another, similar word.' I had to admit; I wasn't certain.

We both watched as the business between the group of men at the bar continued to the background of the trio playing Russian folk songs. Handshakes, bowed heads, and their general bearing signalled some form of agreement and an ending to their encounter. Bearded man leant against the bar and raised a glass to the others before he gulped it down and slammed it down. The Frenchmen were ready to leave, and it appeared as though they were waiting for the musicians to finish as their exit route would take them in front of the stage.

'I will follow them when they leave,' I murmured into Adam's ear.

He turned to me quickly with a look of alarm. 'No, I will go.'

'You cannot leave me here, alone.'

'Then, we must both follow them.'

'No, you should stay and observe the bearded man, or in case Sazanov arrives.' Before he could counter my argument, I put a finger to his lips and said, 'Adam,

I will only follow them and will not place myself in danger.'

He took my outstretched hand, pulled me gently but firmly to him, brushing his lips against my cheek as he murmured into my ear, 'Here, put this in your bag.'

I glanced down to see him holding a small gun in its leather pouch under the table.

'I don't think…' My automatic reaction was to refuse his offer but recalled the last time I had been ill-prepared at Rue Lauriston. Adam was right; I should take it – in case. 'Loaded?'

At his confirmation, I opened my bag and stuffed it in. The musicians had finished their latest number to a smattering of applause, allowing the three Frenchmen to edge their way past the stage and tables towards the exit. Adam helped me throw on my coat. I buttoned up, slung the bag over my shoulder, then hesitated for a moment, blew Adam a kiss and headed for the door.

I shivered and held my hat as an icy gust greeted my exit on to Avenue Hoche. The three men were crossing the road, heading North. I waited for two motor cars to pass, then followed. They turned left and then right after only twenty paces. I rounded a corner to see the last of them disappearing into a street marked Avenue Beaucour. I stopped at the entrance and feigned a problem with my shoe until a couple walking arm-in-arm passed by. The street was dark and narrow, more alley than avenue. It was unlit, save for a faint glow of light about one hundred yards away. A shape that looked like a horse and cart stood under the light, and black silhouettes of men were moving towards it.

There was little cover, except for doorways, but I was wearing my navy-blue coat and hat, and should have been inconspicuous so long as I was careful and kept my distance. I crept slowly along the north side to the third doorway, then stepped into the narrow refuge and peered along to the men about forty yards ahead. They were gathered around the cart. I heard the horse stamping and saw its steaming breath. A man held the halter, while others appeared to remove a canvas sheet from the cart. Two of the men hefted objects on to their shoulders. They were near an expanse of a high wall with no visible doorway or entrance, but they seemed to have disappeared. A light flickered. Two men left standing by the cart had lit cigarettes and were talking; laughing; sharing a joke. I couldn't catch any of the words.

At least ten minutes passed with muted conversation, another cigarette and the occasional snort of impatience from the horse. A raised voice. Movement. The other two men had re-appeared, and, after a brief exchange, they pushed, pulled and encouraged horse and cart to turn it within narrow confines. I made my way quietly and as quickly as I dared to the end of the street, turned to the right, crossed the road and stood by the window of a pharmacist. I had a good view as they emerged from Avenue Beaucour and turned left, back towards Avenue Hoche. I assumed the two men carrying objects had opened a door or a very narrow alley was hidden by the cart. I had to find out, so I retraced my steps and continued to where they had gathered. There was a small arched doorway. I tried the handle, but it was locked. I couldn't see anything on the door or on the arch to indicate what was inside the door. I considered exploring the streets nearby to try and discover where the door might lead but decided we would have better results in daylight.

I returned to *Bar L'Espoir* to find the trio still performing. I tried to make myself inconspicuous and skirted around tables until reaching Adam. My attempt at discretion was more successful than I anticipated as he hadn't noticed my approach. Adam's eyes widened with surprise when I nudged his arm and sat down.

'Entranced by the music?' I said, keeping a straight face.

'It has a certain hypnotic quality.' He turned and acknowledged my teasing with a brief smile. 'But it was something else that diverted my attention away from your entrance. I was writing you a note.'

'What is in the note?'

He considered for a few seconds before answering. 'The bearded man left the bar. I was in two minds whether to follow him. The note would have been to inform you I had followed him and would return shortly. In the end, I decided to stay and wait for your return.' He screwed up a scrap of paper, grabbed a pencil from the table and stuffed them both in a pocket. 'Well, what did you find out? You were gone for some time. Where did the Frenchmen lead you?'

'It wasn't far. They gathered in a nearby alley where there was another man with a horse and cart. Two of them carried heavy objects and disappeared through an entrance in a high wall. After they departed, I checked, and the door was locked.'

'What is on the other side?'

'I don't know. I thought it would be better to investigate in daylight.'

'The heavy objects; do you think they were barrels?'

'Possibly, but I couldn't see clearly enough to be certain.'

Adam took a deep breath and sat back in his seat. 'Barrels. They could be as innocent as barrels of beer. Or. Or they could be a source of death and destruction.'

'Some form of explosive.'

He nodded his head slowly. 'Why? Why would Sazanov…' He left his question unfinished and stared ahead in silence for a few moments. 'Come, that's enough for tonight. I will take you back to the Majestic, get a good night's sleep, and I will pick you up in the morning to explore the alley and mysterious entrance.'

Twenty-One

I slept well, although I hadn't expected a restful night. As soon as I entered my room, I was confronted by a half-written letter to John on my bedside table, abandoned when Adam called a few hours earlier. I re-read it, tore it off the notepad and threw it in the bin containing my other failed attempts. I dithered over whether to put pen to paper again, but I was too tired. I undressed and flopped on to the bed. It wasn't only the letter to John that troubled me; Adam appeared distracted when we parted in a motor-taxi outside the Majestic. No, I decided I imagined a problem where there was none. Adam had plenty on his plate, serving as an aide to General Smuts. I reasoned that I should be thankful he devoted some of his time to investigating Arthur's murder and hadn't relegated me to the side lines.

Whatever thoughts itched and nagged; they hadn't kept me awake for long. I woke shortly after seven, unprepared for sleep with makeup still applied, hair pinned, and nightdress tucked under a pillow. Just as well that I wasn't still in Edith's care, or hotel gossip would identify me, not only as a mad woman for exercising but also a wanton temptress for my nakedness in bed.

My appetite had returned with a vengeance. I breakfasted with Annie and Jane. They stared open-mouthed as I joined their table carrying a main plate piled with bacon, eggs and sausages and a side plate stacked with toast. They were in the typist pool at the Astoria when President Wilson called at the Majestic the previous day. They badgered me for every last detail on his appearance, how his wife was dressed, how many were in his entourage and any notables he met. In exchange for all the information I had, they told me how their visit to the Theatre Trianon Lyrique was spoiled because none of the music hall acts was in English. Their trial by language was cut short due to a bomb scare with cast and audience evacuated to the streets. It turned out to be a false alarm with blame attributed to the 'damned Bolshies'. Thankfully, their night was rescued by the exciting discovery of a jazz band in a nearby bar. I couldn't help but wonder if some part of me envied their innocence.

Adam entered the foyer a few minutes before nine. Any preoccupation or trouble in his thinking appeared to have dissipated as he welcomed me with a bright smile, bowed head and military click of his heels. The air was cold but dry, and with a blue sky, I was happy to agree with his suggestion that we walk to our destination at Avenue Hoche.

We arrived at the junction that led to Avenue Beaucour. We paused at the entrance. Two children were playing with hoops and sticks by a doorway twenty paces from us, but the remainder of the street was deserted. We strolled past staring children to the arched entrance in a plastered and whitewashed wall of about twenty feet in height. The door was old, formed of thick, dark wood panels ribbed with iron straps and a large keyhole that looked as though it had survived several centuries. Adam turned the iron handle. It was locked and we headed off to locate a parallel street to discover what was on the other side of the wall.

The only way to exit Avenue Beaucour was to retrace our steps. It was a short walk to Rue Daru, which ran in the same direction. We stopped at the location, approximating a direct line through to the ancient doorway.

'A church.'

'Not any old church,' I replied. 'It's Russian Orthodox.' A faded and paint-blistered wooden board displayed its name - *Cathédrale Saint-Alexandre-Nevsky*. Even without a sign, it was unmistakably Russian with its colourful domes, golden cross and the icon of a Christ figure above the central arch. 'Ahhhh.' An involuntary rush of air escaped my mouth. The recall came in a rush. 'The name. That's it.'

'What do you mean? Whose name?'

'The name scrawled by Arthur on a piece of paper next to the Rue Gustave Courbet address. It was an abbreviation for church followed by *Nevsky* – not a misspelling of Chersky, as I thought. This church must be connected in some way to their murder.'

Adam pushed at a small iron gate, and we started down a stone path towards the church entrance. The main door was closed. Adam inclined his head, and I followed him around the side. There was little ageing to the stone, and the church was clearly a relatively recent construction. Its clean vertical lines lent a dominant air with spires reaching above the tops of the buildings on either side. Did the land it occupied stretch back to Avenue Beaucour? We rounded a corner and viewed the wall, about twenty feet high, marking the rear boundary. Surely, the same wall, but

I couldn't see the doorway. The middle part of the bottom half of the wall was blocked by a squat, dilapidated construction of darker stone detached from the body of the church, and sunk into the ground with only small, shuttered windows. Much older than the church itself, I guessed it was probably used for storage.

'The doorway will be behind this old storehouse,' I said, pulling Adam's sleeve to follow me.

There it was. With only a ten-yard gap between the high wall and the building, it could only be seen close up. We retraced our steps to an open space and surveyed the scene. The old, sunken structure was the only one in the grounds with a roof apart from the church itself. Whatever was taken from the cart was likely to have been stored in there. We edged around the wall until we found the door, down a flight of stone steps. I was about to descend and check the lock on the door when Adam caught hold of my arm.

'Someone is coming.'

Two men were making for us in a manner that suggested they were not pleased. One, wearing long black robes and a white headscarf, was short, slight and bespectacled. The other, at least twice his size and with wild, staring eyes, was brandishing a large cudgel as though impatient for its use. Adam flexed his shoulders and edged forward to meet them. The two men were shouting, threatening. It looked bad. How could we avoid a bloody encounter? Quickly, I pushed past Adam and performed an elaborate curtsey.

I said, 'Bonjour messieurs, veuillez excuser nos mauvaises manières,' offering my sweetest, most innocent smile. They stopped, unsure how to react to this unexpected show of contrition. I continued, 'My boss here is an architect from America. He is most interested in the beauty of your Cathedral and wishes to incorporate some of its features into a commission he has in Texas. I realise we should have sought your permission before entering these grounds, but - he is American, doesn't speak French and has rather rough manners. Our humble apologies for any offence we may have caused.'

The clergyman held out his arm to halt the progress of his burly companion. He adjusted his spectacles, then examined Adam and me in turn before replying.

'You must leave this sacred precinct directly. Your intentions may be blameless, but this place is a target for thieves and delinquents.' His partner grunted and pointed his weapon at Adam. 'If you wish to study or sketch our church, you should put your request in writing. It will be considered in due course.'

I bowed my head and murmured thanks for his understanding. Reaching behind, I took Adam's hand and led him away, hoping he was also adopting a submissive and meek attitude. When we had gone far enough to be out of earshot, I hissed 'Don't look behind,' in English. He squeezed my hand and laughed.

'I understand enough French to appreciate your genius as an actress. That was well done, Mary.'

He gripped my hand and urged me to quicken. Once in Rue Daru and away from the boundary of the church grounds, he took my waist, twirled me around, then bowed and kissed my hand in an old-fashioned show of gallantry. It all happened so quickly; I couldn't decide how to react.

'What was that for?'

272

'For saving me a bruising encounter with the clergyman's brute of a bodyguard.'

'Oh, I don't think he would....'

'And for simply being an intoxicating mix of beauty, bravery and brains.'

I felt the heat rise in my neck and weakness in my legs. I scoffed and pushed at his chest. 'I... thank you... but...' Off guard, I didn't know what to do or say.

'Come on, let's get back to the Majestic,' he said. 'There's nothing we can do here in broad daylight.' I was saved from further embarrassment. Adam released my hand, turned and started to head back down Rue Daru. 'We return tonight.'

*

I resented inaction, waiting. Adam left me at the front of the Majestic with a polite and friendly farewell. But no more. I tried to dismiss all thoughts of Adam as a girlish fantasy. And failed. I scolded myself, ashamed when I had so recently wept over John's letter. I needed a diversion, something else to occupy my thoughts. I had a return letter to write; I couldn't; I shouldn't put it off any longer. Guilt, shame, remorse flooded my senses. Only a few days earlier, I was with John at a nightclub, idly wondering if there was an attraction between us. And now. Now, I had John's declaration from his hospital bed and in fear for his life. What had he proclaimed? Not simply a passing infatuation. Was it love? Devotion? Yes, to both. And there was I in my fancy new room at the Majestic, daydreaming about another man.

I had an envelope waiting for me in my bedroom – an unusually large one. I recognised Keynes' handwriting, and inside was a note wishing me good health and speedy recovery from all in the schoolroom. I had thought little about my work for the Treasury since my recovery, and I was surprised how much the messages from Derek, Jack and others affected me. It didn't take long to decide I should put in an appearance at Rue Leo Delibes and thank them for their good wishes.

I arrived at the school shortly after eleven. I was about to turn the handle on the front door when it opened, and Pinchin emerged. He didn't see me at first as he was adjusting his hat, and we almost collided.

'Goodness, Miss Kiten. My apologies, I didn't expect to see you here so soon after your... your....'

'Ah yes, I remember you were there when I fainted that morning.' I wondered if *fainted* was the best way to describe what happened to me. Fainting implied a certain elegance in subsiding to the floor. My admittedly hazy recollection involved a graceless crumpling and shattering of crockery.

'Indeed. It is good to see you improved so quickly.' He was edging away from me as though wary of catching my influenza.

'There is no need to worry, Mr Pinchin; I believe that I am no longer infectious.'

'Infectious – oh no, no, never crossed my mind. Must dash, I have a meeting at the Ministry of Finance.'

I had startled him, but even so, his behaviour was a little odd. Usually self-assured and ebullient in his manner, at least when he wasn't working, he seemed preoccupied and concerned about some matter. Perhaps he had a particularly thorny problem to solve. All thoughts of Pinchin vanished as I entered the schoolroom to whoops of delight and applause. I was surrounded by well-wishers and a confusion of questions.

'Cor, I thought you'd had it when you fell over in here,' said Derek.

'Made a right mess,' added Jack.

'Do I have you two to thank for taking me back to the Majestic?'

They exchanged glances. Jack took up the story. 'At first, we didn't know what to do. Me and Derek cleared up the mess and tried to get you to drink water. You were groggy but awake most of the time. Talking a load of nonsense about trains, hospitals and South America.'

'South Africa?'

'Yes, that's it, South Africa. Anyway, it was Mr Keynes who sent Derek out to get a motor taxi for you. Then me and Mr Keynes took you back to the Majestic where we called the doctor.' He glanced to his left. 'And Corporal Hincham helped, of course.'

Hincham was sitting in a leather armchair in the corner of the schoolroom, reading a newspaper. He winked at me. I returned a mock salute. Another man I didn't recognise was sitting at a desk near Hincham, puffing on a pipe.

Derek whispered, 'That's Jeff, Jeff Bruckner. He's a special agent from America.'

I nodded my understanding. I had forgotten the extra security for Keynes agreed by Colonel House. I glanced in the direction of Keynes' office to see the door opening and Keynes loping across the room towards me with a broad smile on his face.

'Miss Kiten, Mary, how good it is to see you up and about. You had us all worried.'

275

'Thank you for taking care of me after my fall, Mr Keynes. It was that new strain of influenza that seems to be sweeping through France and Belgium. I understand the hospitals here are full of those suffering from the infection.'

'It's just as bad in England, according to my mum,' said Derek. 'She says there are half a dozen from our street in hospital. My sister has even lost her fiancé. He was diagnosed with the new 'flu and died less than 48 hours later. She's devastated.' The spirits of those surrounding me were visibly dampened at these words, and a quiet descended on the room after muted words of sympathy to Derek.

Keynes signalled that I should follow him to his office. He closed the door behind me, and we took our seats at his desk, strewn with papers. Two ashtrays, a cup of tea and a pile of books completed the evidence of his recent industry.

'You look remarkably healthy, if I may say so,' announced Keynes as he took a cigarette from his silver case.

'Thank you; I have been lucky to recover so quickly. However, I must beg your indulgence as it will be a few days before I am ready to return to work.'

'Of course, I quite understand.' He lit his cigarette and sat back in his chair. 'You wouldn't know, but there was a minor scare on the Quai D'Orsay a couple of days ago. The American agent, Bruckner, tackled someone as I was about to enter the Hall of Clocks in the Ministry of Foreign Affairs. A rough-looking fellow carrying a gun was arrested. He protested his innocence and eventually was freed, although Bruckner insisted he had murder in mind.'

'Where was Corporal Hincham?'

'He was not at fault. I had instructed him to park the car while I walked a few paces to the door.'

'Do you believe there was an intention to shoot you?'

He drew heavily on his cigarette. 'Ten days ago, I would have dismissed warnings about my safety as fanciful nonsense. Now… I am more careful. Sir Basil has tightened up my security with Bruckner more visible and Hincham with orders not to let me out of his sight.'

'That must be tedious for you. Have you had any news from Chief Inspector Bonnet on the progress of his investigation?'

I knew the answer before Keynes confirmed he had heard nothing. A criminal like Fournier would have covered his tracks well and distanced himself from the incident. Even in the unlikely event of uncovering evidence to charge Fournier, would he disclose who contracted him? Did he even know the ultimate source of the conspiracy against Keynes?

My mind wandered. Keynes was talking, informing about the progress of gathering data on the costs of the war. He also outlined a paper he was writing on his experiences in Paris so far, his opinion on the Allied leaders and how a flawed treaty may impact our future wealth and wellbeing. He was enthused, animated and I understood the importance of what he was relating to me. But I was only half-listening. I remembered the meeting I had in the schoolroom with Bonnet when he broke the news about Crozier's murder. There another conversation I had with Keynes the day before. They were linked. But how? I was missing something. Had I forgotten some detail that might help discover more about Crozier's murder and the attack on Keynes?

'Miss Kiten. Mary. Are you…?'

'My apologies, Mr Keynes. Please forgive me. My illness has left me more tired than I anticipated.' I hesitated, trying to piece together the sense of his last words. 'Yes, of course, I would be delighted if you used my Christian name.'

'And the proofreading?'

'I would be pleased if you entrusted me with proofreading your latest work. It sounds to me more of a full-blown book than a short paper for an academic journal.'

'Excellent. Of course, all will depend on the outcome of this conference.' He drew on his cigarette again and admired his trio of smoke rings. 'I confess, I have little faith that our leaders will steer us to a sensible and workable solution.'

'Will you stay here and promote your views, no matter what the opposition and danger?'

He stubbed out his cigarette, placed his elbows on the desk and rested his chin on fists in a thoughtful pose. 'I have considered that question many times in the past few days. The answer is – I do not know. There are times when I could happily turn my back on all this and return to Cambridge.' He paused and re-arranged some of the papers into neat rectangles. 'Then, on reflection, I despise my cowardice and feel strength in determination to face down the opposition – political, academic and physical.'

'You should take it as a compliment that there are those who would take extreme measures to silence your views. And no one would blame you for seeking safety away from this place. You should not have to work here in fear of your life.'

'Thank you – Mary. I am sorry to burden you with my troubled thoughts. I should confide and consult with my peers, but, along with your other gifts, you have the knack of making me comfortable sharing these sentiments with you.'

I departed his office with a sense of privilege for all that Keynes had revealed to me. Despite my inattention, I had been infected with his enthusiasm for work on a paper or book about the conference. I was pleased he felt able to express his feelings about his situation in Paris. There was doubt in my mind now. Perhaps I should not have washed my hands of investigating the plot against him and left it in Bonnet's hands. I made a mental note that I would seek an answer for Keynes just as soon as Adam and I had solved the riddle surrounding Arthur's murder.

Twenty-Two

We skipped a visit to *Bar Alfredo Quinze* and took our seats in *L'Espoir* a little after nine o'clock. Our considered view was that we were more likely to encounter Sazanov or the bearded man from the previous night there. Our initial reaction was one of disappointment. Customers were scarce, and the stage looked desolate with no sign of entertainers preparing to stamp its bare boards. We spurned our table from the night before for one closer to the bar, hoping to overhear some snippet about Sazanov, Fournier or their henchmen. Our placement made little difference. It was so quiet you could hear the gurgle of liquor as the barman poured it into a glass.

We had discussed plans before leaving the Majestic. We weighed up an exploration of the building in the church's grounds before going to the bars or club. In the end, we decided to look for Sazanov first. After all, there was only a tenuous connection between him and the activities I witnessed the previous night. We would postpone our search of the church building until after midnight. Seated in *Bar L'Espoir*, I began to question our decision, and the air between us bristled with impatience. For my part, I looked forward to a return to the church grounds and I suspect Adam was of the same mind. I was also tired and conscious of aching in my limbs, serving as a reminder of my recent illness.

A TURBULENT PEACE

We departed *L'Espoir* after less than an hour. It was early to visit *Club Margot*, so we made for *Alfredo Quinze* with low expectations of coming across Sazanov or anyone else of interest there. But, to our surprise, it was much busier than *L'Espoir*. A group of around twenty men and women – at least half of them drunk - were celebrating an occasion with noisy enthusiasm. It was apparent they were all French from their words and actions. Some at nearby tables had been caught up in their high spirits, and the place was vibrating with laughter and raised voices. Adam plucked at my sleeve, and I followed to a corner table, a discreet distance from the festivities. We ordered our drinks and watched the revellers while trying to appear disinterested and unobtrusive.

A group of four men were hunched in quiet conversation at a table in the opposite corner about twenty yards distant. Nothing unusual there, except they were the only ones in the bar ignoring the party festivities. My attention was diverted by shouts of encouragement in the main group as a woman was hoisted on to a table, then joined by one of the men. They began to dance to the accompaniment of singing and clapping until the man staggered and teetered backwards. The woman grabbed him; they clung together at an odd angle, then fell heavily in slow motion into a tumble of chairs, tables and saving hands. All was quiet for a few seconds. The fallen woman rose from the melee, dusted herself down and tugged at the jacket of her partner to backslapping and cheers of relief as they emerged uninjured.

I turned away as the waiter placed our drinks on the table. We were raising glasses when an angry shout interrupted our toast. One of the men from the huddle of four was remonstrating with the merrymakers. Regardless of his large stature and air of authority, I anticipated the carousing would continue, and he would be ignored. I was mistaken. Aside from muted muttering, they recovered the chairs and sat quietly and meekly under his gaze. The change in mood was startling and sudden. I will admit the killjoy presented a formidable figure. A tall, broad-shouldered man with a scar down the left side of his face, his expression told of someone who did not expect to be crossed. Had I seen him before? The look was familiar. I turned to Adam, staring at his glass on the table with furrowed brow and an attitude that suggested he was trying to solve complex mental arithmetic.

I said, 'I may have seen that man before.' No response from Adam. 'Do you know him?'

'Fournier.'

'I beg your pardon?'

'It's Fournier, the criminal who controls this part of Paris; Estelle's pimp; the man behind the attack on Keynes; Crozier's murder; and countless other crimes, no doubt.'

'How… how do you…'

'Photographs. He features in a file Sir Basil used for security briefings when we first arrived in Paris last month. Also, Estelle showed me a photograph of him in a newspaper a few days ago.' He paused and toyed with his glass of whisky. 'He had his back to us. I only noticed him when he stood and reacted to the commotion.'

Fournier. I was so focused on watching for Sazanov, the identification of the infamous Frenchman shocked and confused. Then, I remembered. I had seen him before. He was the man who passed me at the door to the school when Keynes sent me back for his notebook. The bottom half of his face had been obscured then, but there was no mistaking the scar, the eye, his stature. Fournier – the man responsible for the attempt to silence Keynes. And what of Pinchin? He had denied Fournier's presence that evening. But Pinchin was the only one at the school. Something wasn't right. I couldn't figure out an explanation. Surely, Pinchin wouldn't be mixed up with a crook.

'Now, I am certain I have seen him before,' I said.

'Then he may recognise you. Keep your head down, and do not look at him.'

'We should leave.'

'Wait until he sits down. If he takes the same chair, he will have his back towards us.'

I feigned interest in the contents of my handbag. I examined my cocktail closely, adjusted the twist of orange and ran my finger around the sugared rim of my glass. Then it struck me as though I had been jolted awake from slumber. I remembered the conversation in Keynes' office when he asked if I had anything to report on the photographer at Rue Lauriston. Keynes overheard Pinchin questioning Derek and Jack, who had seen me talking to Crozier at the Majestic and wondered if there was a connection. So Pinchin discovered my interest in Crozier shortly before his murder. If Pinchin had an arrangement with Fournier.... It seemed madness, irrational. Could Pinchin, his deputy, be one of those conspiring against Keynes? But then, who would be in a better position to scheme and plot than someone close to Keynes. Someone who knew his movements, his arguments and how and when he planned to use them.

'Come on.'

Fournier had regained his seat, Adam started to move towards the exit, and I followed. Outside, I linked my arm into his, and we walked down Avenue Hoche into an empty shop doorway to take stock.

I said, 'Now I've seen Fournier, I think I may know the identity of one who hired him to attack Keynes.'

'Keep that for later,' he replied. 'Keep your focus on the reason we are here – to discover if there is a reason why Sazanov may have been behind the murder of Arthur Burgess and Chersky.'

He was right, of course. His reproach was light and made casually, but it hurt. I was too easily distracted from our purpose.

'The appearance of Fournier here may be no coincidence,' he said.

I nodded, thinking through the implications of Adam's suggestion. The machinations and intrigues surrounding the peace conference could have presented a glut of opportunities for Fournier. So many scores to settle, advantages to gain, and opponents to silence. Who better to do the dirty work than the chief local villain? 'Then we should stay and find out if there is a connection between Sazanov and Fournier.'

'Yes.' He moved towards me and drew me in, wrapping me in his arms. 'It's cold tonight. Perhaps we should return to the bar.'

I was about to voice my opinion when two large and stylish motor cars pulled up outside *Bar Alfredo Quinze*. Eight men disembarked, every one wearing a fur hat suggesting they were Russian. Was that him in the centre? They filed into the bar. It was too brief a glimpse to be sure.

'Do you think that was…?'

'It could be.'

We returned to the entrance. Adam signalled I should wait while he looked inside. He was back in a short time.

'Well?'

'Yes, it's Sazanov, and he was shaking hands with Fournier. You can't get better confirmation of an arrangement between them than that.' He pointed to a bar on the other side of the street. 'Let's retreat and review our options.'

A small, narrow bar suited our purpose; quiet, with a vacant table by the window. Against my better judgement, I ordered a cognac. 'To warm your body and clear your mind,' were Adam's persuasive words. It tasted awful, but it stopped my shivering.

'Shall we abandon plans for the church building tonight?' I asked.

'I don't see why.'

'Shouldn't we see what Sazanov is up to?'

'It's too dangerous for you to go back in the same bar as Fournier. If he recognises you, or one of his men remembers you from Rue Lauriston, then …' He placed his hand on mine and shook his head. 'No, we should stick to our plan. Besides…'

'What?'

'The man following Sazanov into *Bar Alfredo* a few minutes ago was our bearded friend from the other night. So, whatever was arranged when you followed the men to their assignation with a horse and cart, is likely to involve Sazanov.'

We kept faith with the other part of our plan – to wait until after midnight before making any attempt to enter the church grounds. It was an arbitrary time limit, but I held a strong sense of an unspoken agreement between us that we should abide by it. So, we waited and watched by the window of our quiet, anonymous spot across the street from *Bar Alfredo*. Fournier left first. A motor car stopped outside the bar for the four Frenchmen. Sazanov's group was only a few minutes behind as they exited the bar and marched along Avenue Hoche to *Club Margot*. With Fournier gone, should we adjust our schedule? It was almost midnight, and, after a brief consultation, we agreed to put aside a visit to *Club Margot* in favour of Saint-Alexandre-Nevsky church. As we stepped out into the bitter cold air, the first few flakes of snow began to fall. Had we made the right choice?

The snow was not our friend. Footprints would reveal our route, and we would be more visible against a white background in the dark alley and the churchyard. But if we were quick, we could reach shelter before there was a significant covering.

We passed Avenue Beaucour and turned right into Rue Daru, which was clear of pedestrians. The gate to the church was padlocked, but the iron railings were low enough for Adam to vault over. Then he reached, grabbed me under my arms and hoisted me over before I had time to protest or gather my skirts – graceless but effective. The thin layer of snow lent an unnatural hush to the air as we crept to a corner of the church and peered around to ensure we were alone.

We trod carefully and in silence to the storage building. There was no light from inside. Our next challenge was the lock on the door down the sunken stairwell. Adam had brought a trench torch with him, which he shone on the door when we reached the foot of the stairs. It was locked with a chain and small padlock. I hadn't thought how we might overcome locked doors. I suppose I assumed that Adam would use brute force to gain entry.

'Hairpin?' he whispered.

'Hairpin? What... oh, sorry, I see.' I reached back, removed a pin from near the nape of my neck and handed it to Adam. I held the torch while he poked and prodded the padlock. I was surprised when it opened easily in a matter of seconds.

'Where did you learn to do that?'

'Never mind.' He answered. 'Have you got your gun?'

'Yes.'

'A knife?'

'Aye, aye, sir.'

The door scraped and creaked. Too loud. Slowly. We squeezed inside a crack in the open door barely wide enough to fit Adam. Holding our breath, we halted, checked all was still and silent, then inch-by-inch closed the door. A smell immediately gripped my senses, an acrid, pungent scent that stung the back of my throat. Adam pressed the lever on his torch. The space was big, too big for the feeble light of the torch to illuminate more than a fraction of the interior. What appeared to be oiled sheets were piled over two mounds to our left. On our right side were blocks of stone, a jumble of ironware and reams of coiled rope. Storage for stonemasons, I assumed. Adam handed me the torch and heaved at the oiled sheets. They were heavy, and it took some grunting and pulling before he uncovered one of the mounds. Barrels; five of them.

I put a gloved hand to my mouth. 'What is that terrible whiff? It reeks.'

'Ammonia.'

'So... does that mean they contain some sort of explosive?' In my mind, barrels were associated with either beer or bangs. Ever since I overheard the word 'barils' in *Bar L'Espoir*, I had been dreading a discovery of explosives, having seen too much of the grisly damage inflicted on the human body from bombs, mines, grenades and various other explosive devices. The last thing I wanted was a close encounter with those barrels. I shuddered, my knees trembled, and an icy chill pricked my toes, fingers and face.

'Yes, probably some mix of ammonium nitrate.' He lifted the sheets on the other mound to reveal more barrels. 'That is a hell of a lot of high explosives – maybe a dozen barrels.'

'Who would... what could be their purpose... and the target?' I struggled to form words to express my disgust at the intended use of the barrels.

'Who knows, but we should inform the police straight away so they can seal this place off and render the barrels harmless.' He lifted his torch and shone an arc around where we stood. At least one half of the building remained cloaked in darkness. 'We should get out of here, Mary; it's too dangerous. High explosives like ammonal and amatol are unstable.'

'Wait.' I sniffed the air. There was something else in the air - the putrid stench of human waste.

'Come on.'

'If we go now and the police clean up this place, we may foil whatever destruction is planned, but we don't solve the murders. We can't touch Sazanov and Fournier for this.'

'And we can't do anything about them if we are blown sky-high. I don't like it here.'

'Neither do I.' I took a couple of steps into the dark and sniffed again. 'Hand me your torch, Adam. I will be quick. I just want to check over here. It stinks. Can't you smell it?'

There was nothing in the centre to hinder my progress. I made my way slowly towards the far wall. On my right were more blocks of stone. The stench was getting stronger. I followed my nose to a break in the blocks of stone. I moved closer and shone the torch on a bundle of rags, ropes and chains. I put a handkerchief to my mouth and kicked at the rags with my foot. Nothing. Something small and metallic nestled on a soiled woollen blanket. It looked like a tin cup. I picked it up between thumb and forefinger. A spoon was inside. I replaced them carefully on the blankets, and then I noticed a bucket in the corner. Ugh! I had found the source of the stink.

Adam hissed a warning to hurry. I turned to head back, took a step and froze. Had I imagined it? A noise. A low moaning. A groan. Again. I bent and picked at the heap of rags. Something moved. I shifted a heavy layer of rough, damp wool and shone the torch. I scrabbled at the pile with more urgency. More muted sounds. A human voice? Ah! I lurched back. Shock. Disbelief. I called to Adam and held the torch to light his way.

'What is it?' He was impatient, exasperated with my delay.

'A man.'

'What the hell…?'

I knelt and shone the torch at a face - an unkempt, bruised, unshaven face coated in grime. A hand was shielding eyes from the light of the torch. The wrist was manacled and chained. Adam joined me, picked up the chain and followed it to a block of stone. Two lengths of chain were fixed fast in the rock. Both wrists were manacled, and it seemed the chain length gave enough movement to use the bucket.

'Who are you?' I asked.

The only response was an unintelligible croak and feeble attempts with an arm to re-cover himself with the rags I had loosened. I searched for his feet. I found one, then the other, both covered in filthy socks. Mercifully, his ankles were not chained or tied with rope.

'Help me, Adam. His flesh is icy cold. We must cover him well until we can free him.'

He grabbed and hoisted what could have been the man's tattered jacket so that I could place blankets underneath the stone floor; then, we wrapped him tightly. The blankets and cloths were damp and soiled but better than nothing. I put my fingers to his neck, searching for a pulse. It was there but faint.

'Here, try this.' Adam handed me a leather pouch.

Why? I looked closer, and the pouch opened to reveal a small, silver hip flask. I opened it and inhaled. Whisky. Normally, I would run a mile to escape the fumes, but it was heavenly, overpowering all the other odours around me. I knelt on the floor, grabbed a bundle of cloths with one arm, put the other under his body and tried to lift him. He wasn't heavy, but his cocooned bulk was awkward, and Adam had to assist before we had the upper half of his body upright and ready to drink. I put the flask to his lips and urged him to drink. There was no reaction. His eyes were shut, and he appeared to be asleep or unconscious. I slapped his face gently and tried again, pouring a few drops between his lips. There – movement. His lips twitched, the tip of a tongue searched for traces of nectar. I poured a little more. Too much. His body convulsed and a croaking, wheezing noise was his attempt to cough. His eyes opened. I waited until the spasms subsided and he seemed settled.

'Who are you? What is your name?'

He tried to speak. I put my ear to his mouth.

'What did he say?' asked Adam.

'Brinkov. His name is Georgi Brinkov.'

Twenty-Three

I shone the torch on one of Brinkov's wrists. 'Can you unlock his manacles?'

'Probably, but it will not be quick.' Adam guided me a couple of paces away from Brinkov and said, in a low voice, 'We must leave him.'

'We cannot, not like this. He is barely alive.' I couldn't see Adam's face but could sense his impatience, his exasperation. 'You should go and fetch help, now.'

'I can't leave you here, Mary.'

'We should…' I tugged at Adam's sleeve to bring him closer, so I could whisper in his ear. 'We should try to get him to talk and find out what he knows while there is… still time.'

'Then I will stay with him while you go for help.'

'No, it must be me who stays here. Can you imagine a lone woman running through dark, icy streets of this city and at this hour? You will be quicker. And I… I will be better tending to his needs.'

He was not a man to dither and waste time over a decision. His torment was almost tangible as logic fought for the upper hand over sentiment. I reached up, drew him in close so that our foreheads touched and said, 'Go now. We will be here when you return.'

He was still for a second, stood, took a few steps, hesitated, then quickened towards the door. Should I have said more? Had I forgotten something important?

'Rue du Faubourg Saint-Honoré will be the closest... Préfecture... de... Police.' My voice trailed away to a whisper. He had already gone. All was quiet. Still. I shivered. Cold and... afraid.

I rearranged my coat and skirts so that I could kneel and tuck my legs underneath. Then, I tugged and pushed at Brinkov, gently but firmly, until his head rested on my knees. I placed the torch so I could see his face.

'Are you comfortable?'

A faint sound came back, which I took as an affirmative.

'Would you like some more whisky?'

'Who...' a croaking noise followed. I waited. 'Who are... you?'

'My name is Mary Kiten. Arthur Burgess was my – uncle.' He tried to say something I couldn't understand. 'We have met with Madame Chersky.'

I showed him the hip flask. He nodded his approval, a trembling hand reached for it, and his mouth twitched in anticipation. I raised his head, and he sipped, hesitantly at first, then with such urgency that I had to restrain his eagerness and ration his intake. Eventually, he loosened his grip on the flask, and his head sank back on to my lap. He had managed to drink without coughing. I brushed away a straggle of hair and stroked his head to offer some reassurance and comfort. The light from the torch was getting fainter, and I switched it off to save whatever life was left for when it may be needed.

'No! Please. Light.' There was panic in his voice. His hands shook.

I switched the torch on again. 'This light will fade, but my friend will be back soon with more light.' I paused until his breathing slowed, and he seemed to have regained some composure. 'Do you know why you are being held here?' No reply. 'Mr Brinkov, are you…?' He groaned and mumbled something. 'What was that? Please repeat it.'

'Sazanov. His… doing.'

'Have you heard other names? A Frenchman?'

'Yes. Many… French…'

'Is there a man named Fournier among them?'

'Yes. Fournier and…' He gasped for air.

I placed my hand on his head, 'hushed' and 'tushed' and made other soothing noises until he calmed down.

'Why are you imprisoned here?'

'For… for the…' something unintelligible followed.

'Please repeat.'

'For the… boom. The big… bang.'

That made no sense. Why would Brinkov be chained in that place, waiting for the barrels of explosives to be detonated?

'Do you know where the big bang will be? What do they intend to blow up?'

He turned his head. The whites in his eyes showed wide and staring. 'Wilson… at… the Murat….'

'You mean…'

'President Wilson… yes.'

I clawed at the edge of an understanding. A scheme so outrageous, so devious, it was unbelievable. But what other explanation made any sense? 'Mr Brinkov – Georgi – are you saying that Fournier, acting for

Sazanov, intends to blow up President Wilson's residence?'

'Yes… yes.'

'And have you been kept alive so that your body will be found at the scene of the explosion, as evidence of Bolshevik guilt?'

'Yes… da, da.' He managed a feeble wave of a hand to emphasise his affirmation. 'Yes.' His eyes closed, and I felt his body sag, as though the effort of talking had exhausted him.

There it was. Now the words had been spoken and confirmed; it no longer felt extreme or implausible. From there, it was only a short step to recognise that Arthur and Chersky had been murdered because somehow they had learned of the conspiracy. The torch light had faded to a pale grey. I became aware of a chill ache in my bones as a reminder that I was not wholly free from influenza's lingering effects. How long had Adam been gone? My situation suddenly seemed more perilous. I was cradling the failing body of a Bolshevik in a dark shed full of volatile explosives in the middle of a mid-winter night. I prayed Adam would return quickly. A rough mental calculation told me he was unlikely to return for at least another twenty minutes. Too long. The wait would feel like an age.

I shifted my legs to try and ease their ache, closed my eyes and let my thoughts wander, hoping for reassuring and pleasant distraction. A face. John. I still had a letter to write. I shook my head, screwed my eyes tight and willed John to recover from his illness. I still couldn't shake the feeling of guilt whenever John came to the front of my thoughts. I tried to cast my mind back to happier times as a young girl in the company of mother and father, on holiday; in

Germany; a ski resort; in Paris. And then; the war. It was no good. My head would not rid itself of images related to danger, illness and death.

I counted the minutes. Seven. Eight. Nine. Voices. Someone was coming. Could it be Adam, or was it too quick? I turned off the torch. My body shivered. I held my breath and balled both fists. There were at least two voices, perhaps three, and they were speaking in French. Were they police, or…? I soon had my answer as an exchange of complaining and swearing prefaced scraping and a thud as the door opened and light flooded the interior. They cursed as the open door, first accusing each other and then - suspicion. I opened my bag and slowly withdrew my gun. I knew I couldn't fire it. Too dangerous with high explosives only yards away. Where was my knife? If they ventured beyond the barrels to check on Brinkov, I would be in plain sight. I dare not move and, even if I could scrabble away unseen, where would I hide?

'Over here,' one of them called. 'This cover has been removed.'

'Someone was here.'

'Or is here now.' A third, authoritative voice announced. 'Come,' it ordered.

I could hear footsteps, but all I could see were two sources of light moving in my direction. With my head bowed, arms crossed, and body hunched forward, I tried to make myself as small as possible. But I knew that wouldn't do and prepared for the inevitable.

'Eh bien, qu'avons-nous ici?'

I looked up. The light dazzled. 'Keep your distance. I have a gun.' I pointed it towards the light.

Quiet for a moment and then - laughter – sneering, triumphant laughter.

'You must know you cannot fire that gun, Mademoiselle.' A pause. 'It would mean your certain death.' A longer pause. 'Besides, who would you shoot?' The lights moved apart. A glimpse of a shadow moving quickly. Two lights, three voices. Where was…?

Rough hands grabbed my arm. No… Blinded. Dazzled. Black. A thump and crack on the side of my head. I sprawled on the floor, a knee on my back, my wrist in a vice, neck twisted. My gun had gone. Couldn't breathe.

'Got her.'

'Let me see.'

An arm was pulled, and the neck of my coat wrenched back. I was choking, coughing, a sharp tang of bile in my throat. A fierce tug at my hair loosened the pins. My hat was lost. Feet scrabbled, and somehow I was upright with both my arms held tight behind my back. An urge to vomit hit me. I clamped my mouth. A face was near mine, staring at me. A leering, grinning, ugly mask of a face with a scar across one eye. Fournier.

'Ha! You - English woman from the Majestic.' He pulled another man from his right to look directly at my face. I flinched at rancid breath. 'Is this the one who shot Maxim at Rue Lauriston?'

'Yes, that's her, boss.'

'So, it is you.' His face drew closer. I wanted to close my eyes and turn away but forced myself to stare back. 'Why are you here?' Spittle formed at the corner of his mouth. 'Why should this worthless Bolshevik interest you?' He kicked at Brinkov's prone body.

I clenched my teeth. The bile was rising in my throat. 'We… found him.'

297

'We? Who are we? You are alone.'

'The others will be back here soon.' I spat sour dregs from my mouth at his feet.

'Shall I kill her now?' said the man holding my arms. 'We should be gone from here in case she speaks the truth.'

Fournier wrinkled his nose as though considering his man's proposal.

'You are too late,' I said. 'And it will do you no good. We know all about you and Sazanov.'

'What?' He frowned and grabbed my chin in a gloved hand. 'You two - outside. Make sure the door to Beaucour is locked and watch the path from the church. Go!'

Was it a mistake to alert them? The man behind let go of my arms. I tensed. Should I run? Too late. My eye caught the light on a glint of steel. A sharp point pricked my throat. I tried to take a step back, but he grabbed my shoulder.

'Keep still, or I will stick this blade in your neck.' I did as he said. He was too big and strong to risk a struggle. 'Now, tell me what you know about the Russian gentleman you mentioned.'

I tried to speak, but the knife point was pressed under my raised chin. I gurgled, pointed, and he moved it a little. 'You work for him. We know about your murders and plans to use explosives.'

'You say "we" again. Who knows, apart from you?'

'I was not here alone.' I had to spin a convincing story out for as long as possible. If I were not believed or offered no value, he would kill me without a second thought. Of that much, I was sure. 'There were four of us. Some military.'

'Four.' I could sense he teetered on the edge of doubt. He pressed forward. The knife stung. I was cut and could feel a trickle of blood. 'Where are they now? And why would they leave you, a young woman, in a position of such danger?'

'They will be back soon. You can ask them yourself.' I had to say more. 'Some went for the police. Others...' I strained to keep my neck away from his knife. 'Others have gone for help with bomb disposal. At the Astoria, there are - soldiers with experience of explosives.'

'Even if...' He stopped suddenly and lifted his head at a noise – a muffled cry of what: surprise; warning; pain? I held my breath in an unnatural quiet for a few moments. Fournier snatched at my hair, turned me around, crooked his arm around my neck and switched off his torch. I felt the point of his knife prodding into my back. Then another, different, noise from outside; this time a dull thud. He pushed me forward a couple of steps towards the door. A small light flickered outside, then unfurled and spread as the door opened. The silhouette of a man. But who was it?

'Mary, are you there?'

I tried to cry out his name, but all that came was a sharp breath of air. My body sagged as relief eased the tension in my body. How had he dealt with Fournier's men? Why was he alone? The Frenchman clamped a hand around my mouth and shouted, 'Who are you?'

'I am the man who will kill you if you have harmed her.'

Fournier kicked at my legs, forcing me to kneel. He snatched at a clump of my hair and yanked my head back. The cold blade was at my neck again. He turned on his torch and shone it in my face.

'See, she is here. You can have her, but if you want this pretty little neck in one piece, you will do as I say.'

Adam stood, motionless and mute.

'Shine the light on your face and walk towards me,' called Fournier. 'Slowly. Any false move, and I will kill you both.'

He didn't move. Adam's French was rough and ready, at best. Did he understand? Fournier barked his instruction again. Slowly, Adam raised his torch and turned it on himself. He walked towards us. When he was about five paces away, Fournier shouted, 'Stop.' Switched his torch light from me to Adam. 'Hold out your hands so that I can see.'

The left hand was empty. His right was bloody, and he held a knife.

'Drop it.'

Adam stared, his face impassive. After a few seconds, he opened his hand, and the knife clattered on the stone floor. 'Now let her go. She can't stop you.'

'Not yet. First, we must make sure you cannot follow me.' He swivelled the light of his torch to our left. 'Turn to your right. See those chains on top of that block of stone.' He paused. 'I want you to place the manacles around your wrists.'

'Why would I do that?'

I felt him stiffen. A sharp breath. 'I will cut her.'

Thoughts raced. Must be prepared.

'With what? You have the light in my eyes. I cannot see.'

'You…'

'Here, have this.'

Adam threw his torch at Fournier. I screwed my head back and flung my body to the left. Elbow jarred.

Lights scattered. A blurred image of outstretched arms. Grunts. A clash of bodies.

Straining, grappling, juddering. Movement at the edge of my vision.

Cursing. All chaos. Must get… Adam's knife. Dark. Light gone.

The knife. I had it. A torch. I grabbed it.

Breathing, shouting and - a shriek.

Grunting. Panting, gasping, choking.

Gurgling.

Choking.

And then silence.

I pressed the switch and pointed the torch and knife at… a shadow. I was disoriented. Where was he? A man standing with his back to me. Was it…?

'Adam?' I cried.

He turned. 'Yes.'

'Where? Where is…?'

'Fournier. Here.' He pointed to a crumpled figure lying face down in a pool of black liquid. The head was twisted, an arm bent at a grotesque angle.

'Is he…?' I didn't need to ask.

'Yes, he is dead.'

I dropped the knife. My hands were trembling. Tried to take a step towards Adam. Couldn't move. Heavy legs were fixed. Then he was with me, my head pressed against his heaving chest. I clutched tight to smells of wool, sweat and blood. 'Thank you, thank you,' I murmured again and again. He held me and spoke some words I heard without processing their meaning. A thought jolted. 'Where are Fournier's men?'

'I dealt with both.' He took a breath. 'They will not trouble us.'

I raised my head and pushed his shoulder so that I could see his face. 'Where are the police?' Words dissolved in a gasp of air. Couldn't comprehend. 'Why are you alone?'

'It was taking too long; couldn't wait; sprinted back.' He placed his hands on my arms and waited until his breathing calmed. 'The police will be here soon – I hope. There was no urgency at the station. It was taking too long to make them understand my story. I was worried and should never have left you. So, in the end, I scribbled a note for Inspector Bonnet and ran back here.'

I said, 'He talked. Brinkov knew what they intended to blow up and why he was kept alive. It is shocking.'

'I know you don't want to leave him, but we can't do anything more for Brinkov now. And I would be much happier if we waited outside this building.'

*

It was another half hour before the police arrived. We wandered around the church grounds, moving between the doorway on Avenue Beaucour and the front of the church on Rue Daru, unsure where the police would arrive. We barely spoke, thoughts tied up in replaying and unravelling events of the last few hours. Our brief exchanges were about Brinkov, me wanting to check his wellbeing, Adam placating and preventing me from entering the building. In truth, our impatient meandering in the church grounds often took us so close to the explosives we were no safer than inside with Brinkov.

With some relief, I recognised the lumbering figure of Bonnet as he emerged from a motor car on Rue Daru. For all his apparent pedantry, I knew he would act without undue delay and with an understanding of our situation. His appearance and demeanour showed he had been dragged from his bed, but all drowsiness and resentment vanished at the mention of Fournier's death. He gaped as we took it in turns to relate our story from the connection between Sazanov and Fournier; discovery of high explosives; The murders of Arthur and Chersky; the imprisonment of Brinkov; and finally, to the bloody encounter with Fournier and his henchmen. Thankfully, Bonnet didn't waste time on questioning for fine details at that stage. He ordered reinforcements and ambulances, then secured the church grounds before examining the scene himself. Only when the three bodies had been recovered, Brinkov had been transported to a hospital, and the barrels of explosives assigned to the care of a contingent of soldiers, were we taken to Bonnet's office to explain events in full.

Twenty-Four

It was almost six o'clock when our interview with Bonnet drew to a close. The last hour had been taken up with a discussion on when, where and to whom we should present our findings. I took little interest in the conversation, being physically tired and mentally drained. My sole contribution of note was that Bonnet should accompany Adam and me to participate in what they were now referring to as a briefing. Adam agreed immediately, and Bonnet took only a little persuasion. We reasoned that including a statement from a senior officer in the French police may give more weight to our findings. As to the other matters, it was decided that representatives of the major Allied powers should hear what we had to say as soon as possible, preferably that very day. Only the "where" question was unresolved.

Adam and I adjourned to the Astoria with a promise to telephone Bonnet as soon as a place and time were set. I begged to be excused a consultation with General Smuts so that I could rest and close my eyes for an hour. Adam offered a bed in his room next door to Smuts, and I accepted gladly.

My one-hour rest stretched to almost four, and it was after ten o'clock when I was woken by Edith, my one-time nursemaid from the Majestic. Baffled and unsettled by my strange surroundings, I wondered if memories that flickered at the surface of consciousness were the remnants of a dream. But, so vivid, they seemed real. How could I resolve the doubt? I was lying on the top of a bed, full-clothed. My coat was filthy, dress torn, and my head hurt like hell. Then recall came in a rush: the bar; the church building; Brinkov; Fournier; blood. I shivered; my body convulsed and puckered itself into a foetal position.

'You alright, Miss?'

'Yes… thank you.' I remembered Adam's room. Where had he gone? 'What are you doing here, Edith?'

'Mr Visser brought me here, Miss. Said you needed a hand to get bathed and dressed. Also, you had some cuts and bruises that needed seeing to.' I put a hand to my forehead. No blood there, but it felt tender to the touch. 'He's very handsome if you don't mind me saying. Mr Visser that is. From the way he fussed, I'd say he's quite sweet on you. If you pardon me for telling.'

'Yes, thank you, Edith. I'm pleased you told me. Now, if you would help…'

'Oh, and another thing. I nearly forgot. A very important conference has been arranged at the Crillon Hotel for noon. Mr Visser and General Somebody – sorry, can't remember his name – will meet you in the foyer at eleven-thirty sharp.'

Edith's assistance was a blessing. A hot bath was waiting, she had brought a selection of clothes from my room at the Majestic, and her first aid kit was put to good use. I had bruising and a graze around my right temple that no amount of makeup could disguise. But the rest, including sore ribs, bruised elbow, cut and grazed knees and minor knife wounds, would be hidden from general view. I could never have transformed from a sore, bedraggled and broken specimen to the well-groomed, perfumed and sprightly image I presented in the mirror at twenty minutes after eleven without her in attendance.

They were stood together in the grand, marbled reception to the Astoria. Smuts dipped his head in acknowledgement, while Adam smiled, took my hand, kissed it, then led me to a waiting motor car in the street outside.

'Is it all arranged?' I asked when we were all seated.

'I believe we will have a decent turnout, despite the short notice,' answered Smuts.

The phrase *decent turnout* struck me as odd, more appropriate for an entertainment than a security briefing. However, I ignored it as there was something important I had to ask. 'Have you heard about Brinkov? Does he live still? Do they think he will recover?'

'He is in a critical care unit, but expected to survive, so we have been informed,' answered Adam. He continued, 'You should be aware of a decision made while you were resting.' His tone was ominous, suggesting he had unwelcome news.

'Oh yes.'

'General Smuts and Chief Inspector Bonnet will be the only speakers. They will report the findings with a broad, non-specific approach. You and I will remain anonymous, Mary. We will not be introduced and will stand to one side. If anyone asks, you are there as an aide to Sir Basil Thomson.'

'Good.'

'Are you not surprised and annoyed. Don't you want your part in this… this courageous prevention of a major conspiracy to be recognised?'

'I am pleased. The meeting will have a political agenda, and I have little to contribute to politics. I am more interested in justice for the people involved.' The last two years of the war had drained my emotions and left me feeling disconnected and hardened to the world around me. My time in Paris had seen a re-awakening of spirit. I had felt fear, excitement, disgust, passion, loathing and, perhaps, love; all the extremes. I was alive again. It had become more than a quest to avenge the murder of 'Uncle' Arthur. Now those behind his killing had been identified, and I had witnessed the end of some of the perpetrators; there was quiet satisfaction but no elation. My experience had left me with a distaste for those associated with the Tsarist factions and sympathy for the Bolsheviks. But I knew that was no basis for alignment with a particular set of political ideals.

In the corner of my vision, I saw Smuts and Adam exchange a meaningful glance. Was it approval, censure, or some other assessment? It seemed that I had been a subject of discussion while asleep, and I couldn't decide whether I was flattered or offended.

Attendants surrounded our car at the Crillon, and a sharp-suited man, who I guessed was the hotel manager, made a great fuss of Smuts before guiding us to a doorway guarded by two American soldiers. Inside, the room was dominated by highly polished tables in a rectangular formation. I counted sixteen place settings, each with paper, pen, decanter and glass, arranged in perfect symmetry. Sir Basil was stood in conversation with two men I didn't recognise.

Smuts and Adam joined them while I drifted to a corner. Two more men entered, followed by waiters offering drinks. I turned my back and stared out of a window, wishing I wasn't there. How long would I remain in Paris? I smiled at thoughts of Mother and her bustling concern. I wanted to see her, but did I want to make my home in Whitstable again?

'Hello, Mary. It's a surprise to see you here. I wonder if your presence means this is not going to be one of those run-of-the mill briefings?'

'Sandra, it's good to see you again.' We kissed in the manner of politeness. 'I'm here to assist Sir Basil Thomson and I'm afraid I can't help with your query as this is the first briefing I've attended.'

After a few pleasantries, she remarked on the bruising around my eye, which I blamed on an accident in my bathroom. It was a poor excuse and not believed. To avoid further awkwardness, I steered the conversation away from events in the past few weeks to Max, her fiancé back at Princeton. She soon warmed to the subject, and it was clear from the way she spoke that the excitement of Paris had begun to fade. A tall man with slick, black hair approached us and introduced himself as Georges Mandel, explaining he had been asked to represent Clemenceau. Sandra took him to meet Colonel House, who was talking with Lord Balfour. Between them was a familiar face, but whose name escaped me. Behind them, Bonnet was standing in the doorway with an expression of bemusement. His face lit up with relief when he saw me. I signalled to Adam, and we both went to greet him. We ushered him to a quiet corner where Adam answered his questions on the identity of those he didn't recognise. The name of the man I thought familiar turned out to be the new Minister of War, Churchill, standing in for Lloyd George, who had returned to London for a few days. Smuts rapped the table three times, asked those assembled to take their seats, and signalled for Bonnet to join him. Adam stood to the side of Smuts while I took my place a few paces behind Sir Basil at the other end of the room.

Smuts opened by stating that what was to follow was a confidential briefing for those with the two highest levels of security clearance. He followed with a short speech on the 'Russian Question' as a prelude to news about to be disclosed. When he mentioned a conference on an island called Prinkipo to which the various Russian factions had been invited, there was a swell of grumbling and raised voices. Next, Smuts introduced Bonnet and whetted the audience's appetite by declaring the French police had foiled a plot against Woodrow Wilson as well as identifying the suspect of the murder of a senior British civil servant. Bonnet took over and started by outlining the circumstances surrounding the murder of Arthur and Chersky. His delivery was deadpan, which oddly seemed to give the crimes an extra edge of malevolence. He followed with a brief history of the activities of Fournier, his short imprisonment in 1908 and, since that date, an increase in power, wealth and range of illegal activities. He was disarmingly honest in ascribing the inability to convict and imprison Fournier to police corruption and witness intimidation. His account of the arrangement between Sazanov and Fournier was met with muttering and shaking of heads.

In contrast, the discovery of explosives and the imprisonment of Brinkov was heard in stunned silence. He described the bloody encounter with

Fournier and the testimony of Brinkov in such a detached and matter-of-fact manner that it felt disconnected from my own experience. Bonnet finished with his contention that Burgess and Chersky had been murdered because they had learned of the plot against Woodrow Wilson.

Smuts' invitation to ask questions was met with an uncomfortable quiet. Someone struck a match to light a cigarette, and an Italian named Sonnino, stood, bowed his head briefly to Smuts and exited the room without a word. Mandel, the Frenchman, was the first to speak. He wanted to know more detail on the nature of the arrangement between Sazanov and Fournier. *Was it documented? Had Sazanov been questioned?* Bonnet's answer that he had signed testimony from Brinkov corroborated by other independent witnesses received an exclamation of derision and a spate of muttering. *Who were the witnesses? Why couldn't their identity be revealed?* Half an answer, interrupted by another question. *What was the explosive, and how much was recovered?* Initial indications pointed to Ammonal. A substantial quantity; the precise amount... *How strong was the evidence to suggest that President Wilson was the target?* Answers were drowned out by exchanges and arguments developing among the audience.

Eventually, Smuts banged his table and called, 'Order, please'. When the room quietened, he said, 'Gentlemen, let me remind you; this is a briefing only, not a court of law. This Congress has to consider many important matters and, up to the present time, more hours have been devoted to discussing the situation in Russia than any other. The report provided by Chief Inspector Bonnet is for your information. You may wish to consider this when forming an opinion on the various proposals offering a solution to the Russian Question. That is all – no more, no less.'

Churchill rose from his seat, gazed around the tables to make sure he had everyone's attention, then said, 'Thank you, General.' He paused and turned to Bonnet. 'You are to be congratulated on the elimination of a major criminal in this city, Chief Inspector. But as for Sergei Sazanov, I choose to disregard any possibility of his participation in the conspiracy you outlined. All you have to implicate him is hearsay, and the testimony of a Bolshevik named Brinkov. Surely, no one in this room still believes that the word of a Bolshevik can be trusted.' He adjusted his tie, buttoned his jacket, said, 'Good day to you all,' and marched to the door.

Churchill's exit signalled the end of the briefing. Balfour and Mandel were the next to leave. Colonel House shook hands with Bonnet and Smuts, then engaged them in conversation. Sandra approached me with an expression of disbelief.

'Did you have anything to do with this, Mary? I never imagined…' She took hold of my hands. 'When you asked all those questions about Russians.'

'I simply passed on the information. Others did the hard work.' We moved aside to let others pass and exit the room. 'What do you think will be decided about the Russians? I was surprised at the lack of interest here in Sazanov's plan. It was treated as though it was an inconvenience, better forgotten and put aside. Surely, he and his faction will not be forgiven for scheming to bring death and destruction down on your President and those around him?'

At the edge of my vision, I saw Sir Basil look our way, hesitate briefly, then turn, heading for the exit. I wondered if he wanted to speak to me, but I couldn't escape from Sandra, who was answering my question.

'… Prinkipo will not go ahead. Our President favours self-determination and limited involvement in the affairs of other countries. But he is also a pragmatist and has yielded to increasing pressure back home to support the White Russians and crush the Bolsheviks. Your Prime Minister is in a similar situation. Churchill is a fervent anti-Bolshevik. The French and the Italians opposed Prinkipo from the outset.' She shrugged. 'Time has moved on. Now, there is probably no need for Sazanov to stage a dramatic incident to discredit the Bolsheviks. I am sure it is not what you want to hear, but there you have it.'

'So… Sazanov will not be held accountable for the murders committed and conspiracy to commit more. Even if he didn't have to go through with his plan to… The very fact that he…' I couldn't find the right words to express my disgust. 'It is… unjust… incredible.'

'I regret it is the grubby reality of politics. I have seen too much of it here and will be glad when I leave this city.'

I was perplexed; I couldn't understand how any of the Allied powers could trust Sazanov and all he represented. But that was only a dull ache compared to keen hurt at the thought of the man behind Arthur's murder escaping any form of punishment.

Only Bonnet, Adam and I remained in the briefing room. I uttered the first few words of an apology to Bonnet for his ill-mannered and belligerent reception before a hand was raised to halt my progress. It transpired that Smuts and Adam had beaten me to it, and Bonnet was unperturbed.

'Please, do not concern yourself with my feelings, Mademoiselle Kiten. I am more than content that a malign presence has been removed from our streets. I, and the residents of these arrondissements, owe you a great debt of gratitude.'

I considered for a heartbeat and said, 'In that case, allow me to beg a favour. You can consider the debt repaid in full if you would accompany Mr Visser and me to the school on Rue Leo Delibes.'

Twenty-Five

We entered the schoolroom to a scene of academic industry. Foreheads frowned in concentration, eyes stared downward, with pens poised. Hincham had his head buried deep in a newspaper, and a blue haze of unnoticed cigarette smoke hovered around the electric lights. Not a murmur at our intrusion was heard until Jack muttered a surprised, 'Mary', then eight pairs of eyes followed our progress to the door of Keynes' office. I knocked, Keynes looked up from his desk, gaped with mild surprise at our deputation, then signalled we should enter.

'Good afternoon Mary, and gentlemen. You are, of course, welcome. I hope you will forgive me if I say that your sudden appearance has an ominous chime. Is it good or bad news?'

'I suppose you could say it's both,' I answered. 'You know Chief Inspector Bonnet. Have you met Mr Visser?'

'Indeed, I am acquainted with you both, gentlemen.'

Hands were shaken, and chairs provided. Keynes opened the drawer to a filing cabinet and offered whisky or cognac. We all declined. He lit a cigarette, rearranged a few items on his desk, then sat back in his swivel chair, folded his right leg over his left and said, 'Shall we begin with the good news?'

I said, 'I am sorry, Mr Keynes, but the good and the bad are inseparable in this case. We will have to disclose both at the same time.'

'How mysterious and a little worrying.'

I said, 'Please could you invite Mr Pinchin to join us?'

'Gerry?' He shook his head, uncoupled his legs and rose from his chair. 'The mystery deepens.'

He opened his door and gestured to Pinchin, who stood, adjusted his jacket, hitched his trousers and drifted towards Keynes' office. He hesitated in the doorway and looked at each of us in turn with narrowed eyes.

He took the chair offered at the side of the desk. 'What's all this about?'

He directed his question at me, so I replied, 'Chief Inspector Bonnet has uncovered a crime, which will impact the Treasury Unit.'

Bonnet began his report with a summary of the incident on Rue Lauriston. I couldn't detect any reaction from Pinchin at the mention of Fournier, except perhaps for a faint twitch at the corner of his mouth. He continued, 'The mortally wounded attacker worked for Fournier, but to prove Fournier's involvement, we knew would be very problematic.' Bonnet clasped his hands together, breathed deeply and gazed at his audience. 'And then came an unexpected intervention. Awakened in the middle of the night, I had a note from Mr Visser requesting my urgent presence at the Russian Orthodox church in Rue Daru. Apparently, it was an emergency and concerned Miss Kiten.'

'When was this?' asked Keynes.

Bonnet reached into his waistcoat pocket and checked his watch. 'Almost fourteen hours ago, although so much has taken place in the interim, it feels like days, not hours.' He sat back in his chair and continued. 'When I arrived at the church, I found that Fournier and two of his associates had been caught in the middle of a criminal act, one unrelated to the attack on Rue Lauriston.' He paused. 'Mr Visser and Miss Kiten apprehended them. Both are to be commended for their courage in the face of great danger.' He waved a hand towards Adam and me. 'I will defer to Mr Visser at this point.'

'Thank you, Chief Inspector,' said Adam. We had devised a stratagem for the occasion. While Bonnet was happy to lend legal gravity to our presentation, he was unwilling to state any untruths. I had no such scruples. Neither had Adam, who took up the narrative. 'I was unaware of the incident at Rue Lauriston, and my French is mediocre at best, so I was confused by the initial exchanges. However, it soon became clear that Fournier was trying to bargain with us for his freedom.'

'Yes, they were surprisingly forthcoming in that respect,' I said. 'Fournier's associate recognised me from Rue Lauriston, and they clearly thought we would be interested to know who contracted them to attack you, Mr Keynes.' I glanced at Pinchin. He was sat with his head bowed and hands clasped around his middle. 'But that information would be in exchange for their freedom. Of course, we could not contemplate freeing them.'

'What criminal act were they engaged in when you caught them?' asked Keynes.

Bonnet cleared his throat and leant forward. 'I regret that cannot be disclosed at present. All I can say is that it was aimed at the very core of this Congress with a devastating potential impact.'

'At first, we didn't fully appreciate the enormous repercussions of the planned crime we prevented.' said Adam. 'But that was why Fournier was so eager to strike a deal for release before the police arrived.' He was distracted for a moment by Bonnet, who was making elaborate preparations with a pipe retrieved from his pocket. 'We played along with Fournier, tempting him to say more. Eventually, we persuaded him to offer a name as a sign of good faith. The name would be one of those who contracted Fournier to carry out the attack on Rue Lauriston. Not a major figure, we were told, but an important one in the conspiracy.' He paused to heighten a sense of anticipation. 'The name he stated was yours, Mr Pinchin.'

All eyes turned to Pinchin.

'No, surely not,' exclaimed Keynes.

'Of course not… Preposterous idea… Outrageous. How could you think…' Pinchin's bluster and indignation were convincing if a little over-dramatic. 'Why, I have never even heard of Fournier, let alone conspired….'

I interrupted. 'But you have met with him, Mr Pinchin. Fournier was here, with you, when I returned here after work to retrieve Mr Keynes' notebook.'

'You must be mistaken.'

'I don't think so. Fournier himself confirmed my encounter with him. He was departing as I was arriving. You were working late. The only one here.'

317

Keynes stubbed out his cigarette, gazed at Pinchin with a bemused expression. 'Can you be certain there is no misunderstanding? I have worked closely with Gerry for - well, almost four years now.'

'Who better to enlist in a plot to silence you, than one of your closest colleagues?'

Pinchin opened his mouth to speak, but words wouldn't come.

'Then - why Gerry? Why?' Keynes shook his head slowly, pleading to understand.

Pinchin clamped his jaw and folded his arms.

'Do you have no defence; nothing to say in mitigation?'

Pinchin muttered under his breath. When Keynes asked him to repeat, he raised his head and blew a contemptuous puff of air. 'I said, you have no proof. It will never come to trial.'

'Is that true, Chief Inspector?'

Bonnet had finished with his pipe and replaced it in a pocket, ready but unlit. 'Who can say, Mr Keynes. The wheels of justice sometimes turn in unexpected directions. But at this stage, I have no plans to arrest Mr Pinchin.'

After a few moments of awkward quiet, Pinchin spread his arms in a gesture of self-righteous innocence and said, 'So you have nothing.'

I looked to Keynes for an appropriate response, and he didn't disappoint. He stood, moved to the door, opened it and said, 'I don't need a court of law. Your reaction, your expression, your whole body screams guilt. You are fired, Gerald Pinchin. Clear your desk, check out of the hotel and slink back to your hole over the channel. Sir Basil Thomson and Lord Hardinge will be informed. I am sure they can find ways to repay your disloyalty and make your life uncomfortable back in England.'

Pinchin levered himself up, took two steps, stopped as if he would offer a retort to Keynes, then decided against and shuffled off to his desk. His colleagues had overheard his ignominious dismissal and watched in silent incredulity. He cut a desolate, woeful figure, and I couldn't suppress a stab of pity for him. All that dissolved quickly when I recalled his probable hand in Crozier's murder.

Keynes closed the door and sat down, resting elbows on his desk with fingers steepled. 'If Pinchin was the bad news, would I be correct in thinking that the good news is the arrest of Fournier and the consequent reduction in the threat against me?'

'Yes, but it's not quite as simple as that,' said Adam. 'We can safely say that Fournier is no threat to you as he is dead. We should also admit that he divulged no name before his death. You have the persuasive talents of your personal research assistant to thank for outing Pinchin. I have to admit that Mary and I bent the truth a little to expose him.'

'Dead? Mary – Miss Kiten. How did you know? And how long have you known?

'I have suspected Pinchin for only a few days since Fournier was identified to me. However, absolute certainty of his culpability only came a few minutes ago.'

'There must be others. Surely, it cannot be Pinchin acting alone.'

'I think we all agree, Mr Keynes,' said Adam looking at me and Bonnet in turn for confirmation. 'Pinchin was probably only the messenger boy. Those other unidentified conspirators and opponents of your views on reparations will be shocked and feel exposed when they hear of Fournier's death and the disappearance of Pinchin. The Chief Inspector believes they will keep their heads down and give up on further attempts against you. Mary has agreed to explain all this to Sir Basil, and no doubt, he will adjust your security as appropriate.'

I had accomplished what I believed was an outside chance in unmasking Pinchin. Helping Keynes by degrading the danger he faced went some way to compensating for an unsatisfactory outcome to Arthur's murder. It helped appease my sense of antipathy towards grubby political manoeuvring, but only so far. I wanted nothing more to do with the Congress and had begun to tire of the city itself. I had decided. I would leave Paris and return to England. I remained with Keynes after Adam and Bonnet departed so that I could inform him personally. He would be the first to hear and perhaps the easiest to tell. We had developed a bond, Keynes and me. We were not close in the way of friendship and affection, but we were connected.

I said, 'There's something else. Something you should know.'

He arched an eyebrow and turned his head to gaze at Adam and Bonnet as they made their way towards the exit to the schoolroom. 'For my ears only, it seems. I don't know whether to be eager or apprehensive. What is it to be, Mary?'

'It's nothing frightfully important and no cause for alarm. I want to… I mean, I thought it would be polite to let you know first as my… superior.'

'Goodness, you have me worried. Please tell me. Ah, wait, I think perhaps, I understand. Are you leaving us?'

'Yes.'

He puffed his cheeks. 'When? Straight away?'

'No, I expect to remain in Paris for a short time. If it's your wish, I will certainly continue working for you here until you find a replacement.'

He nodded his head as acknowledgement, and I waited as he ran through a familiar routine of lighting up his cigarette. 'We will miss you, Mary, and not only me, everyone in our unit will be sorry to see you leave us.'

'And I… I have enjoyed my time working for the Treasury, but now is the right time for me to return to England.'

'You have endured so much: the incident at Rue Lauriston, the murder of Mr Burgess and the latest escapade with Mr Visser. So, I suppose it is no surprise that you want to distance yourself from the scene of those nightmares.'

'It's not the incidents themselves that I wish to put behind me. Indeed, I have become very fond of some of those closely involved.' I paused and clasped my hands together. 'It has been a long time since I was at home with my mother.' Another short pause as I took a breath. 'There is another reason. I have had a sort of awakening; an awareness of what I want to do with the rest of my life.'

'You are to be congratulated, then. I suspect most people wander through their lives without any great sense of purpose or motivation.' He drew on his cigarette and leaned back in his chair. 'I'm intrigued.

Can you tell me more, or do you wish to keep it under your hat for the present?'

I saw no reason to keep my plans from Keynes and I explained how my experiences, doubts and hopes of the past few years had resolved themselves in recent days. We had a pleasant and fruitful conversation for another twenty minutes or so. Keynes was encouraging and surprised with an offer of practical support. It seemed, after all, that we were destined to meet again in England.

*

I arrived back at the Majestic with four hours to kill before Adam was due to call. He had promised to take me for a celebratory dinner. I didn't argue at the time, but celebration seemed an odd word to mark the terror and bloody killing we had recently endured. Half of me looked forward to the prospect of dinner with Adam. The other half dreaded it. We had both endured extreme danger and he had saved my life. For reasons I couldn't rationalise, our experience together had crystallized my view of Adam. I admired him and would be eternally grateful for his courage and daring, but he was not someone in whom I had a romantic interest. I understood my earlier thoughts about Adam were fanciful, especially when set against my feelings for John. I was tired, weak and nauseous. I didn't know whether to blame the lingering effects of influenza or a delayed physical reaction to my close escape from Fournier's grip. Whatever it was, I couldn't rest; some matters needed my immediate attention. I would have to fight the exhaustion and ignore nausea.

I went directly to Sir Basil's office. The temptation to lie down and close my eyes would have been too much to resist if I had called at my room first. His door was open, and inside two men were shaking hands with Sir Basil. It seemed they were leaving, so I stepped back into the corridor and waited. It was apparent from Sir Basil's respectful attitude that they were important men and both French, as I gathered from their speech. He saw me as his two visitors disappeared down the corridor.

'Ah, Miss Kiten, you must have been reading my mind. I was about to send you a message. Please do come in.'

I wasn't sure if I was reading Sir Basil right, but he seemed flustered. His greeting was polite – perhaps too polite and correct. And there was something wrong with the way he held his body. Too stiff. Almost as though he was treating me like royalty. I aimed to sit at his desk, but he ushered me to his casual seating area. We flopped into capacious leather armchairs at opposite ends of a circular wooden table with intricate carving, inlaid with mother of pearl. He noticed my interest and explained it was a souvenir from his time in Fiji and the South Pacific islands. Fiji was a surprise. Perhaps it shouldn't have been, as many senior British administrators cut their teeth in the colonies. But I had imagined Paris was an exotic and distant posting for Sir Basil. He always gave me the impression of one who would be happily ensconced north of the English Channel and south of Birmingham.

'Miss Kiten?'

'Sorry, Sir Basil, I was dreaming. No, nothing to drink, thank you.'

'You have every reason to feel tired, from what I hear of events in the last twenty-four hours.'

'What have you heard?'

'Your presence at the briefing on the Russian question alerted me, and General Smuts was kind enough to elaborate a little. The two gentlemen you saw leaving were the head of French security for the congress and his deputy. They were here to inform about the discovery of a large cache of explosives and the elimination of a major criminal. Unsurprisingly, they were also keen to take credit for this triumph of intelligence and the extra level of safety it offers to Congress members. Of course, most of the detail and personalities involved were left unsaid, but I know enough to fill in the missing pieces.'

'I don't think I will break too many rules by informing you that Mr Visser and I were at the scene of Fournier's demise. I am convinced a White Russian named Sazanov was guilty of plotting to blow up President Wilson's residence, and I had also hoped that he and his Russian faction would be punished. Sazanov and Fournier were responsible for the murder of Arthur Burgess to stop him informing on their evil plot.' I sighed involuntarily and stifled a yawn. 'After the briefing, I have reluctantly come to accept that we will receive only partial justice.'

'I understand your disappointment, but I am sure Mr Burgess would have been extremely proud of your efforts on his behalf.' He shuffled in his chair and cleared his throat, readying himself for his following statement. 'Please also accept my congratulations on your dedication and bravery. You are a remarkable young woman.'

'Thank you, Sir Basil.' I paused to give him time to recover from his discomfort. 'There are several matters I wish to discuss. If I may…'

'Of course, please fire away.' He ran a finger around his neck to loosen the collar from flushed, pink flesh.

'The first is a relatively simple matter concerning the security detail for Mr Keynes. Fournier and two of his henchmen are dead, one of those who hired him to kill or harm Keynes has been warned off, and the others are likely to withdraw into the shadows. I hope you will agree that the threat has been significantly reduced, and his security can be relaxed.'

'Yes, agreed. Leave that to me to sort out with Hincham and the American chap, Bruckner.'

'The second matter is more... delicate. As you know, it was Arthur Burgess who was responsible for bringing me here. Now he has... passed and the mystery of his murder solved, there is nothing...' My mind wandered and words were stumbling. The armchair was too comfortable, and sleep beckoned. I shook my head and straightened my back. 'In short, I have decided to resign my position, pack my bags and return to England.'

'Well, if you are certain.' Was he pleased with my decision? Glad to see the back of me? He seemed... relieved. A smile softened his face. His whole body relaxed as though a puppeteer's strings had been cut from his arms and legs.

'I would like to stay on to tie up a few loose ends. It would only be a week or so – three weeks at the most – and I wondered if it would be possible to stay in room 44 for that time. I know it's a bit of a cheek with rooms at a premium.'

'That will be absolutely fine, Miss Kiten. The room is yours for as long as you need it.'

'Thank you.'

I hadn't expected such an easy acceptance, and I should have been pleased. But I felt drained. Another yawn stifled. I yearned for my bed. Sleep. But I couldn't – not yet. Something urgent needed my attention. It had scratched my conscience raw for a few days, and I had to deal with it before I could rest.

I said, 'One of the reasons I want to delay my departure is to see Major Parkes on the mend. I intend to visit Major Parkes in hospital. I will go directly from here and, as I have recently recovered from a bout of the influenza, there should be no problem of catching the virus or spreading it.' His demeanour changed again. He had reverted to the stiff and guarded figure I encountered at his doorway. Why was he acting strangely? 'Do you have any message you would like me to deliver to the Major?'

'Ah, well.' He started to lever himself up from his chair, then stopped and remained seated. 'There will be no need for that.' He cleared his throat and flexed his shoulders as though composing himself. 'Miss Kiten.'

'Yes, Sir Basil.'

'I mentioned that I had intended to send you a message. You see… Jenkins returned from the hospital earlier today.' He clicked his tongue and straightened his back. 'There is no easy way to say this, Mis Kiten. I regret to inform you that Major Parkes passed away as a result of his infection.'

'Passed away? You mean… he's… dead? When?'

'I understand it was in the early hours of this morning. Terrible news. You have my sympathy. I am afraid two more deaths were also reported…'

He continued talking, but I wasn't listening to the words. I was lost in my imagining of John in his hospital bed. Desperate to recover. Struck down by a virus after surviving all the war threw at him. And his letter. Was he thinking of me while he lay dying? I winced. Shut my eyes and clenched my teeth. Had I spoken? Sir Basil had stopped talking. Too quiet. Silence boomed. A sharp pain grabbed my breastbone. I gasped. If only... if only I had written a positive reply to his letter. If only...

*

I was marooned in swaying mists and strange noises. The air around was heavy as though I was beneath an ocean. The light had a translucent quality, a creamy silk that murmured as it ebbed and flowed. I was wrapping myself deeper into that welcoming environment when a sharp sound pierced the milky air. A human voice, harsh and guttural. It was distant, and I couldn't make out the words. Was someone calling? The sounds were getting nearer.

'Mary.'

The name meant nothing to me.

'Mary. Mary Kiten.'

It was me – my name. But I didn't want to know. I resented the attempt to wrench me from a place of comfort and softness.

Someone tapped my shoulder. Took my hand in theirs. And a scent I recognised; earthy and warm.

I opened my eyes.

'Mary.'

'Adam.'

'I am sorry to wake you. Edith let me in and made sure you were... decent, before she... I was going to leave you, but... dinner tonight was a stupid idea. We both need to rest after a night like that.' I was lying on top of my bed, fully clothed. Adam had pulled up a chair and was gazing at me. His expression was anxious, puzzled. 'Sir Basil said you were upset; advised me to call on you. Are you… are you - feeling well?'

'No.' I turned my head and ran fingers through my hair. 'I'm tired.'

'I know the cause of your upset.' He hesitated. 'Were you… were you very fond of Major Parkes?'

'Yes.'

'Did you have an understanding? Were you or did you intend to be - together?'

'No, Adam. Not yet.'

'Oh, I see.'

'I liked him very much, but we met only a few weeks ago. Nothing between us was understood or promised. When… when he was ill, he declared his intention, his hopes, in a letter.'

'And did you feel the same way?'

'Not then. I don't… I don't know.'

'So, how did you reply?'

I studied his face. Lines on his forehead suggested more questions to come. How could I explain? Should I even try? After a deep breath, I said, 'Words were too difficult, and I couldn't formulate a reply. I wasn't even sure he intended me to see all he had written. I… I wanted to tell him I felt… as though I may feel the same – given time. If only I had…' I levered myself up on to an elbow. 'I'm sorry, I can't rationalise my thoughts. It was my fault. He wouldn't have been in hospital if I hadn't asked him to accompany me the night he was shot. If he hadn't met me, he wouldn't have caught the disease. Do you see? Can you understand why I find his death so distressing?'

A few moments of quiet followed before Adam replied. 'Yes. But in time, you will see it differently. You cannot be blamed for his wounding or the infection.'

I knew he was right, but it gave me no comfort. I swivelled my legs, gathered my skirts and levered myself off the bed at the side away from Adam. I gestured to the small table and two leather armchairs. I waited until we were both settled, then said, 'Did Sir Basil inform you that I've resigned from my position here?'

'Yes, he did.'

'I will be leaving as soon as I can arrange a passage back to Dover.'

'Do you have plans back in England?

'Yes.' He tilted his head and waited, expecting more. I hesitated, reluctant to offer up any detail of my intentions. But why? It wasn't a secret, and if I couldn't share with Adam, then who?

He said, 'I'm sorry, I don't wish to pry.'

'No, no, it's something I'm only just coming to terms with. I haven't told anyone – well apart from one person. Even my mother doesn't know yet.'

'That sounds – interesting.'

'I'm going to train as a medical doctor. I had it at the back of my mind in Wimereux when I was nursing. And I suppose, even before then as my father was a doctor.'

'An admirable ambition, Mary, and I'm sure it's not an easy one to follow. Despite all the changes brought about by the war, I know many who still regard doctoring as the exclusive domain of men.'

'Yes, I know that attitude only too well.'

'Did anything happen here to make your mind up?'

I didn't have a ready answer. The seeds had been planted back in Whitstable, then all life was put on hold at Wimereux where it was tempting the gods to imagine any future past the next day. Surviving the encounter with Fournier made me realise I needed focus in my life, and I suppose talking with Doctor Morton gave me a prod. If John had lived, how would he have reacted to my intention to become a doctor? I hoped he would have encouraged me; that we could find a way to... Would I even have had the same ambition if we were together? I sighed. 'There was no specific event that decided me. But I'm certain now.'

'How will you see it through? Do you have a place for training?'

'I broke my study at Cambridge in 'sixteen to volunteer, but there are no degrees in medicine available to women there. So, I will apply to the London School of Medicine for Women in Bloomsbury. I am very lucky that Mr Keynes has promised to use his influence to try and secure a place for me there, as well as offering accommodation in his apartment nearby.'

He nodded his head slowly as if analysing my strategy. He clasped his hands together and said, 'I am also making plans for departure.'

'Oh... Where and when?'

'I will be sailing to Cape Town from Marseilles in ten days.'

I was surprised. From all I had heard, the Congress was likely to last the rest of the year. 'Is your work here done?'

'It is almost finished. Our original intention was to be here for December and January, but Lloyd George has pleaded with General Smuts to stay at least until mid-year. He has agreed, but with some reluctance.'

'Then, why do you return to South Africa without the General? Is there a crisis?'

'We are a young country, with many embryonic problems to overcome. The General is needed there and has been requested to return by Prime Minister Botha. I am simply an advance party, preparing his way.'

'It sounds... challenging; exciting. I suppose you must welcome the prospect of going home and leaving this place.'

He looked down, crossed his legs and brushed a hand across his knee as though removing specks of dust from his trousers. The quiet between us stretched. Had I said something wrong?

He raised his head and said, 'I've enjoyed meeting with you. I admire you.' He took a deep breath and leaned forward. 'And I owe you an apology.'

'Why? I don't... understand.'

'I should have told you some time ago that I'm married.'

How to react? I think my main sensation was one of relief. Relieved that we didn't have to be guarded in our conversation and interaction any longer. 'I did wonder when we first met on the train.'

'I've been reprimanded by General Smuts. He was correct in assessing my weakness. It was male vanity that led me to keep that information from you. You are a beautiful and intelligent young woman, and I suppose I wanted your approval; your admiration. It was unworthy. I am sorry. Please forgive me.'

'The fault is not entirely yours, Adam.' I abandoned any notion of saying more. He knew my meaning.

331

The moments of quiet between us lengthened. I struggled to find a way to describe the incidents, excitements and horrors we had both just survived. I suspect he must have felt the same. There was no awkwardness and we ended up smiling at each other. We had shared an experience that was ours alone, and there was no need to give voice to our understanding.

He removed a card from the top pocket of his suit jacket and handed it to me. 'This is my home address in Cape Town. I don't expect we will ever meet again, but if by chance you ever need a place to stay in my country, look me up and you can be sure of a warm welcome. Or, if you feel the urge to put pen to paper as Doctor Kiten then I would be thrilled to learn of your achievement.'

'Of course. You saved my life, Adam. I will never forget.'

He stood slowly, touched my hand with his fingertips, mouthed a silent 'goodbye' and exited the room without a backward glance.

End Notes

Paris Peace Conference, 1919 *

The congress to establish the terms of peace following the armistice of November 1918 was held in Paris. Neither the British nor Americans wanted Paris; favouring a neutral location, but eventually they gave way under pressure from the French.

The formal opening of the Peace Conference was on 18th January 1919. Woodrow Wilson, the American President, arrived in France on 13th December 1918 and had made preparatory visits to London and Rome in advance of the Conference. The delegates from more than 30 countries attended. There was no representation from the defeated Central Powers (Germany, Austria, Bulgaria, Hungary and Turkey).

From the outset, there was confusion over organisation, procedures and purpose. The Big Four countries – Britain, France, Italy and the United States had intended a relatively short preliminary conference of victors to settle on the terms to be offered. The Central Powers would then be invited to negotiate at the main Peace Conference. There were too many participants, too many questions and too little planning. As weeks and months passed with slow progress, the preliminary conference turned into the real thing. When Germany was presented with a draft of the Treaty of Versailles in May, there was no negotiation. They were to forfeit a good deal of territory and pay punitive reparations. They also had to accept sole blame for the War. After bitter debate, it appeared they had little option, and signed the Treaty with only minor amendments. The terms of peace and their overall treatment by the Conference was the cause of great resentment in Germany.

Although it is sometimes referred to as the *Versailles Conference* only the first treaty was signed there. Formal meetings were held at the Quai d'Orsay. In practice all of the major decisions were taken informally between Britain, France and the United States.

The conditions for the armistices that had brought an end to World War I had been set by Wilson's diplomacy and his *Fourteen Points* underlying terms for a peace. The points included Wilson's ideas regarding freedom of the seas, free trade and national self-determination. He proposed a *League of Nations* to guarantee political independence and territorial integrity.

Wilson arrived in France to great fanfare and acclaim, with high hopes to deliver peace and prosperity in the post-war era, as outlined in his points. For most of the conference, he struggled to gain support for his ideas and to ensure that the Central Powers, especially Germany, were not treated too harshly. Prime Ministers Georges Clemenceau of France and David Lloyd George of Britain argued that punishing Germany severely was the only way to justify the immense costs of the war. Clemenceau was also determined to weaken Germany economically and militarily so that they could not threaten France again. In the end, Wilson's attempts to get *Fourteen Points* adopted failed. He compromised on the treatment of Germany in order to push through the creation of the *League of Nations*.

Wilson, his wife and entourage lived in great state at the Hotel Murat, provided by the French government. The rest of the American delegation were also accommodated in some luxury at the Hotel Crillon. Wilson's great friend and chief adviser, Colonel Edward House, had a large suite at the Crillon. House had visited Europe some months before to prepare for Wilson's arrival. *Colonel* was an honorary title and he had never fought in a war. He was small, unassuming, and appeared frail. Wilson relied on House a great deal and delegates in Paris soon came to understand that one had to go via House to obtain agreement from Wilson.

Lloyd George arrived in Paris on 11th January and stayed in style at an apartment in Rue Nitot lent to him by a rich Englishwoman. Lord Balfour, British Foreign Secretary, was housed on the floor above Lloyd George. The Foreign Office was given the task of making arrangements for the Conference and senior civil servant, Lord Hardinge, was named as *Organising Ambassador*. Detailed plans were devolved to Alwyn Parker, the Librarian at the Foreign Office. Chief among the many difficulties faced by Parker was the increasing scarcity of accommodation for the large and growing British delegation.

Most of the British delegation were based at the Hotel Majestic. The nearby Hotel Astoria was also used for accommodation and became the main work location. Readying the Astoria presented a particular problem as it was still in use as a military hospital a few weeks before the start of the Conference. Several other smaller hotels, private houses, garages and industrial units were requisitioned for transport, food storage, printing and other support services.

Sir Basil Thomson of Scotland Yard had the task of managing a security service. Access to the Majestic was strictly controlled and all domestic staff for this hotel were imported from across the Channel. Logic behind this last measure appears flawed as the staff of the Astoria, where the work was undertaken and papers deposited, were all French. The Majestic had a set of *house rules* governing mealtimes, recreation activities and general behaviour such as a warning against slamming of doors. "Like coming to school for the first time," was the opinion of one new arrival.

Clemenceau was President of the Conference with full control of the French position, and he took little advice from those in the military or government. He was said to hold a special dislike for the French President, Raymond Poncaire and kept him in the dark on progress in negotiations. Having experienced two German attacks on French soil in 40 years, he was determined to guard against it happening again.

Clemenceau mistrusted Lloyd George and was dismissive of Wilson's Fourteen Points saying, "God Almighty has only ten." He was known for expressing irritation with slow progress in negotiations in a loud and forceful manner. On 19th February 1919 an anarchist fired several shots at Clemenceau as he was leaving his apartment. He was hit and a bullet lodged between his ribs, just missing vital organs. He survived, but the bullet remained for the rest of his life as it was too risky to remove.

The Russian Question

Russia was a notable absentee from those countries with a formal delegation at the Peace Conference. As an ally at the start of the war, Russia had probably saved France from an early defeat by diverting German resources to the Eastern Front. Russia had fought the Central Powers suffering huge losses, until in 1917 it transformed from autocracy, via liberal democracy, to a revolutionary dictatorship under the Bolsheviks (a small and little-known group of socialists) in only a few months. But Russia was divided, and the Bolsheviks controlled only a relatively small core area of land, including St. Petersburg and Moscow. Great tracts of the country were ruled by rival groups, commonly referred to as *White Russians*.

Throughout the Conference, Allied policy toward Russia was confused and changeable. The view of Clemenceau and many other politicians was that Russia had betrayed the Allied cause when they signed the Best-Litovsk treaty with Germany. Under the terms of the treaty, Lenin surrendered land and resources to Germany in return for external peace, so that Bolsheviks could win the battle within its borders.

In line with his belief in self-determination, Wilson was not in favour of intervention in Russia. He proposed negotiation with all factions, including the Bolsheviks, to take place on Prinkipo, an island between the Black Sea and Mediterranean. He sent an envoy, William Buckler, to meet with Maxim

Litvinov, a representative of the Bolshevik government. Buckler was impressed and came back with a positive report. Initially, Lloyd George also favoured negotiation, understanding there was little appetite in Britain to commit men and resources to another conflict.

In Paris, Russian exiles over a wide political and military spectrum, had formed the Russian Political Conference to represent all non-Bolsheviks. Sergei Sazanov, who had been foreign minister in the tsarist government, was one of their main spokesmen. News of the Prinkipo proposal was deeply shocking to the White Russians and they turned out to demonstrate their opposition on the streets of Paris.

Despite their initial inclinations and encouraging signals from preliminary meetings, Wilson and Lloyd George were outnumbered by those who opposed any form of rapprochement with the Bolsheviks. The press was also increasingly critical of the Prinkipo proposal. The Bolsheviks gave only a partial acceptance of terms to meet there and by the time the White Russians sent their refusal in February 1919, the possibility of negotiations had already disappeared. Wilson was at sea, returning to the USA for a few weeks, while the British Prime Minister had returned to a Britain under threat of a general Strike. Lloyd George's place in Paris was taken by Winston Churchill, the new Secretary of State for War, and fierce opponent of a Bolshevik Russia.

Spanish Flu

The 1918 influenza pandemic, generally known by the misnomer *Spanish flu* or *Spanish lady*, killed at least 50 million people; more than twice the number who had just been shot, blown up or gassed to death in the trenches. It was referred to as Spanish flu because Spain was neutral during the War, and there was no censorship. The outbreak was reported widely in the Spanish press, including King Alfonso XIII's illness, making Spain appear as the apparent focal point of the epidemic.

Spanish flu came in three waves. The first was relatively benign and ran from March to August 1918. A mutation in the virus then occurred and a second, deadly wave began in September and continued until December 1918. A third wave ran from January to May 1919, as armies disbanded from the War. The third wave was not as lethal as the second wave, but more so than the first. Spanish Flu could also induce longer term neurological problems once the normal symptoms such as fever, cough, aches and chills had ended.

It's estimated that about a third of the world's population were infected, and delegates at the Peace Conference were not immune. President Wilson contracted the virus early in April 1919. Although his illness was played down publicly, behind the scenes he suffered coughing fits, a high fever and gastrointestinal problems. It is also reported that he suffered from fatigue, loss of concentration and bouts of irrational behaviour. Wilson eventually gave way to the arguments of Clemenceau and others, abandoning most of his *Fourteen Points*. Whether he would have held to his position for more equitable terms if he hadn't succumbed to Spanish flu, we will never know, but contemporaries and historians have argued that he was never quite the same.

PAUL WALKER

British Women Doctors in WW1

In 1914 there were about 42,000 registered doctors in Britain, of which less than 1,000 were women. They were barred from posts in most general hospitals, with their work confined to general practice and hospitals founded to treat women and children. More than half were trained at the London School of Medicine for Women, the only London teaching hospital to admit them. Most universities refused to accept women to study for medicine.

Shortly after the outbreak of war, two doctors, Louisa Garrett Anderson and Flora Murray called at the French Embassy in London and offered to establish a medical unit in France comprising women doctors and nurses. They didn't bother to approach the British War Office, knowing they would receive a rebuttal. It was common knowledge that the French army had insufficient surgeons and hospitals and their offer was quickly accepted by the French Red Cross. They managed to raise money, recruit staff and buy necessary equipment in short time, then set up their first hospital at Claridge's Hotel in Paris to be run by the Women's Hospital Corps (WHC). It was an immediate success and a few weeks later a second hospital was established by WHC at Wimereux, near Boulogne.

In 1915 it became apparent that there was an urgent need for women doctors to replace the male doctors serving with military units and there was a great expansion in opportunities for women to train in medicine. A War Office inspection of the WHC was positive and they were put in charge of a new military hospital in Endell Street, London, near Covent Garden. This hospital remained in service until October 1919 and treated over 24,000 soldiers as in patients.

At the same time that Garrett Anderson and Murray put their offer to the French Embassy, Elsie Inglis, a Scottish surgeon had formed the Scottish Women's Hospital unit (SWH) and offered 100 beds to either the War Office or British Red Cross. After receiving a sharp rebuff, she turned instead to the French and Serbian authorities, who both accepted her proposition. In France the SWH was housed in a 13th century abbey at Royaumont, near Paris. At its peak, with 600 beds, it was the largest British voluntary hospital in France.

Because the supply of male doctors was dwindling, by 1916 the War Office had reversed it earlier policy and allowed women doctors to be posted overseas attached to the Royal Army Medical Corps (RAMC). Although they were paid, they did not enjoy equal rights with male doctors, had to pay for their own board and could not wear uniform. The medical profession was also obliged to open access to women for university training. During the War women doctors treated every kind of wound and illness and experienced the same hardships and dangers as their male counterparts. However, the end of the war saw a return to reactionary viewpoints; clinical training was restricted once again; and even women doctors with distinguished service in the War were relegated to inferior positions. It took the outbreak of another world war before women doctors held commissioned ranks in the British army.

PAUL WALKER
John Maynard Keynes

Keynes was the principal representative of the British Treasury at the Paris Peace Conference from January to June 1919. He took up an official government position in the Treasury in 1915 after an earlier post in the Civil Service, followed by a spell in academia. He rose through the ranks quickly and his success led to the Paris appointment at the age of 35.

His first notable act in January was to travel by train to Trier in Germany for a renewal of the Armistice agreement. There, he met with a German lawyer, Carl Melchior, with whom he struck up an understanding. They maintained correspondence for many years. Keynes's primary concern was to ensure that the terms of peace with Germany did not endanger post-war economic and social stability. With the reparations set too high, it would undermine ability to repay, damage its economy and impair other economies in the wider world, unable to export to an impoverished Germany. Unfortunately, Keynes was excluded from the highest-level negotiations and was forced to work behind the scenes while Lords Cunliffe and Sumner pressed for punitive damages.

Lloyd George was generally sympathetic to Keynes's view in the early days of the armistice. But the general election of December 1918 showed the British electorate and many in his coalition government were in favour of harsh punishment for the Central Powers. Ever the pragmatist, Lloyd George fell into line, arguing for severity. Wilson was in favour of moderation, but eventually gave way to Clemenceau and Lloyd George's strident calls for large reparations. Eventually, Keynes became so frustrated with the way the terms of peace were being framed that he handed in his notice and departed Paris in June 1919. Keynes was not the only one to express exasperation and misgivings about the way the Conference was heading. Jan Smuts, the South African leader, was a trusted adviser to Lloyd George and respected by Wilson. He wanted a magnanimous peace and urged Keynes to write an exposure of the dangers of the financial clauses in the draft treaty.

Keynes was a member of the Bloomsbury Group and spent much of the 1919 summer at Charleston Farmhouse, the Group's outpost in the Sussex Downs. It was owned by Vanessa Bell and Duncan Grant, and they entertained Virginia Woolf, E. M. Forster, Lytton Strachey and Roger Fry amongst others, as frequent visitors. There Keynes wrote most of a book about, in his words, "… the economic follies and wickedness of the Peace Treaty". *The Economic Consequences of the Peace* was published in December 1919. The book was a best-seller throughout the world and added to a perception that the Central Powers, especially Germany, had been treated unfairly. Its success also established Keynes's reputation as a leading world figure in economics. It is less well known that Keynes was an enthusiastic patron of the arts and the prime mover in the establishment of the Arts Council shortly before his death in 1946.

(As a postscript it should be noted that only a small fraction of the reparations set for Germany in the Versailles Treaty was ever paid.)

PAUL WALKER

* Paris 1919, Six Months that Changed the World by Margaret Macmillan, provides a detailed and authoritative account of the Peace Conference.

Printed in Great Britain
by Amazon